2nd Edition

Z.L. ARKADIE

EDITION NOTE

The second edition of this novel combines *Once Friends* with *Now Lover* to give the reader a more robust reading experience.

First edition published in 2018

Second edition published in 2020

ISBN: 978-1-952101-08-3 (2nd Edition)

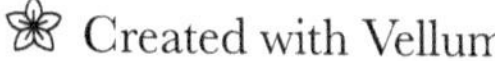

PART I
MY BEST FRIEND'S BACK

CHAPTER 1

JAY WEST

Jay West heard a jingle. Caught between the end of a dream he was already forgetting and consciousness, Jay slowly blinked until he was mostly awake. The stark daylight that filled the room stung his eyes. He turned his heavy-lidded gaze toward the noise. His cell phone was playing a song he didn't recognize, and the ringtone made his already excruciating headache worse.

"Damn it," he muttered as he swung his legs over the side of the bed and bent to rub his aching sinuses. The damn smog was going to kill him one day. *What in the hell happened last night?* Hell if he could remember.

The phone quieted then chimed and vibrated

again. He clutched his stomach, wanting to hurl, but then the bed shifted, so he turned his stiff neck to look behind him. A naked woman, lying under the top sheet, was snoring gently. The phone, the strange woman, his headache, the angst Jay had felt about facing the rest of his day—something had to give.

First things first.

He swiped his cell phone off the nightstand and scowled at the screen. It was Jim Neely, his agent.

"Yeah," he whispered, wishing he had let the damn call go to voicemail. Again.

"Where the hell are you?" Jim barked.

Jay closed his eyes to let the extra ache the volume of Jim's voice had caused pass through his head. He tried to remember where he was supposed to be but drew a blank.

"God damn you, Jay. Are you hell-bent on killing your fucking career?"

Jay's dead gaze fell over the hazy city beyond the tall windows his bed faced. Normally he would close the curtains at night so he wouldn't wake up to so much light. But at the moment, he couldn't remember how in the hell he'd made it to his bed in the first place. He looked at the lower half of his body. At least his pants were on.

"Okay, I'll bite. Where am I supposed to be?" he asked, rubbing the inside corners of his eyes.

"Are you kidding? You're fucking kidding me, right?"

Jay exhaled. "Does it sound like I'm joking?"

He could feel Jim's disappointment and frustration in the moment of silence.

"Why haven't you hired a new assistant yet? I had Carla send you the resumes. Why in the hell haven't you picked one yet?"

The sleeping girl groaned. Jay quickly looked behind him to stare at the back of her head, waiting for her to turn around so he could get a look at her face.

"I'll get one," he barely said.

Jim scoffed, perhaps because he knew that Jay was only trying to pacify him. Jay hated assistants. He'd never had one he could trust or hadn't fucked, which had proven to be a gold mine for the celebrity gossip rags that brought entertainment to those who loved to see big stars like him fall from grace, and boy, was he on a downward spiral.

"Just tell me where the hell am I supposed to be," Jay grumbled.

"AMTA. Get your ass here now." Jim hung up.

Finally the girl twisted until she flipped over,

turning in his direction. He studied her curves and the features of her face. She was young, maybe in her early twenties—he hoped not younger. She was also pretty, just like any other girl who stepped off the bus from somewhere else in America and came to Hollywood to make it big only to discover that there were way too many other pretty fish in the city's enormous pond. The fine lines branching out at the corners of her eyes and puffiness beneath them showed the stress of chasing that elusive stardom.

"Good morning, Jay West," she purred, beaming as she reached to rub what was between his legs.

He guided her hand away. "Sorry, um…" He didn't know her name. "You gotta go."

The glow in her eyes dimmed. He could tell that her hopes of nailing a big-time movie star boyfriend had been thwarted and now she felt cheap.

He hopped spritely to his feet. "Listen, it was fun. But I have a meeting that started an hour or so ago."

The girl glared at him. Jay knew she thought he was bullshitting her, and normally he would sell her a load of crap to get her out of his house as quickly as possible, but it just so happened at the moment, and thankfully so, he was telling the truth.

"Don't worry, I'm glad to go," she said, flinging herself to the edge of the bed. She bent over, snatched a tiny dress off the floor, and then tugged it over her head to put it on.

"Sorry to be so—" Jay said.

"Just shut the hell up already," she snapped. She bent over again and Jay heard the heels of her shoes scraping the hardwood.

He folded his arms, desperately trying to recall how the girl had ended up in his bed in the first place. The last thing he remembered about the previous day was meeting two buddies, Davcy Lyons and Rich Brisbane, at the Hot Spot, which was a club in Malibu. It had been a while since he'd hung out with the two avid partiers, who were also former child stars, only their careers hadn't taken off like Jay's.

Jay had seen a lot of people he knew at the Hot Spot, and of course they were still into the same shit—mounds of cocaine, lots of poppers, ecstasy, and all kinds of other shit. Against his better judgment, Jay had had a few drinks, and although he couldn't remember taking a hit of coke or anything else, he must've and perhaps had taken too much of it.

The girl snatched her small purse off the floor and jumped to her feet. “Have a nice day,” she said coldly and rushed out of the room.

Jay shot to his feet and followed her as he scratched the back of his neck. He wished he could remember meeting her and bringing her back to his place. Before leaving for the party, he questioned whether he had the resolve to go and not get into any trouble. But goodness, he couldn’t believe he had fallen off the wagon in such a big way.

He followed her up the hallway, down the floating stair, and into the foyer. She was almost gone, but he still had a lot of questions to ask her about last night.

“Can I call you an Uber?” he asked in his efforts to at least not make her feel cheap.

She snorted facetiously and jerked the door open. “I drove.”

“Wait,” he said before she stepped out into the bright day.

The women turned and scowled at him.

“Why can’t I remember meeting you or getting into bed with you?”

She grunted and rolled her eyes as though his question had offended her. “Don’t worry. You couldn’t get it up.” She rushed out of the house, slamming the large and heavy door as best she could behind her.

Jay knew her comment was meant to belittle him, but his lifestyle had been affecting his sex drive for quite a while. He felt numb inside as he watched her skip down the white stone steps and get into the driver's seat of a black car with dark tinted windows, which happened to be parked along the circular driveway behind his Roadster.

Jay kept his narrowed eyes on his car. "What the hell?"

The girl's car rolled slowly down the driveway, heading away from the house. As the gate opened, Jay turned his attention back to his car. Had he driven it home last night? And if he had, then he must've been sober enough to do that. He squeezed his eyes shut, trying hard as hell to remember something, anything. Then suddenly and out of nowhere, a familiar and strong urge to run as far as he could away from his life hit him.

Jay closed his eyes and kept taking deep breaths as he thought about waking up next to the girl, the call from Jim, and the fact that he wished his whole body would do something miraculous like disappear into thin air and never return.

When he opened his eyes again, he knew

exactly what had to be done. So he sighed briskly and turned away from the window, deciding to forget about last night so that he could focus on what would be from that moment forth.

Before zooming down the hills on his Harley, Jay had showered but didn't shave. He didn't remember any details about the meeting he was in a rush to get to until he made a left off Santa Monica Boulevard onto Avenue of the Stars. An agent named Mike Gillespie wanted to meet with Jay and his agent, Jim, to see if he would be a good fit to play the leading role in *The Red Scream,* which was touted as the next big blockbuster.

Jay wasn't all that excited about the project. Actually, he had been having a hard time concentrating on work lately, which included remembering his lines and becoming whatever character he was playing. No one said it to his face, but behind his back, the crew, cast, and executives were calling him the line eater because he always needed his lines fed to him. But fuck the part—Jay didn't want it or any other role. He wanted time off and away from Hollywood, and he was going to get both.

Jay made a left hand turn into the driveway of the tall reflective glass building and stopped his motorcycle at the valet station. As soon as he took off his helmet, he heard the gasps, oohs, ahs, and his name, and he also felt all the stares upon him. The abundance of attention never failed to make him feel initially shy and undeserving. Regardless, he stood up straight, lifted his head, and pretended as though he was worthy of the adulation.

Once he was inside the building, his footsteps crashed against the glossy white linoleum at a rapid pace. He found himself fighting the urge to go back home, crawl into bed, and pull the covers over his head. He recalled the look in the woman's eyes that morning as she stood at the door, glaring at him. His heart tightened and a chill ran down his spine. She'd looked at him as if, unlike everyone who was making a big deal about him being in the building, she knew the truth about him. Jay West was a lost and lonely man.

He put his head down as he walked past the receptionist desk. The young blonde didn't bother him. That was the rule. He was top-tier talent and it was her job to make sure she knew it. His foot mounted the first step leading to the elevators, which would take him up to the twenty-eighth floor.

As Jay looked up again, he caught sight of a beautiful woman watching him with the same sense of recognition.

Suddenly he was frozen stiff.

"Jay, is that you?" she said with her cell phone still pressed against her ear.

"Elaine?" he said.

"I'll call you back," she told whomever she was speaking to, and then opened her arms wide. "Jay? It's you!"

When they hugged, he held her as though he was hanging on for dear life. It helped that she squeezed him tightly too.

"You're looking good," he said.

"Thanks, Jay." Her eyes narrowed slightly. He knew Elaine well enough to know she wouldn't return the compliment if she didn't think it was true. She rubbed his shoulder like she used to do sometimes when they were kids. "I was wondering when our paths would cross."

He cut a tiny smile. "Yeah, you have a reputation around these parts."

She chuckled proudly. "It's all true." She winked.

A moment of silence fell between them. He was waiting for Elaine to mention *her,* but she hadn't, so he figured he should.

"So how is Sonja?"

Elaine grunted as she rolled her eyes. "Sonja is Sonja. Actually, she's the reason I'm here."

He was still wondering what she meant by *Sonja is Sonja*. But he was also shocked to hear that Elaine was at AMTA doing business on Sonja's behalf. "So she has an agent here?"

Elaine rolled her eyes. "Had. And he was barely an agent to her."

She went on to explain how four years ago, Sonja had won a contest and her prize was being saddled down with Mike Gillespie, or as she called him, "the laziest creep in the building."

"He sat on her screenplay for four damn years. And if his assistant hadn't called while I was in the room with Sonja, discussing the details of my upcoming wedding…" She touched his hand. "Have you heard?"

He cocked his head and narrowed an eye. "Heard about Mike Gillespie representing Sonja?"

"No, about my wedding?"

"Oh, no," he said.

She turned her head slightly. "Riley didn't tell you?"

Riley was his older sister. "We don't talk much."

"I see." Elaine studied him for a few uncomfortable moments. "Well, if I hadn't heard the conversation between Sonja and Mike's assistant, then I would've never known that jackass held her work for four years without paying her."

"Then she's still writing?" Jay asked, elated to hear it.

Elaine slapped herself on the chest. "I'm her sister. This is what I do. And she never consulted me." She huffed as though she had been waiting all morning to get that off her chest. "Anyway, I got her a nice big fat check. She can thank me when it comes in the mail."

He could see that after all these years, Elaine was still prone to overreact and always looking for a fight. Jay also remembered that she liked to win, and even though she had worked herself up, he could see in her eyes she was satisfied with her victory.

But Jay figured he'd take another stab at the question he had already asked. "Then Sonja's still writing?"

"Uh, no," Elaine said with another cynical roll of her eyes.

"Oh." His curiosity had tripled. "Is she married? Kids?"

"Ha!" She chuckled some more. "No, and never. Frankly, I don't know what the hell Sonja does these days. But"—she raised a finger—"I heard Riley's divorced again though." She leaned back to search his eyes as though she was waiting for him to comment.

He shrugged. "As far as I know, she's still married to Winslow."

She shook her head definitively. "No. That relationship wasn't working. They have to be divorced by now." Again, she seemed to search his eyes for a response.

When he threw his hands up, she sighed briskly, signaling a change in subject. "Well... so Jim Neely's your agent?"

"Yeah."

"He's another burglar."

A laugh escaped Jay. Not until that moment had he realized what had been missing in his life—the Hester girls. "Burglar? I haven't heard that word since I was a kid."

She scowled toward upstairs and said loudly, "This whole agency is filled with them."

Two agents Jay had seen before were walking downstairs but pretending as though they didn't see or hear her. Jay should've been embarrassed, but he wasn't. Elaine had always been crazy in that way, and holy hell had he missed her brand of insanity.

She reached into the side pocket of her suitcase. "Listen, I'm glad I ran into you. I've meant to call you and offer you my services, but these assholes keep me busier than I like by constantly railroading every single one of my existing clients. However"—she shook her finger at him—"you're like family and I want to help you. And to be honest, you look as though you need me."

Jay pictured the face that had stared back at him in the mirror that morning. His eyes were sunken and the skin around them was dark. He had been losing a lot of weight because he often missed meals, so his cheeks were becoming hollow. Jay could accept the truth. Without the makeup, lights, and post-production fixes, he looked like shit.

When he took her card, he felt as though he was accepting his final lifeline. "I'll call to set up something."

She reached out and patted him on the shoulder. "You do that."

Damn tears—Jay fought them as they hugged and held them even after they parted ways. He watched Elaine as she whipped her cell phone out of her leather briefcase and made a call.

"It's me again," she said while walking. "As I was telling you, that's a bad deal, but getting a better one means cleaning up your act."

That was the last thing he heard her say before the sound of her thin heels beating the floor overtook her voice.

Jay was now skipping up the steps, grinning from ear to ear. Running into Elaine had made him change his plans, and what he was going to do next was as clear as a bell. The elevator door opened. People watched him with excitement as they exited and he entered. He crossed his arms as the door closed, cutting off their wide-eyed stares. Up he rode to the top floor, satisfied to know that soon he would be laying eyes on Sonja's beautiful face once again.

CHAPTER 2

SONJA HESTER

TWO MONTHS LATER

Sonja Hester sneezed as Ms. Jenkins said something about Sonja's grandmother being too busy with her wealthy friends to stop by and make sure Sonja did a better job managing the apartment complex. It was the cats. Sonja was severely allergic and Ms. Jenkins had what felt like a million of them skirting, slinking, and lounging throughout the unit. Six minutes ago, Sonja had shown up to her tenant's unit with a snake to unclog the toilet. Every second spent inside the cat-infested domain had been pure torture.

Sonja took a break from craning the snake to

look down. Through watery eyes and past her itchy nose, she saw something white and furry snaking between her ankles.

"Ms. Jenkins, you know I'm allergic to cats." She sneezed again.

Ms. Jenkins waved dismissively in her direction. "You have hay fever, that's all." The elderly tenant swiped the fluffy white cat from off the floor and draped the creature around her neck. "You should take better care of yourself and this complex."

Sonja stared at Ms. Jenkins with her mouth agape. She wanted to scream. She was sick and tired of jumping through the high maintenance tenant's hoops. At least once a week, it was something. Last week, Sonja had snaked a plush kitty toy out of the bathtub drain. Before then, the air conditioner wasn't working until it miraculously did. Before then, the oven wouldn't turn on until again, it miraculously did. Holes mysteriously appeared in the walls. And something was always leaking.

Sonja knew the problems were self-inflicted, and she could prove it! But proving it had never done her any good. Her grandmother, who owned the property, was always on Ms. Jenkins's side, which Sonja found extremely odd. Apparently they had known each other for a long time, but she wasn't quite sure they were friends.

Sonja used the back of her forearm to wipe the sweat off her forehead. "How many cats do you have now anyway?" Her blood boiled as she tried to count them but became overwhelmed once she reached eleven. "You know according to your lease, you're only supposed to have two pets and you had sixteen the last time I knew the damn number for sure."

Ms. Jenkins touched her chest. "Watch your language."

Sonja wanted to blurt something far worse but knew if she did that, her words would get back to Gran and she would've been made to sound like the bad guy.

"And I'm giving these lovely creatures a home. Only a vile person would consider displacing them."

Sonja's glower fell on the fat and pretentious animal stretched around Ms. Jenkins's neck. "Well could you at least lock them away while I'm here?"

Sonja didn't think the woman's eyes could expand wider. "I will not imprison my darlings in their own home."

Sonja sneezed again. Her itchy nose and eyes

were running like a fountain. "Listen, Ms. Jenkins… *ah-choo.*" Her cell phone rang. "Shit!"

Despite Ms. Jenkins's melodramatic gasp, Sonja pulled off her gloves, snatched her device off the back pocket of her jeans, and answered the call.

"Hello?" she barked, still using the back of her arm to wipe the wetness from her eyes and nose.

"Is this Miss Sonja Hester?" a woman asked.

Sonja averted her burning eyes from Ms. Jenkins's scowl. "Yes, this is she." She sneezed again.

"You're being rude, young lady," Ms. Jenkins grumbled, then muttered something about Lorraine, who was Sonja's grandmother, needing to do something about Sonja's unprofessionalism.

Sonja shook her head and allowed her feet to speed walk through the living room and out the front door.

"I'm calling from Mike Gillespie's desk." The woman paused as though she was giving Sonja time to recognize his name.

Now that she was outside, Sonja took a deep breath. Her symptoms immediately diminished, which pissed her off even more. That was it. Her grandmother had to make a choice. If Ms. Jenkins stayed, then Gran would have to hire someone else to run the complex. She had it up to here with the crazy lady who didn't think it was odd to sport cats around her neck.

"Mike Gillespie would like to know if you could attend a meeting tomorrow morning."

"Mike Gillespie?" Sonja asked sharply. She sniffed and swiped her nose.

"Mike Gillespie from AMTA. He represented your screenplay, *Pact of Lies*," she said as if casting out hints.

"Oh, right. The last time I spoke to you, you told me I was no longer being represented by Mike."

Four years ago, she'd submitted a screenplay to a contest, and as third place winner, she received agency representation. Sonja had met Mike Gillespie once. It was pouring rain on that Monday morning, which was the worst time to drive from where she lived to Century City. Regardless of the surface street nightmares, which ranged from the average fender bender to the worst kinds of collisions, Sonja had been in a good mood. As she inched along with the rest of traffic, she dreamt of stardom and proudly telling her grandmother that she could no longer manage the complex and all of Ms. Jenkins's crazy demands.

As she pulled into the parking garage in her

yellow Volkswagen Beetle, Sonja had felt she was at the start of something big. She wasn't just some poor soul there to interview for a hapless assistant position, as she had done for years after graduating from college. Nope. She was the talent—the bread and butter and blood that fed the whole operation and kept the agency alive. She was confident and nervous up until the moment she met Mike Gillespie. The guy was probably five inches shorter than her, his hair slicked back with a greasy-looking substance, and when he spoke, it was as though his words were racing each other. For all of two minutes, he stared at her chest as he said something to the effect that he'd call her if something came up but don't count on it and ended with "good luck."

She had been crushed. And from that moment forward, she vowed to abandon her dream of being the next Charlie Kaufman. Mike Gillespie had been one Tinseltown asshole too many.

"What does he want?" she said with a serious lack of enthusiasm. She stretched her neck to ease the stiffness.

"He and others want to meet with you. Should I pencil you in for tomorrow at eight thirty a.m.?"

Sonya wanted to laugh bitterly and tell the assistant to let Mr. Gillespie know he could drown in toilet water for all she was concerned, but then Ms. Jenkins appeared in the doorway, stroking the fluffy white cat she was wearing around her neck. Suddenly Sonja wanted to get as far away as possible from the scene she was watching.

She turned her back on Ms. Jenkins. "Sure," she said, wishing she hadn't given up smoking because boy, did she want a cigarette. "Why not?"

The assistant said thanks and that she'd see her tomorrow. As soon as Sonja clipped the phone onto her back pocket, she regretted her decision to meet with the creep of an agent. And just like that, she changed her mind. Whatever meeting Mike Gillespie was having would have to go forth without her. *The douchebag.*

"Are you finished with your call?" Ms. Jenkins asked.

Sonja sighed sharply. Her eyes were no longer watery. She had stopped sneezing. Her nose was no longer running. And that tight pressure at the front of her face was gone. She didn't feel like subjecting herself to more misery, so she spun around and glared at the woman who had become her worst enemy.

"Either you put those cats away or you can wait until I call a plumber to come fix your toilet. Your choice." Sonja folded her arms, letting Ms. Jenkins know that she meant business.

"I will not imprison my lovelies," Ms. Jenkins said and set her jaw.

Sonja could already hear her grandmother giving her hell for the choice she was making at that very moment. But for the first time ever, she turned away from Ms. Jenkins and headed back to her office. Her head was spinning and she felt as if she wanted to barf. She had never walked away from Ms. Jenkins's demands, and now her tenant was yelling something about how sorry she would be when Lorraine heard about this.

Sonja wanted to get back to unclogging the cat lady's toilet, but she had made a decision to leave and there was no turning back. She would let the chips fall where they may.

As soon as Sonja made it back to her office, she called Hector, the plumber, who said he could fit her in but he couldn't get there for another three hours. And just as she expected, the wait for his arrival had been a low-grade nightmare. Ms. Jenkins called her desk every fifteen minutes or so.

Of course she wasn't going leave her apartment and walk up the stairs to the manager's office. The fact that the woman wouldn't walk up the stairs had something to do with arthritis or sciatica or fibromyalgia—she had used all three as excuses to make Sonja jump through her hoops.

Instead Sonja finished some paperwork and paid some invoices. By the time Hector arrived, her grandmother hadn't called yet, which relieved a lot of Sonja's anxiety. It took him an hour to take the toilet off the base and remove a wig Ms. Jenkins had flushed down it.

Sonja rubbed the tension at the back of her neck as she listened to Hector explain how something like that couldn't have happened by accident.

"She's *loco*," Hector concluded while spiraling his finger around his ear.

He was right. And Sonja had been off her rocker for tolerating and accommodating Ms. Jenkins for as long as she had. So after Hector left, she picked up the phone and called her grandmother. It was time to have *the talk*.

"WHAT IS IT, DARLING?" SONJA'S GRANDMOTHER asked impatiently.

Before calling, Sonja had rehearsed an argument for putting limits on Ms. Jenkins's power, but now she couldn't remember it. Sonja shifted nervously in her seat. "Has Ms. Jenkins called you?"

"Yes," her grandmother said nonchalantly.

Sonja was taken aback by her grandmother's casual tone. "She called today?"

'Yes."

"About the toilet?"

"Yes, Sonja, is that all you wanted to ask?"

Sonja quickly sat back in her armchair. "And what do you think about what she had to say?"

"Didn't you call a plumber?" Gran asked.

"Yes," Sonja said leadingly.

"And now the toilet's fixed?"

"But she stuffed a wig down it. On purpose."

Gran huffed impatiently. "Is there anything else?"

Sonja scratched the back of her head feverishly. Hell yes, there was something else! She couldn't take it anymore. Something had to be done about Ms. Jenkins. Immediately.

"Gran, listen, Ms. Jenkins doesn't pay rent, yet she's the tenant I service the most. She's rude. And she purposely breaks shit just so she can torture me." Oh goodness, she was whining and that never worked to sway Lorraine Hester to rule in her favor.

"I'm not evicting her," her grandmother bluntly stated.

In the past, her grandmother's tone would've been enough to make Sonja drop the entire conversation and just deal with it, but only one deranged tenant stood between her and her job being tolerable. She heard Regina, her grandmother's executive assistant, mention that they had three minutes before their conference call with T Corp.

"One moment," Gran said to Regina. "Sonja darling, you're calling me with problems and complaints, but I can only support you if you bring me solutions."

Sonja tried to sit farther back in her chair, but she had already pinched it against the wall. "I want to evict Ms. Jenkins."

"That's not going to happen. Is that all you have for me?"

Sonja clenched her teeth and groaned inaudibly. "Okay, then I need to hire an assistant and a full-time handyman."

"Now that I can sanction. Put it in writing."

Sonja jerked her head in shock. "Really?"

"Don't put this on me, darling. I've been waiting for you to ask for what you want. You often behave as if I haven't taught you anything."

Sonja grimaced. "What do you mean?"

"When life gets difficult, you either give up or run yourself ragged trying to control the chaos instead of asking for help. So you asked for help and I'm giving it to you. Now, I'm late for my conference call. Goodbye, my love."

"Bye, Gran," she barely said.

After her line went silent, Sonja sat with the phone against her ear as thoughts raced through her mind. Was that who she was? Someone who didn't ask for what she wanted? Someone who settled? Someone who ran away from difficulty? Was she the person who had given up on her dreams because, except for managing Ms. Jenkins, it was easier to be the mayor of crazy town?

Instead of putting together a budget request report and commencing the search for a handyman, Sonja went back to her apartment and collapsed on her bed. There was a rumor in her family, one that Sonja strongly believed, that the Hester women were cursed to never find love. Sonja's older sister Elaine, who she called Laney, always accused Sonja of using that silly curse as a crutch to justify giving up on love.

Sonja stared at the French doors that led to her small patio overlooking the backyard garden. She didn't have to get up to cherish the view—it was burned into her brain. The complex was certainly a stunning piece of property. Her grandmother had bought the first apartment building on the ten-acre estate in the eighties. It had white stone walls with a red tiled roof and a big limestone bowl-shaped fountain surrounded by cobblestones in the courtyard. Six years later, her grandmother made a deal to buy an identical building next door. Then she purchased the two mini-mansions behind the two structures. Next she acquired the appropriate permits to combine all four properties into one. That was when the major renovation occurred, which included landscaping the grounds to feel and look like paradise.

Sonja walked to the French doors. No wonder she had let herself remain lost on the estate. She admired the cacti and the Mediterranean plants, such as Phormiums, agaves, Cordylines, flax lilies, lavender, and red bottlebrushes. For more color, there were birds of paradise, lilies-of-the-Nile, and an array of colorful roses. Islands of palm trees were surrounded by white rocks. It was daytime now, but at night, the plants were all lit by lights placed decoratively through the foliage. She could've hidden in the beautiful world of the complex forever and the thought of doing that made her stomach feel queasy.

Sonja turned away from the beautiful grounds and faced her closet. The door was open and the first thing her eyes fell on was the navy dress suit she'd bought for job interviews. She hadn't worn it since giving up on her dream of being a screenwriter. Unfortunately she had to start from the dreadful bottom. When it came to Hollywood, those who knew somebody—close friends or family members who were already in—had the best chances of climbing the ladder and making it to the top. A face came to mind, one she hadn't seen since she was fifteen years old. Her old best friend Jay West. He was a big-time movie star, but she would rather eat nails than ask him for a lift up.

She breathed in deeply through her nose and held it. Tomorrow, she would make that eight thirty a.m. meeting. She was one hundred percent sure Mike Gillespie would treat her as though she should be so grateful he'd invited her to grace his presence that she should lick his boots. He would be rude of course. Sonja forcefully released the breath.

Nope.

She couldn't let the fear of rejection win. Sonja stopped painting a future that incited dread and decided to use her grandmother's words to help her face life's uncertainties head-on. Tomorrow at eight thirty, she would be there, and only then would she know what would happen next.

CHAPTER 3

SONJA HESTER

Sonja had hardly slept at all. So many times while lying awake in her dark room, she'd had to talk herself into waking up at six o'clock to get dressed and brave Thursday morning traffic in order to make Gillespie's mystery meeting. Even while stopping and going west up San Vicente Boulevard, she had to fight the urge to turn her car around and inch her way back home.

But she didn't turn around. She made a right onto Avenue of The Stars in Century City, then another right, and drove down the ramp into AMTA's vast underground parking garage. The last time she had taken the drive down the incline and stopped at the security booth, she had been proud to announce to the guard that she was Mike Gillespie's new client, even though he hadn't asked. This time she silently took the ticket from him.

"Who are you here to see?" he asked to her surprise.

"Mike Gillespie," she mumbled.

The guard grabbed a clipboard. "Your name?"

"Sonja Hester," she muttered.

"One second." He ran his finger down a list.

All Sonja wanted to do was flee the scene as she waited for the guy to do something in the booth. She thought maybe Douchebag Gillespie had changed his mind until the guard stepped out, smiling.

He gave her a nametag with Sonja Hester written on it. "This is for you." He pointed toward her right. "Park over there in the yellow section next to the motorcycle. Once you've parked, take one of the elevators which will be right in front of you. You'll need to scan the back of your badge against the red light on the wall for the doors to open. Once you're in, hit L and you will be taken to the lobby. Reception will be expecting you."

Sonja could hardly believe what she had just heard. For some reason, it sounded as if she was receiving special treatment. But why?

Sonja's head felt floaty as she followed the

guard's instructions to a T. The elevator doors slid open, and a young woman with dark hair and porcelain skin gazed at her from behind the receptionist's station.

"Welcome, Miss Hester," the receptionist said with what appeared to be a practiced smile.

Sonja wanted to smile back, but all the curiosity plaguing her brain wouldn't let her. "Um, I'm here to see Mike Gillespie."

"Right, you're here for the meeting."

"Okay," Sonja said if her mind was a million miles away.

She did exactly as the receptionist instructed and took the elevators to the twenty-eighth floor, where she sat in the waiting room to the right. The space looked the same as it had four years ago. The carpet was still red. The chairs were still black leather with metal frames. All that changed was the artwork on the walls. Each picture was a black-and-white still of old Hollywood studios. They used to be portraits of the oldest and newest premium clients. She remembered Jay's picture hanging on the wall and how she'd successfully avoided looking at him.

Sonja stopped shaking her foot nervously as soon as she realized she was doing it. Deep down, she really didn't want to be there. She stared at the iconic picture of the Hollywood sign as she remembered how hard it was to make her dream of being a screenwriter a reality.

After graduating from film school, Sonja had spent about four and half years bouncing around from job to job as an assistant before throwing in the towel. There was the production executive who rarely bathed and was mean as hell, so no one could tell her how bad she smelled without getting fired. There was the crazy producer who barked at everyone, including her tiny designer puppy that she brought to the office every day. Then there was the average big-bellied, balding, aging creep who would let inappropriate propositions slip out of his mouth. If she went to his house, then he would probably get her a meeting with someone big, very big. If she went to dinner with him, then they could talk about her future. But most of them had had a way of testing the waters first, just to see how far they could go and what she was willing to do to make it to the big time. There had been too many of those guys to count.

Thinking about her previous encounters with Hollywood cast a dark cloud over Sonja's head, and she whipped her face around to get a look at the way out of the waiting room.

"Sonja Hester?" a girl with a high-pitched voice asked.

She jumped and quickly turned to face the speaker. "Yes."

The girl, who looked like the receptionist but blond, smiled. "Could you please follow me?"

Sonja stood so fast her head felt dizzy. "Sure."

She followed the girl down the carpeted hallway and through a wide open floor filled mostly with unoccupied cubicles. From what she remembered, the scene usually picked up around nine o'clock. She wondered why the meeting had started so early.

The girl continued her brisk pace but turned to ask, "How was your drive?"

Sonja wanted to make a cynical reply that would truthfully reflect how anxious she felt, but instead she put on a fake smile and said, "Fine."

"Good," the girl sang as though it was the best news she'd heard in a long time.

They walked up a spiral staircase with shiny silver handrails then down a hallway. The closer they got to an open door, the more Sonja could hear multiple voices coming from inside the room. Fear spoke to her again, telling her to turn tail and run like the wind. She took one deep breath then another.

The assistant turned and held out her hand. "By the way, I'm Katie. It was my pleasure to meet you."

Sonja ruffled her brows, then after a few moments, shook Katie's hand. It felt all too much, as though Katie had taken a moment to suck up to her. "Thank you."

Katie pressed her lips into a tight smile then raised her eyebrows as if to say, "And now it's game time."

Sonja followed Katie into the room and was instantly caught off guard by all the attendees sitting around a large oval table. They were all men except for one woman. Sonja attempted to count the number of people present, but her mind kept botching the number.

Then the one woman, who was petite and wore a short blond bob haircut, stood and walked toward her with an outstretched hand. "Sonja Hester?"

"Yes," Sonja barely said as her narrowed eyes fell on one face in particular.

"I'm Fiona Meadows. We're happy you could make it."

Fiona's grip was weak, but Sonja shook her hand anyway.

The guy. Was it…? There was no doubt it was him. Sure, he had grown quite a bit older, but he still had the same floppy blond hair and sky-blue eyes. Scraggly hair painted the lower part of his face, and he was sitting back in his chair as if he were leaning away from the sight of her while watching her with an incredulous expression.

Suddenly it was as if everyone else in the room had vanished.

"Jay?" she said.

He nodded slowly. "Good morning, Sonja." His tone was formal, as though they had never once been the most important person in each other's life.

Sonja could hardly breathe. Her feet felt planted securely on the carpet. She glanced over her shoulder, wanting to make a mad dash out of his presence. When she looked at him again, he was still watching her with the same dubious expression. And that's when all the ill feelings she had for Jay West came rushing back like a tsunami.

CHAPTER 4

SONJA HESTER

JULY 1998

The front door flew open.

"Ouch!" Sonja shook her hand then sucked on the finger she had just pricked with the tip of a needle.

She was sewing the torso to the legs she had already stuffed with cotton. Even though she was anxious to be done, she had taken care to ensure each stitch was straight and strong enough to withstand some intense performances.

"Play with him," her sister Elaine ordered and then zipped upstairs with Riley West on her heels.

Riley was the odd-looking girl whose hair was so

blond it looked white. She lived six houses down the street, and before three weeks ago, she and Laney had been mortal enemies. Now they were self-absorbed, superficial, and inseparable best friends.

Earlier that day, Laney and Riley had taken the city bus from Hancock Park all the way to the Santa Monica Pier. Sonja's grandmother had wanted Sonja to go with them so that she could get some air, but last weekend, Sonja actually had accompanied them. It was a harrowing experience. Laney and Riley wore bikinis under short, see-through white dresses. They walked funny, swinging their tiny hips to attract male attention. And it worked! Only it wasn't the boys their age who were losing their minds over them—it was grown men who were old enough to be their fathers. Sonja found it all so gross. Plus, she knew her grandmother wanted her to shadow Elaine just so she could keep an eye on her older sister. Sonja had no problems reporting back to Gran anything Elaine did wrong, but that morning she had refused to be Gran's snitch. Nothing would change anyway if she went. Just like last weekend, and all those before it, Elaine and Riley would walk out the door half-naked and looking to make anyone of the opposite sex fawn over them like dogs in heat. So Sonja had insisted on staying home and doing what *she* thought was fun instead.

Sonja and the boy who had been dumped into her lap locked eyes. He looked an awful lot like Riley, only younger. He even had the same shaggy blond hair, except his was shoulder-length. She actually would've thought he was a girl if Laney hadn't told her to play with "him."

Both of them seemed trapped in a moment they wished didn't exist.

"Hi," she said timidly.

"Hi." His tone was similar to hers.

Getting him to respond was easier than she thought, but she wondered if they had anything in common. "Are you my age?"

He wrinkled his forehead. "I don't know. I'm eleven."

Sonja smiled. "Me too. I mean, I'll turn eleven in September. What's your name?"

"Jay." He lifted his chin to get a better look at what was in her hands. "What are you doing?"

Sonja glanced at the needle pinched between her fingers. She'd forgotten she was holding it. "I'm making another puppet."

"Another puppet?"

She nodded. "I make them for my shows."

"Oh?" He sounded intrigued. The boy didn't move a muscle though. He stood there as if he was caught between running out the door and staying put.

She scrunched up her nose. "Did you have to go to the beach with those two?" She thought maybe that was why he seemed so weird. Spending all day with Laney and Riley was enough to make anyone feel skittish.

"Yeah," he said with a sigh of dread.

"They like boys a lot," she said.

"All girls do."

She shook her head vigorously. "Not me. I like doing constructive things."

"Oh yeah?" He sounded intrigued.

Her head bounced as she nodded.

"Then you don't like boys?"

She shook her head. "Not like Laney and Riley. Sometimes boys can be fun, as long as we're doing something constructive."

"What do you mean by constructive?"

"My gran said it's doing something that makes me smarter and helps me fulfill my purpose in life."

He crossed his arms. "Jeez, that's heavy."

"I know. Plus, we're cursed anyway," she said, repeating what her cousin Theresa, who was fifteen years old just like Laney, often said. Basically, hunting boys was a lost cause because the Hester girls were cursed to never get married. That's why their mothers were never around. They were always chasing bad men, trying to get the men to love them in order to break an unbreakable spell.

Jay uncrossed his arms and walked toward her. "But curses aren't real."

"Ours is," she said as he sat beside her. He smelled like the ocean and corndogs. Laney and Riley must've spent most of their day at Hot Dogs on a Stick, trying to get the attention of the boys they liked who worked there.

"Curses are only real if you believe them. Just stop believing them."

She beamed. "But I like the curse. I get to live here with my gran because of it."

He grimaced. "Why's that?"

Sonja shrugged because she didn't want to say that her mom liked being with men more than she liked taking care of her and Laney. "I don't know. I just like living here."

"I guess that's cool." He pointed at the puppet in Sonja's hand. "What kind of puppet are you making?"

She raised the puppet higher. "She's called Skinny Pig."

He laughed, and she could tell it was because he liked the name.

"You want to help me? After I make her, I'm going to put on a show."

He tilted his head curiously. "Do you have a script?"

She frowned. "A script?"

"Like a movie script or a TV script?"

Sonja had never heard of a script, but she sort of guessed what he was referring to. "Do you mean like a play?"

He shot his finger toward her. "Yes. Like a play."

"I wrote a play. I always write them." She waited for Jay to laugh at her. Laney always said her plays were stupid and not at all interesting because she was only ten years old and people her age didn't know anything about how the world worked.

"Do you need an actor?" Jay asked. "I've done sixteen commercials and I'm up for a part in a movie called *Space Vermin*."

Sonja scooted to the edge of the sofa. "Cool! Yeah, I do need an actor!"

She was so excited to hear that. Jay was exactly

what she needed—a real actor who could bring her stories to life. She was never any good at performing the lines herself.

They smiled at each other again. It was strange, but Sonja felt as if she had known Jay all of her life and that they would be friends forever.

They spent the rest of the afternoon finishing Skinny Pig, then they built a new stage for the puppet show. They rehearsed the lines Sonja had written and rewrote them until Jay made sure that when he spoke the words, they sounded natural. By nightfall, they had used her grandmother's video camera to record a full production of *Skinny Pig Finds New Friends*. She had never seen her plays on video until then, and instantly she became hooked on recording all of her shows and watching them like she would a TV program.

Jay came back to Sonja's house the next day and the next. Soon they had become inseparable and remained so even after the many times Laney and Riley's friendship crumbled to shreds, re-erected, and collapsed again.

It didn't take long for their puppet shows to become one-man plays starring Jay West. Their productions turned into the talk of the neighborhood, and soon they began to charge local kids three dollars per seat to view Jay's Saturday afternoon performance. The audience was mostly made up of girls who thought Jay was cute and the boys who liked the girls who were infatuated by Jay.

Sonja and Jay also rode their bikes to school together. Whenever Jay's caretaker would let her, Sonja accompanied them to Jay's tapings for a commercial or a guest role on a television show. Since Jay's parents, Carla and Jason, were rarely home, Jay slept over at her house most nights.

Sonja and Jay became very close, like family. He knew how much it hurt Sonja whenever her mother landed a new boyfriend and ran off with him not too long after. And she knew how very lonely it was to live in Jay's home.

"It's okay," Jay would say. "My parents didn't want us, and you know what? I don't want them either."

As one year faded into the next, the girls who liked Jay and the ones he liked back never approved of their special friendship. After all, Sonja had boobs and the kind of body Laney insisted she show off more so that she could land a real boyfriend.

But on September 7, 2001, everything changed. It was Sonja's fifteenth birthday, and they hadn't seen each other or talked for weeks. However, Jay had finally picked up one of the many calls she made to him and agreed to join her for a birthday night movie-a-thon. The movie-a-thon was something they had done on special occasions, like the first day of summer or Christmas break or Halloween night, since neither one of them liked candy enough to go trick-or-treating for it. They would start watching movies at ten o'clock at night and keep going until ten o'clock the next morning.

Admittedly, she was surprised and relieved when he showed up in his plaid pajamas. She figured he had been avoiding her because Ginger, his pretty new girlfriend, didn't like that they were such good friends. Once they settled in in the basement, Sonja sneaked a peek at him while curled up on the other end of the long sofa. Jay, who had been distant ever since he arrived, had the blanket pulled up to his neck. Nevertheless, she was glad he was there.

The movie *Memento* was on, the lights were off, and one large pizza was sitting on the coffee table, untouched. With every passing second, Sonja wondered if she had to fall on her knees and beg Jay to remain her best friend. Finally he shifted abruptly. She thought he was going in for a piece of pizza, but instead he snatched up the remote control and put the movie on pause.

"What's going on between us?" he asked.

Sonja jerked her head back. "I don't know. You're the one who's acting strange."

He floated back against the sofa and squeezed his eyes shut. "I am?"

"Yeah, actually, and it's awful the way you're shitting on our night."

Jay reached out to touch her but then pulled back. "I'm sorry, Son. I don't want to do that."

She smiled tightly as she nodded. There was the thoughtful friend she had grown to adore. "That's okay. I just figured Ginger doesn't want you here but you came anyway and now you're feeling guilty about it."

Jay stared into her eyes for a few moments and then moistened his lips. "Nah, that's not it."

Sonja's lips parted. She wanted to ask him what was it then, but more importantly she wondered why he was looking at her in that way. Finally she swallowed. "Then Ginger's okay with you being here?"

"No, she isn't okay with it, but I don't know." He shrugged. "I don't think I like her anymore."

"Oh." She struggled to speak because she had become breathless. Perhaps because she was so darn thankful and hopeful that she was going to get her friend back.

Jay continued to look her steadily in the eyes as he nodded continuously.

Sonja crossed and uncrossed her legs. "What? Why are you looking at me like that?"

It was strange, because Jay had often gazed at her in that way and until now, she had ignored it.

"What about us?" he asked.

She quickly turned away from his hypnotizing stare and her eyes landed on the TV screen. "We're friends, right?" Her heart fluttered and nervous breaths wafted across her lower lip as she waited for his answer.

"When I first saw you…" he finally said.

She turned to regard him. Even though he was close, he seemed many miles away.

Jay cleared his throat. "I thought you were the prettiest girl I'd ever seen."

That sounded nonsensical to Sonja. She threw her hands up. "But I was only ten, and you were eleven."

"I know. And you told me you weren't interested in boys."

"And you told me you weren't interested girls."

"I never said that."

Sonja pressed her hand over her heart as she tried to remember a conversation that had happened four years earlier. She couldn't.

"I like *you,* but you don't like me back, and that's okay. But that's all I ever wanted to tell you." He cracked a tiny smile, but Sonja didn't think it was a happy moment.

Suddenly she became hyper-aware of everything around them. She noticed the man on the television screen sitting at the diner's bar with a cup of coffee in front of him. She turned, and there was the long set of steps leading up out of the basement. Then there were Jay's eyes, the ones she had looked into a million times and for a trillion reasons.

Could she like Jay in that way? Was she supposed to like him, or any boy, romantically? They had never spoken about sex, but she knew Jay was doing it with all of his girlfriends. She'd never told him what she thought about that. He was way too young to do such adult things, but Jay had always been more mature than she was. At times, him having sex with his girlfriends made her jealous, but then she pictured herself beneath him and those feelings dissipated. She was far from ready to engage in anything like that.

Until now.

But it didn't matter, because one indelible fact had to be taken into consideration. "I'm cursed, Jay. So you can't like me—not like that at least."

He rolled his eyes as he groaned. "You're not cursed. You gotta stop telling yourself that story because you're making it a self-fulfilling prophecy."

"Yeah, but…" She looked down at her lap. She wanted to believe Jay, but her mom and aunt were proving the curse to be true by constantly chasing men who always broke their hearts.

"Listen, Sonja," he said jarringly.

She looked up. "Yeah?"

Sonja crossed and uncrossed her arms after he scooted so close that she could feel the warmth of his energy washing over her. She could also smell the sweet citrus scent of his breath.

"Haven't you ever wanted to kiss me or something?" he asked.

Her head was spinning. "I don't know," she whispered then swallowed to moisten her dry throat.

"Why not?"

Sonja knew the answer, but it was too complex to not sound like a nerd. So she dropped her head and stared at her tingling thighs.

"Come on, tell me," Jay urged, proving he knew her all too well.

She lifted her head and stared into his eyes. "Well…" She closed her eyes, trying to find the right words. "Your girlfriends never last long, and I want to know you forever."

Jay leaned away as if what she'd said stung a little. Sonja instantly kicked herself for being honest.

"Can we kiss and see?" he asked.

She didn't have to ask him to clarify. Sonja knew what Jay wanted to "see." And perhaps she wanted to know too. If they kissed, would she like it? Things were happening to her body in that very moment that she had certainly felt before—like the time she had been locked in the closet for five minutes with Cory Lake and he kissed and licked her neck and rubbed her crotch the whole time. Her panties had been dripping wet and she'd wondered how and why that had happened.

Sonja's lips were parted and she was speechless.

"Can we?" Jay asked.

She felt her head bobbing lightly above her shoulders. And then his lips were getting closer and closer to hers. They touched. Their tongues connected. Sonja closed her eyes as desire exploded through her body. She had never kissed anyone like that before, but instinctively she knew how to partake.

Soon Jay was on top of her, grinding her with the solidness between his legs. With each thrust and rub, Sonja felt sensations so pleasurable that she had to open her eyes to make sure it was actually happening. Jay sucked on her neck as he moaned and rubbed himself against her. Oh, the emotions racing through her—desire, excitement, pleasure, and lust.

Then his fingers touched her down there. Back and forth they stimulated the sensitive area. The impact was immediate. Their dazed eyes connected. What was he doing to her? Her hips, having a mind of their own, gravitated away then back toward his fingers. She shook and moaned, trying not to make too much noise. And then something happened. Sonja pushed the back of her head into the pillow and softly whimpered as the ultimate feeling spread through her young lady parts. And then Jay's lips were on hers and his tongue in her mouth.

In the afterglow of the strange but pleasurable sensations, she and Jay stared into each other's eyes. A line had been crossed, and there was no going back.

Abruptly he sat up and closed his mouth. "I have to go." He stood.

Sonja stared at her crotch and nodded.

"I'll call you later," he said.

"Uh-huh," she said, keeping her gaze on her pajamas.

Then she heard his footsteps as he grabbed his bag and ran up the stairs. She didn't look up until he was gone.

After Jay left, Sonja knew their friendship would never be the same, and she was right. Jay went back to not answering her calls. His career had taken off, so he was rarely home, and when she happened to run into him, he would be at the pizza place on Larchmont with a girl she'd never met or with a new group of male friends. Once she said hello and he barely looked at her and mumbled, "Hi."

After that, Sonja stopped calling him, and if by chance she saw him, she would turn and walk in the opposite direction. Then, after Christmas, his parents' divorce was finalized and he and Riley moved to Bel-Air to live with their mother. Days turned to years until one day Jay West was just a boy she used to know and the best friend who'd broken her heart.

CHAPTER 5

SONJA HESTER

Sonja ripped her eyes away from Jay's face and made herself smile halfheartedly at Fiona Meadows. It took everything inside her to keep her from saying screw it and walking in the opposite direction.

"Hi," she barely said.

"Come have a seat. We're all excited to get to know you better," Fiona said.

The moment felt too surreal to be true. But at least her feet were still working as she followed Fiona to the only empty chair at the table. She hated that she was over-aware of Jay's presence. He was sitting next to the guy at the head of the table, on the opposite side of her. Sonja's head was spinning and she wanted to fan her heated skin but didn't want anyone to see how flustered she was.

The guy in the most important seat touched his chest. "I'm Vincent Adams, president and founder of AEE, previously A&Rt, and I think I can speak for everyone here when I say you've written a spectacular screenplay."

Sonja's mouth was dry, so she swallowed hard. "Thank you."

Don't look, don't look, she kept repeating to herself as everyone present introduced themselves. Sonja couldn't retain any of their names. However, she did remember Mike Gillespie, who was still short but had more of that greasy and stiff stuff in his hair since it had obviously thinned a great deal.

"And so your screenplay, *Pact of Lies*, we want to make into a TV series," Mike Gillespie said.

"However, I will be your agent," Fiona quickly said.

"Unless you prefer to stay with me," Mike countered.

Sonja frowned, confused. It almost sounded as if they were fighting over her.

Fiona delicately held up a finger. "Elaine and I hammered out your contract, and in it, I am your agent."

"Contracts can be modified."

"Give me a fucking break, Mike," Fiona snapped, rolling her eyes. "You sat your lazy ass on this story for years. Probably because you knew she wouldn't blow your tiny dick."

"Fuck you Fiona," Mike barked.

"Enough," Vincent Adams said. His eyebrows were deeply furrowed, indicating he was not at all happy with their bickering.

It was then Sonja realized she had been staring at Jay while the agents squabbled. Suddenly she felt like her fifteen-year-old self again, so very hurt about how he'd walked out of her basement and out of her life forever. However, her brain held on to a name Fiona had mentioned, which made it impossible to listen to what Vincent Adams was saying about the pilot episode.

Sonja raised a finger. "I'm sorry, did you say Elaine?"

Vincent stopped speaking, and everyone looked at her as though they were shocked she had interrupted him.

"Elaine Hester? My sister Elaine?" she asked.

Jay adjusted in his seat. "Yes, Elaine."

She closed her eyes to take a brisk breath. The one thing she hated more than servicing Ms. Jenkins's apartment was Elaine meddling in her life. She waved her finger, knowing exactly one thing for sure. "Sorry, I can't do this right now."

She stood so fast that she became dizzy. Her frowning eyes rolled around the table, observing the shocked faces. The desire to get the hell out of there heavily outweighed rationality, which was telling her that they were presenting her with a once-in-a-lifetime opportunity. But still, she abhorred that Elaine had found a new and improved way to make her feel inadequate. On top of that, she felt ambushed by Jay, who should've had the fortitude to contact her and tell her all about the meeting she found herself part of at that moment.

As though she were having an out-of-body experience, she watched herself walk out of the conference room as fast as her feet would carry her without running. No one seemed to notice as she picked up her pace. Soon she was riding the elevator back to the parking garage.

Sonja couldn't jump into her car fast enough. Escaping became as vital to her as the blood in her body. She started the engine and backed out of her parking space. Her wheels screeched as she turned sharply toward the exit. It wasn't until she was in the sunlight and making a left turn onto San

Vicente Boulevard that she realized what she had done. She would probably never have another opportunity to work in Hollywood again.

Sonja clenched the steering wheel and screamed at the top of her lungs, hoping that would release her frustration, anxiety, and anger. It didn't.

Then she pictured Jay sitting at the table, staring at her just as absentmindedly as she was gazing at him.

"Shit," she whispered. "What the hell happened back there?"

THERE WAS SOMETHING FAMILIAR ABOUT THE motorcycle parked in front of the complex. Wasn't it the same one she'd seen in the parking garage at the AMTA Building? And then she saw Jay West standing in front of the red wooden gate.

"Oh my…" she whispered. Her heart started pounding out of her chest.

Sonja chewed nervously on her bottom lip as she waited for the gate to open. She glanced at him, he waved at her, and she swiftly faced forward again. Thankfully, she had been granted entrance, so she drove up the concrete path while asking herself what she should do. Should she go straight to her apartment and ignore that Jay had not only followed her but beat her home? Or should she storm to the red gate, fling it open, and give him a piece of her mind?

Instead, as soon as she got out of her car, she clutched her stomach and walked slowly to where he was. The only thing she felt was numb as her hand grasped the brass handle and she opened the gate.

"Sorry," was the first thing Jay said to her.

She stared into his crystal-blue eyes. She had forgotten how pale they were. However, he was far from the shaggy-haired, fresh-faced boy, the one who always had a pinch of something she couldn't define in his eyes, that she used to know.

"What do you want?" Sonja snapped. She sounded mean, even though she didn't want to, but it was where her disposition was defaulting to at the moment and she found herself unable to change it.

"Can we talk about what just happened?"

She narrowed an eye. "Is that all?"

"I got the feeling that you're pissed off as hell at me."

Sonja folded her arms and glared at him. "I

haven't seen you in nearly fifteen years, and when I do, it's at a meeting at AMTA?"

He closed his eyes and nodded as though he was feeling the impact of her words. "Like I said, I'm sorry about that. I would've called you and said something, but I wasn't sure you would talk to me."

They stared into each other's eyes. Sonja didn't know whether to hug him and say it was good to see him or make him work harder for her forgiveness.

She unfolded her arms. "It's fine. I accept your apology."

He cracked a tiny smile. "That's a relief. And listen, Son, I can't change what happened fifteen years ago, but I found your screenplay and it's solid. Elaine negotiated you premium terms, so be angry with me all you want but don't let this opportunity slip through your fingers."

She winced as she remembered walking out on all of those important people seated around that table. She dreaded the moment Elaine heard about that. The thought of sitting through another one of her sister's lectures about how she was purposely choosing to live an unremarkable life made her want to escape to Timbuktu. However, at the moment, she wasn't sure Elaine was wrong. If Jay had never shown up, she would've been happy to let the opportunity fall by the wayside. The fact that she had been so afraid and setting herself up to comfortably continue down the road to nowhere while her hopes and dreams dissolved more and more with each passing day made her tug the gate open wider so that Jay could enter.

"Follow me," she said.

CHAPTER 6

SONJA HESTER

"Nice place," Jay said as his observation moved from the kitchen to the living room then to the hallway that led to two bedrooms and two bathrooms.

"Thanks," Sonja muttered because she was so nervous. She took a deep breath to gather her bearings. "Would you like a cup of coffee?"

He shrugged before his hooded eyes landed on her. They were staring into each other's eyes, and all the work Sonja had done to breathe steadily went down the drain.

"Sure," he said finally.

"Okay." She ripped her eyes off him and made a beeline to the kitchen. "What kind of coffee do you like?" she asked, discarding a used pod out of the Keurig machine and then inserting a new one.

Jay had found his way to the living room and sat down on the sofa. “What do you have?” He crossed his legs, setting his foot right above his knee.

“Buttercream coffee, French Roast, chocolate pecan…”

“The soft stuff?” He chuckled.

He was grinning when she looked at him, so she smiled too. Sonja turned her head slightly. "I have red wine?"

He shook his head. “I’ll have whatever you’re having.”

“Okay, buttercream coffee it is.”

She kept the machine purring so they couldn’t engage in small talk, which gave her a little more time to figure out how to start the conversation between them. But she totally forgot the approach she had chosen to take as soon as she caught him staring at her.

Jay raised his eyebrows. "You look good, Sonja." He said it like he meant it sincerely.

“Thanks. Would you like cream and sugar?” she asked.

“No.”

“No cream or sugar?”

He shook his head. “None.”

“Okay,” she said out of breath and added a teaspoon of cream to her coffee before bringing their drinks to the living room.

“Smells good,” he said as she handed him the coffee.

"Tastes good too." She sat down beside him. She took a quick breath as she handed him the coffee.

They sipped their coffees at the same time.

“You’re right. It does taste good,” he said.

She smiled, then they were back at it again, looking into each other's eyes and grinning. It felt strange because they were no longer kids. They were adults and she was experiencing him as such. However, she couldn't help but notice all the strain on Jay's face.

“You look tired,” she said then inhaled sharply. She hadn’t meant for those words to escape.

Jay snickered. “That’s because I am.” He dropped his leg from his thigh and onto the hardwood floor. “I’ve been working like crazy to get this project off the ground.”

Sonja hung her head, allowing shame of how she walked out of the meeting to pass through her.

"Well..." She sighed. "Opportunities come and go."

Jay patted her thigh. "Don't worry, Son, you're still in."

She jerked her head back. "Really? I figured they would never want to work with me again. I mean, that was pretty intensely insane behavior I displayed back there."

He snorted cynically. "It wasn't as bad as that shit show Fiona and Mike put on."

Sonja floated back against a pillow while carefully cradling her cup of coffee. "Oh right, that was pretty bad."

"It can get worse," he said.

A sense of relief ran through her. She wanted to say good, but the fact that it could be worse wasn't good. They fell silent, so Sonja took a few sips of her coffee as Jay set his on a coaster on the coffee table.

"Sonja." He turned his body to face her. "I just want to say that I'm sorry. I was the one who left you high and dry back then, and..." He pressed his lips together and stared into her eyes.

She closed hers and remembered what she had planned to ask earlier while making their coffee. "Was I wrong?"

“Wrong about what?”

She opened her eyes. “How close we were as friends?”

Jay’s mouth opened then closed. He leaned toward her. “After what happened…” He cleared his throat. “I didn’t know what to do.”

"It was just one moment. It shouldn't have cost so much." Her voice was shaky as she fought back the tears. Even though she was as still as a mountain, Sonja's heart was beating a mile a minute.

Jay sighed heavily as his eyebrows gathered inward. “We were only fifteen. It was a lot.”

“But you used to have sex with all of your girlfriends.”

He shifted in his seat. “Yeah, but that was different.”

She knew her eyes asked him to explain further.

“It was different with you.” He scooted to the edge of the sofa. “Think about a defibrillator, okay?” he said, gesturing intensely.

“Okay,” she barely said.

“My heart had stopped, and each time I had sex with a girl, it was as if the paramedics would yell, ‘Clear!’ and they’d shock my heart, and nothing would happen.” His glossy eyes connected with hers.

Sonja's head felt floaty as she was captivated by Jay's analogy.

"Until we were on that couch. When I kissed you, it shocked my heart and that time it started beating."

The silence between them was awkward. If only Sonja hadn't known exactly what he was talking about. She wanted to confess that she'd had to grapple with the same emotions, only she'd managed to stuff them and store them away by the next morning.

Jay sat up straight. "So we were once friends"—he shrugged—"do you think we can get back to that?"

Sonja didn't have to think twice. She smiled. "Of course." She examined his face as he grinned at her. His eyes were watery, but goodness he looked so beat. "It's just… I haven't written anything in a long time."

"Why not? You used to write all the time."

She sighed and shook her head briskly. "I don't know."

And that was the truth. Something had turned off inside her after she wrote *Pact of Lies,* and whatever that was had never turned back on.

"Okay well…" He opened the messenger bag

he'd set on the floor and took out a small stack of papers. "You should read this contract. Elaine negotiated you the moon."

Sonja rolled her eyes. "She's always sticking her nose where it doesn't belong." She shook her head as the next thought came to her mind. "Last month I received a check for seventy thousand dollars! I mean, I'm not complaining about the money, but I really hate it when Laney thinks it's okay to pick up the parts of my life where she thinks I'm failing." More anger surged through her body and she shook her hands. "I mean, it feels like judgment to me. And you know what? She never does anything for free. She's going to come collecting sooner or later, just watch."

Jay chuckled. "Yeah, I figured she hadn't changed much. But in this case, I'm glad she stuck her nose where it didn't belong."

"No, she's…" she said, reading the first paragraph of the contract. She widened her eyes at Jay. "Co-creator?"

He winked.

She read some more then stifled a gasp. "Executive producer?"

Jay pointed at the contract. "And co-lead writer."

"Come hell or high water, my sister almost always gets what she wants."

"Almost and not always?" Jay asked.

Sonja rolled her eyes. "Next year she'll be on her fifth wedding day, so no."

Jay flinched slightly. "Fifth wedding day?"

Sonja raised four fingers. "Four men have asked Elaine to marry them, and all of them have literally left her standing at the altar."

Jay chuckled. "I'm sure that supports your cursed theory."

"Hmm…" Sonja picked up her cup of coffee and took a sip. Actually, she hated retelling that factoid about Elaine's hard luck and wished she had never mentioned it. But her thoughts about the Hester girls being cursed had evolved over the years.

"What, you don't believe you're cursed anymore?"

She pursed then relaxed her lips. "I don't know. But over the years, I've realized it's just not some outside force making my sister's fiancés change their minds about marrying her. Elaine can be mad psycho."

Jay laughed, and Sonja joined him. All the nervous energy between them had dissipated. As soon as their laughter simmered, Sonja remembered something she had wanted to say to him for a long time.

She delicately touched his wrist. "By the way, I wanted to offer you my condolences about your father and mother."

In 2007, his father had been found dead after overdosing on painkillers, sleeping pills, and heroine, and three years later, his mom had died of cancer.

Jay remained silent as he nodded. He was still the same in that whenever he felt as though he were going to cry, he clenched his lips and bobbed his head until the sadness passed.

They let the silence linger for a while.

"I really missed you"—his eyes smoldered—"a lot."

Sonja skipped a breath as she searched deep inside to see if it was safe to say what she felt. "I missed you too."

They smiled, then to get rid of the awkwardness between them, Jay got right to business. Sonja finished reading and signing the contract, and Jay informed her that pre-production officially started in five days in Vancouver, Canada.

"Yikes!" She sat upright. "Canada?"

"It's economics. The dollar is stronger there. Plus it's a great place to be when you're in production."

Sonja nodded. "I know. It's just... I never thought I'd be part of one of those productions."

He nodded thoughtfully. "Well, I gotta tell you, Son, it's not going to be glamorous. There are a lot of egos on set. You think Elaine's crazy? Multiply that by ten."

Fear made her eyes grow wide. "Are you trying to discourage me?"

"No way. I want you there!" He winked as he flashed his winning smile. "But don't worry, because I'll protect you from the big bad assholes."

Sonja tossed her head back and laughed even though she was acutely aware that she was uncomfortable about finding him attractive. She was so relieved when Jay ushered them into serious time and got right down to business, explaining their impending schedule.

For the first four weeks, they would be staying in the villas on the studio compound, banging out eleven first season scripts. During that time, casting would be filling roles. He listed all the actors they would be soliciting before auditions started. They wanted a balance of new and established talent.

Once the screenplays were submitted and the cast set, they'd have two more weeks to prepare for production. However, they would only shoot five episodes, which meant the fifth script had to end on a cliffhanger. They would spend another six weeks in active production. After wrapping, the project would go into post-production and air mid-January of next year.

"Wow," Sonja said, staring into her empty cup sitting on the coffee table in front of her.

Hearing that solid schedule should've made her jump for joy, but instead her heart was beating so fast, she felt the reverberation in her throat. With every fiber of her being, she resisted the urge to tell Jay to tear up the contract so that she could go back to life as she knew it—servicing Ms. Jenkins's apartment as though she were the woman's own personal handyman and butler, working at the family-owned coffee shop on days when Robin had to show her art at a gallery, and living from day to day, assured of one thing—life would never change.

"That's a long time away from home," she said. Jay was about to say something, but she raised a hand to stop him. "I know. That's how it goes in the business."

He quickly drank the last of his coffee. "I was going to say wherever I am is home."

They shared another laugh. Jay had always been quick with the snappy jokes and she was so happy to hear them again.

He stood. "But listen, I can see on your face that you're terrified, but you got this, Son. And I would stay here and convince you some more but"—he patted the bag strapped across his body then looked at the face of his expensive watch—"I have to get these contracts to Vince Adams before he catches his flight."

Sonja took a breath as she stood. Their faces were close. For a moment, it felt as if they should kiss or something, but reason washed the feeling away.

"Well, thanks for the pep talk." She smiled warmly.

He affectionately cupped the side of her face. "Any time."

Sonja's smile wavered as her head felt as though it were floating so high it would smack into the ceiling. She took a step back. "Right." She knew she looked as conflicted as she sounded.

Jay chuckled as if he were the only one in on a joke he had just told himself. "I'll call you later."

“What for?” she said before realizing it.

His smile grew wider. “Why not?”

He headed to the door. Tongue-tied, Sonja watched him wave one last time before walking out of her apartment. She stood still for a long while, sifting through all the answers she had to the previous question he'd asked. The one that resonated the most was the fact that she needed time to figure out why her head floated when he touched her face. They were becoming friends again, not lovers, never lovers.

Sonja wiggled her head. “There,” she said in a high-pitched voice. “All’s normal again.”

And just like that, she felt the same as she did the day after she and Jay had fooled around on the sofa fifteen years earlier. The floaty feeling she had meant nothing.

CHAPTER 7

JAY WEST

Jay met Vincent Adams at the Santa Monica airport, where he dropped off the signed contract and agreement. He also had to assure the big-time executive that Sonja was indeed up for the job. Vince was alarmed by how she'd run out of the meeting and wondered if she had the resolve for taking on a project as massive as theirs while wearing all the hats her sister had negotiated for her.

"Because I had her pegged as a whole different kind of person," Vince said.

Jay nodded humbly and then put a hand on Vince's shoulder. "All I can ask is that you trust me."

Convincing Vince was his best performance yet, since he barely had faith in himself to pull off the colossal project. He was shocked he had made it that far and credited Elaine for it.

He took his hand off Vince's shoulder. "Plus, I'm the one who messed up by blindsiding her with the whole meeting."

Vince frowned. "She didn't know about the meeting?"

That was when Jay explained as much as was necessary about his and Sonja's past, which made Vince's frown even more intense.

Vince sighed briskly. "You came to me with a proposition, and I put a lot of trust in your word. Don't fuck this up."

All Jay could do was nod stiffly. He was in the business of fucking things up, especially the career he'd wanted to throw away up until the moment he ran into Elaine at AMTA. The last two months of negotiating the contract with Elaine and using her connections to bring people in on the project had been like new blood for Jay. Being bossed around by Elaine Hester made him feel as though he was back in the family again.

When he had first approached Jim Neely and Mike Gillespie with the idea of producing Sonja's script, they'd staunchly said no. They didn't want to have anything to do with Elaine or anyone related to her. So Jay had had to call their devil and pitch his idea of making Sonja's script to her. Elaine didn't have to be convinced.

"I just finished reading the thing, and lo and behold, the girl has chops. You would never think it by her severe lack of motivation." She snorted, and Jay could visualize her slightly rolling her eyes as she did whenever she criticized Sonja. "But if you want to make this, then I'm going to help you do it."

And that was the start of the most intense project he'd ever been part of during his long career as an A-list actor. Jay had never worked behind the camera, but Elaine was there to make sure he proceeded methodically and smartly.

"Rule number one," Elaine said, "make sure you know exactly what you need before you get other parties involved."

And so every day for two weeks straight, he sat down with accountants and production finance professionals to bang out a budget, getting a line item number on everything from ink pens to top-tier talent. They also figured out ways to get a better return on their investment. And so three things were determined by the conclusion of those meetings. Jay would finance the majority of the project in order to maintain creative control. He would also play the lead character and pay himself from profits. Finally, they would make the story into a TV series to maximize profits.

Jay and Elaine had close relationships with Vincent Adams of AEE, whose popular Prime D TV Channel had limited but premium commercials due to its high ratings. So by chance and without an appointment, since they were in Elaine's office together, she decided to place a conference call to Vince to pitch their idea.

"Just like that?" Jay asked.

"Hell yeah. Vince doesn't care. He's a shark always in search of a project that's going to take his network to the next level," she said as the phone rang twice before his assistant answered.

Jay thought for sure they would end up going through the same Hollywood bullshit rigmarole—Vince's assistant would tell them Mr. Adams isn't in the office and she would call back to set up a meeting, which would take another three days, then in a week or two, they would have to fly out to New York and meet with Vince in person. But that didn't happen.

As soon Vince learned it was Jay and Elaine on the line, he took the call and asked them every single question he could think of that was related to budget, which, thanks to Elaine, they were prepared to answer. He liked what he heard and asked for a copy of the screenplay, which Elaine's assistant had already scanned, so it was emailed to him immediately.

Two days later, Jay got a call from his agent asking him what the hell did he think he was doing, arranging the project behind his back, and a few hours later, Elaine informed him that Vincent Adams was in.

That was when shit started hitting the fan. First, Mike Gillespie caused problems with AEE by insisting that Sonja's screenplay was still represented by AMTA and would be so until the end of the month, which was only three days away. Gillespie threatened to sell the script if AMTA weren't cut into all aspects of the deal, and that's when he prodded the razor-toothed bear named Elaine Hester.

Elaine had dinner with the president of the agency. The next morning, Jay was told that Fiona Meadows would become Sonja's agent from then on, which made Vince happy. Fiona also represented one of Vince's favorite writers, Dexter Frampton.

Dexter was the reason why, after Vince's flight

had departed, Jay was waiting in the sky-deck at Santa Monica Airport for another plane to land.

Jay and Dexter Frampton were also pretty good friends. They had worked together on *The Fall and Rise of Nobody*, which was a limited series that had aired on Prime D TV. Dexter would be staying at his place until they flew out to Canada on Wednesday.

As Jay's grimace fell over the empty runway, he thought about calling Sonja, but he didn't know what to say. She'd smelled delicious that morning. Her sweet perfume had made him want to taste her. And hot damn, she was still beautiful, and exciting, and confusing, yet emotionally honest—all the traits he had treasured about her from the moment she had introduced him to her puppet, Skinny Pig.

Jay slid his phone out of his pocket, opened his contact list, and found Sonja's name. He had been happy the day Elaine had given him her number; however, she'd made him promise to not call. She'd said Sonja was a saboteur and she didn't want her torpedoing the deal before it got off the ground. But now, as he stared at her name on the screen, he reminisced about their time together fifteen years ago.

He had touched a whole lot of girls down there

and satisfyingly watched as they enjoyed what he was doing to them. However, when he did it to Sonja, all he'd wanted to do was insert himself inside her and make love to her until their souls merged and he was safely tucked away in her skin.

And then there was her exotically beautiful face. He could still picture how her dark brown ringlets fell over the honey skin of her face. These days, she wore her mounds of curly hair pulled back in a bun. Fifteen years later and she was still trying to downplay her sex appeal.

Jay ran his finger over the S-O-N-J-A. One mere fact had made him leave Sonja high and dry on her birthday back then. He had been barely a teenager, yet he was in love with the closest person he had in his life, and that had scared the hell out of him. It still did.

He saw a sleek airplane fly in. Jay closed his phone case and put the device back into his pocket. He hadn't deserved her then and he sure as hell didn't deserve her now. Ever since he'd started working with Elaine, he hadn't sniffed a grain of cocaine or chugged an ounce of vodka. He wanted to remain sober long enough to convince himself that he had put his demons behind him. The memory of waking up next to a woman he didn't recognize flashed through his mind. Jay squeezed his eyes shut until it went away.

When he focused on the airplane again, the door was open, and down the ramp walked Dexter Frampton. Even from a distance, he could tell Dexter hadn't lost any of his annoyingly good looks.

Despite their friendship, Jay hadn't been overjoyed when Dexter's name came up as co-lead writer. When Jay first met the guy, he'd thought Dexter was an actor. How could a dude who looked like that not be vain enough to get into the behind the camera side of the business? His lack of vanity had impressed Jay, and he was positive Sonja would be enamored by him too.

But there he was, the same old Dexter Frampton, strolling off the ramp as though he were walking in a men's fashion show. Jay didn't like being jealous, so he straightened out his scowl and hurried off to meet his friend while vowing to be professional, which meant introducing his competition to the one woman who had come the closest to winning his heart.

CHAPTER 8

SONJA HESTER

Sonja was angry with herself that morning. She'd spent the remainder of yesterday waiting for Jay to call, since he'd said that he would. But he never did. Once again, Jay West had let her down. She could've stewed in disappointment if she hadn't found other constructive things to do.

First, she'd gone searching for her passport. The quest took her mind off her old friend for a few hours. Then she sat on the sofa and talked herself into getting a grip. Why was she so desperate to hear from Jay anyway? He wasn't the same boy she used to know, and she was a different girl. They weren't going to jump on Jay's moped and ride to the marina to go whale watching because they both thought large mammals were cool. Nor were they going to ride their bikes up to Hollywood Boulevard because they loved to see how many tourists would recognize Jay West as the kid who played the annoying neighbor Dudley Crawford on *Family Magic.* They weren't going to amuse themselves by giving the guys dressed up as superheroes a scenario to act out for them, like saving a child in a stroller who's on a collision course with a Mack truck. And they certainly weren't going to peddle their bikes to Succulent Treats, also on Hollywood Boulevard, to buy a dozen warm cookies and gobble them down while watching the parade of tourists.

Yep, they were adults now, and as far as their relationship went, all they had left were memories. So Sonja had stopped agonizing over Jay not keeping his word and spent an hour on the phone with Elaine and their cousins, Robin and Theresa, planning her farewell dinner. They'd settled on scheduling it for Tuesday night at Elaine's house in Cheviot Hills. Even though the back and forth with her type-A family members had given Sonja a headache the size of Texas, she'd spent the rest of the evening getting reacquainted with the screen-play she had sat down to write a little over five years ago.

And now she was driving to her grandmother's office, which was near Sunset and Doheny, in the middle of Friday morning rush hour traffic. She was too nervous to be miserable about it. She'd received a call from her grandmother in the middle of having her morning coffee, asking that they meet in her office that morning. Gran's tone had been dry and serious, which usually meant Sonja had done something wrong.

Finally, she pulled into the special parking space for guests of LH Real Estate Group, which was in a wide open subterranean parking structure beneath the building. Sonja closed her eyes and rested her head on the back of the seat. She figured her grandmother wanted to talk to her about handing over the responsibility of running the complex to Robin until a new full-time manager could be hired. But then she recalled her grandmother's tone. No, Lorraine was unhappy about something that she didn't want to discuss over the phone. *What could that be?*

Maybe her grandmother wasn't as pleased by Sonja's new opportunity as she'd let on, and the thought of Gran not being happy for her made Sonja jittery. It probably wasn't good that her gran's approval still affected her contentment. At some point, she had to stand on her own two feet and stand firm in the decisions she made for herself. However, Lorraine Hester was such a remarkable woman in every way imaginable.

Lorraine Hester had left her tiny town in Michigan for Midland, Texas when she was sixteen years old. Her father was a drunk, and she and her mother were his victims. Gran had never gone into detail about how she'd suffered at his hands, but she had zero love for the man and rarely mentioned him. Before escaping home, Gran had one of her friends make her a false ID that made her eighteen years old. Gran used that to get a job at Drillers diner, which was near an oil rig in town.

Gran had never said much about her first two years in Midland, other than to say they were hard and she tried to keep a low profile the best she could. Sonja had seen photos of her grandmother when she was in her early twenties. She'd had a wavy bob haircut, a graceful ballerina's neck, delicate pink lips, and a fawn's eyes. She had been a stunning creature then and still was at the age of seventy-nine.

Sonja hated to think of how often, as a young single girl from another state, Gran had had to fend off the men who worked on the rig. Regardless, she was eighteen when she met and married her first husband, Harlan Duke, the oil baron who one day happened to choose her diner to lunch in. After she walked over to take his order, the first thing he said to her was, "You're the prettiest thing I've ever seen."

"I'm not a thing," she replied.

He didn't laugh, which she liked because she wasn't trying to be funny. Instead he studied her with one eye narrowed, and Gran stared back at him, refusing to the be the first to look away. He next asked if she liked steak.

She shrugged. "Sometimes."

And that was when the oil baron, Harlan Duke, who had a reputation for loving money, cars, and gorgeous women, asked her on a date.

She said no thank you, even though she was living in a trailer where the water didn't run and the circuit box blew out every other week. Gran said she felt no attraction at all for the arrogant man who was twenty years her senior and, according to kitchen chatter, three times divorced. As far as she was concerned, a man with three ex-wives had to be an awful lot like her father, who didn't know how to get along with women.

Harlan was handsome though—tall, lean, dark

hair, and keen hazel eyes. But Gran had never put much stock in the way a person looked. Her father was considered handsome too, and knowing him had taught her that monsters could not only be beautiful but also look absolutely normal.

But every day for one month, Harlan came to the diner during lunch and sat at a table in her station. Mostly he sat alone, but sometimes he held meetings with other big-wigs. When he sat alone, he would read his paper and pretend to not watch her thwart advances from roughnecks. Then one day, one of the guys called her a shabby piece of ass before he grabbed her and pulled her into his lap. Gran elbowed him in the throat, which allowed her to scramble out of his grasp. But the guy wasn't done with her. When he went to kick her in the gut, Harlan was there to catch the man's foot, punch him in the jaw, and fire him from his job.

A few weeks after the incident, Harlan had asked her out again.

"I'm under no obligation to go on a date with you because you stepped up for me." Harlan bowed his head graciously and was about to say something when she said, "But I think I'm ready to have that steak, if you're still offering."

On their first date, Harlan bragged about how

he'd acquired his first oil rig. Gran sat and listened attentively as he described how he out-negotiated, pulled strings, and outsmarted his competitors. He had found a few investors willing to give him enough capital to make the bank loan officer, who he had promised a large cut of the first year's profits, happier about giving him a substantial amount of cash, which he hadn't nearly enough capital to back. The more Harlan talked about how he'd become a rich man, the more fascinating she found him.

"I loved his mind," her grandmother had said, which was why after their fifth date, he asked her to marry him and she said yes.

According to Gran, Harlan had taught her a lot of what she had come to know about business. It didn't take long for her to learn that money, cars, and women weren't what he valued. He loved playing and winning at the game of being an industrialist. In Gran, he had found the perfect wife. She listened carefully as he expounded his deals for the day. He even asked her opinions about his business and would validate her when he thought she was right and teach her when she could've used more illumination on the subject at hand.

She'd said Harlan was a good guy. He was kind

and fair. He didn't need to prey on the weak to feel powerful. He was the ultimate human being, which was why it shook Gran to the core when one night, only three years after they were married, Harlan lay down beside her to sleep and never woke up. The doctors said he had suffered a massive brain aneurysm.

After she'd mourned and buried her husband, Gran learned he'd left everything he owned and every dime he had to her. And that's when she began a fierce fight between his business partners and ex-wives, who claimed to have had children by him. But Harlan had taught Gran the biggest lesson that guided her success until that very day.

"A man's got to know when he's outmatched and use this here"—he would nudge himself on the temple—"to win the war."

Harlan's partners wanted the rigs, all of them. Gran had two strikes against her. She was a woman with no allies. She was also seven months pregnant with their first child. So she sold her husband's major stake in his business to the highest bidder.

What a story her grandmother had, and that was just her first husband. Harlan Duke was Theresa and Robin's grandfather. Roy Davis, a fair housing attorney from Los Angeles, was Sonja and Elaine's grandfather.

Sonja took a deep breath as she opened her eyes. She wiggled her head and shoulders to get loose, and that made her feel a lot better about cutting the cord that attached her to the one woman she wanted to be like but was too afraid to become.

The time on the dashboard said she was seven minutes early, which meant she was right on time. Without another delay, she got out of the car, walked into the lobby, and rode the elevator up. Gran must've arrived not too long ago because Sonja could smell her floral scented perfume in the hallway. She was going to miss that scent, and thinking about it made her heart break a little.

Gran's operation took up the entire eighth floor. The action started early at LH Real Estate Group. The agents and brokers were in their offices, closing deals, and their assistants, who worked in cubicles in the center of the space, were sweating it out with them.

Sonja waved at Regina, who was on the phone at her desk right outside her grandmother's office. Regina waved back and pointed at the open door. Sonja showed the pretty woman, who looked impeccable with her hair tied back in a bun and wearing a turtleneck silk shirt under a black blazer, a thumbs-up.

As soon as Sonja saw her grandmother, she felt her eyes brighten. "Morning, Gran," she sang as all the trepidation she had regarding their meeting dissipated.

Gran watched her with a stern expression from behind her enormous black wooden desk. She looked stylish in her flawless white blazer and rounded rimmed glasses. "Close the door behind you please."

Caught off guard by her grandmother's tone, Sonja hesitated but did as she was asked.

"What's going on?" she said as she sat in the chair across from her gran.

Gran opened the top drawer of her desk and pulled out a stack of white pages that looked as though they had been handled. "What is this?" She dropped the papers onto her desk.

Sonja craned her neck forward to get a better look. She frowned as she picked up the top page and read it. "Is this my screenplay?"

Gran's eyes remained cold. "I've never read it until last night."

Sonja sat very still even though she wanted to

run out of the office and get as far away from what was happening as she could. When she wrote the screenplay, she'd banked on her grandmother never reading it. Gran had always been too busy to read anything that didn't pertain to her business. Sonja surely didn't want her gran to know how she'd embellished the relationship between her and Ms. Jenkins, as well as her first late husband. Gran would've disapproved. Especially since recounts of her past always came with a strange warning label like "the past can be harmful to my business, so let's not talk about it outside of my presence."

"I've never found beating around the bush worthwhile, so I'll get right to it. You cannot make this story," Gran said and pressed her lips into a hard line.

Sonja looked from left to right, wondering if the moment was really happening or if it was a bad dream. She threw a hand up. "I know Gran, I crossed a line. But it's just fiction and the names and places have been changed. So what's the problem?"

Her grandmother folded her fingers in front of her. "I have my reasons."

Sonja wiggled her head. "I think I deserve to know at least a couple of them."

"You don't," her grandmother said in a frank and haughty tone.

"Well, is it the murder?"

He grandmother pressed her lips together and looked at her defiantly.

"Gran, come on. Tell me something."

Finally her gran adjusted in her seat. "Is that what you believe? That I could murder someone?"

Sonja's breaths came rapidly. She wanted to vomit out about a dozen explanations about why she wrote the screenplay the way she did. "Of course not."

"It doesn't take much to figure out that your story is about Betty and myself."

Sonja groaned before she sighed. "I know. But I wrote that five years ago." She shook her head. "Ms. Jenkins started giving me a hard time and you always took her side. So"—she shrugged dismissively—"I just indulged my frustrations. It's not real, Gran. It's just a story. No one is going to believe it's real."

Her grandmother watched her with narrowed eyes as she shook her head. Finally she looked off. "You can't move forward with your project."

Sonja's mouth opened, but nothing came out. She cleared her throat and tried speaking again.

"What's going on? Why are you having such a visceral reaction to a made-up story?"

Gran looked into Sonja's eyes as if she wanted to say something but couldn't.

"What is it?" Sonja urged.

Goodness, if looks could kill.

"I didn't know you were so interested in my past," Gran said.

Sonja could hardly tolerate the coldness. Never in her life had Gran spoken to or looked at her in such a way. She so very much wanted to cave and tell her grandmother that she would do what she asked. But the threat of losing her new job as a real writer, and with Jay too, made her realize how badly she wanted it and how much she was willing to fight for it.

Sonja sighed and readjusted in her seat. "Gran, I signed a contract."

Gran stabbed the script with her index finger. "If this story is made the way it reads, I will be very unhappy with you Sonja Lorraine Hester—very unhappy."

Sonja's heart felt as though it dropped to the pit of her stomach. "Gran, you're going to have to be more specific. What exactly do you want changed about the story?" She watched her grandmother, eagerly awaiting her answer.

Gran, who had been sitting so still, finally sighed as she took off her glasses. "I find Ida and Rose irreconcilably problematic."

Sonja pushed herself to the edge of her seat. "But without them, there is no story." Oddly, she felt as though she were fighting for her life.

"If that's the case, then perhaps you don't have a screenplay to sell to Hollywood."

Sonja wiggled her head as if what her grandmother had just said had sent shock waves through her body. "What? Do you want me to renege on the contract I just signed?"

Her grandmother sat back in her big leather chair, looking way too relaxed for the gravity of the moment. "Of course not. But this is business, darling, that's all. And your story does my business a disservice."

"How?" she asked, shaking her hands out of frustration.

"Listen to me," her grandmother said.

Sonja understood that Gran was waiting for her to get ahold of herself and listen carefully. She scooted back in her chair, working hard to be the picture of calm. Finally she folded her arms. "Okay. I'm listening."

"I want you to be clever and figure out how to keep your deal without making the story that you have written. So I'll end this by saying, either you fix this problem on your end or I'll be forced to do so on mine."

Sonja's frown intensified. It was as if she wasn't talking to her grandmother anymore, instead she was being threatened by a mob boss. And yes, just like a lieutenant facing a death threat from the Don, Sonja felt a cold shiver run up and down her spine.

SONJA FELT AS THOUGH SHE WERE ENVELOPED BY A dark cloud as she walked back to her car and sat in the driver's seat. *What in the hell just happened?* She clenched the steering wheel, so confused. On one hand, her grandmother had told her to fix it, and on the other, she'd threatened to stop any possibility of Sonja's success. *What a mind-fuck.*

However, Sonja felt as though she had no other option than to figure out a solution. A face popped in her head. She snatched her phone out of the cup holder between the two front seats to call Jay. But she froze and cursed under her breath after realizing she didn't have his number.

"What next?" she whispered.

Just as she searched her recent calls for Laney, her cell phone rang in her hands. It was an unknown caller, but she recognized the local area code and answered, hoping it was Jay and not the average scammer.

"Hello?" she said.

"Sonja?"

It was him. She slapped her hand over her heart. "Jay. We have to talk. Now."

CHAPTER 9

SONJA HESTER

Sonja agreed to drive up Doheny and meet with Jay at his place. He also wanted her to meet her co-lead writer, Dexter Frampton, who would be staying with him until they flew out to Vancouver next Wednesday.

She wasn't surprised that Jay lived in a white stone mansion that looked more like a modern and angular office complex in the Bird Streets. She plugged in the code he had given her to open the gate. She followed Jay's directives to a T after she was granted entrance, driving past a lawn that had all the charm of a mall-park, especially with the infinity fountain that spurted water from the edges and had two large black iron balls in the middle of the pool. After passing the lawn, she kept driving straight until the road curved. Next she made the only right turn onto a ramp that led into an elevated parking garage.

After pulling into a space, Sonja looked through the floor-to-ceiling glass windows and saw her final instruction. Jay and another guy were sitting across from each other on cushiony chairs on the terrace.

Suddenly, Sonja's nervousness intensified. The drive up the hill hadn't taken long enough for her to figure out a strategic way to break the news to Jay about her grandmother. The fact that she was sitting in her position hadn't quite sunk in. And she still wasn't clear what her grandmother found so offensive about her screenplay. Was it the murder or the fact that a character who read a lot like Ms. Jenkins was in the story? Perhaps she had inadvertently captured a truth that her grandmother wanted to hide.

As soon as she stepped out of the car, both men were watching her. Sonja still couldn't believe that she was in touch with Jay again, and in a big way. He watched her as if he was seeing her from the inside out and didn't want to miss a thing. Existing under his intense gaze made her skip a breath. Without looking down, she had to assess whether her outfit made her look her best. She had on her designer black skinny pants and black cap-sleeved ruffled-front blouse. Whenever she was summoned to her grandmother's office, she had to dress for work. So she looked good.

Sonja put on a smile while coaching herself to get a grip. The guy she was having a strange reaction to was Jay West—a person who had a habit of abandoning her whenever he felt like it. He was barely good for her as a friend, and she would've been a fool to consider him for something more than that. And so her eyes fell on the other guy—Dexter Frampton, she presumed. He smiled at her appreciatively and he was more than cute; he was beautiful. For a second, Sonja wondered what part of heaven he had fallen from. He had bright blue eyes and caramel skin. His lips were pouty, pink, and kissable, and his angular face resembled a Calvin Klein model's.

Sonja sighed when she reached them. Both men stood at the same time, but it was Jay who drew her in for a hug.

"You look good," he said then kissed her temple.

Her heart betrayed her by fluttering. "Thanks," she said, feeling heat rising up her neck and burning her cheeks.

"Hi, I'm Dexter."

She shook his outstretched hand while noting that he was even more beautiful up close. *Wow.*

"Have you eaten?" Jay asked.

Suddenly, Sonja's stomach cramped, reminding her of how hungry she was. "No, I haven't."

"That's great. Cam is going to serve breakfast soon. Have a seat."

She sat in a chair beside Dexter, and for a moment, it looked as though Jay was bothered by it.

Jay readjusted in his seat then circled his shoulders. "Dexter and I were talking about ways to end episode five."

All the anxiety from her meeting with her grandmother came rushing back. Sonja groaned internally in anguish.

"You said we needed to talk. What's going on?" Jay asked, apparently sensing her agony.

She slumped in her chair. "I just met with Gran."

"Lorraine?" he asked.

"Yeah." She sighed. "She read my script and didn't like that the grandmother was the murderer, nor does she like that Ms. Jenkins, a tenant who lives in my building, is depicted in the story."

"Ida Lawry is based on this tenant?" Dexter asked, frowning curiously.

"Yes," Sonja said, wishing he would stop asking the questions that exposed the sensitive parts her grandmother had a right to complain about.

"And Rose Ready is based on your grandmother?"

"Yes," she replied sharply, then massaged the tension at the back of her neck. "And so because those two characters are based on her and this tenant, Gran wants me to write Rose and Ida out of the story or renege on the contract."

Jay and Dexter looked at each other. It was obvious they were having the same trouble wrapping their minds around her grandmother's request. Actually, it was quite bold, and pretty entitled, of Gran to make such a demand.

Jay grimaced as the tip of his finger tapped out his frustration on the table. "That's kind of an irrational request, don't you think?"

"Very," Sonja replied.

"Is the entire story based on her life?" Dexter asked calmly.

"Well, sort of. Yeah," Sonja said, wondering where he was going with his line of questioning.

"Did she give you permission to write it?"

Sonja felt her eyebrows squish together. "No."

Dexter rubbed his face with both hands.

"She doesn't have a case, does she?" Jay asked.

Dexter sighed briskly. "I don't know. Maybe, but I can tell you that Vince isn't going to want the headache. I know him. He'll drop the project if she starts a fight."

Jay cursed sharply under his breath.

"Listen"—Dexter looked at her with penetrating focus—"you said the screenplay is based on the truth. Tell me the story about your grandmother and let's see what we can do to fix this."

She started from the beginning, retelling all that she knew about her grandmother and her first husband, Harlan Duke. At some point, she took a break so that they could move to the dining table on the opposite side of the balcony for breakfast.

Jay's cook, Cam, was an attractive brunette who had bought herself the perfect pair of breasts. Sonja found herself wondering if she and Jay had ever slept together, especially because of the way Cam's eyes danced and her lips pulled into a giddy smile whenever she looked at or addressed him. They were served Denver omelets and home fries with the fresh coffee Sonja had been craving.

"So tell me more about this tenant of yours?"

Dexter asked. He was eating while tapping something on his cell phone.

"Well… she's an old acquaintance of my grandmother's, only I have no idea how they ever became friends and I kind of believe they can't stand each other."

Dexter lifted his beautiful eyes off the phone, and his glower landed on her. "Why do you say that?"

She cleared her throat. If only Robin was there, or Theresa. One of them would be able to confirm that she was actually seeing what she was seeing—Dexter Frampton could be the most handsome man in the world. She would actually bet her entire bank account on it.

"Are you okay, Sonja?" Jay asked.

When she turned to look at him, he was frowning as though he were guzzling baking soda.

"I'm fine." She cleared her throat again and refocused on Dexter. "I say that because Ms. Jenkins, the tenant, only likes to gossip about how my grandmother cares about money over how happy tenants are, even when my grandmother ensures that I hop to it whenever Ms. Jenkins calls." Sonja's body shivered as every fiber of her being remembered how much she hated waiting on that woman.

"She has, like, a million cats and I'm allergic and she knows it. It's as if they know to attack me whenever I go into her apartment. I swear she's trained them to be an army against me."

Jay snickered, but Dexter's serious expression remained.

"I see," Dexter said. "And why do you think your grandmother dislikes Ms. Jenkins?"

It took Sonja a moment to recover. Whenever she had the opportunity to vent about Ms. Jenkins, her emotions always got away from her. She suddenly realized how unhealthy that was, both emotionally and physically.

"Well"—she exhaled forcefully—"the opposite of love is indifference, and as far as my grandmother is concerned, Ms. Jenkins is like a bill she has to pay, nothing more or less."

"That's not the Lorraine I remember. Your gran was always sincere with the people she let hang around." Jay smiled slightly. "She was the one adult who used to ask me how I was doing and expected to hear the truth."

Sonja and Jay stared at each other, smiling. She wondered if he wanted to kiss her too.

"So I've been sitting here doing some research," Dexter said. Sonja ripped her eyes from Jay's in time to see Dexter look up from his phone. "Ever heard of the NewsBank Database?"

"Um," she said, blinking hard, trying to erase from her mind the way Jay had been watching her. "No."

"It holds just about all the articles from every newspaper or magazine that ever existed, no matter how large or small." He sat back comfortably in his seat. "I did a search for oil baron Harlan Duke and foul play. Only one article came up. It was written in 1999 and conclusively claims that Harlan Duke died in his sleep, not from poisoning. And"—he raised a finger pointedly—"there's a quote here from Cyrus Wright, one of his business partners that says, 'Harlan has been missed by all of us. He was a good man, and a friend to everyone who crossed his path. For Christ's sake, let him rest in peace.'"

"Okay, that doesn't sound like murder to me. So maybe murder isn't what has my grandmother so rattled."

Dexter stopped looking at her so intensely as he sat back in his seat again. "Here's what gets me. Your grandmother had a foot *in* the big boy's club." He shook his fist for impact. "The third largest oil field in the country is in Midland, Texas."

Sonja shook her head. "I know where you're going with this. Yes, my gran is extremely ambitious, but they didn't want a widow involved in what they considered men's business back then."

"But your grandmother migrated to Los Angeles and not only became involved in men's business but dominated. LH Real Estate Group did over sixty-three billion in sales last year."

Frustration raced through Sonja's body. "Yes. She's very successful. What does that have to do with anything?"

"Your grandmother sounds like a fighter, that's all."

"She was young. She developed into a fighter."

Dexter sat up straight. He must've sensed Sonja's defensiveness because he had a cautious look in his eyes. "I'm sorry if my questions offend you. I'm just trying to figure out if there's any way you can pull another story out of the same world you created."

A familiar feeling gripped Sonja. It was as if her mind had suddenly hit the same brick wall it had been smashing into for the last five years. "Another story?"

"Yeah. Your grandmother sounds as though she's insisting you change the story. I don't have a problem with giving it a try. But if my instincts, which are pretty good, serve me correct, you do."

"Huh?" she asked, now more confused than ever.

"Well… I've been around a lot of writers, and you're one of the best. I've read your screenplay five times and each reading has given me the same visceral reactions. You've written the story from a raw place inside you. Could you do it again?"

Sonja looked at Jay with her mouth caught open. He seemed eager to hear her answer. She focused her gaze out over the valley of sporadic clusters of skyscrapers surrounded by shorter edifices. The day was smoggy, but the entire scene was uniquely LA. Was it time to confess what she had known for so long?

She swallowed even though her throat felt tight. "I can't."

Jay's neck craned forward. "You wrote the screenplay, didn't you?"

"Yes," she said emphatically. "But I've had writer's block ever since." When she sighed, it was as if her entire body could finally relax after so many years. "It's like I got fixated on the details surrounding the nature of Gran and Ms. Jenkins' association and my brain has been telling me, 'Either you stick with it or I give you nothing.'"

Dexter nodded as if he understood exactly what she was talking about. "Could I suggest something?"

She shrugged, willing to hear whatever he had to say.

"Have you ever been to Midland, Texas?"

Sonja gulped as she felt her head floating away from her body. "Um, no."

"Have you ever spoken with anyone who knew your grandmother when she lived there?"

She shook her head.

Dexter sighed briskly. "I'm not going to pretend I don't like the story as is. On a scale from one to ten, it's a solid ten. Screw with what you've already written and we could end up kissing zero. Or…" He raised his eyebrows twice. "You can evolve the story and, in the process, discover something Vince will still get behind."

"I agree," Jay said, nodding. "Plus, I have a lot of money tied up in this project too."

"Then you both should go to Midland. In your case, a dose of reality may help cure your writer's block."

"I'm in. I can have us flown there today," Jay said.

Sonja's mouth fell open. The idea of actually banging around in her grandmother's past scared the daylights out of her. However, Dexter was right. Her mother had emotionally abandoned her from the moment she was born, but her gran never had. Sonja felt she knew all there was to learn about Carrie Anne, her wayward mother, but never enough about the woman who had saved her soul. She wanted to know more. She needed to. Sonja had no doubt that the fact she'd kept her grandmother on an unreachable pedestal had something to do with whatever was causing her writer's block. The time had come for her to learn all she could about Lorraine Hester.

So she closed her mouth and swallowed the lump of fear that sat heavily in the back of her throat. "Okay. I'll go."

CHAPTER 10

SONJA HESTER

Jay arranged a flight out of Santa Monica Airport, which was supposed to depart with just the two of them in four hours. Sonja had tried to convince Dexter to join them, but his friend Daisy Lord was having a grand opening event for her new restaurant on Abbot Kinney Boulevard in Venice on Saturday night and he didn't want to miss it. Apparently this woman was the wife of a billionaire named Jack Lord. Whenever Dexter mentioned Daisy, Sonja saw the secret hidden behind his glossy eyes. He was in love with her, but his affection was unrequited.

And so after Jay had packed a suitcase, they got into his way-too-expensive sports car and drove to her place. Sonja had to admit that when the gate to the complex opened, she preferred the uniqueness of where she lived over Jay's cold mansion made of stone, glass, stainless steel, and granite.

Once they were inside her apartment, she had no time to linger. First she changed into something more comfortable. They had checked the weather before leaving Jay's. It's hot in Texas. As soon as she threw her suitcase on the bed, the doorbell chimed.

"Jay, could you get that please?" she called, knowing it wasn't Ms. Jenkins. She never walked up the stairs.

"Sure thing," he replied.

A few moments later, she heard Jay and Robin greeting each other like the long-lost friends they were. Of course Jay sounded more excited than Robin, who was not an expressive person to begin with. Her cousin had earned the nickname Wednesday—the unsmiling daughter from the *Addams Family*—in junior high school. Even though she'd inherited Gran's porcelain skin and light ash hair, in the tenth grade, Robin had started dying her mane jet black and kept it cut in a strict bob. She had stopped coloring her hair two years ago, but she maintained the same haircut. Now she could pass for a Russian spy named Natasha.

Sonja put her a pair of jeans into the suitcase

and clamped it shut as she listened to Robin explain to Jay that she was thinking about putting her artwork on hold to work for Gran full time. It was shocking to hear.

"Wow," Sonja said as she hurried out of the room, carrying her suitcase. "You're going to abandon your hopes and dreams to work for Gran?"

Robin looked at her with a blasé expression. "Hopes and dreams? That's kind of dramatic."

Sonja's heart was beating a mile a minute. At the moment, she felt as though she was running off to Midland, Texas, while Robin was dancing off into the sunset to live happily ever after with Gran.

"Don't worry, Son, you're still her favorite," Robin said.

"Here let me have this." Jay took the suitcase out of Sonja's hand before she could properly hand it over.

Sonja scratched her shoulder, embarrassed by the fact that she was jealous and, as usual, Robin saw right through her.

"It was good seeing you, Robbie. The three of us should grab lunch or dinner before Sonja and I head off to Canada on Wednesday," Jay said.

Robin folded her arms tightly against her body

as her eyes veered down to the suitcase. "I'm sorry, but where are you two going?"

"Midland, Texas," Jay replied.

Robin frowned at Sonja as she leaned back. "Wait? Isn't that where Gran's from?"

"Gran's from Michigan," Sonja replied.

Robin narrowed an eye. "Really? Are we going to quibble over semantics?"

Sonja grunted and rolled her eyes. She was forced to divulge to Robin all that had come out of her talk with Gran that morning, which in turn had sparked their trip to Texas.

"But it's not really so hard to change the story, is it?"

Sonja honestly hated when her cousin looked at her that way, as though she could see all of her insecurities, fears, and issues. "Yes. And that's why we're going."

"Does Gran know you're going to Midland to dig around in her past?"

Sonja wanted to blow a gasket. Robin sounded so self-righteous. "No."

"Son, there's a reason why she hasn't told you all the shit you've been dying to know."

Sonja stood there, blinking at Robin like a fly

that had just realized it had been sprayed with insecticide.

"You know what?" Robin waved flippantly at Sonja. "Maybe this is something you have to do. You're, like, obsessed with the curse, Ms. Jenkins, and my grandfather's death. Maybe you need answers so you can stop inventing them."

Suddenly, Sonja was flooded by a sense of relief. "You won't tell Gran then?"

Robin shook her head disapprovingly. "No. And I can stay out of her path until you get back but…"

Sonja heaved a sigh of relief. "Thanks."

Robin raised a finger in warning. "Just get this over and done with already." She grabbed the doorknob. "And don't worry about your commitment to show me around the office today and tomorrow. I'll figure things out. I just need passwords to—"

"Everything you'll need is on the computer in a file named Universal Key. I'll text you the password to get onto the computer."

With one last eye roll, even more unsmiling than usual, Robin said, "Thanks." She turned back to Jay. "Good to see you, Jay."

Sonja rushed over to put a hand on her cousin's shoulder. "And thank you for not sounding the alarm."

Robin sighed. "Oh, Sonja." She patted Sonja's hand as she looked her in the eyes. "You know you're rolling the dice here, and the only reason I'm not going to let Gran know that you're invading her privacy is because I'm positive you're not going to find anything more than what you already know."

Now it was Sonja who was searching Robin's eyes. She knew her cousin well enough to know that she was bullshitting herself. "Do you really think there's nothing to find?"

Robin tilted her head, and then opened her mouth and closed it.

"We have to get going, Son," Jay said.

Robin blinked as though she had to turn off the thoughts in her head. "Just call me if you're there past Monday. Gran is going to Palm Springs with Velma and Clark this weekend, so she'll be preoccupied."

"Okay," said Sonja.

She and Robin kissed each other on the cheek, and her cousin bid her safe travels. As Jay drove, he fielded calls from his agent, who was the most persistent guy Sonja had ever listened to. He kept running down lists of projects he wanted Jay to consider.

"Do you have a pen or something to write this down with?" his agent asked.

"Yep," Jay said, lying.

And then his agent ran down a to-do list as long as a basketball player's leg. Meanwhile, Sonja couldn't stop thinking about what Robin had said—that there was a reason Gran hadn't told her all the shit she had been dying to know. Just as someone would be obsessed with the assassinations of famous public figures of old or whether some powerful secret society controlled the world, that was how fanatical she had been about her grandmother's past. Deep down, she knew her grandmother was hiding something.

Gran was one of the most transparent people she had ever known. So why wouldn't she tell Sonja how she and Ms. Jenkins had met? Even Ms. Jenkins, who couldn't wait to criticize her gran's management skills, would never answer the same questions Sonja posed to her grandmother. It was as clear as glass that both women were harboring secrets. It was all too weird, and no one could deny that—not even Robin, who was always a proponent of letting the past drop and moving forward because the present was all that mattered.

Right as Jay ended the call with his agent, his phone buzzed again and he answered it.

"How are you, Jay?" a woman's voice purred over the car speakers.

Jay frowned at the control panel that gave the name of the caller, then he glanced at Sonja. "Hey, Plume."

"Why haven't you been answering my calls?"

Sonja knew precisely who Plume Ashbury was. She was the hot and sexy movie star most men fantasized about.

"What do you want Plume?" he asked impatiently.

"I told you what I want, asshole. Why in the hell haven't you called me back? It's, like, an issue with you, dude. Didn't your mother teach you how to return phone calls?"

Jay sighed. "I'm busy. If you don't want anything specific, then hang up."

Sonja had heard somewhere that Jay and Plume were an *it* couple. It could've been something she'd gotten from one of those celebrity gossip shows that happened to be on television when she wasn't quite paying attention to what she was watching.

"Well, we should go out to dinner tonight or

something, you know—keep shit fresh," she said, sounding like a valley girl.

"I can't. I'm busy."

"Jay, are you with somebody? I feel as though you're with somebody." She giggled. "So who's your flavor of the week?"

Jay scrubbed a hand through his hair. "Plume, goodbye."

He pressed a button on the steering wheel, ending their call abruptly. The phone rang again, and Jay used his free hand to power down his device.

Awkward silence loomed in the car. Sonja wanted to ask if he was still involved with Plume, because the actress had sounded as though she was asking if he was with another woman. But she did mention keeping their relationship fresh. Perhaps Jay and the actress had an open relationship. At least Sonja didn't have to worry about crossing the double yellow line with him. She was a strict follower of the girl code, which meant she never screwed around with another woman's boyfriend or husband no matter what kind of relationship they had.

"It's not real you know, Plume and I," Jay said.

"What's not real?" Sonja asked.

"Our relationship."

Disappointment and relief hit Sonja in the heart as if someone had pummeled her with a two-by-four. "Oh…"

"I hate this shit, you know, being Jay West."

"But you are Jay West." Sonja said.

After a long moment of silence, he gripped the steering wheel tighter and glanced at Sonja. "So I've been wondering something."

Sonja sat up straight. "Wondering what?"

He was still frowning as though he was one extremely unhappy man. "If I hadn't run into Elaine, would you have ever tried to contact me?"

She turned to watch the sidewalks and low buildings go by. It was seventeen minutes past noon, so there wasn't much traffic. His question made her notice all of those little details.

"I don't know," she finally said. "Perhaps we would've run into each other at Riley's next wedding ceremony."

He chuckled, and so did she.

Sonja sniffed cynically. "She always invites me, but I never show up because I know me being there isn't the point of the invitation. She's looking for me to go back to Elaine and report that she's found a new man to marry, who's actually gone through with the ceremony." She shook her head. "Elaine never hears about Riley's weddings from me though."

He turned to look at her since they were stopped at a light. "She invites me too, but I show up"—he winked—"and you're never there."

Their eyes connected for longer than she was comfortable with. Sonja looked down at her fingers folding and unfolding on her lap as she pictured running into Jay wearing an impeccable tuxedo at Riley's wedding. He would've been irresistible. Perhaps one look and she would've forgotten how he had abandoned her, breaking her heart until it shattered into grains of sand.

Jay grunted grievously. "Son, when are you going to forgive me?"

They were driving up to the airport checkpoint as she looked at him. She felt how wide and confused her expression was. Robin would always tease her about being unforgiving. "You're like a dog with a bloody bone when it comes to excusing those who wronged you." Sonja knew it was because she hated how it felt to be hurt. To her, it was the worst feeling in the world.

Sonja was still trapped in a moment of unresponsiveness when Jay had showed the guard his ID. He drove into a private parking lot.

"So what's your answer to my question?" he said as he pulled into the valet station.

Sonja heaved a sigh. "I'm working on it, Jay. I'm working on it."

What an intense gaze he had, staring deep into her eyes that way. It felt as though they had been connected for a lifetime. For a second, she wondered what would it be like to be under Jay West, the man. Was he a sensual lover? Was he intimate when he made love? Or was he wham bam thank you ma'am?

Finally, he cracked a half smile. "I'll take that answer." He winked. "For now."

Sonja smiled back, then it was on with the show. They left Jay's car with the valet and exited the parking lot through a private corridor. They handed off their bags to skycaps and were on the airplane in less than fifteen minutes.

The speed with which she got from the parking lot to sitting in a big leather chair in the aircraft was miraculous, as far as Sonja was concerned. She had never taken a private flight before. Jay, on the other hand, had known just about everyone they came across, from the valets to the pilots and of course the stewardesses prancing about in the cabin, opening and closing cabinets and batting their eyelashes at Jay in the process.

"Not flying alone this time?" one of the stewardesses asked Jay.

Sonja wanted to say that the fact that she was sitting there was the obvious answer to her silly question.

Jay pointed a hand at Sonja. "Laura, this is Sonja, an old friend of mine and the creator of a new project we're working on."

The pretty raven-haired woman glanced at Sonja for what felt like half a second. "Oh," she said dismissively and gave Jay her full attention. "Would you like champagne and a fruit and cheese platter before takeoff?"

"None for me. Sonja?" Jay said.

Sonja looked up and waited until the woman reluctantly acknowledged her. "I'm full for now."

"Then we'll wait," Jay said.

Laura pursed her lips and strutted away. Sonja listened until the sound of her short heels beating the aisle stopped, a door slid open, and Laura was out of the cabin.

"Have you been involved with her or something?" she whispered.

Jay chuckled. "I plead the Fifth."

Sonja grunted and rolled her eyes. "Well at least that hasn't changed about you."

She was waiting for Jay to say something snappy back, but instead he looked out the window. She hadn't meant to upset him. Heck, she'd thought he would love to brag about his conquest, even though knowing he couldn't keep himself from screwing the stewardess made her more certain she'd never start anything romantic with the likes of him.

Finally the pilot announced they were on the way to the runway. Laura and her co-stewardess, Sarah, were back to make sure they had their seatbelts on and other parts of the cabin were secure and ready for takeoff. That was when Jay informed both women that he would call when they wanted their services. Other than that, they should stay out of sight. If looks could spew fire, Sonja would've been burned to a crisp by both stewardesses.

Goodness, he banged them both! Sonja sank into her seat and closed her eyes, trying not to think about Jay and those two girls in the horizontal position, doing things only in X-rated films.

"Hey," Jay said.

She opened one eye to look at him. "What?" That came out sharper than she wanted.

Regardless of her tone, he was watching her with an alluring smile. "You're going to sleep already?"

"Just resting my head, that's all," she said more softly.

"It's still hard to believe that you and I are taking this flight together."

She released an appreciative sigh as she resettled in her seat. "I know."

"So"—he waved his fingers toward her—"tell me more about yourself."

His charming grin made her smirk. "There's not much, but what do you want to know?"

"You don't have a boyfriend?"

She shook her head. "Nope."

"That's hard to believe."

Sonja shrugged. "It really isn't so unbelievable. LA is full of beautiful single women."

"True," he said, nodding. "But you left out one factor."

She turned her head in a curious manner. "And that is?"

He leaned toward her as though he was sharing a secret. "Crazy," he whispered, circling his finger around his ear.

Sonja rolled her eyes. "Yeah well, that goes both

ways. There are enough insane men in this city to fill a dozen asylums."

Jay tilted his head back and belted out a good laugh.

"But you're sane and beautiful"—he shot his index finger at her—"and that makes you a unicorn."

Now it was Sonja's turn to laugh out loud. "And how do you know I'm sane? I mean, I've spent the better part of my twenties obsessing over my grandmother's past. And then I wrote a screenplay about it. And after that, I haven't been able to write another screenplay because I can't stop obsessing over shit that really isn't my business." She raised a finger pointedly. "But deep down inside, I feel it is my business for some strange, unknown crazy person's reason."

She blew a hard sigh. The words had come so fast that she had hardly taken a breath.

Jay gently patted her knee. "Yep. You're right. That's pretty nuts."

She tilted her head to study his playful grin. "Ha, ha, ha." She rolled her eyes.

"Come on, Son! You know that doesn't make you a crazy person. That makes you interesting."

She had no comeback. The way Jay was looking

at her made her all giddy inside, so she had to remember that she was quite sure he had banged the stewardesses.

"Right," she said in a more serious tone.

He grunted as though he was intrigued by something. Sonja wanted to ask what was he thinking, but she didn't. They had already gone too far with their flirting. But he was studying her curiously again, and she blushed under his scrutiny.

"One of them but not the other," he finally said.

She felt her eyebrows pull together. "Huh?"

"I saw you go into a shell earlier."

Sonja cocked her head to the side, still totally confused. "When did I go into a shell?"

"When Laura was treating you like shit and flirting with me."

Her mouth fell open, then she swallowed. She had no idea what to say to that.

"I notice everything, Son. I'm an actor. I'm supposed to pay attention to the crazy shit people do so that I can bring it to a scene."

Sonja crossed her arms. "Okay, well… which one of the stewardesses have you banged?"

"Laura."

She shook her head judgmentally, then stopped abruptly. She seriously disliked judgmental people.

But it didn't keep her from wanting to light him up for being a man whore. "So do you do that often? Fuck your stewardesses?"

Jay stared at her for a long moment then solemnly turned toward the window. "Yeah, I used to." He looked at her again. "I used to do a lot of shit I'm not proud of."

Sonja felt terrible about leading him to this point of unhappiness. "I'm sorry. I shouldn't have judged and—"

He shook his head emphatically. "No way. You have nothing to apologize for."

She cracked a playful smile. "Nothing? Everyone has something to apologize for, whether they know it or not."

"You're right," he said, mirroring her smile.

They stared into each other's eyes, even after the pilot said that they were ready for takeoff and floored it, and even as they were zooming down the runway and gathering enough speed to lift off the ground.

Sonja cleared her throat and looked out the window, battling an intense desire to kiss him. No. As the aircraft climbed, she realized she wanted to do more than kiss. She wanted to make out with him feverishly. She wanted to experience Jay in a way she never had before. When she turned back to face him, he was still smiling.

"What are you thinking?" he asked.

"Nothing I'm ready to share."

He lifted his eyebrows twice. "For some reason, I like the sound of that."

The airplane jerked, and Sonja was certain that her cheeks were burnt red as she held on tightly to the armrests.

CHAPTER 11

SONJA HESTER

The four-hour flight went way too fast once they got down to business. Jay had rented a house on Airbnb as Jake Johnson, a name he actually had a real ID and credit cards for. He'd also ordered groceries through Instacart and rented a vehicle. It was a sports car, of course. Even when they were kids, Jay had preferred everything fast, from his bikes to his girlfriends.

They strategized their first move.

"I mean, do small towns ever change?" Sonja asked.

Jay cracked an amused smile. "That's right, you've never been to Midland."

"Have you?" she asked.

"Never. But have you ever been to Texas?"

Sonja shook her head. "I guess I don't get out of California much." Now that she admitted that, she felt so embarrassed. Sitting across from the big-time actor who could schedule a private flight at a drop of a dime made her feel as though her life had been more stagnant than she thought.

"Hey, Sonja?" Jay said with a delicate voice.

She looked up.

"There, that's better." He smiled.

Sonja hadn't realized she had dropped her face due to all her regrets about the stuff she'd never done. It wasn't as if she hadn't the means and opportunity to get out and see the world. The days had just gotten away from her. One day, she looked up and she was snaking Ms. Jenkins's toilet yet again and hating every minute of it.

They decided to change the subject and get caught up some more. He told her all about his experiences working with Elaine for the last two months. Basically, she was a bossy hard-ass who got shit done.

"How's Theresa these days?" he asked.

Sonja smirked. "She's still the same. Alpha to the extreme and can't stop exercising to save her life."

Jay laughed. "But she hasn't gotten married yet either."

"Ha!" Sonja scoffed. "She's like a praying mantis ready to rip a guy's head off simply because she's hungry."

Jay clutched his stomach and laughed even harder. Sonja remembered how much she used to love making him laugh. She told him more stories about Theresa. Like how she'd brought one of her many boyfriends to a family dinner and broke up with him before the night ended because he drank too much wine.

"Then she broke up with another guy because she could do more push-ups than he could. And then another guy because he said that her sister and cousins were knockouts."

"Well, you are," Jay said in a frank tone.

"Thanks, but that's not a reason to break up with your boyfriend." Sonja shook her head. "I don't get her. If she doesn't want to have a boyfriend, then why keep picking them up? Now *she's* crazy."

"And what's Robin's story?" Jay had made himself comfortable in his seat.

When she'd first seen him yesterday, she'd thought his face displayed some serious exhaustion, perhaps from all the stress of being a movie star, but as she smiled at him in that moment, the puffiness underneath his eyes evened out and his skin glowed. It was clear Jay was really enjoying their conversation, and just talking about her unique and borderline insane family members made her feel that they were best friends again.

"Well, Robin is still an enigma," she said. "I've been trying to figure her out since we were two years old."

Jay's laugh indicated he knew exactly what she meant. "A few years ago, I went to this concert in Paris. The singer was—"

She pointed at Jay. "St. Vincent?"

He snapped his fingers. "Yes. She's Robin's twin. Yours too, but more Robin."

Sonja grinned. She knew why her eyes were tearing up. Somewhere in Paris years ago, Jay had been thinking about a Hester girl. It made her feel closer to him, and she liked it.

Suddenly a door opened and the sound of heels came closer. Laura stopped in the aisle, very close to Jay's shoulder. "We'll be landing soon. Please buckle your seatbelts," she said, and only to Jay.

Sonja knew the woman couldn't help herself from being rude. After all, her key to Easy Street—a hot actor with a stellar bank account—wasn't interested in biting her hook, at least not at the moment. So Sonja decided to not sweat it and do what she was told and buckle her seatbelt.

Once Laura was satisfied, she sauntered away. But then she quickly came back.

"Oh by the way," she said, handing Jay a folded sheet of white paper. "This is where we'll be staying tonight." She glanced at Sonja. "Come over if you can get away." She fled just as quickly as she had showed up with her invitation.

Sonja turned away from Jay to lift the shade over the window, pretending she wasn't bothered by what had happened. After all, Jay was a single man, outside of his bogus relationship with Plume Ashbury, although she was positive the stewardess had no idea Plume and Jay were merely a Hollywood farce.

Jay cleared his throat. "Son?"

She stopped trying to focus on the landscape below and made herself smile when she looked at him. "Yep?"

They were staring into each other's eyes again, and it made her uncomfortable, so she looked down at her lap.

"About this…"

Through her peripheral vision, Sonja saw him holding up the paper, so she lifted her head. "What about it?"

Jay dropped the sheet into the storage compartment next to his armrest. "There." He smirked.

Sonja wanted to grin like crazy, but she didn't want to expose her deepest desires, the ones she wasn't quite ready to accept herself. "It's okay. You're a single guy."

"But I'm on this trip with you, and like I said, I've changed my ways. And look, I've made our reservations, bought our groceries, and"—he winked like the charming pro he was—"I'm making dinner."

Finally Sonja could let her smile shine through, and she stretched it wide, from ear to ear. "I've never heard of an A-lister making their own reservations and buying their own groceries, let alone making their own dinner."

He chuckled as he scratched the back of his head. "That's because I spend more time being between assistants than actually having one."

Sonja raised a hand. "Don't worry. I won't ask why."

Once again, Jay laughed his head off, and yet again, she loved watching him.

THE LANDING WAS BUMPY, BUT FINALLY THEY WERE back on the ground. It was early evening but still hot outside. However, the private terminal they used to exit the airstrip was overly air-conditioned. Since they passed literally no one in the terminal, the appearance of Jay West didn't cause a ruckus until they arrived at the car rental counter. Finally, after six selfies and handshakes, they loaded their bags into the small trunk of a very impractical sports car and sped off the airport grounds.

Sonja felt like a fool for picturing Midland, Texas, as the same small town her grandmother had lived in. With the proliferation of the internet, smartphones, strip malls, superstores, and designer coffee, of course Midland would change. She quashed her plan to ask people who were near her grandmother's age if they have ever heard of Lorraine Hester or Harlan Duke. Now, looking at the rows of tan stucco track homes and passing their fifth Starbucks, Sonja felt as if learning anything about her grandmother would be like finding a needle in a haystack.

She ripped her eyes off a McDonald's, with its gym-sized playland, to tell Jay they'd have to think of another plan of attack when his cell phone rang and Bluetooth picked up the call.

"Hello," Jay said, keeping his eyes on the road.

"Where the fuck are you?" a voice blared through the speakers.

"Jim. What do you want?" Jay asked.

"Fuck it, I don't want to know where you are. Listen, Nora's going to be your assistant. I'm sending you her number. Run every damn thing you're doing through her so she can keep your calendar."

Jim didn't wait for Jay to respond as he kept going on about what he preferred as far as his project with A&Rt. He was still encouraging Jay to postpone *Pact of Lies* so that he could consider hotter projects that would "take his career to the next level."

"How many levels are there?" Jay muttered, but it seemed Jim didn't hear him because he kept talking.

Sonja watched how Jay leaned to the left, pressing his body against the crevice between the car door and his seat. He used to do that years ago. Whenever his caretaker ran down the list of auditions he was scheduled for while handing him scripts for each, he would lean away from the source of the information. Back then, Sonja didn't have enough life experience to know why he would do that, but now she did.

"Got it?" Jim barked.

Jay stared straight ahead.

"Jay, are you there?"

Jay cleared his throat and shifted abruptly in his seat. "Jim I don't want to talk about this right now. I'll call you back when I can."

Jim's voice exploded over the speakers right before Jay ended the call and promptly powered down his device.

Sonja sat very still, waiting for the tension that the previous moments had caused to dissolve. "Are you okay?" she finally asked.

Heavy silence lingered for a few beats, then he put on a smile that was an inch too high to be real. "Yep!" he optimistically declared.

Sonja watched him with her lips parted. "So your agent doesn't want you to do this project?"

"I don't give a damn what he wants, the little shit. He should be glad he hasn't been fired, which is something I should've done a long time ago."

She felt as though she should rub his shoulder to comfort him, but she didn't want to cross a line that she so badly wanted to breach. So she stared ahead vacantly as the navigator announced that they had arrived at their destination.

Jay made a left into the driveway of a red brick house with white shutters, tall windows, and a large wooden door. There were lots of well-manicured trees and bushes in the yard. The place was nice, especially for the price per night.

He shoved the gear into park, turned off the engine, and looked at her with the sexiest bedroom eyes she'd ever seen. "Hey?"

She could barely breathe. "What?"

"Don't let anything Jim said make you think I'm not fully committed to you because I am." His eyes seemed to penetrate her deeper when he said *you.*

"Oh." She felt warm in her light cotton dress even though the air conditioning had done its job of making the car nice and cool.

Then his eyebrows lifted slightly and his eyes gleamed some more. Sonja felt as though he was hypnotizing her into betraying sound judgment. Sonja couldn't be attracted to Jay in that way. It wasn't feasible—at least that was what she felt, but she didn't know why.

So she swallowed and decided to guide them down the right path. "I wasn't worried about that." Her voiced cracked, so she cleared her throat. "The fact that we've, I've, probably taken on more than I can chew worries me."

He smirked. "Don't worry about a thing. You and I have always made a formidable team, remember?"

Oh goodness, her head was spinning as she recalled the plays they used to write and produce together and all the money they made from the neighborhood kids. "I remember."

She hadn't realized how close his face was to hers until he leaned back. "So let's get inside and figure this shit out."

With some distance between them, Sonja felt as though she could think more clearly. "But I'm not even sure what we're looking for anymore?"

Jay's winning smile was back in full force. "Oh, that's easy. We're looking for any kind of inspiration."

Sonja chuckled. Jay always had a way of having no plan sound like the most exciting idea in the world.

Jay punched in a code to extract a key from a locked box. Sonja was relieved when they stepped inside a cooled house. Even though he'd paid for the house, he insisted she make herself comfortable in the master bedroom. There was nothing Sonja could say or do to change his mind. So shortly after turning on the lights, they parted ways to wash off the flight. The plan was to meet in the kitchen to make the steaks, baked potatoes, and salad for dinner, and then spend a good chunk of the night figuring out a strategy to learn more about Lorraine Hester's past.

Sonja had stripped out of her clothes and gotten in the shower. As she let the warm water run down her body, she tried to wrap her mind around the unbelievable day she'd had. First she had been summoned to her grandmother's office, where Lorraine had threatened to drop the hatchet on her budding career as a screenwriter. It was at that moment Sonja realized how badly she wanted to change her life, so she brought the issue to Jay and Dexter. And then she and Jay ended up on a private flight to Texas.

Being alone with him had done unexpected things to her body and mind. At the moment, she was fighting the desire to fantasize about Jay stepping into the shower behind her. Without saying a word, he would spin her around, kiss her so deeply that her head felt as though it was spinning off her neck, and titillate all her sexual hotspots, making orgasms rush through her with the velocity of Niagara Falls. Sonja gasped as though she had just taken her first breath. Being around Jay had awakened desires that had been dormant within her for years, and she had no idea what to do next other than focus. So after lathering her hair with shampoo, she forced herself to think of ways they could proceed with their research.

Sonja's thoughts raced back to when she'd become overly interested in her grandmother's past. It all started after she'd decided to give up on her ambitions of becoming a screenwriter, because too many assholes were blocking the path to success, and asked her grandmother for a job.

"I didn't know you were interested in real estate," Gran said.

"Well, I'm not," Sonja replied. "I just want somewhere to land until I figure out what to do with myself."

Her grandmother didn't lecture her about getting back in the ring and trying until she landed a knockout punch—that was the sermon Elaine had given her. Instead her grandmother had said, "As long as you continue moving toward something."

Sonja had assured her grandmother that the job would be short-term because she was definitely planning on enrolling in a graduate program somewhere. However, she was still lost when it came to picking a subject of study. All Sonja knew was that she was both restless and lost inside, which made for the worst kind of inner turmoil.

But it so happened that Leslie Smith, the then-manager of the complex in which Sonja lived, had just received her broker's license and was moving into a full-time job at LH Real Estate Group. So Sonja filled her position as the manager of the complex.

It was funny, because when Sonja started the job, she would see Ms. Jenkins out and about every now and then, and the woman always greeted her with a smile. And she was no bother until Sonja saw that all of Ms. Jenkins's utilities—cable, internet and even her telephone account—were all in the name of LH Reality. Then Sonja discovered that her gran's assistants were also paying Ms. Jenkins's cell phone account, grocery service, and scheduling her house cleanings and car service for the rare times that she left the complex to do things like acquire another cat or take one of them to the vet or something. She found the fact that her grandmother was basically taking care of Ms. Jenkins's every need very odd. So she decided to bring it up with Ms. Jenkins, as well as pull an Elaine on the woman by simply trying to sell her on the principle of empowering herself by taking care of her own bills. Ms. Jenkins basically told her to stop being nosy and mind her own business.

Sonja had kicked herself for trying that strategy. Hell, it never worked on her, so why did she think it would work on someone else? And when Sonja asked her grandmother why she was taking care of the woman, her grandmother, in not so many words, told her the same thing.

The next time Sonja saw Ms. Jenkins, she asked her when and where the woman had met her grandmother. Ms. Jenkins's eyes expanded like balloons as she smashed her lips together and stormed off. Sonja marked the weird reaction and tried to ask her grandmother the same question.

"She's merely a tenant who needs help," her grandmother said in a tone sharp enough to slice through steel.

Sonja didn't believe her one bit.

Then one day, she had received a call from Ms. Jenkins to unplug her kitchen sink. The whole ordeal was a crazy disaster. Ms. Jenkins had more cats than she could remember, and Sonja didn't know she was so allergic until then. Cats were everywhere, skittering and scattering across on the counters, around her feet, and of course Ms. Jenkins was wearing a gray cat around her neck. Sonja was thankful that she actually knew how to take the pipes apart and unclog a sink. She'd learned how to do it in college while living in the dorms. Whenever something went wrong in the bathroom, they could've waited forever for maintenance to come and repair the problem or she could just do it herself. Her grandmother had taught her to not sit around and wait for someone to fix something she could handle herself.

Sonja took a break from her memory as shampoo rolled into her right eye.

"Ouch," she cried, rubbing it. "Shit."

She decided to concentrate on the matter at hand. Plus, she had already extracted what she needed from her memory and couldn't wait to sit down and discuss with Jay what she thought should be their first plan of attack.

JAY STARED AT SONJA, BLINKING, WHEN SHE

appeared in the kitchen. She would never admit it, but he had given her the reaction she was seeking. Her curly locks were damp and fluffy, her running shorts hugged her ass and crotch in the right places, and her T-shirt was loose enough to not be overtly sexy but just enough to make him want to snatch it off her and suck on her tits.

He closed his mouth to clear his throat. “Um, the steaks will be done in about twenty minutes.”

“Good,” she said then strolled past him to hoist herself up on top of the island made of gray granite. “Listen, I think I’ve come up with a starting point.”

He frowned as though he had no idea what she could’ve been talking about.

“Ms. Jenkins,” she said leadingly.

He blinked hard a few times. “Oh, the tenant.”

He was apparently distracted by her, and for a moment, she wished she had been less overt with the sex appeal. "Yeah. I can't shake the feeling that she's been blackmailing my grandmother into paying all of her bills for years. There's a secret. We have to find out what it is."

Jay kept his stern expression. “A secret about what?”

She folded her arms. “That’s the million-dollar

question. But I think it has something to do with Gran's first husband."

He walked over and sat on the island beside her. "Whatever you want."

They were staring into each other's eyes yet again. And Sonja realized the desire she had worked so hard to manage was charging back to the surface. She noticed how his eyes rolled down to her chest and beyond before rising again to her face.

"I ordered a bottle of wine. You want a glass?" he asked.

Sonja shook her head. She wasn't a big wine drinker, especially since it only took one glass to dismantle all of her inhibition. "Nah, but you can have a glass."

His lopsided grin was perhaps the most seductive expression she had ever seen—at least it felt like it at the moment. "I'll pass."

Sonja's heart was thumping as she looked down at her burning thighs.

"Sonja," Jay whispered.

When she raised her head to face him, Jay's lips were right there. After one breath, their mouths bridged the distance between them. In the next breath, their lips were connected. Sonja's heart fluttered and her soul ignited into flames of passion.

Finally she had given her body what it so desperately desired.

With every swirl and brush of their tongues, she wanted more of him. His hand was squeezing her breast as though it had finally been granted permission to indulge. The way he sucked, bit, and kissed the skin of her neck, then lifted her shirt to sink her nipples into his warm mouth sent sensations to her pussy that she'd forgotten existed. A whimper escaped Sonja as Jay swept her off the countertop as though she were as light as a feather. Through the warmth of their tongues and lips and their breaths clashing, she heard her grandmother's voice telling her to always be responsible in such moments. That was when she regained reason and took a deep breath.

"Jay," she said, dropping her face to block access to her lips. "What are we doing?"

CHAPTER 12

JAY WEST

They had made it to the start of the hallway. He had planned to carry her to the master bedroom. But what Sonja had just asked was valid—what in the hell was he doing? His dick was throbbing, and his body was shivering. If he didn't enter her soon, then he would burst. And she felt so soft in his arms. Her ass in those shorts, and her fluffy damp hair, and he'd been wanting to suck on her breasts all day. Damn, she had the perfect set. But then he smelled the meat in the oven. He didn't want to turn back or put her down. But the decision wasn't his.

"I want you, Sonja," he said with a little pleading in his tone.

"I know but…" She was breathing heavily.

"We're not kids anymore."

The way she searched his eyes always turned him the hell on. It was as though he couldn't hide anything from her. Sonja was the only woman in the world who could discover his secrets, which meant that he didn't have to hide anything from her.

"I know we're not kids anymore."

"So what does that mean?" he asked impatiently.

She nodded stiffly.

His eyes widened. "Yeah? We can do this?"

"Do you have condoms?" she whispered.

He paused because he didn't want to answer that question. He didn't want Sonja to think he was so presumptuous as to believe she would give him the privilege of making love to her. He also didn't want her to believe that he was still as promiscuous as he used to be. But he didn't want to make a U-turn and go in the opposite direction of where they were taking their night.

"Yes, I have some." He felt just as eager as he sounded.

"Okay," she whispered thickly.

Cautiously, he went in for another kiss. Her lips were so soft. She tasted so sweet. He was so close to receiving the one thing in life that had always eluded him.

"But," she said between kisses.

He didn't want her talk, so he kissed her again.

"Jay, the oven," she managed to say.

The food could burn for all he cared, but she was right. He cursed under his breath.

He moved fast, practically running with her down the hallway. Once he made it to her room, he spread her out on the bed and lowered himself on top of her, grinding his erection against her pussy. He wanted her to feel his rock-hard thickness. It throbbed so badly for her.

After one last deep caress of her tongue by his, Jay jumped to his feet, ran to the kitchen, and fumbled with the knobs of the oven until he'd finally turned it off. He nearly sprinted down the hallway, eager to taste her and be inside her. After he stormed into the bedroom, Jay stopped in his tracks. His jaw dropped. Sonja had stripped out of her shorts and top and was completely naked.

"Fuck," he whispered, then swallowed the desire trapped in his throat. She was a goddess. Jay closed his eyes, considering his best approach. He wasn't standing before just any woman.

"Are you okay?" she asked in her sweet voice.

No, he wasn't okay. He didn't want to fuck up the moment. He didn't want to make a mistake that would ensure that after one time, he would never be able to have her again.

He wanted to taste her tender clit and kiss her perfect ass, but his desire to be inside her was too strong. So he snatched the buttons on his jeans and pushed them down until they bunched around his feet. He felt as though it was all taking too long as he finishing stomping out of his pants and kicking them away. He snatched off his T-shirt and tossed it somewhere.

Sonja inhaled sharply. He was fueled by the lust in her eyes.

"Don't forget the condom," she whispered.

All Jay could do was nod, then he ran out of the room, darted into his bathroom, and took a box of condoms out of his leather overnight kit. When he re-entered the space where Sonja was waiting for him, her eyes veered down at his thickness. He was so hard that his dick was pinched against his belly. He ripped the condom open, grabbed hold of his dick, and slid the rubber over it.

"Shit," he said. He needed to get ahold of himself.

Then she spread her legs, and her glistening

wetness hastened him. It was go time and he moved swiftly toward her. And now his body was against hers, then her warmth, wetness, and tightness gripped his firmness. As though his spirit had left his body, he experienced intense pleasure with each thrust. He'd never reached such a physical and emotional state, and he fought the urge to cry.

Their gazes stayed locked as blood rushed through his penis. With each pump, he tried like hell to enjoy it while not blasting off. Then she closed her eyes and pushed the back of her head deeper into the pillow. Seeing her enjoying him turned him on more than he could know. So he lost control. As sensations raced through his dick, he shook, grunted, and groaned, then cried out for the divine.

Sonja Hester

It was the sixth time Sonja had climaxed in the last fifteen minutes or so. It was impossible to keep track. Jay was eating her out as though he had been starved for her pussy, and she had no idea her body could experience so many orgasms in so little time. However, after she released the sheets she had been clawing along with the tension in her body, he pelted kisses up her belly then devoured her nipples. It was strange. Jay acted as though he couldn't get enough of her.

"I want to taste you some more," he announced then kissed and licked toward her pussy again.

She was about to make a request when her stomach growled.

Jay looked up with a naughty smirk. "But I guess we should eat dinner first."

They laughed together, then he helped her out of bed. Her legs shook as she put her shorts and T-shirt back on. It was clear to Sonja that they would be doing it again, and again, and again. She was all in when it came to sex with Jay. The point of no return had been passed.

They did a lot of kissing as Jay took the steaks and baked potatoes out of the oven. Surprisingly, the meat was cooked perfectly, and though the potatoes had been in the oven longer than they should've, they weren't overdone. They made out some more after Sonja helped Jay plate dinner. He grew another erection as he sat at the table, and she almost lost her head enough to spread her legs over his lap and insert him inside her.

"Sorry, not without a condom," she said, despite how desirous she felt.

"You're definitely Lorraine Hester's granddaughter," he said with a smile.

She chuckled as she sat in the chair beside him. "Responsibility first and always. It's impressive how much you remember about Gran."

"I always wished she was my grandmother. I knew if she were, I wouldn't have had to continue with the acting nonsense."

"But you're so good at it. How many times have you been nominated for an Academy Award?"

His knife ripped through his steak. "Three." He sniffed bitterly. "That's why Jim won't stop bothering me. He wants to win one."

Sonja snarled. "Then maybe he should become an actor."

Jay watched her with a silent smile again. "You know the day I ran into Elaine at the agency, I was on my way to tell Jim to kiss my ass because I was done with it all."

Sonja's eyes widened with surprise. "You mean you were done with acting?"

"Yeah," he whispered and looked deeply into her eyes. "But then Elaine mentioned your script and I knew I couldn't quit, not yet." He cupped the side of her face. "It was fucking fate."

Sonja felt her breathing speed up. She never believed in fate until now. "Yeah, it was."

They allowed the silence to linger between them as Sonja raked her knife through the tender meat. So many things were racing through her mind and body. Sitting there unable to get making love to Jay out of her head was pretty awkward.

"How are you feeling about what we did?" As usual, he did a great job reading her mind.

Sonja shrugged as she pushed a few pieces of meat across her plate with her fork. "I don't know." She sighed. "Well… I guess I do know."

"I don't want what we did to mean nothing."

Sonja looked into his glassy eyes. "What we did meant a lot actually, more than I was ready for."

Jay slouched in his seat. "I get it, Son." He sat up again and looked her square in the eyes. "But listen, you don't know what kind of life I've had." He sat back again. "I've been in rehab four times, and after the last time, I think it finally fucking took. I had some clarity."

"Clarity?" she asked.

"Why I needed the bad shit that I needed. And how I have to rewire my brain to want something different. It's hard work, especially when I'm doing something I fucking loathe."

"Acting?"

He nodded. "I hate it."

She swallowed the lump in her throat. "What do you love then?"

She sat on the edge of her seat as she waited for an answer, mainly because it seemed as though they had the same problem when it came to life. Sonja couldn't figure out what she wanted to be or who she really was either.

The corners of his mouth turned down as he looked off thoughtfully. "You know what I like to do?"

"What?"

"I like to cook."

"Then you want to be a chef?"

"I don't know." His eyebrows furrowed. "I think so."

She nudged him affectionately on his rock-solid bicep. "Then what's stopping you? After all, you're Jay fucking West."

He tilted his head back to laugh. Goodness gracious, he was sexy.

Jay flexed his forehead twice. "But do you know what I want now?"

By the look in her eyes, all she needed was one guess. No words needed.

They were kissing.

He was carrying her.

Soon they would make love again, and again, and as many times as they desired.

CHAPTER 13

SONJA HESTER

Sonja slowly opened her eyes. The room was dusky and perfectly air conditioned. As her mind stirred, it asked her one question. She slid her hands down her sternum to touch her wetness. Sonja grinned and twisted her body as she yawned. Yes, last night did happen.

Suddenly the smell of bacon and fried potatoes hijacked her senses. She turned toward where Jay had been lying when he held her. He was gone. Excited about seeing his face, she hopped to her feet and put on her shorts, T-shirt, and flip-flops, and then she scurried to the kitchen. Jay was at the oven, pushing hash browns around a skillet with a spatula. His face lit up when he saw her, and the appreciation his expression held made her heart flutter.

"Good morning," he said.

She grinned from ear to ear. "Morning." She sounded so girly, which was not like her at all.

And then she did something else that was different and walked over to kiss him for no reason other than he was Jay, a man who was once her best friend but last night became her lover. He liked it so much that he wrapped his arms around her, tugged her closer, and deepened their kiss.

Sonja's head spun in a way it hadn't since the first time Jay kissed her, and last night when they did more kissing and making love than sleeping.

"So what does this mean?" Jay whispered.

"I don't know," she said before their lips met again.

"I want you, Sonja."

Their mouths melted together.

"You have me."

He leaned back to look in her eyes. "Do I?" His tone was so passionate, so eager to know the answer.

Suddenly she was back in touch with the fearful parts of herself, which she had neglected from the moment she chose to make love to Jay. These parts protected her from giving her heart to a man only to end up like her mother. When her inner guardian spoke, its unrelenting tone reminded her that men leave unless she was willing to give up her independence, hopes, and a lot of dignity in order to convince him to stay.

And so she journeyed through his eyes and into his soul. This man wasn't any Joe Blow off the streets—it was Jay. As she took a deep breath, Sonja became acutely aware of his arms around her body, his nearness, and the warmth emanating from his skin. She pictured herself standing with him like that every day of their lives. Sonja admitted to herself that because of the fear within her, she didn't know how to be his partner. Hell, she didn't know how to be anyone's mate.

Jay continued searching her eyes for an answer, so Sonja dropped her head and confessed, "You have me now. Let's just start from here."

Jay pressed two fingers under her chin and gently raised her face. "Okay." He pressed his lips against hers tenderly. "We have nothing but time."

He kissed the stream of happy tears that rolled down her cheek.

Of course they made love again. Last night's sex was bolstered by them being unable to keep their hands off each other, but that morning's session was directed by a force Sonja had never known existed. Sonja and Jay had reached the elusive apex of lovemaking. She actually felt her soul merging into his—and at the moment of synthesis, with his erection shifting in and out of her wetness and their mouths kissing feverishly, she actually felt herself floating.

They could've lain in bed all day and repeated reaching that addictive state which was the mere definition of making love, but instead they showered, dressed, and ate breakfast. They were on their way to a museum in town, figuring since museums were dedicated to the past, in a city which appeared to be looking toward the future, the institution would be a great place to start.

With one hand he guided the steering wheel, and the other held her hand. Sonja looked out the window, narrowing her eyes at the huge Walmart and then another Starbucks. She was convinced now more than ever that they were searching for a needle in a haystack, and for that, she was losing interest in the reasons that had brought her to Texas in the first place.

"Hey?" Jay asked.

She turned quickly enough to meet his gaze before he was forced to watch the road again. The familiarity of his eyes made her smile. "What?"

"What are you thinking?" he asked.

She shrugged indifferently. "I don't know. Maybe we should just either call my grandmother's bluff or scrap the entire project." She sighed. "I *have* been obsessed for too long. I think it's time to start focusing on other things."

"Yeah, like what?" Jay asked.

Sonja blinked at the stark daylight beyond the windshield, trying to come up with an answer. "I don't know," she finally admitted. "I have to give it some more thought."

Jay grunted thoughtfully as he nodded. "Son, may I share something with you?"

She felt her eyebrows pull together. "Sure."

"I'm talking as someone who's done the wrong fucking thing for too long." He glanced at her as her frown intensified. "I've come to learn that it's good to take your time when it comes to life. There's not much worse than running for too long up the wrong road, and then realizing you're unhappy as hell."

He swallowed hard. "Then you stop, turn back, and you can't even see where you started from."

She squeezed his hand, and he did the same. "I'm sorry. I know you hate being an actor, but you can be sixty years old and it'll never be too late to be something else."

The navigator announced that it was time to make the final turn to their destination. Jay did.

"I know," he said, looking ahead at the parking lot. "But first let's see what we can find at the museum before we start changing our paths." He winked at her.

"I'm all for that," she said, smiling at him appreciatively.

Jay stopped the car in a parking space, and then put on a pair of shades and a red baseball cap with a white visor. "Are you ready?"

She took notice of an exhibit on the lawn featuring a derrick and shifting pumps. People surrounded the gate, observing the hammers as they went up and down, seemingly mesmerized by the movement. She hadn't expected so many people to be visiting the museum on an early Saturday afternoon.

"Are you sure you're going to be able to get away with this?" she asked.

"Get away with what?"

She shoved a hand in his direction. "Being Jay West."

He tugged the bill of his cap and smirked. "I'm going incognito. So come on, let's get this show on the road."

Jay hurried out of the car and was over to open her door before she could criticize his not-so-clandestine disguise. He hooked his arm around her waist as they walked to the entrance of the museum. She became anxious every time a teenage girl or an older woman looked in their direction. She recalled how excited the workers at the car rental place were to meet him. He had probably been posted all over their social network feeds within a matter of minutes after they had left.

Sonja was relieved once they made it inside. Jay paid for their tickets with cash, and off they went, hoping to find some information on Harlan Duke. Jay kept his arm around her waist, and they tried to avoid as many people as possible. After a while, Sonja felt as if they were moving from one exhibit to the next and learning nothing more than what they already knew.

And then she heard, "Oh my God, it's Jay West!"

Jay and Sonja quickly turned toward whoever said that. It was a guy who appeared to be in his early twenties. Suddenly, young girls' screams drowned out the gasps and people repeating his name. Jay and Sonja looked at each other with wide eyes. It was too late to run. His fans were caving in on them.

"Don't let go of my hand," Jay kept telling her.

He was signing as many autographs as he could with his right hand while Sonja clung to his left. They never stopped walking toward the exit, although they were moving at a snail's pace. It felt as though pure mayhem had broken out. Heck, Sonja hadn't known that many people were in the museum. When they cleared one group of manic fans, they walked right into another one.

"Excuse me! Get back! Mr. West!" a loud man's voice called.

Suddenly the path ahead of them thinned out and two security guards were heading their way, waving Sonja and Jay toward them. Jay tightened his grip on Sonja's hand and waved at the crowds as he rushed through the path that had been opened for them. They made it through a door and went down a short hall before entering an office.

A woman wearing a black pantsuit with a white shirt watched them with a scowl until it seemed she forced herself to smile. “Mr. West, you should’ve called and informed us of your intention to visit our museum.”

Jay flashed his winning smile as he shook the woman’s hand. “I’m sorry for being so careless.” He thumbed over his shoulder toward the door. “I hope no one got hurt back there.”

After a moment of seemingly getting lost in Jay’s charm, the woman took notice of Sonja, then combed her fingers through her hair. “No one got hurt.” Her eyes fell back on Jay. “By the way, I’m Francis.”

Jay’s smile grew broader. “Francis, we’re here for information on a man named Harlan Duke. He was an early pioneer of Midland and we want to know more about him.”

“He was an oil baron here back in the fifties,” Sonja added.

Francis’s scrutiny bounced between Sonja and Jay before her gaze fell on the security guard.

"Nate, I can take it from here." She crossed her arms.

The way Nate looked at them made Sonja feel as if they were the strangers who had just walked into a saloon back in the days of the Wild West.

"What do you want to know about Harlan Duke?" Francis asked as soon as they were alone.

Jay and Sonja gave each other quick, relieved looks.

"As much as we can," he said.

She folded her arms again. "But why?"

"Um…" There were right and wrong answers to her question, only Sonja had no idea which side the truth would land on.

"I'm researching for new projects," Jay said, "and I heard this guy Harlan Duke was an early pioneer from the oil boom in this town, so we came here to learn more about him."

"Right," Sonja said, relieved Jay was able to think faster on his feet than her. "But you don't have any information about him. We thought that was strange."

Francis studied them with lowered eyebrows. "I see." She folded her arms. "We have information on Harlan Duke, but he's only included in our private collection."

"Okay..." Jay said.

"You would need permission to—"

Jay threw his hands up. "Ma'am, a guy like me doesn't come all this way without permission. I know his late wife, and she's onboard."

Sonja fought the urge to widen her eyes in distress about the fib Jay just told. She didn't want to tip Francis off.

The woman had just unfolded her arms and was still studying them scrupulously. "All right then. Follow me."

Soon they were on the move again. Sonja could hardly believe their luck as they followed Francis up a long hallway. She felt good. She felt as though they were getting somewhere.

"Next time, you probably should call ahead and make an appointment," Francis said.

"We'll definitely do things right in the future," Jay said. "And I want to thank your guards for keeping us from getting trampled."

Francis turned back to look at them. Her eyebrows were raised in a scolding manner. "It was a very dangerous situation you put everyone in."

"I know," Jay said.

"This is not Hollywood. Actors of your caliber don't show up here every day."

Jay nodded graciously. "You're right, and again I apologize."

They stopped in front of a door, and Francis slid a key out of her pocket. "Your apology is accepted."

She opened the door, and they followed her into a room she called the special archive center. Metal cabinets were stacked against the walls. In the center of the space was a circular station that had six computer stations and one long table with chairs.

"This is impressive," Jay said, looking around.

His compliment seemed to decrease the amount of frigid energy Francis was throwing. She smiled proudly. "We like to mix the old with the new. So what have you already heard about Harlan Duke?"

"There were questions surrounding his death," Sonja said. Her heart was beating a mile a minute. She felt too eager and tried to talk herself into a calmer state.

Francis looked at her as though she had just noticed her. "I see." She walked over to one of the file cabinets and pulled open a drawer. "We've attempted to feature Duke during our True Pioneer week, but each year, we've been blocked by a major donor."

Sonja frowned. "Who's the donor?"

She slipped a thick manila folder out of the files. "I don't know. That information is undisclosed."

"Does this donor pay by check?" Jay asked.

She opened her mouth, then closed it. "Again, that information is undisclosed."

"Then secret donations are common?" he pressed.

"They are very common." Francis held up a thick folder while flashing a sneaky smile. "But I can share this with you because this information has been featured in other exhibits. Harlan Duke is just one of many search names attached to the photos."

Francis brought the folder to a long table and opened it. She started from the beginning, when Harlan Duke and others came to Midland to strike oil. There was one collage of those who'd accomplished what they came to town for in 1943. She showed them pictures of oil fields that had belonged to Harlan and his competitors.

"What about Harlan's fourth wife?" Sonja asked, eager to hear something about her grandmother.

"Fourth wife? Harlan Duke was only married to one woman during his short life," she said.

"Then he was only married to Lorraine Hester?"

Francis frowned. "Lorraine Hester?"

"Yes?" Sonja didn't mean to sound so unsure, but Francis's reaction confused her.

"No, that wasn't his wife, but I remember that name," she said.

Sonja jerked her neck. "What?"

"Excuse me?" Francis was on alert again, reading Sonja's energy with caution.

Jay touched Sonja's shoulder. "It's okay, babe, our research led us to some wrong conclusions." Then he put his hand on Francis's shoulder. "But that's why Francis is here to help us."

Sonja gulped then made herself smile, trying to keep herself from showing how her inner house made of sand was crashing into dust inside of her.

Francis raised a finger and shook it. "One second then."

Sonja held her stomach, wanting to barf. She was sure she'd heard Francis correctly. Her grandmother had not been married to Harlan Duke. That fact had been part of the only story of her gran's past that had been told to her repeatedly.

Jay grabbed Sonja's hand and nodded encouragingly at her. She wanted to groan, but instead she nodded back.

"Here it is," Francis said then slammed the drawer of the file cabinet shut. She brought a white binder to the table and flipped through the pages of old photos, which were protected by plastic film. "Lorraine Hester was a waitress at Drillers and was rumored to be the mistress."

Sonja's mouth fell open. "Harlan Duke's mistress?"

"No. Cyrus Wright's mistress."

Sonja struggled to maintain her composure. She cleared her throat and squared her shoulders. "Harlan Duke's business partner?"

"Yes. Um..."—she frowned—"I have a picture of Lorraine Hester here."

She flipped through more pages until the tip of her finger landed on a page and slid across a picture of two women with their arms around each other's waists. They were standing in front of a cash register, which sat at the edge of a lunch counter. Francis leaned closer to get a better look at the picture then grimaced at Sonja. Sonja and her grandmother had the same strong features, like her graceful neck, oval face, and bright doe eyes.

"Lorraine Hester is my grandmother," Sonja

admitted, answering Francis's curious expression. She pointed at the other woman in the photo. "But who's this?"

Francis's mouth fell open, then she closed it. "Um… that's Dora Duke."

"Cyrus Wright, is he still alive?" Sonja asked quickly, because it was apparent they were rapidly losing Francis's willingness to assist them, and even Jay's charm wouldn't be able to get her back.

Francis's hands were jerky as she pressed the binder closed then tucked it under her armpit. "I don't know if Cyrus Wright is alive or not, but there's nothing more here to show you."

Sonja and Jay looked at each other.

"Well, thank you for your time," Jay said.

Francis became even more frigid as she pursed her lips tightly then said in a cold tone, "Nate will show you out."

Nate quietly escorted them to the loading dock at the back of the building. Jay waited there while Sonja drove the car around to pick him up. They were able to leave without causing a ruckus.

With Jay back in the driver's seat, they were on

the highway heading back to the house. Sonja clutched her stomach because she felt sick. Francis must've gotten it wrong. Her grandmother lying about being married to Harlan Duke didn't make sense. And what an elaborate tale she had spun about how they met and slowly fallen more into a partnership of appreciation and trust than love.

"So how do you want to proceed?" Jay asked.

Sonja groaned. "I don't know." She smashed her hands over her face. "I mean, is this what Gran didn't want me to know? That she lied about being married to Harlan Duke and instead she was banging his married business partner?"

"I'm sorry, Son," Jay said.

She closed her eyes and took deep breaths. "And a mistress? That doesn't sound like Gran at all."

"I agree." Jay's definite tone made her feel more sure of her belief that what Francis had told them wasn't true.

But then she remembered something. "You know how they say apples never fall too far from the tree?"

"Yeah?" he said.

Sonja took a deep breath. "Elaine and I have different fathers. They both were married, but neither of them was married to my mother." She rubbed her face hard, perhaps to rid herself of that shameful reality.

"You never told me that."

"That's because I'm ashamed of it."

"Don't hide because of something your mother did. Let your mother deal with her own shame—that's if she has any," Jay said.

She sat very still and, after taking a breath, dropped her hands from her face. "You're right."

Jay reached over to take her hand but then quickly clutched the steering wheel as he craned his neck forward to put his face closer to the rearview mirror. "What the hell…?"

Sonja whipped around to look out the back window. A man was driving on their tail while waving one hand out the window. She narrowed her eyes to focus on the face behind the windshield.

"That's the security guard," she said.

"From the museum?" Jay asked.

"Yeah." She put a hand on his bicep. "Pull over. Let's see what he wants."

JAY ROLLED DOWN HIS WINDOW. THE MAN WAS definitely Nate from the museum.

"Hey," Jay said with puzzlement in his tone.

All Sonja saw was the man's torso as he handed Jay folded sheets of paper and said, "Go there now if you want more answers."

"Where is this?" Jay asked, unfolding the pages.

When they looked at the open window, Nate was already walking back to his car. They sat in a state of awe until the man's car drove past them then turned left at a median crossing in order to head back toward the museum.

They studied the two pages in Jay's hands. The first page had directions, and the second was someone's attempt at drawing a map. It was evident that whoever had drawn it had scribbled it in a hurry.

"So what do you want to do?" Jay asked.

Sonja closed her eyes to think. She was dead set on finding Cyrus Wright and asking him some questions. But first they had to find him. At least now they had a lead, which had literally fallen into their laps.

"I think we should go check it out," Jay said.

"But what if it's a trap?"

Jay caressed the side of her face as he stared into her eyes. "Son, I'm not going to let anything happen to you." He nodded. "Okay?"

Sonja trembled because the person she had, in

that very moment, decided to put her trust in was the boy who was once her best friend. But goodness that was long ago. When his lips moved in to connect with hers and their tongues delicately swirled, her head spun.

All she could say was, “Uh huh.”

CHAPTER 14

SONJA HESTER

"Are you sure you're reading that right?" Jay asked.

Sonja squinted at the words on the sheet of paper in her hands. "Yeah, I think so."

"You think?" He was snappy and rightfully so.

Where in the hell had Nate led them? They had driven sixty-three miles out of town on the interstate, then onto an abandoned highway. They were passing through more desolate flatland comprised of yellow grass and thorny bushes. Then they made a left at the creek and were supposed to drive until they saw a log cabin. They had made that turn a half hour ago.

Sonja used her finger to trace each step of the directions on the page. "Yes, I'm reading it right," she snapped back then rubbed the inside corners of her strained eyes.

"Sorry, Son, I apologize for my tone."

She sighed and looked at him. "It's okay, I get it. This is frustrating as hell."

Jay took her hand. "Let's keep going. This road has to run out at some point."

"Do you think we were purposely led astray?" she asked, but her words trailed off as the terrain suddenly offered a different picture. Sonja leaned forward toward the line of thick green trees, which appeared as though they were marching in a single-file line. Then she saw white smoke snaking up behind them. "I see something!"

"I see it too," Jay said.

They looked at each other with slight smiles. After driving past the wall of the trees, they saw their destination. Sonja had pictured a small and neglected cabin, but beyond the lawn of maintained wild grass was a home made of pale wood and with lots of windows that was a cross between a lodge and a chateau.

As the car rolled up the dirt driveway, the wheels kicked up a minimum amount of dust. Sonja could also see that the smoke came from the back of the house, which made more sense since it was nearly a hundred degrees out.

"This place is nice," Jay said.

"Yeah," Sonja whispered, keeping her focus on the house. She assumed that whoever owned the house not only had means but sought isolation as well. "Do you think Cyrus Wright lives here?"

"Maybe. We can't know until we know," he replied as though he hadn't a concern in the world.

Sonja gnawed nervously on her bottom lip as Jay killed the engine after carefully parking behind a red pickup truck, which sat beside a line of well-manicured hedges.

"Are you ready?" he asked.

She turned to face his intense expression. He was definitely in charge, and more importantly, he appeared much braver than she was. Finally she nodded.

"Stay close," he said before he got out of the car and ran around the front to open her door. She took his hand as they walked toward the front steps. "Let's come up with a secret phrase just in case either of us feels uncomfortable."

The closer they got to the front door, the harder Sonja found it to keep her breathing steady. "Good idea."

Jay kissed her temple. "Everything's going to be fine."

She exhaled briskly. The visit to the museum had been so overwhelming and the drive so stressful that she felt as if she could rest her head on his chest, close her eyes, and sleep while walking.

"How about we ask if they have any pets as a 'get the hell out of here' question?" Jay asked.

Sonja was so nervous that she quickly forgot the question, but there was no need to let Jay know. She looked up at him with a manufactured smile. "Okay."

He guided her close and kissed her temple again. "Don't worry, babe."

She was too nervous to focus on the fact that he'd called her babe and what that meant. They walked up the wooden plank steps, and Jay held her hand tighter as he rang the doorbell. He still looked like the picture of calm. They raised their eyebrows at each other and he winked before facing forward again. Sonja almost passed out as she watched the door creep open.

Sonja was shocked and relieved to see a woman about her grandmother's age.

"Well, you made it," the woman said as though it sort of bothered her that they were there but she knew they had to come. She wore loose-fitting jeans and a button-front white light cotton shirt with cap sleeves. She looked like she belonged in the middle of nowhere, living in comfort on such a grand estate. The corners of the woman's mouth were turned down as her probing eyes rolled up and down Sonja's form twice before landing on her face. "Does Lori know you've been in town asking all your questions?"

Sonja frowned. "Lori?"

"Your grandma, Lori?"

Sonja's eyes expanded as though she had been caught with both hands in the cookie jar. "Oh. Um. Well…"

"Never mind." The woman grunted then glared at Jay. "And you're that actor."

Jay stood up straight. "Yes, ma'am."

She narrowed an eye. "I like what you do, especially when you played Hawk in *Nowhere to Return*."

He glanced at Sonja, and she saw the element of surprise in his expression. "Thank you."

She put her focus back on Sonja. "Well, y'all come in and let's see what I can and can't tell you."

Jay nodded at Sonja, which told her that he felt just as safe about entering the stranger's house as she did. The woman held the door open as they walked inside.

"Sorry, I never got your name," Sonja said.

"That's because I haven't given it," the woman said.

Sonja and Jay raised their eyebrows at each other again as the woman closed the door.

"This way," she said.

The house smelled like potpourri and catnip. The sun-filled rooms, exposed brick, and an overabundance of knit throws and fluffy pillows gave each room that cozy and warm feeling.

The woman led them into a small room on the back end of the house and right off a formal dining room. As far as furniture to sit on, there were only two leather armchairs and a cloth sofa with a matching ottoman that doubled as a coffee table. Sonja noticed the woman's short, curly gray hair and small but sturdy frame after she sat in the center of the sofa. She and Jay got the message, and each of them took a seat in one of the chairs. The woman crossed her legs and arms, and Sonja found herself appreciating her vitality.

"What do you know about your grandma?" she asked, eyeing Sonja like a hawk.

Sonja readjusted her bottom against the firm

leather cushion as she remembered to breathe. For some reason, the woman's inquiry felt like the trick question at the end of an exam. "Um"—Sonja cleared her throat—"She left home when she was sixteen and came to Midland, Texas. That was in 1954, and the first job she found when she came to town was a waitress."

She paused to gauge the woman's reaction. Her expression said that she was patiently waiting to hear more.

Sonja blew a brisk sigh because she had already learned that the next thing she knew about her grandmother wasn't true. "And two years later, she married Harlan Duke."

The woman narrowed both eyes but kept her lips clamped.

"I believe that was in 1956, and three years later, Harlan died," Sonja mumbled because the lady had uncrossed her legs and arms.

"Is that all?" her host asked.

Sonja glanced at Jay. "Yes, ma'am."

"Okay well, Francis let me know that she told you your grandmother was never married to Harlan. But they were as much of friends as they could be. Harlan used to love to come into Drillers and give everybody advice on how to live better."

She grunted. "Lorraine was the only one who'd listen to him though."

Sonja felt her heart drop to her stomach. "My gran said she loved his business advice."

"Yep," she said, dipping her head. "I reckon that's why Lori's a rich lady today."

Sonja swallowed hard as she smiled weakly. She had heard the worst things about her grandmother that afternoon, so it was refreshing to hear something good.

"But Harlan only married one woman and for a very short time. See, their parents put them together. Harlan's family was in the oil business, and so was hers. But he bought his wife Drillers to keep her busy." She sniffed as she looked off nostalgically. "Harlan and his wife liked each other a whole lot, but they didn't love each other at all."

Sonja followed the woman's gaze out the window. It was only then Sonja noticed a glistening lake beyond the yellow grass.

"But I guarantee you, even though your grandmother was a sight for sore eyes, sort of like yourself, he wasn't interested in her either. Harlan liked the licentious things in life, the kinds that weren't free."

Sonja glanced at Jay and then scooted closer to

the edge of her seat. "Earlier, I was told that my gran had an affair with Harlan Duke's business partner—"

"Cyrus," the woman said before Sonja could say his name.

"Yes." She felt a knot form in her throat.

The woman nodded firmly. "That's correct."

Sonja felt her soul take a nosedive and recover before slamming into the ground.

The woman shook her head emphatically. "Listen here…" She crossed her legs again. "I reckon if your grandma wanted you to know the truth about Cyrus, she would've told you, but you've probably already learned more than you should, so I'm just going to tell you it all. Your grandmother had an affair with that man, but not because she wanted to." She dipped her chin and looked at Sonja with a warning in her eyes. "One look at Lori and that man didn't want to keep his pet in his pants. He made it to where if she didn't lay with him, she would lose her job and even that trailer she lived in. Lori had built a home for herself in Midland but"—she shook her head—"he just couldn't give her any peace."

"I don't understand," Sonja said.

"Cyrus liked to take whatever he wanted, when

he wanted, and he didn't give a damn how he got it." She turned away. "I can't prove it, but I know he had something to do with Harlan's death."

"But you said he took her?"

The woman faced her again. "Yes. He went to her place whenever he felt like it. Sometimes he'd leave her alone for months. He liked to get rough first." She dropped her head. "Lori always had bruises."

Sonja could hardly believe what she was hearing. As a matter of fact, she wanted to pinch herself to make sure she wasn't having a nightmare. "I'm sorry, but are you saying that my grandmother was violently raped?" Just speaking those words made her want to dry heave.

The woman's eyes softened. "That is what I'm saying, darling."

Sonja slapped her hand over her mouth. "Oh my God."

"Whoa," Jay said and then rubbed Sonja's arm consolingly. "Maybe we've heard enough for one day."

"No." Sonja took a deep breath and sat up straight. "I'm fine. Please continue."

The woman looked off, shaking her head. "I may have said too much. I'm sure Lori didn't want to tell you because she was ashamed of what he did to her, especially when she became pregnant. Lori always believed it was her fault."

"But it wasn't," Sonja said.

"Of course it wasn't, darling." She faced Sonja. "But Cyrus paid her to leave town. The next I heard, she'd taken up with a lawyer, bought a lot of property, and was doing pretty well for herself." She said it as if her grandmother's success was some sort of consolation.

Sonja was too angry and hurt to reply.

"When was the last time you saw or spoke to Ms. Hester?" Jay asked.

The woman's face tightened, then she pursed her lips to form a fake smile. "I haven't seen Lori in years."

Jay narrowed his eyes. "What about when you spoke to her?"

"A few times." She glared at him as though daring him to ask another question.

"But I wonder"—Jay leaned forward, resting his forearms on his thighs—"about Cyrus's wife. Did she ever find out what happened to Lorraine?"

The woman rubbed the side of her face. "Everybody knew."

"Oh and another thing." Jay sat upright. "Are

you Dora Duke? We saw a picture of her earlier. Shave twenty years off and you look just like the beautiful woman in that picture."

She grunted then smirked. "You're very charming, Mr. West. I suppose it's a trait you honed in Hollywood. I haven't worked at my diner in forty-five years."

Sonja tried to remember the face of the other woman in the photo with her grandmother, but she couldn't. She was thankful Jay did though, and she sat on the edge of her seat as he maintained his steady and expectant grin.

"Then you are Dora Duke?" he asked.

The woman pursed her lips as though she had to think about her answer. "I go by Dora Watkins these days."

Sonja couldn't stop shaking her head, mainly because the moment was too unreal to be true.

Now that the cat was out the bag, Dora shared more photos with them. They stayed for at least an hour, listening to Dora's tales. She showed them Harlan's first oil pump and pictures of the young women who'd worked at Drillers. They had a lot of Christmas parties and New Year's celebrations, birthday parties, and just friendly moments in general. Sonja searched for Ms. Jenkins's face in each snapshot, but she wasn't there.

Sonja was about to ask Dora if she'd ever heard of Betty Jenkins when Dora pulled one of the last photos in the box and held it close to her face. "Now this here is Cyrus and his first wife, Hazel."

She set the photo on the coffee table, which already had a sea of pictures displayed on it. Sonja recognized Hazel right away. Sure, her face was plumper and eyes, though sad, were brighter, but it was the cat herder herself, Ms. Jenkins.

Sonja stabbed her finger on Hazel's chest. "I know her. She's Betty Jenkins."

"No, darling, that's Cyrus' first wife, Hazel." Dora sounded a bit confused.

Sonja closed and opened her eyes several times, then she explained to Dora how Hazel was living at an apartment complex her grandmother owned in LA. She told her how her grandmother was paying all of Ms. Jenkins's bills and now she might know why. Dora listened attentively as Sonja tacked on the part about the screenplay she had written, and how the characters were based on her grandmother and Ms. Jenkins. The surreal part was that she'd thought she'd made up the story, but the more she learned during her Midland trip, the more she realized that she had guessed the truth.

"Well, that's mighty interesting." Dora then told them how in 1999, Hazel had finally left Cyrus, but not before trying to point suspicion in his direction for Harlan's death. "I always suspected it was Hazel who sent the bottle of cyanide to the police with a note asking them to check it for Cyrus's fingerprints and then exhume Harlan's body and examine it for poisoning."

"But do you believe Harlan was poisoned?" Jay asked.

Dora seemed to sink deeper into the sofa. "I didn't. Until Cyrus bought Harlan's interest from me and sold everything to the Clark Brothers."

"Francis showed us pictures of those guys," Jay said.

"Well, they were two vicious jokers. They were after Harlan's business the second he struck oil."

"I take it they didn't find poison in Harlan Duke's body?" Jay said.

Dora sat silently with a grave expression. "No." She squeezed her eyes shut and then opened them. "Harlan's coffin was empty. It seems as though Cyrus was way ahead of all of us." The anguish on her face gave way to a slight smile. "But Hazel waited the old bastard out."

She told them how after Cyrus sold everything to Harlan's rivals, he spent his days drinking and sleeping with prostitutes. When Hazel finally left him, it was forty years later and she took all the money he had left, and no one had seen her since.

Sonja slapped her hand over her heart as she turned to Jay. He shook his head, apparently knowing exactly what that look on her face meant. They had identified the part of the screenplay that alarmed her grandmother. In the story, Ida Lawry stole every cent her husband had before disappearing and showing up in the life of self-made billionaire, Rose Ready. The two women were from the same town, and Ida threatened to reveal Rose's darkest secret, which was that she'd murdered her husband, though not so she could claim his wealth. Rose had killed him because he was abusive. Sonja couldn't believe it. Even though the pieces fell in different parts of the true story, they were all there in *Pact of Lies*.

CHAPTER 15

SONJA HESTER

Shortly after they tied all the pieces together, Sonja and Jay excused themselves. Dora revealed one last thing before they left. Francis, the museum manager, was her daughter-in-law. Paul, Dora's son, had actually been burning trash in Dora's backyard when his wife called to tell him about her visit from Jay West, the actor, and Lorraine Hester's granddaughter. Apparently the only reason Francis had agreed to talk to them was because they had recently been approached by a producer about making a movie about Harlan Duke, focusing on his short life as an oil tycoon. She'd figured Jay West had been offered the role and was there to do some personal research. However, Francis knew she had it all wrong after

Sonja revealed she was Lorraine Hester's granddaughter.

Dora's son, Paul, immediately told Dora what had happened, and she asked Francis to send Sonja and Jay to her house. Since it had been revealed to them that Lorraine was Cyrus's "mistress," Dora felt she owed them the truth. She didn't want Sonja to believe that her grandmother was a harlot.

Dora said one more thing before she and Jay got back into their car. "I didn't know Hazel was with your grandmother. I'm going to keep that to myself, but Lorraine should know that I know."

And that was all Dora had to say on the matter.

Sonja and Jay were silent as they drove back to the rental house. It was only a quarter after seven and still light out. So many thoughts were bumping around Sonja's mind, but one thing was obvious to her.

She turned to Jay, who was peering straight ahead. "Jay?"

He glanced at her then took her hand. "What is it?"

"We're going to have to change the story or scrap the project."

Jay sighed thoughtfully. "I know. We have the rest of this weekend and Monday at least to switch the elements of the story around and present a new screenplay to Vince." He glanced at her. "Do you want to run that race?"

Sonja groaned because she was confused. Did she? "I don't know."

"Well, it's your choice. Don't do it for me. Do it for you." He squeezed her hand tighter, which let her know that whatever she decided, he wouldn't abandon her.

She asked if she could close her eyes and think for a while. Jay had no problem giving her mental space.

Something was happening inside her. Sonja was sure now more than ever that she wanted to write stories. But she had lost the desire to rummage through her grandmother's life. The truth had set her free, and now she was at a different point in existence. What was happening to her was strange. She wanted to go to Canada. She wanted to expand her horizons.

Sonja opened her eyes and turned toward Jay. "I want to do it. Let's do it."

"Rewrite the story?"

"Yes."

He cracked a satisfied smirk. "I was hoping you would say that."

THEY DECIDED THAT JAY'S HOUSE WOULD BE A better place to shut themselves in and create for the next forty-eight hours, so he scheduled a charter flight to take them back to LA. With continuous movement, they made it back to the rental house, packed their things and went straight to the airport. While they waited for takeoff, Jay called Dexter to let him know their plans to write a major revision to the story. Dexter welcomed the changes by saying he was always up for a new challenge.

Sonja sent a text to Robin, asking her to meet them for breakfast at Jay's in the morning so that she could catch her up on what happened in Midland. Before the pilot announced they were next in line to charge down the runway, Robin texted back, *Okay. Send address.* Sonja had enough time to forward her the same text Jay sent her on yesterday with his address.

On this flight, Jay sat beside her instead of across from her, and she rested her head on his shoulder. She was so drained that all she wanted to do was sleep, but Jay reminded her that she should eat something first. The last meal she'd had was breakfast, and not since boarding the plane had she had any water.

Sonja was also relieved to have two nicer flight attendants, ones who didn't try to secretly or overtly flirt with Jay. Right away, they served dinner, starting with roasted butternut squash soup. As the main course, they had port-braised lamb shanks on top of a fluffy bed of mashed potatoes, along with garlic-and-sherry-vinegar string beans. Their final course was a dessert tray of tarts, vanilla cream desserts, tiramisu, éclairs, berry bowls, and mini cheesecakes.

Sonja and Jay were so hungry that the only talking they did during the meal was moaning about how good all the food tasted. And when their bellies were full, the stewardesses dimmed the cabin lights. Instead of joining the Mile High Club, Sonja fell asleep in Jay's arms.

THE FOUR-HOUR FLIGHT WENT BY SO FAST THAT IT felt as if they had just closed their eyes when it was time to wake up. The small amount of shut-eye made Sonja feel slightly better, but once they got back to Jay's place, they found Robin in the living room, sitting on the sofa across from Dexter.

"Robin?" Sonja said, her surprise evident in her tone.

"Gran called me. She saw this." Robin displayed the face of her smartphone for Sonja to see.

Sonja had to blink her tired eyes to bring the screen in focus.

"Shit," Jay muttered.

Someone had snapped a photo of them pushing their way through the crowd at the museum.

Sonja's stomach tied in knots. "Gran saw that?"

Robin pressed her lips in a hard line as she nodded. "And there are a lot more." She turned to Jay. "You're way too photogenic for your own good."

He chortled tiredly.

"Um…" Dexter cleared his throat. "It's good to see you both back."

Sonja looked at him and could clearly see that he had been rattled by Robin's unique beauty. The red in Dexter's undertone was on fire and his eyes were gleaming. Robin usually had that effect on men.

"We should go somewhere and talk," Sonja said.

Robin couldn't stop herself from grunting when Jay put his arm around Sonja, kissed her, and said they could take the living room. He and Dexter went to the den, which was down a hallway to the left and around the corner.

"Are you and Jay a couple?" Robin asked once they were alone.

Sonja folded her arms. "Yes."

"Oh." She frowned. "Isn't he with Plume Ashbury?"

"Not for real. I mean, it's a fake Hollywood relationship."

Robin also folded her arms as she cocked her head to the side. "Are you sure?"

Sonja felt her frown intensify. "Why? Have you heard something?"

Robin wiggled her head. "No, but Jay is a notorious party boy."

"He's different."

"How do you know?"

"He told me."

"And that's enough for you?"

Sonja closed her eyes and shook her hands

vigorously. "Robbie. Please stop." She opened her eyes. "Didn't you come here to talk about Gran?"

Robin studied her for a moment then sighed as she released the tension from her body. "Let's sit."

They moved to the sofa and sat next to each other.

"So, yeah, Gran knows you've been in Midland." She sighed as her eyes widened. "And she's pissed."

"I found out a lot about her but…" Sonja closed her eyes and shook her head. "I wasn't going to tell her what I know."

"Well, what do you know?"

Sonja started from the beginning. Robin had also heard their grandmother spout the same false version of the past she had told Sonja. She told Robin about the rape and even who Ms. Jenkins really was.

"Ah," Robin said gravely. "It sounds like your script nearly hit the nail on the head."

Sonja swallowed and nodded. "So how mad was Gran when you talked to her?"

"From a scale of one to pissed? Pissed."

Sonja grimaced. "Well, I wasn't going to tell her that I know the truth."

"That's pretty patronizing of you."

"How so?" She was frowning so intensely that her skull ached.

"You chose to go poking your nose in Gran's past. And I get it," Robin said, throwing her hands up. "Gran sort of had it coming. I mean, she told you to figure out a solution." She scoffed. "She should've guessed you were going to do just that."

Sonja's headache got so bad that she rubbed her temples. "Listen, you're going to have to be direct with me. I have no idea what the hell you're saying." She dropped her hands from her head and squared her shoulders. "Why do you think I need to tell Gran?"

"Because you know her lies. Are you really going to sit there and look in Gran's face and not say anything, knowing what you know?"

Sonja braced herself. "Did you hear what I told you?" Her voice cracked.

Robin rubbed Sonja's thigh consolingly. "Yes, Son, and I know it's hard." She sighed. "And hell, if I were in your shoes…"

"But you kind of are in my shoes because I told you everything."

"No, no, no, no, no!" Robin said, shaking her head. "Don't put this on me. This is your shithole. You dug it. Now fill it."

She wanted to choke Robin for speaking in riddles again. If only her cousin wasn't right. There was no way she could look her grandmother in the face and pretend she didn't know everything. Although she needed no explanation from Gran. After what Gran had endured, she had the right to revise her history.

"You're right," Sonja finally said.

They sat in comfortable silence for a while.

"So who is Dexter Frampton?" Robin asked.

Sonja jerked her head back in shock. "Are you asking about Dexter because you're interested?"

Robin rolled her eyes. "Forget I asked."

"No, he's beautiful, isn't he?"

Robin shrugged.

"And listen, you're beautiful. He's beautiful. The two of you can make lots of beautiful babies together."

Sonja laughed as her cousin hopped to her feet. "I'm leaving."

"Come on, don't leave," Sonja said even though she was sleepy and eager to get in bed with Jay.

Robin shook her finger at Sonja. "You just be careful with Jay."

Sonja groaned as she rolled her eyes. "Okay. You're right. Time for you to go."

Robin was right on her heels as Sonja walked toward the door. Robin wasn't one for sticking around when a boy she liked was in the vicinity. Sonja couldn't count Robin's ex-boyfriends on one hand because she had none. Although she wasn't a virgin. Robin had just never let a guy stick around long enough to strike up a relationship with her.

However, never had her cousin ever inquired about a member of the opposite sex. Dexter must've really made an impression on her, and of course Sonja's curiosity wanted Robin to give her the play-by-play of the interactions she'd had with Dexter before Sonja and Jay showed up. Instead they hugged at the door and said they would see each other soon.

With Robin gone, Sonja went to the den to meet Jay. Dexter had already gone to bed, so Jay escorted her to his room. The mood had been set. There was no doubt about what would come next. They hadn't partaken in each other's bodies since that morning when Sonja had reached divine heights.

However, even though her body and soul craved more of Jay, she couldn't get Robin's warning out of her mind. Robin was one of those fascinating people who famous people liked to know, so she knew just about everyone in the entertainment business from LA to New York and across the Pond to London. If Robin had heard anything about Jay's reputation, then she would've gotten it from a credible source.

Jay's room was large and modern but very sterile like the rest of his house. Each room could've used a woman's touch. They had both stripped off their clothes and met under the sheets of his bed. The mattress was comfortable and the linens nice and soft.

He gathered her in his arms and guided her ass against his erection. She breathed heavily as he grinded against her indulgently while sliding his fingers through her warm slipperiness. She would've already given in to his attempt to make her horny, but she couldn't rid herself of Robin's warning.

"Hey, what's going on with you?" Jay kissed the back of her shoulder.

His lips made her body shiver with delight. "Nothing." When he grinded her again, she said, "Well, something."

"What is it, baby?"

She could tell Jay was so close to flipping her on her back and sliding himself inside her. "It's just that Robin told me I should be careful about you."

Suddenly she didn't feel his erection dipping deep into the crack of her ass.

"Why did she say that?" There was no more seduction in his voice.

She flipped over to face him. The lights were still dim. During their lovemaking the previous night, Jay had kept the environment dusky. It was clear to her that he liked to see all the parts of her body that got him hot and bothered.

"You know Robin," she said.

He shook his head against the pillow. "No, I don't." He sounded irritated.

"You said yourself that you have a reputation."

He looked so solemn as he stared into her eyes. "You're not going to hold that against me, are you?"

Sonja smoothed the side of his face. "Absolutely not."

"Because I've changed."

"I believe you."

Jay flipped onto his back and stared at the ceiling. "How far do I have to run from this shit?"

"What do you mean?"

He turned to face her. "Fame sucks ass. My parents did this shit to me. And what did they give me for it? They're fucking dead. My dad committed suicide, and when you slice it all up, my mom fucking let herself die. She didn't even try to fight cancer. She drank, smoked, and bumped coke up until her last breath."

Sonja tried to think of the right words to say, but in a sense, they shared the same wound. Her mom sucked. She hadn't seen Carrie Anne in years. She could be dead for all Sonja knew, and more than that, Sonja couldn't have given two fucks if she was dead.

"You know what I really want to do, babe?" he asked.

"What?" she asked breathlessly.

"I want to run away with you. I want to make up for living the last fifteen years without you. Because at the moment, I can't fucking think because you're all I want."

Jay snatched a condom off the nightstand, rolled it over his erection, and climbed on top of her. She let him spread her lips and insert his fingers into her vagina. He moaned greedily when he felt how dripping wet she was.

"Hell, I can't wait anymore," he whispered as he plunged his erection into her smoldering depths.

Sonja gasped when she felt his thickness. She loved how his size stretched her wide. She felt his every thrust sparking pleasurable sensations through her pussy. And he knew what the hell he was doing too. Jay liked to take it nice and slow. He loved to angle this way and that so he could try to get her off in more ways than one. Sonja felt as if her pussy were a five-course meal prepared by a world-famous chef and he was savoring every swallow of her.

And then something happened from some mysterious spot within her vagina. It started slowly.

"Oh my God, I'm coming," she whimpered as a full-on orgasm blasted off inside her. She shook and shivered as she clung to Jay.

"Shit," Jay said once the tension relaxed from her body. He shifted in and out of her like a powerful jackhammer until he came.

They kissed and groped, caressed and petted. They couldn't keep their hands or mouths off each other until finally one or both of them had fallen asleep.

When Sonja and Jay woke up the next morning, they made love again. Not only could they have stayed in bed all day, they could've remained together between the sheets, making love, sleeping, and eating, all year. But they couldn't. They had work to do.

Jay's cook was back and made them breakfast. This time, Sonja could see that Jay and Cam were actually friends, and when he asked her how she'd achieved the flavors in her eggs Benedict, she step-by-step listed her recipe.

Dexter had been up for hours, and when he joined them at the table, he had a story checklist ready to go over with them. "What we'll do first is discuss the elements we want to keep and get rid of the shit we can't use."

So they sat at the table for hours, working together like a well-oiled machine.

CHAPTER 16

SONJA HESTER

Cam had served them a late lunch of sushi and various kinds of Asian flavored salads. It was remarkable how well all three of them worked together. They had changed the murder victim four times and built a world around the death of each particular character. They had continuously created themselves down a dead-end road.

It was going on ten o'clock at night when a bright idea came to Sonja. "What if he's not dead? He's like one of those guys with a lot of money who make tons of promises to a lot of people while he's alive. And then in a later season, he's murdered, but by then, everyone is a suspect, even the son who comes to town asking questions."

"My part," Jay said, grinning at her.

She grinned back. "Yeah, you were too much of a choirboy. Now you can be just as bad as the rest."

"I like it. Let's bang out an outline before bed." Dexter tapped his finger on the tabletop three times. "By the way"—he kept his eyes glued to his computer screen—"Sonja, is Robin single?"

Her lips slowly reformed into a smile. She had been wondering if he was going to ask about Robin. "Perpetually."

He looked up, frowning as though her answer had puzzled him.

"Robin is perpetually single," she repeated.

"A woman as beautiful as she is?"

"Yep."

"Why is that?"

"She's not cuckoo, she's just hard to get. But she did ask about you tonight, and she never does that."

Dexter's miraculous blue eyes looked so defenseless. "Does what?"

Her smile grew wider. "Ask about someone she's attracted to. It seems you made an impression on her." She narrowed an eye curiously. "What did you guys talk about?"

Dexter rolled his eyes slightly. "Not much. But

she did mention a dinner you're having on Tuesday night. She asked if you had invited me?"

"What dinner?" Jay chimed in.

"Oh, my family's throwing me a going away dinner before we head off to Canada." She squeezed Jay's shoulder. "You're invited, hon." Then she winked at Dexter. "So are you."

Dexter's incredibly glassy eyes turned even more brilliant. He tried to hide them by sticking his face close to his computer. He cleared his throat. "Another thing," he said in his all-business tone.

"Yeah?" she said, trying to sound extra nice to get him to look up.

"We don't go to sleep until we have a new script ready to send to Vincent Adams." He looked up. "Are you both with me?"

Jay raised his eyebrows at Sonja. "We can fit in fifteen-minute quickie breaks, can't we?"

Dexter's face turned red, but Sonja could see in him exactly what she saw in her cousin. They both had a secret sexy side that only a profound intimate encounter with someone they were deeply attracted to could bring to the surface.

Sonja playfully nudged Jay's shoulder. "Jay, come on. You're embarrassing Dexter."

"I'm fine," Dexter said, his eyes still on his computer. "Quickies are allowed if they don't interfere with getting shit done."

"All right, then no quickies," Jay said jokingly.

Sonja chuckled.

Dexter remained serious. Sonja only knew one other person who could keep a stone face like that and she had asked about him, and he had asked about her. But Sonja wondered if they were opposite enough to not send the other running for the hills. She had a feeling that one day soon, she would get the chance to see.

"All right then." Sonja stood. "Let's go to the kitchen and make coffee." She winked suggestively at Jay.

He hopped to his feet. "Dexter, this is going to take us about fifteen minutes."

Dexter rolled his eyes. "And not a minute longer." He shook a scolding finger at Jay. "I mean it."

Jay swept Sonja off her feet. "Let's go break some records, baby!"

Sonja laughed her head off as he scurried away, carrying her over his shoulder. The fact that his strength made her feel as light as a feather was so hot. When they reached the kitchen and he spread her out on the massive white quartz-topped island, things got hot and heavy real fast. Within fifteen minutes, they had managed to please each other's body and desire as well as make a large pot of coffee for the start of a long night.

Sixteen Hours Later

When they got down to business in Jay's office last night, the space was tidier. Now sheets of paper covered the floor, some crumbled and others not. Sonja's eyes were so tired that it hurt to concentrate on her computer screen, yet she was captivated by the world they had created and couldn't look away.

They had first written a detailed outline with Jay acting out most of the scenes for precision and deliverability, just as he used to do when they were kids. The three had laughed a lot. They'd shared moments of extreme appreciation for the creative process whenever one of them had a moment of pure brilliance. And Sonja and Jay's first quickie was actually their last. Who could think of sex when what they were doing was just as fulfilling?

Finally Sonja reached the last word of the fifty-page pilot episode.

"The end," she sang while her heart pounded with exuberance.

Jay raised a finger as his face inched closer to his computer screen. His lips moved as he read silently. Finally his finger came down and he sat up straight. "Done."

"Been done," Dexter said.

"Dude"—Jay heaved a balled up sheet of discarded paper at him—"do you always have to be an overachiever?"

"Yes," Dexter said calmly.

Jay laughed.

Dexter snickered then folded his arms as he sat back in his seat. "Shit, I can't believe we did that. We make a great team."

Sonja couldn't stop smiling. "So is this how it's going to be in Canada?"

"It's going to be a lot more chill than this, but yeah." Dexter sat up. "That's if Vince approves the story."

"He will." Jay sounded sure of himself. "And if

he doesn't, I'll fund the whole production and find another network to air it."

Dexter smirked. "That's pretty gangster, man."

Jay flicked his thumb up. "Going gangster or going home."

Dexter swiped his phone off the desk. "I like the sound of that. Let's call Vince and get it over with."

CHAPTER 17

JAY WEST

It was three o'clock in the afternoon when they ended their call with Vincent Adams. He wasn't thrilled about the changes being sprung on him, but he was impressed they had managed to crank out a new pilot script in less than twenty-four hours.

"It better not be shit," he said before announcing that he'd get back to them before Wednesday to let them know if they still had a deal or not.

Jay knew they were lucky that Vincent Adams enjoyed the excitement of working under the gun. He had often repeated in meetings that without risks comes zero rewards, and the guy hated formulaic bullshit.

Sonja had crawled into bed with him, and she was naked. His hand ran up and down the soft skin of her curved hip. He burned to have her at least once; however, less than a minute after Sonja's head hit the pillow, she was snoring gently.

"Shit," he muttered as he guided her closer to his hard-on.

It would take a while before he stopped wanting Sonja every minute of the day. He recalled seeing her around the neighborhood fifteen years ago after he had decided to put some distance between them. If Sonja was a needle in a haystack, his eyes would've been able to find her. He used to love her so much.

He'd always wanted her, but he knew she hadn't been exposed to the same shit he'd had to endure early on. Being a child star in a land of predators made every day feel as though it was one he had to survive. But he had been lucky to have Margareta, the woman who was his nanny and guardian. She had been good at protecting him. All he'd had to do was tell her that some sick individual had touched his dick and she would figure out a way to get him out of that job.

However, although Margareta could save him from the creepy old guys, she wasn't so successful at teaching him how to wait it out with girls his own age. He felt as if every hyper-sexualized girl who needed to be banged to feel loved would find him to do the job. It took years for him to learn that he hadn't obliged them because he was a sex-starved boy who couldn't control his dick. He'd given the girls what they'd thought they needed because he too craved shots of intimacy with his hits of dopamine. Not only that, but he had been angry at his mother and disappointed with his father for abandoning him. But he'd had Sonja, Riley, and all the Hester girls in his life too. For some unknown reason, he'd always believed they were too good for him, which was why he had slowly pulled away from all of them.

Jay guided Sonja closer against his body. "If you don't get to know what's loveable and good about yourself, then you will never stop running up the road to complete and utter destruction," Dr. Reynolds, the one therapist who had changed his life, had said.

Jay had thought it was too late to make amends with Sonja when he finally realized that he did deserve her. He'd also realized, around the same time, that instead of rubbing her pussy the night of her birthday get-together, he should've gorged on the entire pizza and struggled to stay awake from one movie to the next with her. He'd repeated that night over and over in his head many times and each had a different outcome.

Jay knew one thing for sure—Sonja was the one for him. God had made her specifically for him, and vice versa.

Finally Jay fell asleep, and he must've done it with a smile because he had never been happier.

"Hey, Jay," someone whispered sharply.

Jay was being shaken. The lights were on and he felt groggy as he turned and opened his eyes. "Jim? What are you doing here?" The potency of Jim's cologne blew him away. Then Jay looked at Sonja, who was still sleeping. "Shit."

"Why the fuck haven't you answered my calls?" Jim barked.

Jay put a finger to his lips and shushed his agent. He was steaming mad as he carefully got off the bed and turned the light back down.

"This way," he snapped and led Jim out of the room, closing the door behind them.

“I’m your fucking agent, for fuck’s sake,” Jim said way too loudly for Jay’s current condition.

Jay had been sleeping hard and his body hadn’t caught up to the situation yet. “What time is it?”

Jim thumbed over his shoulder. “Is that the Hester bitch?”

Fueled by ire, Jay grabbed Jim by the collar and shoved him against the wall.

“What the fuck is wrong with you?” Jim yelled.

“Call her a bitch again and I’ll split your head in half.”

“What the fuck—”

“And say fuck in my house one more time and I’ll toss you out the front door.”

Their glares were stuck on each other. Jay meant business and was waiting for Jim to test him.

“Okay,” Jim said defiantly. “Let go of me.”

Jay got ahold of himself and released his agent.

Jim circled his shoulders and stretched his neck by moving his head side to side. “Don’t ever put your hands on me again.”

“Don’t ever call the woman I love a bitch and I won’t have to.”

“Love her? You just met her!”

Jay shook his head. The fact that Jim didn’t know about the past he shared with Sonja was reason enough to get rid of the guy. Jay remembered telling Jim about Sonja and her screenplay on three occasions. "I didn't just meet her. I've known her just about all my life."

"Elaine Hester's sister?"

"Yes."

"You've known Elaine Hester that long?"

"Yes, why?"

Jim rubbed the back of his head. "Shit. Why didn't you ever tell me this shit?"

Jay shook his head. The problem with Jim was he was an egomaniac who heard what he wanted to hear when he wanted to hear it and the man could conveniently forget shit.

Jim dropped his head as he kept shaking it. "This shit isn't going to turn out good for either of us."

"What shit?"

Jim stood up tall, widened his stance, and folded his arms. "Your contract expired last week. If you had a fucking—"

"I said—"

Jim raised a hand. "Sorry." He sighed gravely. "If you had an assistant, then we could've gotten this settled already."

Jay felt another weight lift off his shoulders. "I'm not under contract?"

Jim's expression became more pinched. "Listen, I got the fucking contracts outside in my car."

Jay shook his head. "I'm not signing anything."

Jim threw his hands up in defeat. "And hey, I'll give you your fucking"—he shook his head—"shit, sorry, your damn pet project with V-Adams."

"Give me?" Jay muttered thoughtfully. He was half asking Jim the question while coming to a realization.

Jay had been dealing with self-serving assholes like Jim all of his life. Recently Jay had learned something about the comfortable uncomfortable. It was when the brain got so used to bullshit, abuse, and all the things that made a person unhappy that their need for bad shit became second nature. Then if the opposite came along, that person would reject it even though it was good for them. Telling Jim to go stick his contracts where the sun didn't shine felt uncomfortable, but Jay knew that was the only answer he needed to give in order to be a better advocate for himself.

"Listen, we'll talk about it later. I'm going to go get the contract. Comb over it and get it back to me before you go to Canada." Jim pointed at Jay in warning. "Just don't let that bit—" He stopped himself then sighed hard. "But Elaine Hester is a bitch, dude."

"She's family, so don't call her a bitch either."

"Jay?" Sonja called from the room.

He turned toward her voice. "I'll be back soon."

"Come now, please?" she said.

He didn't hesitate to leave Jim and rush to Sonja's aid.

When he entered the room, Sonja was holding out her cell phone. "I heard your conversation and called Laney. I think you should talk to her."

Once again, Jay knew he was hesitant because of the beast named the comfortable uncomfortable. So he got a grip and calmly took the phone from Sonja. "Hello?"

"If you sign his contract tonight, I'll kill you," Elaine said. "But you take it and give him reason to believe you're going to sign it. I'll work magic for you while you're in Canada."

Jay felt another hundred pounds lift from his shoulders. "Thanks, Elaine."

"Yeah," she muttered and hung up.

Sonja was watching him with wide, conflicted eyes when he handed the phone back to her. "Did I cross the line?" She lifted one side of her mouth squeamishly.

When she took the phone, he took her by the wrist and tugged her against him. "Does it feel like you crossed the line?"

He heaved his hard-on against the top of her pubic bone. Damn the sensations that raced through his dick.

He was ready to fuck.

"No," she said with a sigh.

"No." He repeated and smashed his lips against hers.

It was time to fuck.

CHAPTER 18

SONJA HESTER

Sonja and Jay had only stepped over AMTA's contract, which was on the floor by the door, and come out of the bedroom for one reason—it was Tuesday at ten thirty in the morning and they had a conference call with Vincent Adams. He was over the moon about the script, treatment, and outlines of the first five scripts they had written. He actually had been worried about whether or not Sonja and Dexter would make an effective writing team, since she had no professional television writing experience. However, the creative packet they had sent proved him wrong. And right there on the spot, Vincent Adams approved shooting the entire first season while they were in Canada and gave them an extra two weeks to do it.

He also wanted to restructure his deal with Jay so that his company took on more of the financial burden and payoff.

"You can work out those details with Elaine," Jay said then smiled and winked at Sonja.

She smiled back. Her sister was undoubtedly the constant pain in the ass, but she always had his and her best interests at heart, along with those of anyone she'd made a commitment to.

After wrapping up their phone call, Sonja and Dexter celebrated with a glass of champagne. Keeping his commitment to sobriety, Jay drank sparkling water. Since Cam had the day and the next three months off, since Jay was off to Canada, he made a hearty brunch for them.

Sonja learned more about Dexter as they sat around the patio table, eating. He had two daughters and an ex-wife. His girls were lucky enough to have two parents who were devoted to living in peace not only for their sakes but also for their own. Dexter had dated plenty of women since his divorce and had fallen in love with one unavailable woman, but that was it.

"Are you still in love with this woman?" Sonja asked.

"I love her as a friend, but nothing more."

She narrowed an eye suspiciously. "Okay, but what if this woman divorced her husband tomorrow? Would you go after her?" Sonja felt as though she was guarding her cousin's heart. Dexter was slated to attend her going away dinner later that night and it was evident that he was interested in Robin and vice versa.

Dexter shrugged. "I don't know. I'm not in love with anyone else. I probably would try to figure out if she and I are seriously compatible. But I don't have to consider a real answer to that question because her husband is never going to leave her and she certainly isn't going to leave him."

"Her husband is Jack Lord," Jay announced. "Your grandmother has to know him."

Sonja shook her head. "She may. I've always tried to stay out of my grandmother's business."

"Yeah," Jay said with a sigh. "Real estate is definitely not your thing."

She smirked seductively. "And what's my thing?" She batted her eyelashes.

Dexter threw up both hands. "Hey, you guys, give it break already. Single guy at the table here."

Sonja and Jay chuckled.

"But not for long," she sang.

Dexter's brows furrowed as he leaned in Sonja's direction. "Do you really think Robin's into me?"

"I'm positive."

"Because she showed me no signs of it."

"That's because her nickname is Wednesday, you know, the daughter in the *Addams Family*," Sonja said with a chuckle.

Dexter maintained his curious frown. "Why is she that way?"

Sonja knew why, but she didn't think it was her place to tell him. "I guess if you're interested in her, then you're going to have to take the time to discover the answer to your question."

Jay knocked on the table a few times. "I can tell you this, Dexter, Robin isn't a praying mantis. She's just one of those people who are too deep for their own good." He looked at Sonja. "Is she still an artist?"

"Yep. Her work is at galleries all over LA and New York. She sells a lot of her pieces and they're not cheap, but she rarely spends the money. And…" She was about to say more about her cousin but decided to stop there.

"And what?" Dexter said.

Sonja shook her head. "Like I said, Robin's interesting, but she's for you to get to know."

Dexter rocked back and forth as he nodded. His slight smile had revealed his thoughts. “Damn, I’m more intrigued than I was last night.”

Sonja took the final bite of the delicious potato soufflé Jay had made. "Well…" She wiped her mouth after swallowing. "I have to get going, but I'll see you both tonight at seven. Elaine's house is in the Palisades, and for the love of everyone's sanity, please don't be late. Theresa, Gran, and Elaine will be there, and they're the trifecta when it comes to shaming people for being late."

Jay took her hand. “How about I go back to the room with you?”

She let go of his hand. “No, because I have to leave now. And get dressed.” Sonja still had on a pair of his pajamas, which were way too big for her.

“Just one more time,” he said.

“No. Tonight after dinner, okay?” She kissed his forehead.

Dexter looked away bashfully, so Sonja didn’t let Jay take their kiss too far.

“Later,” she said after their lips parted, and she traipsed off, waving at both men still seated at the table.

ONCE SONJA GOT HOME, THE FIRST THING SHE DID was pack for three months away from home. Her present and future felt less surreal as she filled her suitcase with clothes suitable for Vancouver's weather. She brought lots of jeans, comfortable vintage T-shirts, and red, black, and gray Chucks. She made sure she had at least thirty pairs of panties so she wouldn't run out quickly, and she packed feminine products for four cycles. Sonja didn't neglect packing for possible nights out.

After filling two suitcases, she stood in the middle of her room, racking her brain as she tried to remember if she had forgotten something. At the moment, nothing came to mind. She was able to take a deep breath and finally focus on the monumental task ahead of her. She was to meet her grandmother for a drink at Elaine's place an hour before dinner started. Sonja wasn't sure if the conversation was only going to be between Gran and herself or if others would join them. She had decided to leave the decision in Gran's hands.

So now that she was packed and ready to go, she showered, put on a black satin spaghetti-strapped midi-dress, fresh makeup, her favorite perfume, and a pair of strappy sandals. She also packed a bag for the night because she was spending the night at Jay's place. They would return to her apartment a few hours before her flight to get her things. He had insisted, even after she had assured him that she could carry her luggage to her car, stuff it in the back seat, and drive over to his house after the party.

"No way. Give me this, babe. Let me make it easier for you," he'd said.

When Jay called her babe, it felt as though he had been calling her that forever. It also felt as if they had been a couple for way longer than a few days. Sonja grinned as she locked the door to her apartment. She liked the fact that Jay seemed so familiar to her. She liked it a lot.

Then Sonja so happened to look down in the courtyard. Ms. Jenkins was sitting on the wrought-iron bench, and their eyes met. Sonja's heart raced and her feet remained glued to the floor. Ms. Jenkins called her favorite way-too-fluffy white cat onto her lap, picked up the creature, and calmly walked back to her apartment. Sonja remembered to breathe once the woman was gone.

She thanked her lucky stars that she would be gone for a while, and when she returned from Canada, Sonja knew she would have to move. She walked quickly to her car, hoping that Ms. Jenkins wouldn't decide to ambush her. The woman had done it many times before, pretending that she was going inside her apartment only to sneak up on Sonja before she managed to escape. Her heels beat the ground feverishly as she rushed to her car, got in, and left without a hitch.

CHAPTER 19

SONJA HESTER

It took her an hour and a half to drive fourteen miles across town to the Pacific Palisades. There was nothing worse than LA traffic. She hated it.

Thanks to Elaine, she had seventy thousand dollars in the bank and would soon receive an even bigger check for knocking out the pilot episode. The rest of the season would bring in even better checks. Holy hell, she had hit it big, and working with Dexter made her job so easy. So on one hand, being richer and more successful made traffic more tolerable, but on the other, she realized she was no longer beholden to that city. She could leave and drive in only when absolutely necessary.

Elaine had a three-acre property with a Spanish-style mansion in the mountains. Her sister liked it that way. She could afford to live right off the water, but she didn't want to oversell herself as an independent woman. Elaine was waiting for the right man to marry her before she moved to a house that cost way too much money—but not in the Palisades. She had her sights set on Malibu. Image meant everything to Elaine.

Sonja parked in the guest lot at Elaine's house. Her grandmother's Bentley was already there, but she didn't see Theresa or Robin's cars. That was a relief.

Sonja had a key to Elaine's house, just like Elaine had one to her apartment. However, she did ring the bell four times before entering just to signal she had arrived. As usual, Maria Lopez, one of Elaine's house managers, met Sonja in the foyer.

"*Buenos tardes, mija,*" Maria said.

They hugged.

"*Buenos tardes.*"

"Your grandmother is on the patio," she said.

Sonja thanked her then took one of the longest walks of her life. She stopped under the veranda to watch her grandmother sitting at a rectangular wrought iron table, gazing out the picturesque

Pacific Ocean, unobstructed by power lines or other homes.

"Hi, Gran," Sonja said.

Her grandmother turned around to watch her with a tight smile that said she wasn't angry or happy with her. "How are you, darling?"

Sonja kissed her then sat in the closest chair to her. As though her buttocks hitting the seat cushion alerted Maria that they were ready for a drink, she rolled out a cart of wine selections. Both ladies had the cabernet franc.

When they were alone again, Gran kept her narrowed eyes directed toward the view of the water. "I never liked the beach."

"Oh," Sonja said as though what her grandmother had said truly shocked her. The truth was, it was an exaggerated reaction to a declaration she cared very little about.

"Malibu, Palisades, Brentwood, Bel-Air, Trousdale Estates, they're all designer neighborhoods. But Hancock, Beverly Hills, that's where it all started." Gran took a sip of wine. "When I came to this city, I was a young girl with a lot of cash and a broken spirit."

Finally Gran turned to look at her and Sonja gulped nervously. She knew her grandmother well enough to understand that the big talk had already started.

"Gran, I'm sorry," she said.

Gran brought her glass to her lips. "The past can be brutal, can't it?" She took a sip.

Sonja adjusted in her seat. "I guess. But we've changed the story completely." She took the draft she had printed that morning out of her oversized brown leather purse and handed it to Gran. "I made a copy for you."

Gran looked at the pages as though she was being forced to take bad luck. "I don't need to read it. I trust you've changed your story to my satisfaction." She took a deep breath through her nose and released it slowly. At least she was smiling. Sonja took that as a good sign. "One day, when you were a little girl, I opened a cabinet and there were spiders everywhere. I jumped and screamed and scrambled, looking for insecticide. But you said, 'Don't worry, Gran, I'll get them for you.'" Her smile broadened and her eyes softened as her gaze drew in Sonja's face. "And my heart stopped as I watched in horror as you rustled up spiders with your hands and ran them through the kitchen and the front door to set them free. I remember thinking, look how brave she is, and look how she protects me."

Sonja felt her heart swell and tears rush to her eyes as her grandmother caressed her hand. She couldn't remember that moment exactly, but she recalled the emotions she must've felt.

"Years later"—Gran tilted her head and smiled—"when I finally saw a therapist, I told her that story about you and the spiders. And she explained how because of my problems, I had inadvertently taught you to be brave and overprotective of not only me but of your safety. You see, darling, I was your safety and you were sheltering me. I didn't know what shelter meant until I met Roy, your grandfather."

Sonja gulped as the energy soaring through her body made her sit up straight. All her grandmother had ever said, other than he was a great lawyer, was he'd died way too young and she'd loved him way too much.

Gran looked off at the ocean with a nostalgic grin. "He was the first man who showed me that men were not put on earth to scar our souls. He was smart, empathetic, kind, and compassionate. He used those traits to acquire and conquer. He was

God's perfect human being, and that's why he was taken from this corruptible Earth so soon."

Sonja sat very still as tears slowly rolled down her cheeks. She would've wiped them away, but one shift in her position and she feared her grandmother would stop talking, and Sonja didn't want her to. She wanted to hear it all.

"Did you know he had spent almost every waking hour fighting for fair housing for those who didn't know how to do it for themselves?"

Sonja nodded. Her grandmother had told her that many times before.

"You have his heart. You've sensed my pain, my torture, and you have spent your young and beautiful life fighting for me." Tears streamed from Gran's eyes, so Sonja jumped up. Before she could frantically grab the nearest napkin, her grandmother lifted one off the table. "As you can see, I've found this myself."

Sonja's mouth fell open as her mind connected that moment to the things her grandmother had just said and to a lot of incidences in the past.

Gran patted her eyes and cheeks, sniffed, and set her napkin on the table beside her glass of wine. "I assume you've discovered the truth about Harlan Duke?"

Sonja swallowed. “Yes.”

“I’m sorry for lying to you.” She smiled slightly. “I’m afraid you’ve gotten your creative talents from me.”

Sonja tried to smile but couldn’t because she had another confession to make. “I also learned the truth about Hazel Wright.”

Gran paused. “All of it?”

Sonja nodded.

“Then you know what’s being done is what must be done.”

She nodded again. “But Cyrus is awfully old. Do you think he still wants to hurt Ms. Jenkins”—she wiggled her head—“or Hazel Wright?” Calling Ms. Jenkins by another name felt weird.

“He’s an evil man, darling. But I fixed him.” Gran’s eyes narrowed in an expression Sonja had never seen from her before. “I fixed him good.”

“Wow. What did you do?”

Gran patted Sonja’s hand. “As you know, answers never come that easy. But I welcome you to put your investigator’s hat back on and go seek the answer.” She leaned closer to Sonja and lowered her voice. “But I guarantee it won’t be as easy this time.” She sat back. “Dora was never good at keeping secrets, nor keeping secret the fact that she'd spilled a secret."

Sonja jerked her head back. "Wait, Dora told you about my visit?"

"Dora and I are still great friends." She cracked a tiny smile. "And so are Hazel and I."

Sonja recalled how Ms. Jenkins had looked at her from the courtyard earlier. "Ms. Jenkins knows I know, doesn't she?"

"Yes." Gran lifted her wine off the table. "You know, her annoying tenant facade was all my idea."

Sonja's mouth fell open. "What?"

"You were asking too many questions. You were on her tail just when I was putting the final nail in Cyrus's coffin."

Sonja felt intrigue flash through her. She would love to know exactly what her grandmother had done to "fix" the abusive man. But she closed her mouth and shook her head like a rattle. "Then Ms. Jenkins, or Hazel, isn't a maniacal tenant who's addicted to cats?"

Gran chuckled. "She's indeed addicted to cats, but she's not maniacal at all."

Sonja grunted thoughtfully.

Her grandmother took a sip of wine. "I always knew the two of you were made for each other."

Sonja tilted her head and frowned. “Ms. Jenkins and I?”

Gran lifted her eyebrows twice. “No, darling, you and Jay.”

Sonja couldn’t stop a grin from forming. “Then you approve?”

“Absolutely,” she said emphatically

Sonja went on to tell Gran about the last two days they’d spent rewriting the script, while leaving out all the sex they’d had. She mentioned Dexter, then she remembered to ask her grandmother if she’d ever heard of someone named Jack Lord.

Gran’s expression crashed into a frown. “Yes, why do you ask?”

Sonja almost felt as though she had stepped in deep shit by saying the man’s name. And she surely didn’t want to mention that the man who would be arriving soon for dinner, and was attracted to Robin, had a thing for the man’s wife. “Dexter knows him. Since you and Mr. Lord are successful in the same field, he thought you may know him too.”

Gran hummed thoughtfully. "I'm never surprised by how small the world is. You know, I had a conversation with Jack Lord on Friday. He's offered to buy my company"—she raised her eyebrows as she tilted her glass toward Sonja—"and for a considerable amount of money." Gran took a drink.

Sonja felt her eyes grow wide. "But you're not going to sell your company, are you?"

Gran took another drink. "I've been working my whole life. Brick by brick, building a tower that took me as far away from my roots as I could get. Maybe it's time to stop and enjoy my handiwork, and that includes my beautiful granddaughters and the wonderful women you've all become."

So many thoughts swirled in Sonja's head as she took her first sip of wine. It was divine. Elaine always had the good stuff. "But what will you do if you don't work?"

"I love golfing. I love the heat. I've been thinking about relocating to Palm Springs. I turn eighty years old next year. It's about time I see the whole wide world before I'm ninety."

Sonja pressed her lips together in a smile, but goodness, why was she so conflicted? Thinking about her grandmother somewhere out in the world where anything bad could happen to her did cause Sonja a bit of anxiety. But what her grandmother had said to her moments ago made so much sense. Sonja's grandmother had been hurt to her core by

Cyrus Wright, and yet Lorraine Hester had made it. She had excelled in more ways than one. To think of her grandmother running freely in the wind, still beautiful, so vivacious, and so full of great wisdom made Sonja's heart swell with happiness.

So Sonja smiled from ear to ear as she tipped her glass toward Gran. "I think that's a great plan. You should do it."

Gran winked. "I just might."

GUESTS ROLLED IN FIFTEEN MINUTES BEFORE SEVEN. Sonja was so relieved to see Jay and Dexter arrive early. Just as she'd anticipated, Dexter and Robin's eyes lit up when they ran into each other in the foyer.

Then Theresa arrived in a red dress that hugged every inch of her toned, celebrity trainer's body. When they made their way to the table for the starter course, she insisted on sitting next to Jay and kept touching his shoulder, arm, or hand whenever she engaged him in any sort of conversation. It was her standard behavior and it had never bothered Sonja in the past, but it did then.

Sonja had the misfortune of sitting next to Gary, Elaine's current fiancé. He always seemed slightly tipsy, although she wasn't sure if he had actually had a few or if it was his usual disposition. Regardless, she'd never seen how he was in the least bit compatible with Elaine. Sonja sneezed because his stinky, strong cologne was almost as bad as Ms. Jenkins's cats.

Robin and Dexter ended up sitting across from each other, and both of them tried like crazy to avoid gazing into the other's eyes.

As they were being served the second course, which was a cucumber and melon salad, Theresa revealed that she had an announcement. "I'm moving to Seattle."

"And for what reason might that be?" Elaine asked in a deadpan tone.

"Job," Theresa said, apparently irritated by Elaine's question.

"You do know the sun hardly shines there and the lack of sunlight will depress you."

"Of course you're going to squat and shit on my future."

"This is the dinner table and we have guests," Gran warned.

Theresa rolled her eyes.

"But really, Terry, what sort of job is taking you to Seattle?" Robin asked.

"I'm going into business with a friend. We're opening a fitness supercenter."

"Carly?" Elaine asked cynically.

"Yes."

"Didn't she screw your last boyfriend?"

Theresa huffed.

"Didn't she?" Robin asked.

Theresa rolled her eyes as she wiggled her head. "Yes, but she's a hell of a trainer, and this is all about business."

"Her actions speak to her character," Elaine said.

Theresa threw her hands up. "Why are you shitting on my parade, Laney?"

Elaine calmly wiped the corners of her mouth with a cloth napkin. "I'm not. I just think you're not making a smart decision, and I suspect you're partnering with her because she has money and you need some."

Theresa shrugged defiantly.

"I'll give you the money and we'll go into business together," Elaine said and then rang the bell for the third course. "And I won't fuck your boyfriends."

Theresa opened her mouth to say something but then closed it. "Really?"

Elaine shrugged. "Diversify our assets, right, Gran?"

"That's right," Gran sang.

"All right," Theresa said as she picked up her glass of wine and tilted it toward Elaine. "First thing in the morning, Carly gets the boot."

Elaine raised her glass too. "Good. Come by my office at eleven. We'll hammer out contracts and shit."

"I'll be there."

They both drank to that.

"I'm selling the house," Gran announced out of the blue.

Sonja was the only one of her sister and cousins who looked at Gran with a smile.

"And the business," Gran added.

Robin gasped. "The business?"

"And I'm moving to Rancho Mirage."

Theresa, Robin, and Elaine were still staring at Gran, speechless.

"Wow, Ms. Hester, you've lived in that house for as long as I can remember," Jay said. "It's going to be strange driving through that neighborhood and knowing you're not there."

"Gran, you can't sell that house. Our memories are there. It's where we grew up," Theresa said.

"Yes, you grew up. We all have." Gran's eyes smiled as she looked around the table. "I look at you women, and I'm so proud of you."

"We're proud of you too, Gran," Robin said.

"I know you are. But I'm done making you proud. For the remaining years of my life, I'm going to make myself happy."

The room fell so quiet that they could have heard a pin drop.

"Wow," Jay finally said. "Good for you, Ms. Hester."

"It's Lorraine, Jay darling. As I said, we're all grown up."

He cleared his throat. "Good luck on your future happiness, Lorraine."

"But what about the coffee shop and the complex?" Robin asked.

"I have a novel idea," Theresa said and pressed her finger against her lips animatedly. "Robbie, why don't you just do one thing? Just your art."

"I can't count on that."

"Bullshit. You sell everything you make."

"I'd like to see your art," Dexter said.

Robin looked at him with wide, conflicted eyes.

"Let's just change the subject." She looked at the table just as one of the servers collected her plate.

"Well, is anyone going to mention the elephant in the room?" Elaine asked.

"Elephant?" Sonja's stomach tied itself into knots because she figured Elaine wanted her to spill the news about her recent trip to Midland.

"Sonja and Jay are an item," Elaine announced.

Sonja stifled a sigh of relief.

"Really?" Theresa leaned away from Jay. "Why the hell didn't you say something?" She glared at Sonja then turned her pinched expression back to Jay. "Or you?"

"Why don't you just stop flirting with every pretty thing that has a penis?" Elaine said.

"I don't flirt."

"Ha!" Elaine scoffed. "Anyway, this night is about sending our little bird out into the world to kick ass. How about a speech before we dig into our main course?"

Sonja sneezed as the last person was served. Her allergies had reached their breaking point with Gary's cologne. "First"—she looked at Theresa—"could we switch seats?" She sneezed again.

Theresa grimaced at Gary, who threw his hands up and said, "What is it?"

Sonja hated that he talked like a wise guy from a mobster movie.

"Your cologne, baby," Elaine said. "Sonja has allergies."

"But she likes my cologne. I've worn it around her before."

By Elaine's narrowed eyes and pinched lips, Sonja could tell that her sister did not like what her fiancé had said. She snapped her fingers at the servers. "Switch their plates."

"It stinks, dude," Theresa said as she got up to make the switch.

Once Sonja was in Theresa's old chair, she and Jay squeezed hands under the table. Being seated next to him as the servers finished resetting her plate felt so good.

"Well, Jay, you've got our girl, so don't fuck up," Theresa said.

Jay's eyes sparkled as he said, "I don't plan on it."

He and Sonja kissed for the audience, and Theresa, Elaine, and Robin clapped while Gran watched with a delighted smile.

"Okay now, speech," Robin said.

Sonja had no idea what to say. Her eyes fell on her sister's and cousins' faces before landing on

Gran's. They had guests tonight, but she couldn't think of a better send-off than a crazy Hester girl dinner. Then suddenly, the right words dropped into her head.

"I don't know..." She dropped her face for a moment to simper. "I'm just happy to be here with all of you. I feel as though we're all on the precipice of change. Gran picked up our mother's slack." Sonja tilted her glass of wine to Gran, who was sitting opposite Elaine at the head of the table.

Everyone else at the table followed Sonja's lead.

"To Gran's handiwork," Sonja said then winked at her grandmother.

"To Gran's handiwork," they all repeated.

And everyone drank to that.

PART II
WILL HE STAY FOREVER?

CHAPTER 20

SONJA HESTER

It was quiet-on-the-set as the final scene of season one came to an end. Jay's performance held the attention of everyone in the room. Even Sonja couldn't take her eyes off him. Whenever she watched him perform, it was as though she was seeing him for the first time. His acting was impeccable and his presence divine. He was a damn fine actor for someone who loathed it so much.

Plume Ashbury was also in the scene. They were only seconds away from their final kiss of the season, and the thought of them locking lips again turned Sonja's stomach.

"I want to trust you, but I don't know how," Jay said, delivering a line Sonja had written.

Plume grunted and called him an arrogant bastard and a self-proclaimed magistrate of wrong and right. Sonja had written that line as well, and if Plume had known it, she would've tried to have it cut from the script. The actress had been giving her hell ever since their informal meeting in front of the elevators on the day Plume arrived at the compound called Production City.

Sonja, Jay, Dexter, and two other people on their creative content team had already been there for four weeks. Sonja had been at the bungalows where their offices were located since before sunrise. Due to a last-minute addition to the final script, Jay and Dexter had left around noon with a location scout to find settings that would support the changes. She didn't expect to see Jay until he returned to their room later that night, which was fine with her. Sleep had been a precious commodity since the day they arrived, and she got more of it when he wasn't around. The more time they spent together, the more inseparable they became. Dog-tired from work and with only six hours before doing it all again, they would either watch a movie or stay up way too long talking about their pasts and wishes for the future, making up for fifteen years of lost conversations. And they would always make love.

It had been after seven at night when Sonja left the bungalows. She could hardly keep her eyes open as she dragged through the cool evening air back to the residence building. The next day's production call time was set for six o'clock, and she wanted to spend as many seconds in dreamland as she could. Sonja was waiting impatiently for the elevator doors to open when Plume stopped beside her, chatting loudly on her cell phone.

Sonja recognized the movie star immediately. She would've quickly introduced herself or smiled or something, but she sensed Plume was purposely avoiding eye contact. Then the elevator doors slid open, and Plume raced past her to enter first. Sonja froze, shocked by how rude that was.

"What I want to do is cut off his balls for being a dick and force-feed them to him," Plume barked and pressed a button on the elevator panel.

Sonja stuck an arm between the doors to stop them from closing.

Plume looked at her with a grimace as Sonja walked into the small space, then she went back to telling whomever was on the other side of the phone that the guy, whom she wanted to force-feed testicles to, had a new girlfriend who was jealous of her because she was Plume Ashbury.

As they rode up the elevator, Plume lost reception.

"What?" she snapped and tried calling the person back. "That turd hung up on me."

Sonja rolled her eyes and said after a brisk sigh, "This is an elevator."

"What did you say?" Plume snapped.

"She didn't hang up on you. The call dropped because we're in an elevator."

"Did I ask for your opinion?"

Sonja groaned and allowed herself to the feel the exhaustion in her body. She did not want to get into a verbal spar with Plume Ashbury, even though she wanted to let Plume have it for being so entitled that she believed the world revolved around her wants and needs, including cellular service in elevators.

Thank goodness the doors opened.

"Who the hell are you anyway?" Plume said.

Sonja could hardly keep her heavy eyelids lifted as she looked at her. She didn't owe Plume an answer, so she walked out of the elevator and down the hallway.

However, Plume stayed on her heels. "Your job is in jeopardy. What's your name?"

Sonja picked up her pace as she shook her head. She could hardly believe what was happening. One of their star actresses was chasing her. It felt like a bad dream.

"You're crazy," Sonja muttered.

"I'm crazy? You're fired!" Plume's voice filled the hallway.

Sonja felt shaky. She was exhausted, plus Plume was like a high-strung Chihuahua snapping at her from behind. However, Sonja controlled her nerves and calmly stuck her key in the door. "You can't fire me."

"Are you with *Pact of Lies*?" she asked.

Sonja grunted as she turned the key.

Plume's hand came down on her shoulder. "Do you know who I am?"

That did it. Sonja felt anger surge through her. She was so close to letting Plume having it, but her room door opened and Jay was standing there. Plume immediately went silent. When Sonja turned to look at the actress, Plume's mouth was caught open and her eyes were wide.

Finally Plume cleared her throat. "Jay?"

Suddenly Sonja was being guided into Jay's

embrace. They kissed briefly, and that made her feel safe and secure inside. "Are you okay?"

Sonja nodded. "Now I am."

"Plume, meet Sonja Hester. She's the one calling the shots," Jay said, scowling at the entitled actress.

Plume's eyes narrowed as she studied Sonja. "We'll see about that." She spun on her heels and stormed off down the hallway, finger stabbing at her cell phone as though she wanted to kill it.

Sonja and Jay didn't stick around to hear who Plume had called. He guided her inside, kissing her as he assured her Plume was the last person on Earth she needed to worry about, especially since she had the power to fire her whenever she deemed necessary. He then guided Sonja on top of their bed and they made love.

Sonja had no idea who Plume called to voice her complaint to, but she had hoped that by call time the next morning, the actress would've had packed her things and headed back to LA. But nope. Plume was on set bright and early and, from then on, determined to give Sonja hell.

Her assaults were never direct. The actress would gossip about her with just about everyone working on the production, sometimes convincing people that Dexter was the one who really wrote the scripts and Sonja was only around because she was boning Jay. Generally Sonja had a strong spine, but people avoiding eye contact with her or pretending as though she wasn't there weighed on her.

On Friday, nearing the end of the first full week of production, the director, Adam Weingart, exploded at Sonja for demanding he stop shooting because Plume and another actress, Alexandra Little, were delivering lines that weren't in the script. Plume had chosen to omit lines Sonja had written. Plume had gotten sophisticated about figuring out who'd written what by getting her hands on the script outlines, which noted which writers wrote each part of the episode. Weingart called Sonja a stupid cunt who had no business being there in the first place and shook with rage as he demanded she leave his set and never come back.

Sonja had walked back to the residencies with her head hanging in shame and her heart aching. Plume had planned her assault perfectly. Dexter and Jay were on location with another director, Rex Donaldson, who was shooting a separate scene for a different episode. Plume knew Sonja would have no protection.

But oh, the humiliation. Sonja felt she would never recover from all the eyes watching her, judging her as Weingart laid into her. And that sneaky smirk on Plume's and Alexandra's lips. Before Sonja turned to leave, Plume winked at her. At that moment, Sonja was determined to give up. Why take their bullshit and humiliation when she had already been paid for writing the story? On top of that, she had been surviving on coffee and four hours of sleep for a week. She would've packed her things the moment she got back to the room, but instead she flopped on the bed and, within minutes, had cried herself to sleep.

When Jay awakened her, it wasn't with his usual hard-on. He had a stern expression as he said, "Get up, Sonja, and go fire Weingart now."

She was still groggy when she sat up. "Huh?"

Standing before her, Jay widened his stance and folded his arms. "Do you want to do this?"

"Do what?"

"All that we're doing here."

She blinked a few times to let the lightheadedness pass. Jay kept his expectant gaze on her as she turned to check the time on the nightstand. She had only been asleep for little over two hours.

"You heard?"

"Yes. Answer my question, babe. Do you want to be a head honcho on this production or not?"

"Of course I do," she said. "You know I love it, but these people have been so nauseating…"

Finally Jay smiled and held his arms out toward her. In his hug, Sonja felt the safety and security she wished she'd had when Weingart was tearing her a new one.

Jay stared into her eyes, looking so deep into her that she was sure he could see her soul. "Babe."

"Yes?" she said breathlessly.

"As long you're the executive producer, producer, head writer, and creator of this show, everybody on this fucking set has to respect you as though you're a god. They don't have to like you, but they have to fucking respect you. Got it?"

Sonja gulped. She didn't have it yet, but the longer she let his words saturate her, the more she got it.

Jay drew her in closer. "Elaine negotiated those terms for you for moments like this." He pursed his lips.

Sonja dropped her head. "Okay, I'll talk to Weingart tomorrow."

"That's not how it's done, babe." With two fingers under her chin, he gently lifted her face.

"Leonard is waiting for you in the hallway." He raised his eyebrows as though he meant business. "He's going to escort you to the set, where you're going to fire Weingart's ass in front of everyone and tell him to leave the compound immediately. He's gonna be a dick about it, but don't let whatever the hell he says get to you. You tell Leonard to get him out now." He nodded briskly.

"I understand," she said, answering his expression.

"Good. And after he's gone, you look every one of those fuckers in the eyes, especially Plume, and let them know they're all replaceable. Got it?"

Sonja took in a deep breath and nodded.

"Good. And to show them how much power you have, you're going to shut down production for the rest of the day. Tell them they'll make up the time tomorrow morning at six a.m. with Shelly Blasingame as the new director. And then you walk out of there like you own their fucking world."

All of his instructions made Sonja's head spin. But she knew she had to do it. There was no other way to rebound strongly from the humiliation she'd suffered earlier. Out of all of Lorraine Hester's granddaughters, she was the only one who had difficulty asserting herself, but regardless, she did it.

It was the hardest thing Sonja had ever done, but she followed Jay's instructions to a T. Of course, Weingart didn't go silently. He called her every derogatory name in the book and told her how she'd never work in "this town" again. However, holding her composure was easier than she'd thought it would be. She calmly and firmly instructed Leonard to get him off *her* set. When the director was gone and she was still standing, she saw in everyone's eyes they were starting to see who was in charge.

That afternoon had been the start of something new for Sonja. When it came to work, she had donned her shark's teeth and hadn't taken them off for two months. Sure, Plume had remained a thorn in her side. Ambitious and backbiting assistants, other prima donna actors, and just about everyone else who worked above the line, except her writing team and Jay, drove her up the wall. But now…

Sonja took a cleansing breath. One last scene and it would all be over.

Finally, Jay and Plume's characters kissed. Sonja felt her mouth form a frown. At least they were kissing goodbye. It was up in the air whether Plume's character, Dani, would return for another season. The evil genius in Sonja was already making plans to permanently be rid of Dani. The filming process was hard enough. She didn't need the actress exacerbating things.

But they had a whole two months to decide. Come tomorrow morning, post-production would be placed in AEE's hands and she and Jay were catching a flight to Costa Rica. They'd made plans to spend the next sixty days zip-lining through jungles across South America and then some in Asia. Sonja couldn't wait.

She smiled as Shelly Blasingame called cut and, "That's a wrap!"

The set erupted in applause. Someone turned up the lights. Sonja clapped while watching Jay until his searching eyes found her face. They grinned at each other. She was lost in his bright and handsome face, but not so much that she couldn't feel her eyes sparkle with glee. She waved him over by curling her finger. Her mouth couldn't wait to taste his. Jay took one, two, three steps in her direction before Nick, one of the many production assistants, stepped in front of him and spoke. Sonja watched them like a hawk as her body ached for his sweet embrace.

Then he mouthed, "I'll be back." He returned

the thumbs-up she gave him before he followed Nick.

She figured there was another fire to put out. Every day, at least one or two forest-sized blazes needed to be extinguished. She would have to indulge herself in Jay West later.

As soon as he was out of sight, she became wrapped up in the whirlwind of hugs, handshakes, smiles, and double cheek kisses. Bottles of champagne were passed around and glasses filled to the rim. Seeing all the ordinarily stressed faces smile and glow felt good.

About a half an hour later, everyone decided it was time to take the celebration to the wrap party at Bixby, an upscale bar and grill downtown. Sonja walked slowly behind the large crowd heading to the black party vans.

"Coming, Sonja?" Shelly asked.

Sonja stopped walking and looked behind her, gnawing anxiously on her lower lip. She'd thought she would run into Jay near the loading zone, but he wasn't there. And now that she thought about it, she hadn't seen Plume either.

Sonja walked backward while waving to Shelly, who had become a good friend. "I'll catch up with you guys later."

“Okay, but hurry. We’ll miss you,” Shelly sang before she entered the van.

Sonja trotted back to the bungalows. She was sure Kelly, the production manager, was the one who'd needed Jay's immediate attention. Kelly was always concerned about how every penny was spent, and that wasn't going to change just because it was the last day of production. However, right before Sonja reached the cluster of bungalows reserved for the production management team, she saw Kelly and her two assistants walking in her direction.

“Are you going to Bixby?” Kelly called.

Sonja felt heat rising up her neck and into her face as she pasted on a smile. “Um, sure.”

“Good, because we did so well with the budget that all drinks and eats are on us.” Kelly sounded pretty proud of that.

Sonja stretched her fake smile, hoping it masked her impatience and worry. Something deep down inside was telling her something was wrong. “Great!”

“And you deserve it, kiddo. We had our doubts about how you would shake out in the long run, but I’d work with you again in a heartbeat.”

Sonja wanted to respond graciously to Kelly's

compliment, but her paranoia was through the roof. Plume would've loved to get her grimy hands on Jay, and it would've been just like her to use her highly refined manipulation skills to trap him in her wicked web, especially now that production had wrapped.

"Hey, have any of you seen Jay?" Sonja asked as casually as possible.

"Not since earlier today," Kelly said.

"Nick whispered something to him and—"

"Oh, Nick is in the prop room," Penny, one of the assistants, said.

Sonja clutched her chest as relief washed over her. "Thank you," she said and took off.

"See you at Bixby," Kelly called after her.

Sonja raised a hand but kept moving. She realized how eager she must've appeared to them. It wasn't Jay she distrusted. Three weeks into production, Jay had confessed to her that Plume had sneaked into his trailer while they were shooting on location and, naked as a jaybird, slid into bed with him. When he realized she was there, he insisted that she leave, but she refused and threatened to make a scene if he forced her. He had to pretend he was okay with her being there before escaping to the bathroom, locking himself inside, and calling Dexter for some help removing her.

Sonja had heard from PAs and Shelly about more instances of Plume coming on strongly to Jay, though he had shot her down in every situation. But Sonja always wondered how long his defenses would last. Plume oozed sex appeal. She never took a low-key day when it came to her looks. She loved to wear extra-tight jeans, low-cut blouses, and stretch pants that crept into the crack of her ass. She was definitely the camel toe queen. A few times, Sonja thought she had caught Jay ogling Plume's accentuated parts.

"I'm not into her that way," he'd said when Sonja asked him about it. "But I still worry about her sometimes."

Sonja was lying on his bare chest, listening to his heartbeat, as they spoke. "What do you worry about?"

He was silent, so she lifted her head to see his face.

Jay smiled gently. "I never told you why they put us together, did I?"

"I don't think so."

"You remember the hell they gave me for offending a fan?"

"Sorry, I never gave a damn about celebrity gossip."

Jay chuckled then kissed her. "That's one of a million reasons why I love you."

He told her how, while he was incognito at a mall in the Valley, some fans had recognized him and begged for autographs. He asked them if it looked as though he wanted to be bothered with them. One woman in the group called him a spoiled actor, and that set him off. He was caught on many cell phone cameras, yelling, "It's my fucking job. *You* learn *my* fucking lines and deliver them. There's no privilege when it comes to work. There's work when it comes to work. And I'm off, so leave me the fuck alone."

Sonja's jaw dropped. "You said all of that?"

"Verbatim."

The incident started a debate on every single morning show in existence, and it even spread to the news channels. His popularity plummeted, and his sordid past with drug addiction was back in the tabloids.

"Even with all the crazy shit Plume was into, she managed to have a clean, girl-next-door reputation," he said.

And so, to allow some of her favor to rub off on

him, their people put them together, promoted the hell out of them by making her the beauty that tamed the beast, and in less than six months, everybody loved him again.

"And that's why I never read or watch that shit," Sonja said.

He winked at her. "And I still find that sexy as hell."

They got lost in each other's eyes for a moment before Sonja asked the question that was still plaguing her. "But what is it specifically that you worry about when it comes to Plume?"

Jay studied her, as though he was evaluating how much he could trust her with what he was about to say. "She's self-destructive, just like I used to be, so we used to help each other a lot."

"Then you guys had an emotional relationship?" The thought didn't bother Sonja too much. She knew Jay was all hers.

"Our publicists put us together, but we became friends. Good friends." He told her how he'd had to stop Plume from committing suicide so many times he couldn't count them all. "She's found me many days after I'd gone a bender and picked me up out of whatever hovel I had landed in."

"I get it then," Sonja said.

"You do?"

"Behind closed doors, you both could be your imperfect selves and not be judged for it."

Jay nodded thoughtfully. "Yeah, that's it. There's a lot of pressure being a celebrity that everyone knows."

Sonja snorted cynically. "People love erecting gods, but get off on tearing them down just the same."

Jay gazed at her as though it his first time ever seeing her, and then they made deep and passionate love.

Sonja yanked open the door to the prop room. Deep down, the intimacy that Jay and Plume shared made her afraid he would leave her for his fake ex-girlfriend. But no… to banish her paranoia, Sonja squeezed the sides of her head as she walked into the dim room. She released a quick breath. There was nothing to fear. For three and a half months, Jay had loved her like no man ever had. She was paranoid and being silly. Just as she was about to race back to the carport to catch one of the vans leaving for Bixby, she heard a crash then a hushed giggle.

Sonja's heart dropped to her stomach as she turned toward where the sounds came from and slowly walked that way. The closer she got, the more moaning and heavy panting she heard. She could positively identify the female as Plume. Fueled by anger, Sonja picked up her pace. Her heart was already broken as she pictured Jay and Plume going at it like sex-starved porn stars. She raced past props on shelves and then racks of costumes.

"Jay," she shouted as she made a sharp right. When she saw the couple, she gasped and slapped a hand on her chest.

"What the fuck?" Plume said.

She was buck-naked on Nick's lap in a black leather swivel armchair.

"Whoa," Nick said, trying to use Plume as a shield.

"Um, sorry."

Sonja ran away so fast that all she could hear was her footsteps and the fading sound of Plume going off about how crazy Sonja was.

The brisk evening air clashed with the heat coming from Sonja's throat. When she got far enough from the prop room, she bent over to catch her breath. After recovering, she did what she should have done in first place. She slid her cell phone out of the pocket of her gray bomber jacket and rang Jay. The call went straight to voicemail. She tried again. No luck.

She swiftly tapped out a text message, which asked *where are you*?

Suddenly, a cool breeze blew across her face. Even though it was quickly gone, she stood still and allowed herself to listen to her deep inner voice.

A giggle escaped her. She slapped a hand over her mouth and laughed harder. She was being utterly ridiculous. Jay was more than likely at Bixby's, waiting for her.

She had missed the vans, but another one should be arriving at the compound soon. But she had gotten herself so worked up that she could smell her own stress sweat, so she rushed to her room to take a quick shower and change. When she opened the door and stepped inside, she noticed the space felt emptier.

Sonja closed the door and walked swiftly to the bathroom. All of Jay's toiletries were gone. She opened the closets. His clothes weren't there.

"What the hell?" she whispered.

Sonja took a moment to collect herself. Jay certainly hadn't vanished off the face of the Earth. Never in a million years would she believe he would pack and leave without telling her, so she examined the room. All the drawers were closed. There were no hangers on the floors. Basically, it didn't appear he'd left in a rush.

"Nick," she whispered and raced out of the room again.

He was the last one to see Jay, and she didn't care if he was boning Plume or not. They were going to stop their intercourse long enough to give her some answers.

She ran out of the lobby and back into the evening. Just before cutting a left and heading down the path that led to the prop room, she saw Nick walking toward her with a dubious expression.

"Hey, Nick," she called just in case he thought about fleeing her.

"Hey, Sonja. I'm sorry about that." He looked over his shoulder. "She just grabbed me and asked if I wanted to… you know, fuck."

She closed her eyes and waved her hand frantically, wishing she could unhear what she'd just heard. "TMI on that. Where did you take Jay earlier?"

His mouth fell open as if he was surprised and relieved she didn't want to talk about him getting it on with a lead actress in the prop room. "Um…"

He cleared his throat. "Some guy from his agency wanted to talk to him."

She frowned. "His agency?"

"Yeah."

"And that's it? Did you see where they went?"

He scratched the back of his head. Sonja could finally see how flushed his skin was. "Um, he got into a car and left."

Sonja sighed then shook her head. What in the world was going on with Jay?

"Is that all?" he asked.

She nodded.

"Are you going to Bixby?"

She shook her head then whispered, "No."

He folded his arms and widened his stance. "I've been wanting to tell you that you've done a kick-ass job with production." He cracked a smile. "Beauty and brains are a rare combination."

Sonja blinked a few times. Was this guy really coming on to her? After she'd caught him screwing Plume in an armchair? Frankly, she had nothing else to say to him, so she calmly turned away and walked back to her room. She had one more call to make. Perhaps her sister Elaine would have some answers.

CHAPTER 21

SONJA HESTER

The night before, Sonja had eventually called a cab to take her to Bixby. Even though she knew he wouldn't be there, she searched the bar and restaurant for Jay. When she didn't find him, she couldn't stay to enjoy the party.

On the way back to the hotel, she'd called Elaine and asked her if she had sent some guy to the compound to collect Jay.

"I haven't heard from him, but you do remember, right?" Elaine asked.

Sonja scrubbed her scalp, racked by anxiety and frustration. "Remember what?"

She was overly familiar with the tone of Elaine's voice. Her sister wanted something Sonja wasn't supposed to refuse, especially now that she should've thanked Elaine profusely for her brand new career.

"Aren't you my maid of honor?"

She sighed briskly, wondering if that was a trick question. "Aren't I always?"

"I spoke to Robin, and she told me you're traipsing off to the jungle."

"I don't know about that anymore."

Elaine was silent.

"Hello?" Sonja asked.

"I'll call you back. Gotta go." She hung up.

That was the last time Sonja actually wanted to speak to Elaine. Next, she'd called Dexter and left a message. He had flown back to New York shortly after production wrapped. She was hoping he could shed some light on whatever business Jay had that was so important he couldn't tell her he was leaving.

After that phone call, worry continued to attack her until she developed a throbbing headache. There was nothing more to do but go back to her room, book the first flight she could find out of Vancouver, pack, and head to the airport.

As Sonja waited for her early morning flight to board, she felt as though her head was being squeezed by a vise. Her weary eyes searched every face see in the terminal, hoping one would be Jay.

She hadn't eaten, and her body still sought to make up for all the sleep it had been denied over the months. She felt like a zombie, trapped between being alive and dead. Finally her flight was called.

As the plane soared through the sky, all she could think about was what to do next. Even when she tried to get some shut-eye, her brain wouldn't allow it. She hoped Dexter would've returned her call by the time she landed. Since her car was parked at Jay's place and she had the gate code, she would go straight to his house.

Sonja tried to keep her insecurities from narrating the situation. Jay hadn't just up and left because he wanted to get away from her. She tried to think about all the nights they'd spent in bed, barely awake but unable to sleep because they had so much to talk about. They were still best friends who laughed at the same things, even when no one else was laughing. Every now and then, before the weather had started cooling off, they would sneak off to a watering hole on a stranger's property to swim.

They still spent their leisure time watching movies together. They would have conversations about what was going on around them and in the world. Every other morning at four forty-five, they would gear up and go for a three-mile run. Every night, no matter how exhausted they were, they felt compelled to make love. Snapshots of their limbs intimately entangled and him inside her filled her mind. Yes, they had once been the best of friends and still were, but now they were lovers.

Sonja remembered the time he looked in her eyes and said, "No matter how perfect you are and how great we are together, a year ago, I would've run from all this. I've made a lot of movies where the guy's an uncommitted jerk until the woman comes along and changes him. You do enough of those movies and you start to believe that shit. But you couldn't have changed me. No one could've. I had to resolve a load of deeply buried issues just to figure out how to be good enough for myself."

That confession had sparked a conversation which lasted until call time the next morning.

Sonja shook her head. They were a new couple but a solid one. He wouldn't just disappear without a reason.

THE WEATHER WAS NICE IN LA. SONJA WAS BACK IN her hometown and that felt good, but her body was hanging on by a wing and a prayer. The Uber she ordered arrived within five minutes. The driver was a woman named Heather who told Sonja about all the accidents Heather had narrowly missed that night. The pipes at her son's school had burst that morning and flooded all the classrooms, so now he was home for the rest of the week. She was trying to give him something constructive to do. Regardless of Sonja's barely-there state of being, she found herself chuckling at Heather's stories.

"You must really be somebody to live here," Heather said as they entered Jay's neighborhood.

"My boyfriend lives here," she said in a defiant tone. She wouldn't stop thinking of Jay as her boyfriend until he officially broke up with her.

"Oh, you used all that you have going on to hook a rich man." Heather chuckled.

"He and I grew up together."

"Oh! Is he famous?"

"Jay West?"

"The actor?"

"Yes."

Through the rearview mirror, Sonja saw Heather's eyebrows ruffle. "Isn't he marrying Plume Ashbury?"

"No, he's not."

"I listen to the Scope Report with Nicole Howard while I'm driving around. I thought she said Plume Ashbury was rocking a big diamond that Jay West gave her after proposing."

Sonja adjusted uncomfortably in her seat, stopping short of revealing that the last time she'd seen Plume was yesterday evening, riding a PA's dick in the prop room. So there was definitely no marriage in the cards for her and Jay.

The navigator told Heather that Jay's house was three hundred feet to the right.

"I wouldn't put much stock in celebrity gossip," Sonja said. "They've been given too much liberty to be wrong."

"Humph," Heather said thoughtfully.

The car stopped in front of Jay's house, and Sonja got out of the back seat to punch in the code. The gate rolled open.

"Well, you definitely have access to the man's home," Heather said. "It's cool to meet Jay West's real girlfriend."

Sonja didn't know how true that was anymore, but she made herself smile. "Thank you for an enjoyable ride."

"Any time."

Heather gave Sonja her card and drove her to

where her car was in Jay's parking structure. She took Sonja's luggage out of the trunk and pretended to be doing something while Sonja waited in front of the glass doors after pushing the doorbell button on the wall. The lights were dim inside. Jay was probably asleep.

Sonja pressed the button again, hoping someone would answer. Heather hadn't left yet. It was apparent she was waiting to see if Sonja truly had access.

Thinking fast, Sonja punched the same code she'd used to open the gate into the keypad on the wall. The lock clicked, and after a twist of the handle, she was in.

Sonja turned to wave goodbye to Heather, who waved back then finally drove out of the structure. Blowing out a brisk sigh of relief, Sonja picked up her suitcases and headed inside. Jay's house still felt sterile and cold as she headed down the hallway, looking into the rooms.

"Jay?" she called as she continued up the corridors and down the stairs.

She went into Jay's bedroom. The bed was perfectly made, and there was no sign that Jay had ever been there. Perhaps she had gotten it wrong.

But he had indeed packed his things and left the compound.

Sonja presumed he had to return home at some point, so she dropped down on his bed. As soon as her butt hit the mattress, all the heaviness returned to her body. Even though Jay wasn't there, she could feel his presence and smell his scent. Both made her take off her clothes, crawl up to the top of the bed, pull the covers over her, settle her face against the pillow, and close her eyes.

Something was ringing. Sonja slowly blinked. The daylight was bright. The sound came from her cell phone, and once she realized that, she moved quickly to answer it. Her heart was beating a mile a minute as she fumbled through her purse. Then she saw who was calling.

"Elaine?" she said, noting the desperation in her own voice.

"Jay's signed with AMTA, and right now he's on a new project."

Sonja's gaze rolled around the room as she digested what she'd heard. "He's still with Jim Neely."

"Yes."

"But that's not possible. He was certain about ditching that guy. He was certain of it."

Elaine sighed. "I don't know what to say to you other than if I were you, I'd be pissed too. But I'm going to need you to come to my office this afternoon. I want to discuss your contracts and obligations in person."

"What?" Sonja rubbed her face. "But he was determined to sign with you."

"He changed his mind. Let it go."

"Let it go?" She shook her head briskly. "And that doesn't sound like you at all. What the hell's going on?"

"Nothing's going on. Get over it, and let's move on. You did well in Vancouver. Lots of doors have opened up for you, and you're going to walk through every single one of them. So you're my priority. You're my family."

"But Jay's family too, and you know it."

"Holy shit. You're like a dog with a bloody bone here. He's chosen the dark side. That's it. Like I said, focus on your shit and let it go."

She closed her eyes to massage her temples. Speaking of dogs with bloody bones, Elaine was the leader of the pack. It wasn't like her to back down from a fight.

"Today at three, okay?" Elaine said.

"I can't believe you gave up on Jay."

Elaine groaned as though someone had stepped on her wedding cake. "To have *my* representation is a privilege. If Jay couldn't see that, then it's his problem, not mine."

"Like I said, you gave up on him."

"Screw Jay," she said so loud that Sonja had to pull the phone away from her ear. "All that's important is that you have a career, and that's what we have to talk about, so be here at three."

Sonja couldn't stop rubbing her temples while trying to make sense of all that was illogical.

"No one knows more about being abandoned by a guy than me," Elaine said in a gentler tone. "But what do you want to do: spend precious time figuring out what's going on with Jay or strike while the iron's hot?"

Realizing her eyes were closed, she opened them and released all the tension in her body. "I'd rather spend my precious time figuring out what happened to Jay."

She waited for Elaine's response, postured to defend her position. Seconds ticked by.

"Laney?"

Elaine sighed. "I'm here."

"I just want to talk to him. At least have a conversation with him. And where is he anyway?"

"He's on location."

"Where?"

"I don't know, but I'll find out and have Eden update you when she calls."

She slumped in relief. "Thank you."

"Just be here at three, okay?"

Sonja turned to look out across the city below. The last time she'd indulged in the view, Jay had been in bed with her. Her mind wanted to remind her that he had abandoned her before in nearly the same way, but her heart said they'd been kids then. She focused on how close they had become.

"Okay," she barely said, holding back tears. "I'll be there."

"Hang in there, kiddo. Love you," Elaine said, continuing to exhibit her rarely there softer side.

Sonja shut her eyes, but the tears rolled out anyway. "I will. Love you too."

Their call ended, and she saw a text message from Dexter Frampton. It said, *in meetings all day but Jay is no longer affiliated with production. We have to write him out. Terrible news. Abrupt. Don't know what happened. I'll see you.*

That was a stab in Sonja's heart so deep, she was throbbing in pain. Paralyzed by indecision, she sat there a while. Something was definitely off, but the fact that Jay had chosen not to confide in her hurt the worst. She read the message from Dexter twice before she noticed the hour. It was almost two p.m.

Sonja sprang to her feet and rushed to the bathroom to shower. She felt comfortable in Jay's house, but not enough to stay. He was on location, which meant he'd probably be gone for a few months. Hopping from one role directly into another wouldn't have given him much time to learn his lines, but Jay's photographic memory gave him an advantage over most actors. When they were kids, they used to call it his Superman power. He could learn his lines in a snap. So he would have no problem getting right into the groove of a new project.

As the water rolled down her face, Sonja decided she would cry no more. For the last three months, Elaine had been locking horns with Jim Neely and AMTA over Jay's contract. Accepting defeat wasn't Elaine's style—at least until now—so she suspected her sister was keeping something from her. But it also wasn't like Elaine to spill secrets.

Sonja heard her cell phone ring from the other room. Dripping wet, she turned off the shower faucet, snatched a towel off the bar, and raced as fast as she could, being careful not to slip and crack her head open, back to Jay's bedroom to answer it.

"Hello?" she said.

The caller wasn't Jay, but it was the closest thing to him she was going to get, at least for now.

CHAPTER 22

JAY WEST

3 Days Later

Jay walked briskly across the plain, weighted down by armor. He was playing a soldier in a fictional world where dragons soared high in the sky and trolls with poisonous bites roamed the miry earth. The action was live and it was almost time to deliver his next line. He hated that he was so good at acting and couldn't sabotage his performance by pretending he sucked at it. He had too much pride for that.

Jay stopped in his tracks and turned to face Ben Aiken, the other actor.

"You want to stay alive?" Jay asked with an edge. "Humph?"

Ben gazed off, doing a fine job of playing an anxious sidekick. "How did we end up here?"

His English accent was just as precise as Jay's.

"That's not a question a man who wants to live asks," Jay said and stormed up the trail, leaving the other man behind.

Ben jogged to catch up with him. Jay acknowledged the character's decision to follow without looking at him.

"Cut!" The director's voice blared through large speakers. "That's a wrap."

Jay felt a sense of relief, happy he'd managed to get through another long, cold day of filming. Every cell in his body missed Sonja. The last three and half months he'd spent with her had been the best days of his life.

Ben patted him on the shoulder as the PAs took the microphones off them. "Good job, dude."

Jay barely muttered, "Thanks."

"What they say about you is true, huh? You just got here and you're killing it. I'm the one who's fucking tripping over my lines."

Jay knew Ben was fishing for a conversation. Jay hadn't said much to anyone on the set because he was pouting about his circumstances. He hated sulking, it was counterproductive, but he was trapped in a hellish reality so he couldn't stop doing it.

"There. You're free to go," the production assistant said.

"See you tomorrow at call time," he said to Ben and stormed off.

"That's it?" Bens said to his back.

Jay grimaced. "That's it."

"You're going to have to lighten up soon."

"Maybe, but not today."

He hadn't been hanging out with his cast mates or the crew since he started on the project. He wasn't on location by choice, and he couldn't leave, even though that was the one thing he wanted most.

His trailer was about a hundred feet ahead, and he was hoping to make it there without being bothered, but Rodriga Deleon, a Spanish actress, appeared out of nowhere.

She kept pace with him. "Are you returning to your den or will you join us for dinner tonight?"

Jay's gaze stayed on his trailer. "What do you want, Rodriga?"

"Ay yai yai, testy. You want to fuck?"

"No." He picked up his pace.

She grabbed his arm to slow him down. "Hey, what's wrong with you?"

Now he had to look at her. She was still pretty, but she was a lot shorter than Sonja and didn't have the same organic beauty as the woman he was in love with. He and Rodriga had probably had sex four or five times in the past. They could've done it more than that, but he could only remember doing it with her once. The other times he had been high and drunk and trying to figure out why in the hell was he still breathing.

"Does it look like I want to fuck?"

"What is the matter with you? You are like black clouds raining on parades."

Jay looked at her with narrowed eyes. She was lucky not to have his burdens pressed upon her, and a small part of him envied her because of it. Her dark hair, supple skin, and bright green eyes used to get him hot and bothered. But it wasn't only because of Sonja his dick didn't jump to attention at the thought of banging her. He was a young guy, but he didn't feel the desire to make love with someone he wasn't in love with. He didn't want to run his tongue around her soft nipples or taste her nectar. He didn't want to take a deep whiff of her hair, taste her sweet mouth, and sink himself deep into her wet, warm pussy. Unfortunately for lust, he was too in touch with his soul.

Rodriga nudged his shoulder. "Come on, Jay. You know you want me. I want you too."

He didn't want to be an asshole, so he eased out of his grimace. "Listen, I had dinner brought to my trailer. I want to be alone. And I'm not interested in having sex with you now or ever."

She blinked as though what he'd said wasn't getting through her thick skull. She wasn't used to guys turning her down. Sex and her looks were her power, her glory. He thanked his lucky stars he wasn't responsible for making her feel validated for both.

"Good night," he said sharply.

"Then I'll eat with you, in your trailer." She batted her eyelashes seductively.

Jay shook his head briskly and walked off. "No." He raised an arm and waved goodbye. "See you tomorrow."

She didn't respond, but he knew she was still standing there in awe.

When Jay made it to his trailer, he locked the door and fell on his bed. Everyone knew he didn't want to be there, but no one had asked why.

His reckless behavior had stripped away all that was perfect in his life. The smell of finely seasoned steak and spicy potatoes made him hungry as hell, but he wasn't ready to eat yet. Instead, he stared at the recessed lighting in the ceiling, recalling the moments after the director wrapped the last scene of *Pact of Lies.*

He had been relishing Sonja's smile, the one that could compete with the stars, when Nick approached him and told him he had an urgent message from his agent's office. Jay had gone back to that moment way too many times to count. He fantasized about walking over to Sonja, wrapping her in his arms, and tasting her mouth. *She had the softest lips he'd ever kiss.*

During *Pact of Lies*, he had been in constant contact with Elaine, negotiating his release from AMTA, who was fighting tooth and nail to keep him. He was high off being done with production and catching a flight to Costa Rica with Sonja in the morning, which was why he didn't think twice about meeting the messenger at such an odd hour of the day. He had hoped it was a final contract sent from Elaine.

Well… it wasn't.

The messenger—a middle-aged, stocky, and balding guy—kept his eyes cast down as he showed Jay the video playing on his device. "If you don't want anyone to get hurt by this, then get inside the car that's waiting in front of the residence hall."

"What?" Jay looked at the door that led back to the set as he realized he wasn't going to get what he wanted so badly. "Who are you?"

The guy slipped his phone into his pocket and pursed his lips. Jay read the obstinacy all over his face.

"Did Elaine send you?"

The guy put up his fat hands. "I'm only a messenger."

"But you're the one who showed video of me doing shit I've never done."

"Do what you want. The car leaves in five minutes."

Jay scratched the back of his neck. There was no time to think it through. The shameful shit he saw someone who looked a lot like him doing… But shit, there was no disputing that the man on that video was him. Suddenly he burned with embarrassment because the slimy messenger had seen him like that.

"But it's going to take me longer than five minutes to pack."

"That's already been done."

Jay thumbed toward the residence building. “The shit in my room has been packed already?”

“Yes.”

“Who the hell walked into our room and packed my shit without my permission?”

The guy shrugged and walked away.

Jay reached out to stop him and ended up with one arm behind his back and the guy’s forearm against his neck. But it only took a split second for him to turn things around. The guy’s technique was shabby. Jay maneuvered through his captor’s weaknesses, and after a shift here and a twist there, he was the one with an arm around the guy’s neck and a stronger grip on his arm.

“Who sent you?” Jays demanded.

“I don’t know,” the guy squealed.

Jay realized he was slowly killing the guy and threw him to release him. “Don’t ever put your fucking hands on me again.”

The guy stretched his neck. “Duly noted. And I wish I could tell you more, but I’m only a messenger.” The guy checked his watch. “Now you have three minutes before that car leaves.”

Jay watched the guy walk away. All he cared about was Sonja seeing that video. He needed to know more about its origins, so he ran to the car, making it in the nick of time. He had his cell phone in his hand, about to call Sonja, when the driver asked for his device.

"Are you fucking kidding me?" Jay asked.

"No," the driver replied.

He was another slimy looking guy. It killed Jay to hand it over, but he did it.

While on the private jet heading back to LA, Jay suspected Jim was somehow behind the ordeal. He became angrier as the hours passed. If Jim thought he was going to blackmail Jay into remaining a client, he was wrong. But he would have to face other repercussions if that video got out. Jay didn't want to think about them, at least not yet. It was after ten o'clock at night when his flight landed and a car drove him to AMTA's building. That was when he knew for sure Jim was the culprit.

Jay stormed out of the car, through the nearly empty building, and into Jim's office. He was surprised to see Elaine at the window, arms folded and looking out, while Jim sat his desk, typing rapidly on his keyboard. The disconnect between the two was apparent and the tension thick.

"I'm here," Jay gruffly said.

Elaine turned around, and the look in her eyes could've frozen fire. Then she set her glare on Jim.

"He's here. Now where the hell did you get that video?"

With a smug grin, Jim sat back in his oversized chair and folded his fingers behind his head. "Sit. The both of you."

"No," Elaine said.

Jay felt like a plump squirrel trapped in the sights of two hungry hawks, but he took a seat just to get the show on the road.

Jim shrugged. "This is a free country."

"Where did you get that fucking video?" Elaine said, enunciating every syllable.

"I don't know where it came from, but we're paying for it."

"Who is the 'we' you're referring to?"

"The agency."

"I don't remember doing any of that shit," Jay said.

"Well, you didn't look sober, buddy," Jim said.

Jay didn't like his tone. He sounded like someone who had hit the lottery—not the mega pot, but one big enough to make him do a happy dance.

"Just give me a second." With her hands on her waist, Elaine walked over and sat in the chair next to Jay. "So you're saying this agency is being extorted?"

"Apparently so."

Jay shook his head briskly. "But that's not me in that video. It can't be me."

Elaine put a hand gently on his shoulder. "Can I talk to Jay alone?"

"He's my client, Elaine."

"He's my family. So get the fuck out and let me talk to him."

Jay nodded briskly. If anyone could dig him out of the deep shit-hole he was stuck in, it was Elaine. "I want to talk to her."

Jim watched them with narrowed eyes. Elaine didn't shrink under what was supposed to be an intimidating glare.

Suddenly he stood and aimed a finger at Jay. "Just so you know, we're paying to keep his dirty deeds under wraps, so he stays my client and does whatever the fuck I tell him."

Jay expected Elaine to explode, but instead she kept her composure and crossed her legs. "I got that loud and clear."

Jim seemed anxious about leaving them alone, but he did it anyway.

Once it was just the two of them, they sat in

silence before Elaine raised a finger and walked to Jim's computer. She tapped a few keys before muttering, "Fucking amateur."

Jay raised his head. "Was he recording us?"

Elaine sat back down. "Trying to." She sat up tall in her seat. "Jay, that is you in that video. There's no doubt about it."

Jay kept shaking his head. He didn't want stop, because if he did, it felt as though that would be an admission. But finally he had to. "I know it's me, but I don't know how that happened."

Elaine sighed briskly then took her cell phone out of her purse. She played the clip and stopped it on the woman. "Do you recognize her?"

Jay studied the naked woman. Her lips were parted and her eyes closed as she was being pleasured by Jay and another guy. He stared at her eyes, mouth, and the shape of her face.

"Play it a little further," he asked.

The video rolled on. It was tough to watch, especially knowing the guy was doing shit to him. He wanted to shrink enough to disappear in his chair.

"I wouldn't know what to do with that, Elaine."

"With what?"

"A dude."

"Then focus on her."

And then the woman opened her eyes.

"Stop the video."

Elaine halted the video.

Jay shifted his face closer to the image. "That's the girl who woke up in my bed."

"Woke up in your bed?"

"The morning I bumped into you at AMTA, there was a strange woman in my bed. I didn't know how she'd gotten there. I didn't even remember meeting her."

Elaine nodded thoughtfully. "If I remember correctly, you used to be really good at remembering things. Is that still so?"

"For the most part."

"Did this woman sneak into your home and climb in bed with you?"

Jay shook his head briskly. "No, I don't think so. The night before, I went to Hot Spot to meet some friends."

"What friends?"

He examined Elaine's intense expression. "Davey Lions and Rich Brisbane."

She grunted thoughtfully, but her expression didn't give him any clues about what she was thinking. "Could they tell you what you did that night?

Now he felt like a dope. He sighed dejectedly. "I never asked."

"Why not?"

He shrugged. "Embarrassed, I guess."

She shook her head as though she wasn't so happy with his answer. "Did you do any drugs that night?"

"I don't remember."

She scrunched up her face. "You don't remember taking drugs?"

Jay rubbed his scalp. "I don't remember a damn thing, and don't think I haven't tried. I've tried a fucking million times and nothing."

Elaine kept a straight face. "Do you remember taking drugs that night?"

He closed his eyes and tried to force himself to remember. "No, I don't."

"Jay?" She took his hand.

He cleared his throat. "Yeah?"

"You've taken a lot of drugs in your life, haven't you?"

He hesitated, wondering where she was taking her line of questioning. "You know I have."

"Have you ever forgotten the moment you put the drugs in your body?"

He closed his eyes and sighed gravely. "Not really."

She smiled tightly. "You only forget what happens after you put the drugs in your body, isn't that so?"

Jay's mind was processing so fast, he could feel it running hot. "But damn. Shit."

"What is the last thing you remember from your visit with Davey and Rich?" she asked.

Jay took a deep breath and closed his eyes. His memories of that day were hard to capture, and the ones he had were faint, like whispers.

"Do you remember getting into your car and driving to Malibu?" she asked.

He saw himself walking into the parking garage, putting the key into the ignition, and driving the distance. "Yes."

"Arriving at Hot Spot?"

"Yes, and I shook hands with Davey and Rich. We ordered drinks."

"Did you have that drink?"

He squeezed his eyes tightly, trying to force some sort of visual into his head. The tightness in his head hurt so much that he had to release the tension.

"I can't remember," he said breathlessly.

"Okay." She patted his thigh. "Listen..." She waited until he made eye contact. "I've spoken to Sonja about your plans to become a fucking chef, even though you're one of the greatest actors out there. When you became my client, I was going to talk you out of it."

"It's what I want," he said.

She rolled her eyes dismissively. "Right. So I know you don't give a damn about your career right now, but I care about Son's. Don't you?"

"You know I do," he replied sharply.

"If that video gets out, Vince will have to pull *Pact of Lies*. Especially since you chose to sell him majority interest in the series so you didn't have to be involved in post-production."

Jay dropped his face and massaged his temples. "I fucking know." He was looking more and more like an incompetent imbecile with lousy business acumen.

She patted his thigh again. "Buck up, Jay. We're not going to wallow in shame. Let's stay solution oriented."

He raised his head and rolled his shoulders. She was right. "What do you think is the solution?"

"We need the first season of *Pact of Lies* to air in its entirety. Season two needs to be shot without you. Once it airs and the ratings are in, feel free to blow your career to pieces." She sighed as if she abhorred the idea of what she'd said. "But I know Jim. He doesn't want you anywhere near me or my family. So he's going to ruin your relationship with Sonja, and we're going to let him."

Jay shook his head adamantly. "No."

"Yes," she said just as ardently.

"No fucking way. And Sonja would agree with me."

She threw her hands up. "Where the fuck do you two think you live? Disney World?"

"No, but—"

"You let me handle this. I have shit coming down the pipeline that's going to obliterate Jim's shoebox-sized world. But you stay away from her and cooperate with Jim until I say otherwise. Understand?"

Jay kept shaking his head. His heart was already aching, and not one cell in his body wanted to comply with her command. But he knew Sonja wanted him and her career. If there was a way she could have both, then he couldn't be so damn selfish.

"I understand," he said.

She breathed deeply through her nose and once

again patted his thigh. "Good boy." She sounded as though she was talking to his twelve-year-old self and not the man who was thirty years old. "And don't worry about Jim. I'm way fucking smarter than he'll ever be."

That was three days ago. Jay had to look away from the light above his bed. It was burning his eyes. He had only been away from Sonja for a short time and he ached for her. How in the world was he going to get through seasons one and two of *Pact of Lies*?

Elaine was right about Jim. Jay told himself it was best that he'd ended his relationship with Sonja. Elaine had caught Jay by surprise, but he trusted she had Sonja's and his best interests at heart. She'd convinced Jim that Jay should cease his role and association with *Pact of Lies*. Then Jim handed him a script and told him a driver was taking him straight to the airport to catch a flight to Ireland.

Jay sat up abruptly. He did that a lot recently—make quick movements then realize he had nowhere to go. He was trapped. As soon as it was permissible to be back in Sonja's life, he planned on running straight to her. Of course she would hate him by then. He hoped no other guy would come into her life and sweep her off her feet. The thought gave him anxiety.

There was hard knocking on his door. At first he ignored it, but the pounding got louder.

"Hey, Jay!"

He hopped to his feet. It was CJ, the production manager.

"What is it?" Jay asked as he swung the door open.

"There's someone here for you," CJ tried to whisper.

"What's the fucking secret?"

Then the person stepped from behind CJ. "It's me."

CHAPTER 23

SONJA HESTER

2 Days Ago

"He's in Iceland," Eden said.

Sonja released a slight sigh. "Where in Iceland? Do you have an address?"

"Sorry, it's a closed set."

"A closed set?" she asked.

"I can't give you the location or the name of the project."

Eden said that sort of snootily, which made anger surge through Sonja. "Well, do you *know* the location and name of the project?"

"No, I don't. Elaine just told me to tell you Jay's in Iceland."

"Iceland?"

"Yes. When you come in today, I'll have your schedule for the next two months. You'll also meet with five candidates."

Sonja rubbed her tired eyes. "Does Elaine know where Jay is?"

Eden paused. "I don't know."

"Could you ask her?" Her voice was restrained and calm, but any moment, Sonja was ready to blow.

"She's in meetings until three when she meets with you. I've been tasked with helping you find an assistant. Do you—"

Sonja ended the call. She hated being rude, but if Eden had been nicer, she would've felt more guilty about it. A fire was brewing deep in her belly. And like a beacon, it was guiding her to her next step. She had to know exactly where Jay was and why he hadn't even come home before flying out of the country.

And that measly call from Eden confirmed to Sonja that Elaine knew more than she was letting on. She knew her sister too well, and Elaine was merely trying to pacify her, which meant she was in damage control mode. Sonja had learned a long time ago how to read Elaine's actions. Something had gone remarkably bad as far as Jay was concerned, and Sonja wasn't going to sit around without ever knowing what happened.

Sonja paced as she pondered her next move. Jay was part of a production somewhere in Iceland. She wondered if the set was indeed closed or if Eden had lied to her.

Then Sonja remembered that when she worked as an assistant, she had access to a database that listed all present and in-production Hollywood projects. However, she couldn't remember the name of the database or how to access it. She had been working for Limelight Productions, which was located on Wilshire Boulevard in Santa Monica. Of course, that was over five years ago and turnover in the industry was rampant. She was betting not one person who worked there then was still employed by the company, including the president and vice president. Those two guys had been real jerks.

As she darted to her suitcase, her plan to drive over to Limelight was thwarted by common sense. She wouldn't even get past the receptionist. Her name wasn't big enough to grant her access and get answers without an appointment. That meant she needed some muscle. Elaine would've been perfect, but she wasn't an option. Then another face popped into her head.

"Damn it." She kicked herself for not thinking of them before all the pacing and worrying.

One Hour Later

Sonja had her luggage in the trunk of her car and was driving to the address Robin had given her. Earlier she had contacted her cousin. After Sonja had explained everything, from Jay's disappearance to Elaine's weird reaction, Robin agreed that something was off and told her to hold tight while she made a few phone calls. A half an hour later, Robin connected her with an actor named Delta Foster.

"Great. I'll swing by and pick you up," Sonja had said.

"I can't go with you. I'm five minutes away from a meeting with a realtor and a buyer. Gran's made a decision, Son. She's selling the coffee shop and…"

"And?"

"The complex."

Sonja felt her stomach take a nosedive, but she hadn't the focus to raise an objection. Plus, one of her first major projects, which she had planned before all hell broke loose, was to move. She and Jay had talked about it extensively. They both loved the idea of buying a house in the desert, only they hadn't decided on whether to purchase one together or two separately. But a lot between her and Jay was now up in the air.

Sonja parked in front of a private gym in West Hollywood, on Sunset Boulevard. According to Robin, Delta had said he only had five minutes and one call to make for her. He sounded like a certified asshole, but even Sonja knew the guy was a big star, probably a hair more popular than Jay. However, Robin had promised that if Delta didn't work out, then she would try someone else.

Sonja swiped her credit card, putting an hour on the meter. Her legs shook a little as she walked to the entrance of the gym and rang the doorbell. She was in such a state not because she was nervous but because she feared the actor wouldn't be able to help her. Every moment she spent not knowing Jay's whereabouts made her feel as if the possibility of finding him was getting further out of her reach.

"Knockout Fitness," a male's voice said through the speaker. "Who's your appointment with?"

"I'm here to see Delta Foster."

"Follow the signs," the guy said.

It took less than a second for the door to buzz open, and Sonja entered, thinking customer service wasn't the establishment's forte. The signs took her down a hallway with a hint of a sweet odor, like incense or something, but it wasn't doing a good enough job of masking the putrid stink of man sweat and heavy cologne. Then she made it to a desk where a skinny man and even thinner woman were engrossed in something behind the counter.

"Delta is in the massage room," the guy said without looking up.

Sonja's blood boiled. She wasn't ready to be treated rudely for a third time today. "And where might that be?"

Even though the woman still refused to acknowledge Sonja's presence, the guy looked up. "It's down past the treadmills, make a left, and the third door on your right. You'll see the sign that says massages on the door."

The fact that he'd said all of that without even a hint of a smile made her blow up inside. "Is that all you have to say?"

He snarled a little. "Sorry?"

"Your customer service sucks. You're rude as hell."

"Are you here to see Delta or bother me?"

She could've wrung his skinny little neck, but instead she chose to employ the tools she had acquired by dealing with Ms. Jenkins over the years. She patted the counter and said, "You're right. It's not my job to teach you some manners."

Sonja moved briskly past men stomping it out on treadmills and lifting weights. She was still fuming, and she wanted to burst into a million pieces.

The door to the massage room was cracked.

"Hello?" she said as she opened it carefully.

"I'm here."

A tall and handsome hunk was lying on a massage table with only a towel draped over his bare butt. His face rested on top of his folded hands, and his eyes were closed.

"Are you Delta Foster?"

"You're Robin's cousin?" he asked.

Sonja's mouth fell open. The answer to his question was simple, but the way he lay there without looking at her made her not want to have anything to do with him. Enough was enough.

"You know what? Forget it." She spun around so fast her head became dizzy. She was determined to get out there as fast as her feet could go.

"Wait a minute!"

She heard him scrambling. When Sonja turned, he was sitting up and adjusting the towel over himself.

"You know what? It doesn't look like you're interested in helping me." She sternly pointed toward the front desk. "They were rude as hell. My sister's lying to me. Nobody is willing to help me," she said, throttling her hands.

"Then you are Robin's cousin?" There was a hint of a smile on his face.

"Yes," she snapped.

"You're looking for Jay West?"

"Yes." She sighed, letting go of a portion of her frustration and anger. "I just want to know where he's filming. He's supposed to be in—"

"Iceland," he said.

She was relieved that he knew that. "Yes."

"You're pretty," he said.

Sonja frowned because she hadn't expected him to say that. "Okay…"

"Pretty is underrated. It's more attractive than beautiful and sexier than hot. You're soft. Delicate. Like pink cashmere and a first kiss."

And all her negative feelings were back with a vengeance. "Can you help me or not?"

"I can, and I have," he said, apparently not at

all provoked by her tone. "Jay's not in Iceland. He's in Ireland, and you won't be able to get on the set. Not if I'm not with you."

She felt the tension in her face. "What?"

"It's a closed set. They're not going to let anyone near it"—he held out his hands—"except me."

"You're offering to go to Ireland with me?"

"Yeah, why not?"

She folded her arms and regarded him shrewdly. "That's a big help. What do you want in return?"

"I don't have anything better to do for the next seventy-two hours."

"That doesn't answer my question. What do you want from me?"

"I like your cousin." He shrugged. "Maybe this will convince her to give me a snowball's chance in hell."

Sonja gnawed nervously on her bottom lip. She doubted that anything could make Robin change her mind about him. Something about Delta was remarkably odd and not in a good way. His comment about pink cashmere and first kisses was weird as hell. But she was desperate, and after all, he was *the* Delta Foster.

“Okay. Let’s do it.”

He was about to say something when the buzzer rang. Over the speaker came the snarky voice of the guy at the front desk. “Your other masseuse has arrived.”

“What other masseuse? I only ordered one, but I don’t need her. Send her away,” Delta said. “And, Peter?”

“Yes, sir.”

Sonja rolled her eyes at the front-desk clerk’s servile tone. Now he’d decided to prove he knew how to respect people.

"If you treat any of my guests rudely again, I'm going to fire your ass."

Peter went dead silent for a few moments. “Yes, sir.”

“Now give us some privacy.” The intercom clicked off. Delta winked at Sonja. “I own this place.”

Sonja’s mouth dropped open. “Thanks.”

She’d needed that. And suddenly she was less nervous about hanging with a guy who’d said she looked like pink cashmere and a first kiss for the duration of the flight from LA to Ireland.

Sonja waited at the juice bar, where she'd been told to order whatever she liked. She had the vanilla, banana, and kale with almonds and granola crunch smoothie. She was surprised by how fast she sucked it down. The drink tasted divine, plus after going without a solid meal within the last forty-eight hours, she was starving.

When Delta finished in the men's locker room, he had on a blousy tank top that revealed all the muscles in his chest and arms. His pants were super tight spandex, showing off the cuts in his legs and protruding package. One look and she wanted to warn him to give up on his hope of ever landing Robin. She had never seen her with a guy so vain. As a matter of fact, Robin would be completely turned off by it.

"Want another?" he asked, pointing at her empty cup.

She rubbed her belly. "Actually, I'm full, but that was really good."

"We aim to please." He clapped his hands and rubbed them together. "All right, so here's the update. I can't get a pilot until eleven p.m. You're welcome to hang with me at the beach until then."

Part of Sonja wanted to go home, check her mail, and decompress for a while. She could finally relax some now that she had a line on Jay. The other part of her realized she had missed her meeting with Elaine, which meant her sister would be on a warpath that wouldn't be halted until she found Sonja.

Her cell phone rang in her purse and she fished it out, knowing it was Elaine or Eden but hoping it would be Jay.

It was Elaine, and that fact made the answer to Delta's invitation easy.

CHAPTER 24

SONJA HESTER

Sonja transferred a few outfits, clean underwear, and hygiene essentials from her luggage into her weekender bag, which Delta's driver put into the trunk of his Bentley. Two of the gym's employees were tasked with driving her car, which carried the rest of suitcases, back to her complex, parking it, locking it, and dropping the keys in the manager's office mail slot, where Robin would eventually secure them. The plan was to spend the day relaxing at Delta's beach house in Malibu. They'd have lunch in a few hours and grab dinner before heading to the airport.

"So, Sonja," Delta said while sitting next to her in the back seat of his car. "What do you do for a living?"

Of course Robin hadn't told him about her recent project in television. It wasn't her style to talk someone up, because she never saw the point of it.

"I recently finished the first season of a new TV series in Canada."

He turned his body to face her. "Oh yeah?"

"Yeah."

"Are you an actress?"

"Nope. The creator. I was also a producer and the head writer."

"Whoa, those are heavy titles."

"My sister negotiated them for me."

"Your sister's Elaine Hester?"

She wasn't surprised he knew of Elaine. However, she wondered how he had connected them so quickly. "Did Robin tell you I was her sister?"

"Do you have a problem with it?"

"No," she said, shaking her head emphatically. "But..." Her instincts were sounding off like a fire truck blaring down Fairfax Boulevard. "Did that influence your decision to help me?"

He smiled slightly.

"It did, didn't it?"

Delta scratched his temple nervously. "She's going to be taking over my agency."

"What agency are you with?"

"AMTA. Your sister bought the company."

"What!" Her jaw dropped as her mind raced. What the hell was Elaine pulling? She was supposed to be working against AMTA because they were holding Jay's, and a number of other clients who wanted to leave them for her, contract hostage. "How do you know this?"

"I'm not supposed to know. No one is." He looked at her with an expression that asked her to be cautious with what he'd just revealed. "But I know."

"But how?"

"Like I said, I can't tell you."

Sonja sighed as she turned to watch the city pass by her window. She needed a moment alone with her thoughts and couldn't stop shaking her head. What in the hell was Elaine trying to pull? First of all, purchasing a multimillion-dollar operation was not the kind of life-changing decision Elaine would keep from her. Secondly, that wasn't the decision a woman like her—someone who had issues appearing "too powerful" and deterring potential loser husbands, the ones who actually gave a damn their wives were less successful than they were—would make. And now Sonja was trying to figure out if it was Jim Neely who'd sent Jay off to Ireland or her own flesh and blood. And had Elaine tried to throw her off Jay's scent by telling her he was in Iceland instead of Ireland? And then there was Delta, pretending he was so interested in Robin that he would fly to the other side of the world with her just to win Robin's elusive favor.

"Hey? Are you okay?" Delta asked.

She turned to face him. "What do you want from Elaine?"

"What do you mean?"

"I'm putting it all together in my head. You must've dug deep to find out this information about my sister. Flying to Ireland with a woman you've never met, who happens to be the sister of the person who just bought your agency, sounds like a power play. What you're doing for me is pretty big, which means you 're going to want something of equal or greater value."

He smirked. "I need a new agent or out of my *fucking* contract."

She was happy he'd answered without pause. "I don't usually get involved in my sister's business—it's usually the other way around—but she owes me for lying to my…" She sucked air through her teeth to control her anger. "She'll owe me. So yes, I'll convince her to give you what you want."

He studied her with narrowed eyes. "You didn't even ask why I need out of my contract."

"I don't care."

He extended his hand to her. She shook it.

"At least you're asking for something I can help you with," she said.

He looked her incredulously "What do you mean?"

"You don't have a snowball's chance in hell with Robin."

"No?" He sounded surprised.

Sonja's eyes widened. "Oh, you were serious about wanting to make me happy so you can have a chance with her?" She wiggled her head. "I'm baffled. Have you ever met her?"

He shifted in his seat. "Yeah, of course. But I have multiple goals here."

"Sorry, but you're not even close to her type. But take it as a blessing. Robin's meant for a guy who's not so fragile."

"But I'm handsome. In good shape. I'm nice." He threw up a hand pointedly. "And I'm not fragile."

She'd offended him. "Sorry about that. I meant,

you strike me as someone who doesn't know himself well. You strive to be liked for who you are, only you have no idea who you truly are."

"I'm not following you," he said.

She shook her head like a rattle. "Basically, Robin's not a beefcake-and-stud kind of girl."

He squeezed his biceps. "I'm not a beefcake. I make sure I don't overdo it in the gym. I have just enough to attract any girl."

Sonja closed her mouth after it had dropped. "Wow."

"What?" He was definitely frustrated.

"You're missing the point."

"You're saying I have no chance with Robin?"

"That's what I'm saying."

"Then I'm not missing the point."

"You're missing the point of why you don't have a chance with her."

Sonja wanted to laugh but settled for a chuckle. She was engaged in the craziest conversation she'd had in a long time. Honestly, it was a welcome distraction from worrying about Jay.

"Then what about with you?" Delta asked.

"What about me?"

"Do I have a chance with you?"

Now she laughed her head off. Delta was definitely egocentric. However, the endearing part was he was clueless about it.

"I'm not interested, but thank you," she said instead of asking him why in the world he thought she wanted to travel across the globe to find Jay. It wasn't because she had nothing better to do. She was in love with him!

Delta sighed hard and fell back against the seat, resting his head. “What is it with women?”

“I’m hard-pressed to believe you have a hard time finding women.”

“Ones like you.”

“What are ones like me?”

“Smart, confident, who have their shit together.”

She nodded at his tank top. “Have you ever thought about leading with something besides your biceps?”

His curious eyes followed hers before he looked up. “Hey, I work hard to look this good. What, you want to fuck a fat guy?”

“If I’m into him, it doesn’t matter.”

“Bullshit.”

“Okay…” She turned to face him. “But this isn’t about me. It’s about you. And you say you want a deep woman, right?”

He shrugged indifferently. “Sure.”

“Then tell me about yourself?”

At first he looked dumbfounded, as though no one had ever asked him that question. “I’m an actor.”

“Tell me something I don’t know.”

Suddenly she saw his brain working behind his eyes, as though he was struggling to come up with an answer.

She was just about to let him off the hook when he said quietly, “Sometimes I wish I was somebody else.” He searched over both shoulders as though he was in a crowded room and afraid someone had heard him.

“Why?” she said, keeping her voice sympathetic.

“I do the same shit over and over and keep getting the same results.” He sighed then covered his eyes with his forearm. “Sometimes I wonder what if I just showed everyone exactly who I am. Then maybe all this shit inside me won’t torment me like it does.”

Sonja was speechless. She’d misjudged him. “Have you ever thought about quitting?”

He removed his arm. “Quitting what?”

“Acting.”

"Hell no. I have the best job in the world. I just want to be myself and not fucking douchebag Captain Universe or Skylar Dank."

"The *Defenders of Justice* and *Dark Times* films."

"You've seen them?"

She smiled. "Every single one of them. You were great in them."

"I didn't take you for the type who's into that shit."

She chuckled. "None of it's just shit. It's storytelling. And all stories are reflections of who we are as human beings. That's why I love them."

He looked dazed, and she shrank under his adoring stare, wishing she could take back whatever had made him look that way. Leading him on was not her intention.

She readjusted in her seat. "You're not one of those people, are you?"

"What sort of people?" he asked.

"Someone who can't have a great conversation with someone of the opposite sex without thinking they're falling in love?"

He snickered. "I'm one of those people."

She laughed, respecting his honesty. "Well then, don't be. At least not with me. I like our conversation. I don't want to be careful about what I say."

"I love art," he said.

She cocked her head.

"You asked me to tell you something about myself. I'm a connoisseur of the best art."

Sonja grinned from ear to ear. "Now we're getting you closer to deep."

They shared a laugh and a moment of drinking in the lightness their conversation had created. It was the perfect time for Sonja to ask if he could tell her more about the film Jay was working on.

"They're in Cork, Ireland. Matthew Barbary's the director and it's fantasy, like *Lord of the Rings*." Delta smirked. "It's one of those parts I wished my agent would get off his ass and pursue for me."

"Is that why you want out of your contract? You don't like your agent?"

"Yeah, he doesn't like me, so he doesn't get me projects anymore. He's taken it upon himself to tank my career."

She gasped. "Wow! Do you know that for a fact?"

He nodded firmly. "I do."

Finally they made it to the gates of Delta's beach house in Malibu Colony. Sonja knew so much about the neighborhood because it was where Elaine wanted to move once she'd finally hooked her perfect man. As it stood, her sister believed the community wasn't the place for a thirty-five-year-old single woman who had never been married.

"Who wrote those rules?" Sonja had asked her once.

"People who aren't like you," Elaine replied.

She knew her sister hadn't quite meant that as an insult and if she had, there would be no offense taken. Those rules were stupid.

Delta's place was a comfortable and contemporary beach palace with a view of the Pacific Ocean. Sonja admired the fluffy white furniture and the large white faux fur rug over the light wood floor. He also had nice contemporary wall hangings and customized lamp fixtures.

"What a nice place you have. Did you do the decorating?" she asked.

He cracked a lopsided but proud smile. "That's another thing I'm into."

She scanned the décor one more time. "Good job."

"Come with me. I want to show you something." Delta waved her in his direction, seeming almost child-like as he skipped up the hallway.

As Sonja followed him, she admired the tastefully decorated rooms. Down a set of stairs, they entered a space with four tufted gray leather sofas forming a square in the center room and facing a wall of artwork. He stopped in front of paintings with bold colors, millions of brush strokes forming the visible objects. Sonja squinted at the one Delta was showcasing and made out a woman lying across a mountain range. Her body stretched wide from east to west.

She stood beside him. "Did Robin do this?"

"Yeah," he said breathlessly. "Honestly, this is why I fell in love with her."

Sonja studied all the elements on the canvas. All these years and she never really stopped and taken a long look at Robin's creations. "I didn't know she felt this way."

"What way is that?"

"Sad." She felt Delta's stare on the side of her face.

The doorbell chimed.

"I'll be back," he said and trotted away.

She walked to another one of Robin's paintings. How could she have missed the sadness? All of the emotions that Robin rarely showed were right there in front of her, and boy, did they speak loudly. Sonja ran her fingers across the canvas.

"I see you," she whispered.

She had been giving Dexter advice about how to be less egotistical, but she was the one who'd caused the woman to stretch herself across a mountain. Robin had always given way more to everyone in their family than she took. Sonja was determined to stop contributing to that.

"Sonja?"

She quickly twisted around. "Elaine? What are you doing here?"

Elaine slapped a hand on her chest. "Me? What are you doing here?"

Sonja's lips clamped together.

"Why the hell weren't you at my office?" Elaine asked.

"Did Robin tell you I was here?" Sonja saw Delta standing behind Elaine. He looked worried.

"Should she have?"

"No."

"I sent an assistant to your house and I found two of his guys"—she thumbed over her shoulder—"parking your car. What the hell, Sonja? I'm taking your career seriously and apparently you're not."

Sonja wanted to unload on her sister, but that wouldn't have been a great idea. Suddenly she felt as though all her hopes of seeing Jay had been thwarted. If Elaine knew she was on Jay's trail, then she would do whatever it took to stop her. That was something she knew for a fact.

She pointed at Robin's paintings. "Well, I met Delta at one of Robbie's galleries and we became friends. He called me earlier to tell me that he'd finally made space on the wall for these and asked if I wanted to come over and see. So I said yes." Her tone was so frank and guiltless, she wondered if she should've been an actress.

Elaine twisted to look incredulously at Delta then back at Sonja. "Are the two of you fucking?"

"No," Sonja said emphatically.

"I wish," Delta said.

Elaine thumbed at him. "See, that's the kind of answer I expect from him."

Sonja noticed the dumbfounded look on Delta's face. He looked like a little boy being shamed for doing something bad.

"I'm sorry, but you don't get to choose my friends or insult them," Sonja said.

Elaine wiggled her head as though she were stunned. "What the fuck is wrong with you?"

"What's wrong with me is that you're here."

"Are you still interested in your brand-new career? Because you can't go back to managing the complex. Not for long at least. Gran is selling it."

Sonja checked in with her heart. "I know that. And yes, I'm interested in my career. But heck, I'm supposed to be on vacation with Jay right now."

"No, you were supposed to be in my office at three. This is not a fucking 'do whatever the hell Sonja feels like' affair. You have to fly out to New York tomorrow morning."

"New York? Why?"

"You'll be there for three weeks. Your accommodations, flight, and car are scheduled. They need you to guide the cuts for the final episodes as well as get working on season two. So do you even fucking care?"

Sonja folded her arms. She hated when her sister talked to her that way, and she wanted to scream that it wasn't Elaine's job to guide her life because Mom hadn't done it.

"Hey, well, I'm going to pack for my flight to Montreal." Delta raised his eyebrows twice at Sonja.

She studied him as he flexed his eyebrows again, and a sense of relief washed over her. "Okay, thanks for showing me this. It means a lot to me. And um, have a good trip."

He smiled at her. "You too. Maybe I'll fly into New York next week and we can have lunch."

"She'll be busy," Elaine said.

Sonja wanted to choke her sister. "That'll work. Let's do it."

She hugged Delta on the way out, telling him she'd had a fantastic afternoon and asked him to please text her the recipe for the vanilla, banana, and kale with almonds and granola crunch smoothie.

"Where do you get one of those?" Elaine asked, finally losing the attitude.

Sonja raised her eyebrows at Delta, signaling him to answer. She knew Elaine asking that question was her way of saying sorry for being a dick to him.

"I own in a gym in West Hollywood."

She grunted passively. "Okay, Sonja, let's go."

"Give me a minute. I want to say goodbye to Delta."

"Then say goodbye."

"Alone."

Elaine narrowed her eyes to slits. "Fine." She whipped herself around and walked up the hallway.

They listened to her tiny heels beat the hardwood floor and heard, "Hurry up, Sonja," before the door slammed.

"Thank you for doing this for me," she said.

"You're welcome, but I don't think she's going to do anything for me but kick me out of the agency. She blames me for you being here."

"Don't worry about my sister. I'll handle her."

"You sure?"

She could tell he was panicking. "I'm sure, and um, I'll have a messenger come pick up my bag later. I don't want her to know I was planning on catching a flight."

He looked worried. "How late is later?"

"The next couple of hours? I have a service I used to use when I managed the complex. They're pretty quick."

"Oh, the complex your sister was talking about?"

A sense of loss flooded her. "Yep."

"Okay, well, the house manager should be here by then."

And on that note, they exchanged contact information and hugged before parting ways.

After buckling up in the front seat of Elaine's Mercedes-Benz, Sonja turned to meet her sister's inquisitive gaze.

"So when did the two of you become friends?"

Sonja was thankful she'd notice the date under Robin's signature on the paintings. "February of last year."

Elaine grunted curiously then started her car and drove off of Delta's property. "I didn't know Delta Foster had a house in the Colonies. He was married once, wasn't he?"

Sonja fought the urge to look down. If she did, then Elaine would know she was lying. So she decided to take an uneducated guess. "Yes, he was."

"Right. It was an arranged marriage to Francesca Bell." She shook her head. "I'm telling you, AMTA pulls that shit a lot. Isn't he represented by Jerry Cleaver at AMTA?"

Sonja smiled slightly. "Yes, I think so."

"He's an imbecile who's always looking for the easy route."

"That's what Delta said. Maybe you can take him in as a client."

Elaine sighed briskly. "No, I can't. But if he's having problems with Jerry, I know some people who can look into it."

Sonja was thankful for that, but it irked her to no end that Elaine was pretending as though she wasn't the one who could fix it all.

"You know what gets me though?" Sonja said abruptly while searching past Elaine and assessing oncoming traffic. Her sister was a horrible driver.

"Isn't that the million dollar question?" Elaine said, never missing a moment to take a jab at her. The person Elaine cut in front of honked, so she rolled down the window to flip the other driver off.

Sonja grunted and shook her head. "Road rage? Really?"

"It's not road rage. I had the right of way," she snapped.

"You turned in front of her."

"She was speeding."

"She seemed to be going the speed limit to me."

"Shit, can you ever be on my side?"

"I'm always on your side when you're in the right, but now you're clearly in the wrong."

And then, since Elaine wasn't driving the speed limit, the yoga-pant-wearing, house-mommy type ripped her car from behind Elaine's, rolled down her window, and yelled, "You fucking bitch!"

Sonja sighed as she waited for the two of them to finish. What she had to say next was not going to improve her sister's mood. Finally, they had screamed enough bitches and fucks at each other for the other driver to speed off.

“Did you see that? People are crazy these days.”

Sonja wanted to say that Elaine didn’t have to engage, but she knew all Elaine would do was make excuses for her behavior.

“When were you going to tell me you’re buying AMTA?” she asked instead.

“Huh? What?” Elaine’s head bobbed like the flippers on a pinball machine. “Who told you that?”

“My friend told me.”

“What friend? Delta?”

She crossed her arms. “I’m not supposed to say.”

“You said enough already. How in the hell did he find out?”

“Then it’s true?”

Elaine glared ahead, squeezing the steering wheel as though it were Delta’s or Sonja’s neck. “No one’s supposed to know.”

“Well, I get that. What I don’t understand is why you bought it.”

"Because I had the money and it was a great opportunity. But the fucking joke is on me."

Sonja jerked her head back. “Why do you say that?”

Elaine took a long moment of silence. “That place is hemorrhaging money.”

"Why? Are things being mismanaged?"

"Yes, but that's not why they're going bankrupt."

"Why then?"

Her body stiffened. "It's none of your business."

"But Jay's with AMTA. Why are you letting Jim Neely tell Jay what to do?"

"Because the deal isn't finalized yet," she said tetchily.

"Well, when will you own it?" Sonja sat on the edge of her seat, waiting for an answer.

Silence lingered. She felt the intensity emanating from Elaine, so much so that she was shocked when her sister finally said, "I don't… I don't even know if I want it anymore. Or if I can get out of the deal if I don't want it." She squeezed the wheel tighter. "I may be stuck with a lemon."

"Does Gary know about your big purchase?" Gary was her fiancé.

"Sure. He's the one who encouraged me to buy it."

She hadn't often seen Elaine so dejected. Apparently the lemon was really sour. Sonja also realized that Elaine was embarrassed, which was why she didn't want to share the details.

So she affectionately squeezed her sister's shoulder. "Don't worry. I have faith in you."

Since they were stuck in stop-and-go traffic, Elaine looked at her with a slight smile. "I have faith in you too. But just so you know, the wedding is off until I can get a handle on things."

Sonja nodded. "Okay, and sorry for making this difficult for you today. I should've showed up for our meeting."

Elaine made a guttural sound. "You wouldn't be you if you didn't make it difficult for me."

This wasn't the time to discuss Elaine letting go of trying to control Sonja's life, but soon, very soon, Sonja had to lay it all on the table so they could hash it out. Instead she gazed out the window. The waiting game had started. She probably wouldn't hear from Delta or even Jay for a few days, and now each passing second felt like an eternity.

CHAPTER 25

JAY WEST

Standing at the door was a person Jay hadn't seen in many years.

"Delta?" All of a sudden, he felt a lot better. "Dude, I thought you were an urban legend."

Delta slapped CJ on the shoulder twice. "I'll take it from here, buddy."

"Just don't get caught. It's my ass if you do."

"Then I won't." He shut the door in CJ's face.

The two men hugged. For Jay, seeing a face that wasn't affiliated with the production felt like freedom.

"What the hell are you doing here?" Jay asked.

Delta stood there with a wide expression, trapped between amusement and confusion.

"Is everything okay?" Jay asked.

"No, um, I was in the neighborhood. And heard you were here. Since I wanted this job and they gave it to you."

"Oh, believe me, dude, you can have it if you want it. I'm ready to get the hell out of here. Hey"—Jay turned toward the seating area at the rear of his trailer—"come on in. Let's sit and talk for a minute."

Delta threw up his hands. "That's all I have."

"Me too," Jay said.

Jay offered Delta a Coke and a few snacks that the onsite chef had made for him.

Delta pressed his thumb against his nostril and sniffed. "I'll take some coke."

"Not that kind of coke. A Coca-Cola."

"Oh." He dropped his other foot on the floor so hard that the trailer vibrated. "No, I'm good. Unless you have some vodka or something."

"I'm sober, so I don't have anything stronger than a soft drink." Jay grabbed a Coke out of the fridge and sat across from Delta. "So really, to what do I owe the pleasure of this surprise visit?"

At least he hoped it would be pleasurable. With Delta, one never knew. The guy was the embodiment of a damaged human being. The fact that he expected cocaine was a sign that not much had changed since the last time they were in the same room. Between Delta's shit-eating grin and glazed eyes, Jay figured the guy just wanted to get high.

Delta took off his coat and tossed it on the cushion beside him. "Dude, as I said, I was in the neighborhood. How's filming going?"

"It sucks balls, but"—he shifted abruptly and ran a hand through his hair—"it's my job."

"What are you complaining about? This is the Holy Grail here."

Jay rolled his shoulders, trying to stay as loose as he could. Delta was throwing out some uncomfortable energy that he could do without. "You're not here to bust my balls, are you?"

"Nah, not here to bust your balls. Your balls are un-bustable." He dropped his foot again. "Jay West always rises to the top, like fucking helium." He laughed.

Jay frowned, studying Delta. "Are you high, dude?"

"No," he said emphatically. "Why you ask me that?"

"'Cause you're not making fucking sense. Is this a jolly visit or is this about something else?"

He stared at Jay with narrowed eyes, then bent over to slap him on the knee. "Nah, not high. And

I'm jolly, dude." He settled against the sofa again. "So what's been going on with you?"

Jay hesitated but decided to go along with whatever vibe Delta was tossing out. He was going through a whole host of shit, but Delta wasn't the sort of guy it was safe to lament to. "Not much. Work. Just finished shooting a TV show."

"No shit? Where and with who?"

"*Pact of Lies* in Vancouver with AEE."

"Fuck… Vincent Adams?"

"Yeah."

"You're always a lucky fucker."

Jay studied his folded hands, recalling how he had been forced to drop just about all affiliation with the production. At least his LLC kept a quarter of the investment in the series, and his returns hadn't been chump change. It was Elaine who had actually set up the LLC for him.

His goal was to abandon the front of the camera and rely on a financial portfolio of mostly behind-the-camera investments. Then he would enroll in culinary school and eventually open his own restaurant. He had gone over the plans that would dictate the next stage in his life a thousand times. The worst part was picturing himself in a cooking class as all of his colleagues treated him like a pariah because of that video. The thought made him feel even more trapped in his current situation, so he cleared his throat, rounded his shoulders, and took a big drink of his beverage.

"Yeah, well… what about you? What are you working on?" he asked.

Delta slumped in his seat. "I can't get a job to save my life."

Jay wasn't surprised. Delta had burned a lot of bridges. Although he wasn't in the position to judge him. He could've done the same thing. The difference between them was Jay had been working since he was a kid. He could blow up his life off the set then show up the next day, ready to work hard enough to not cut into the schedule. He'd heard a lot of horror stories about Delta. He was known to pass out in his trailer, which delayed production. He'd fuck all the actresses and actors and have them fighting amongst each other, causing chaos. And just like Jay, when he came to set high, he'd always forget his lines and be unable to perform even after being fed them.

"Yeah, well, I'm not returning to *Pact of Lies*. I played a leading role. Maybe I can put in a word for you." Jay didn't even know why he said that. He didn't want Delta to fuck up his reputation because he was the one who'd referred a faulty product.

Delta's face lit up. "Oh yeah? I'd appreciate it, and I'll owe you."

"Yeah well, my girlfriend created the story and she's the head writer." Jay loved talking about Sonja. But then he remembered. "Shit."

"What?"

"I can't call. They collected all of our cell phones. Plus reception sucks out here."

"They took my phone too." His eyebrows crushed into an intense frown. "So is your girlfriend Plume?"

Why did everyone still think he was with Plume?

"No. Plume and I have been off for a long time. And in actuality, we were never really on. You know how it goes when my people and her people make us a match made in hell."

Delta snickered. "I definitely know how that goes. That means you have a real girlfriend these days?"

"Yeah," Jay whispered.

At least he hoped he still did. Seeing Delta made him remember there was a real world out there, and somewhere in it, Sonja was confused. She must've been heartbroken too. But the part that worried him the most was that she would get over him. One thing about Sonja was it never took her long to land on her feet. Now that she was a mainstay in Hollywood, it wouldn't take long before she attracted a shitload of suitors. She wasn't the kind of woman who latched on to any old guy, and that gave Jay a sense of relief. But at some point, she would say yes to someone.

Delta clapped once. "Hey! Are still with me?"

Jay snapped out of his daze. "Yeah, sorry about that."

"That's cool. But do I know your girlfriend?" Delta asked.

Jay shook his head, happy about his answer. "No, you wouldn't."

"Then she's new to the biz?"

"Yeah."

Delta looked at him with that shit-eating smirk again.

Frankly, Jay was tired of looking at it. He slapped his thighs while scooting to the edge of the sofa. "Well…"

"Hey"—Delta stood suddenly—"could I use your bathroom?" He sniffed and wiped his nose, which proved Jay right. Someone must've given him nose candy before he showed up uninvited to Jay's trailer.

"Sure." Jay pointed toward the restroom. "It's on the opposite of the trailer."

Delta smirked again. "This fucking trailer's a palace. Always the best for Jay West, huh?"

Jay narrowed his eyes, tired of Delta's fucking sarcastic and jealous remarks. He fought the urge to toss the guy out and let him find somewhere else to piss, but instead he let him go scurrying down the trailer. He'd be gone soon anyway.

At least Jay was finally hungry. He stood to shuffle to the kitchen so he could take a few bites of his dinner, but stopped when he heard a buzzing sound.

Zzzz…

Jay stood still.

Zzzz…

He twisted around until his eyes landed on Delta's coat.

"That fucker," he muttered. Delta had lied to him.

Jay contemplated his next move. He had been willing to put in the time away from Sonja for the sake of both of their careers, but that was before it became so easy to contact her.

He made a beeline to Delta's coat and took the device out of the pocket. The cell phone was still buzzing. Jay was about to end the call and make one of his own when he noticed who the call was from.

He quickly tapped Answer. "Dexter?"

"Hey, Delta?"

"No, it's Jay."

"Jay? Jay West?"

"Yeah, it's me."

"Are you with Delta?"

Jay realized he'd better keep his voice down and whispered, "Yeah, he just showed up at my trailer on set."

"What the hell happened with you?"

"Long story, man, but why are you calling Delta?"

"I was going to talk to him about playing your old part. You left us high and dry."

Jay sighed briskly. If there was anybody he could trust, it was Dexter. "I'm being blackmailed."

"What the hell are you talking about? Who's blackmailing you?"

"I don't want to put the show or Sonja's career in jeopardy. But who referred Delta to you?"

"Plume did. Who's blackmailing you?"

"I don't know," Jay whispered. All of a sudden, that answer felt extremely insufficient.

"Why didn't you call me? Let me know this?"

Jay checked over his shoulder. "He doesn't know I'm on his phone. He told me he didn't have it on him. Production has mine."

"All right then… what's the name of the project you're working on?"

Jay told him, and Dexter asked him to hold tight. He'd be in touch shortly. That gave Jay enough time to put the phone back in Delta's coat pocket. He had to quickly cycle through his anger to get back to levelheaded. His gut was on the nose —Delta hadn't shown up out of the blue. Jay didn't know what the hell he and Plume were pulling.

The door to the bathroom opened, and Jay turned briskly in that direction.

"Is that a jetted tub you have in there?" Delta said.

"You should go." He swiped Delta's coat off the sofa and tossed it to him.

Delta caught it. Jay kept his eyes on Delta's face, pretending to not notice Delta's gaze drop to the coat pocket. The guy's skin was flushed and eyes wired. No doubt he had done a few bumps of coke off the sink. He'd probably left a deuce in the toilet too.

He put on the garment. "I was leaving anyway."

Jay folded his arms. "Good luck. Thanks for the visit." His tone sounded just the way Jay wanted it to—like he didn't mean it.

Delta grunted then strolled out as if he owned the world.

Jay went straight to his bathroom. He was right.

"What an asshole."

He flushed the toilet.

At least now he could finish dinner. Jay kept track of the time, waiting for Dexter to figure out a way to contact him. He made a pact with himself to give Dexter at least an hour, but after that, he would take matters into his own hands. But he was halfway through dinner when there was a knock on his door. It was Matthew Barbary, the director, with a cell phone in his hands.

"Vincent Adams wants to talk to you," he said.

Jay's smile kept growing as he took the device from Matt. The cavalry had arrived—at least that's what he thought.

CHAPTER 26

SONJA HESTER

Sonja had only been to Manhattan twice: once during high school as a contestant in a playwright contest, and second when Gran took her on a tour of what she had deemed one of the greatest cities on earth. Sonja had never seen it the way Gran did. There were too many people in the streets, and she hated feeling like an ant under the gargantuan skyscrapers. Plus, she could never sleep well in New York City. The energy and ambient noise felt ever-present, even during those rare and precious moments of silence. But what she hated the most and already had it up to here with was how pedestrians cut each other off or nearly collided without a single *sorry* or *excuse me*. They were all too used to being in each other's way, and where she came from it was the complete opposite.

She had been in the city for six and a half hours and already felt overwhelmed. After her flight landed, she'd tried to call Delta to learn how close he was to actually having a conversation with Jay, but her call went directly to voicemail.

Then she made a mistake and chose to be adventurous by taking the subway instead of a cab from JFK to Brooklyn. She made an even bigger mistake when she got into an empty train car while everyone else packed into the ones in front of and behind it. Sonja found herself riding alone with a person who appeared homeless aside from his brand new and expensive red tennis shoes. The guy had a stench that could kill a skunk. He rocked back and forth, staring at the floor with laser focus, while repeating, "I'm going to hell."

It took an hour before she was able to escape into another car so crowded that she felt like a sardine. What made matters worse was at certain stops, the train sat there for more than fifteen minutes and others it left in less than one minute. The subway was unbelievably unreliable, and Sonja vowed to never grace its presence again *ever*. When she made it to her stop, she walked another two and a half miles to Dexter's brownstone, kicking herself for giving up her accommodations at a luxury hotel in the city for a place that had the accommodations of home.

When he had offered her a room with its own bathroom, she took it. She thought Brooklyn would've been a lot less busy than Manhattan, and it was, but not so much that it made a dent in all the reasons why the city made her so restless. Regardless, she arrived at Dexter's two hours later than planned, sweaty, worn out, and starving. Thank goodness the babysitter she had agreed to relieve handled her tardiness graciously. Sonja even offered to pay the college-aged girl an extra fifty bucks for being late, but she wouldn't accept the cash.

“Mr. Frampton wouldn’t want me to. Plus, the girls are no bother.” She escorted Sonja through Dexter’s brownstone, decorated with large brown leather furniture and lots of lacquered wood.

The babysitter introduced Sonja to Mariana at the dining room table, surrounded by colorful textbooks while typing on her computer. Her intense gaze stayed on Sonja’s face long enough to say a quick hello with a weak lift of her hand before she went back to typing pretty quickly for such a young person.

Next they climbed the stairs up to the third floor and went into the room of Dexter's oldest daughter, Maribel, who was lounging with two friends, all of them still wearing school uniforms and watching a TV show featuring a lot of teenagers. Maribel greeted her a lot like Mariana, with a small smile and lift of the hand. The fact the girls seemed so independent put Sonja at ease. She had been worried. Never had any kid been under the care of her watchful eye.

"Oh, and my name is Carmen," the babysitter said.

Shit, Sonja had shown up so flustered that they had forgotten to introduce themselves to each other. They shook hands.

"I'm Sonja."

"I know. I go to NYU. I'm majoring in film. Mr. Frampton said you're his colleague so"—she smiled broadly—"please remember this face. I'll be needing a job when I graduate."

Sonja tilted her head, confused. Was she really at that status already? Were people now going to suck up to her just to dip a toe in the most coveted business in the world?

"Just kidding," Carmen said, laughing.

Sonja's mouth fell open. "Oh?"

"Wait? You're not offended by my shameless self-promoting?"

Sonja shook her head. "Not at all."

She pushed a hand toward Sonja. "Okay then, I'm not kidding."

Sonja chuckled. "Then I'll remember your face and the fact that I owe you fifty bucks. Deal?"

They shook hands again.

"Deal."

Sonja asked Carmen if there was a good place nearby to order food for delivery, and she said there were French rolls and stuff for sandwiches in the refrigerator.

"What about coffee?" Sonja asked.

"Mr. Frampton only has the best. You'll see a coffeemaker and the coffee on the counter. But I already made a pot."

Shortly thereafter, Carmen collected her book bag and headed to class.

Sonja had to knock on Maribel's door to ask which room was for guests. The twelve-year-old quietly escorted Sonja to the bedroom on the second floor. The space was nice. Maribel kindly accepted Sonja's thanks before hurrying back to her room.

After racing downstairs to make herself a sandwich and a cup of coffee, passing the studious Mariana in the process, Sonja took a quick shower, put on fresh clothes, took her computer out of her suitcase, and got right to work. She hadn't thought she would have much to lend to the final editing process, but goodness, scenes had been added and others left out that were critical to not only the rest of the season but also those to come.

After six o'clock, she tried calling Delta again, and like the times before, she was sent right to voicemail. That was strange, and she wondered if he had actually gone to Ireland. Sonja had a lot on her mind when she went back downstairs to get another cup of coffee.

"Are you my dad's girlfriend?" Mariana asked, disrupting Sonja's thoughts.

Sonja almost poured the coffee on the counter as she twisted to see the young girl sitting in the dining area. "Huh?"

"Are you sleeping with my dad?"

"Um, no," she said emphatically. "He and I are just work colleagues."

"Then you're not sleeping in his bed tonight?"

Sonja put the carafe back where it belonged and approached Mariana with a smile. She didn't know why, but she was glad the girl was finally speaking to her.

"May I?" she asked, touching the back of an empty chair beside Mariana.

Mariana nodded.

"No, I will be sleeping in your guest room."

"It's okay if you do. My mom dates and stuff, but my dad never does."

Sonja nodded. "Oh, I see." She touched her chest. "I haven't had a boyfriend in years either."

"I don't have a boyfriend. Lots of girls at my school do though. But there aren't boys at our school. They're all across the street." She shrugged. "I don't think I want a boyfriend, but they say when I grow up I have to have one."

Sonja thought that was the most ridiculous thing she'd ever heard. "Who are the they who say that?"

"Everybody does."

"Well, you know what?" Sonja leaned closer to her. "I've never listened to everybody. I've only listened to myself." She sat back. "Not to say I don't consider others' opinions and experiences. Life is about gathering information. The older you get, the more you have. Does that make sense?"

Mariana smiled delicately. "It's like the more you learn, the more you know."

Sonja jerked her head back in surprise. "Yeah. You're smart."

The young girl grinned bashfully.

Sonja took a sip of her coffee. Goodness, she didn't know where Dexter got the coffee, but Carmen was right. It was some of the best she'd ever tasted.

"You know, if you drink too much coffee, you won't get to sleep," Mariana said.

Sonja couldn't help but smile at such a sophisticated young lady. "Don't worry. I don't plan on sleeping for a while. I have a lot of work to do."

"My dad works a lot. So does my mom."

"My gran used to work a lot too."

"Who's your gran?"

"My grandmother."

"Where was your mother?"

Usually when someone asked about Carrie Anne, Sonja's chest tightened and her eyes welled up. To Sonja's surprise, that didn't happen this time.

"My mom wasn't a good mom. She still isn't, so my grandmother, her mother, raised me."

"Why wasn't she a good mother?"

Sonja hadn't expected Mariana to ask that. "Um, she… um…" How could she put it without letting her rage speak for her? "She didn't want to be a mother, I guess."

"My mom's a good mom."

Sonja smiled. "I believe you."

Mariana stared at Sonja for a few beats then looked down and up quickly. "Do you work in TV like my dad?"

Sonja's smile broadened. "Yep, I'm a writer."

"So am I," she excitedly declared.

"Oh really? What do you write?"

Mariana then showed Sonja what she had been working on for some of the time she'd been sitting at the table. She was writing a school-age romance about girls in a private school like the one she attended. It was six pages of revealing details about four girls, who called themselves the Kittens, shunning a girl named Francine because she wouldn't sneak over to the boys' campus and pass a note to a boy one of the Kittens liked. The Kittens called the girl a wimp, and one of them pulled her hair all during class.

Then one day, the boy sneaked over to the girls' school to tell Francine he liked her. When the Kittens found out, they tried to beat her up in the bathroom. That was the day Francine learned she had special powers to push them away with the palm of her hand.

Sonja raised her eyebrows. "Wow. This is really well written."

Mariana blushed. "Thank you."

Sonja narrowed an eye inquisitively. "So are you Francine?"

She giggled, shaking her head. "No, I'm the super power."

"The super power?"

"Dad said it's called symbolism."

Sonja was even more impressed with Mariana. "What does the super power represent?"

"Helping people who are bullied."

Sonja lifted her coffee cup toward Mariana. "I like it."

Mariana smiled from ear to ear.

Sonja's cell phone rang, so she fished the device out of her pocket and saw that it was Delta. She gasped then calmed herself. "I have to take this. Good talking to you, Mariana."

"I liked talking to you too."

Soon walked up the stars while answering the phone. “Delta? Did you make it to Ireland?”

“I did,” he said with a lackluster tone.

“And?”

“I mentioned you, and he said he didn’t want to talk about you. That you two were done and that’s that.”

Sonja felt her heart break into a million pieces. “Are you kidding me?”

“I’m sorry, beautiful. I asked if he was serious and he said he was. The guy’s not looking good either. I think he’s on drugs or something.”

"What? Drugs?" She shook her head. "No, he's not doing that." She had made it back to the guest room and sat at the foot of the bed.

“They just called my flight number. If it’s worth anything, the guy’s an idiot. I would never leave someone like you high and dry. But I’m coming to New York on business. That show you work on, *Pact of Lies*?”

Sonja pressed a hand over her aching heart. “Yeah?”

“I may be replacing Jay as the lead character.”

She closed her eyes as the impact of hearing that Jay was solidly out of her life hit her. “What? How?”

"It's a long story. Let's have lunch soon. I have to go." He ended the call.

Sonja sat with the phone still against her ear. She didn't want to exist in her skin. What the hell was wrong with Jay? Did he have multiple personalities? She kept shaking her head until at some point, she stopped.

SONJA HAD HEARD THE DOORBELL RING AND DEXTER announce himself to Mariana. About twenty minutes later, he was standing at her door.

"Hey, there you are," he said.

Sonja looked up at him.

"Have you been crying?"

She sniffed and nodded. "Yeah."

He folded his arms. "What's going on?"

She told him about meeting Delta yesterday and how he had been gracious enough to fly out to Ireland to talk to Jay on her behalf. She broke down again as she recounted that the guy who she'd thought loved her had rejected her.

Dexter frowned as though he were chewing on a juicy lemon. "Is that what he said?"

"Yes, that's what Jay said."

"Not Jay. Delta?"

She cocked her head. "Yes. You don't believe him?"

Dexter interlaced his fingers behind his head as he took a deep breath. Something was obviously bothering him. "That doesn't sound like Jay to me."

"Me neither but—"

"You gotta watch out for Delta, Son. The guy has tanked his career. And he doesn't have an honorable bone in his body."

Sonja was confused. "He said that he was being considered for the Michael Lockwood replacement part."

"Yeah," Dexter said dryly.

She studied Dexter carefully. It appeared his body wanted to say more than his mouth was willing to speak. "Is there something you're not telling me?"

He sighed. "Tomorrow, you'll be at the office and we'll get you up to date on how we move forward without Jay. But you know…" He scratched the back of his head.

"But I know what?"

His eyes shifted to the right. "Plume is the one who referred Delta to us, not his agent. Just so you know."

Sonja sat up straight. "When did she do that?"

"The day before yesterday."

Sonja thought about the conversation she'd had with Delta in the car yesterday. "You know, I don't think I ever mentioned the name of my show to him. Which probably isn't as suspicious as it sounds, but why wouldn't he say anything to me? And you know, he's the one that told me about AMTA."

"What did he say about AMTA?"

"My sister's buying the company. I asked her about it and it's true. Only she said it's a bad deal because they're hemorrhaging money."

Dexter folded his arms tighter. "I see."

"Yeah…" She observed him carefully. "What is it?"

"Nothing," he said, then jerked his hand up to scratch the back of his head again. "I have to get the girls fed, but let's see what happens tomorrow. And I don't know, maybe we can get in touch with Jay too."

Sonja's eyes narrowed. Her intuition was sounding off like the fire truck that had just blared by. "What aren't you telling me?"

He wiggled his head. "Nothing. It's nothing. I just don't trust Delta. I don't want him on my set, and I'm going to do all I can to make that happen.

I'm hoping I have your support." He tilted his head. "You want to support me on this, I promise."

After a moment of hesitation, she finally nodded. "We're a team so…"

Dexter nodded briskly. "Now let's go get dinner."

CHAPTER 27

SONJA HESTER

Sonja, Dexter, and the girls walked down the street to a restaurant that served the most delicious Cuban food she'd ever tasted. The girls mostly talked about school and upcoming events and projects. Sonja gathered they loved having Dexter's attention but were also interested in showing off for her. She loved it and laughed and smiled on cue.

They talked about all the family trips they had taken, then Dexter entertained their requests for an upcoming spring break vacation to anywhere in the world. After a long list of options, Maribel convinced them to go to Disneyland in California since they'd never been there but they'd been to Disney World six times.

Just when they thought the decision was made, Mariana suggested Tokyo. According to her, they were on the cutting edge of culture.

"And how's that?" Dexter asked.

"Hello Kitty. *Hello*," she said as though it was obvious.

"And Yayoi Kusama, Daddy. We missed her last exhibit here because Mom dragged us to San Juan again," Mariana said.

Dexter looked at Sonja. "Luddie's mother's been sick for a while."

"And they have the live Hello Kitty exhibit," Maribel added.

"And all the best graphic novels," Mariana said, then turned to Sonja. "Do you want to come with us?"

"She's not Dad's girlfriend, silly bird," Maribel said.

Sonja was about to say something to graciously bow out of their fun offer when Mariana said, "I know. I'm the one who told you. I just like her. Don't you?"

Maribel shrugged. "I guess so, yeah."

"Wow, Son. They rarely like any of my friends." Dexter winked at Sonja.

"Not true, Daddy," Mariana said.

And then they went on listing all of Dexter's friends that they liked and disliked. To her surprise, they mentioned Jay. They said Jay West was cute, nice, and plain old perfect. Sonja hoped she could still agree.

Due to live music and an insane neighborhood dance party that was started out of the blue by people walking in off the street, they got home late. The buzz of the city didn't help Sonja get to sleep at all. She was sure she would never last two weeks without developing a severe case of the shakes.

Piecing together her conversations with Delta and Dexter kept her up as well. She went back over all of Delta's reactions to when she told him that she'd just finished working on a television project in Canada. He'd shown no signs that he already knew she and Plume were affiliated with the same production, but after all, he was an actor. And he was associated with Plume? He had to have heard something about her even if it were only a tiny bit. Sonja didn't believe the world revolved around her, but she couldn't imagine Plume not mentioning her to Delta. And now she was nearly certain Delta had played her. There was no way she was going to skip the chance to call him on his shit.

Sonja sprung out of bed to swipe her phone off

the dresser. She sent a text to Delta, letting him know she would like to meet him for lunch whenever he made it to town. Not too long after, he replied with *1 p.m. today* and gave her the name of the restaurant.

SONJA WAS ALREADY UP WHEN HER ALARM CHIMED AT six o'clock. She hadn't slept a wink, and although she was so exhausted that she could barely carry her shoulders, it was time to barrel through her first day on the job in New York City. She dressed in flared black polyester trousers, a button-front, cap-sleeved blouse, and shoes that had a sensible heel. She would've rather worn a dress, but it was pretty nippy out for her native Californian blood.

Before she could even get out of the room, she was on a conference call with Eden, who was introducing her to Taylor Minks, her new assistant. They went over Sonja's calendar for the day, which was more than she knew would occur. Part of her wanted to complain about all of it. Another part of Sonja blamed herself for merely making Elaine happy by accepting those many hats she'd contractually negotiated for her. But the part that won out was the fact that keeping busy made her think less about how Jay had abandoned her yet again.

"I have lunch with Delta Foster today at one," she finally said.

"Hear that, Taylor?" Eden said.

"I'm on it," Taylor said. "Miss Hester—"

"Call me Sonja."

"Sonja, where will your lunch being taking place?"

Sonja gave her the name of the restaurant, and Taylor said she would call and make sure Delta Foster had actually made a reservation.

"And your car will be waiting for you at the lobby of the Mandarin Oriental at eight a.m. to take you to AEE Headquarters. That's an hour from now. By the way, how did you like your room? Should I find you more comfortable accommodations?"

"That's very good, Taylor," Eden said.

Sonja wiggled her head. "Hold up for a second." Jeez, they were going so fast she could barely keep up.

She told them she wasn't staying at the hotel but at Dexter's house in Brooklyn. The silence that lingered spoke loudly.

"Hello?" Sonja said.

"Why would you do that and not tell me?" Eden groused.

"I'm on it," Taylor replied. "I'll cancel the reservation and see what I can do about getting a refund for the night."

"Thank you," Sonja said. Boy, did she get lucky. Taylor was the kind of assistant she could live with. "But you don't have to worry. Dexter's car is taking us both to AEE this morning."

"That's good." Sonja could hear the relief in Eden's voice. "I just don't want to screw up with you again."

"I don't know what you mean by again, but none of us are error-free so…"

"Well, I still need to apologize for telling you that Jay West was in Iceland and not Ireland. Elaine wasn't happy I did that."

Sonja squeezed her temples, then massaged them. Damn, she had pushed Jay to the back of her mind and now he had risen right back to the forefront. "That was a mistake?"

"Yes. And I'm sorry."

"Okay, thank you," she strained to say. "Taylor, we'll speak later. I have to go."

She wanted to just end the call but had better manners than that. She waited for the assistants to say goodbye, then she promptly ended the call. Sonja sat for a moment to recover. Nope, she couldn't let herself miss Jay. So she hopped to her feet, packed her computer, grabbed her purse, and left the isolation of her room.

When Sonja made it downstairs, Dexter and the girls were halfway through breakfast. She wasn't that hungry, but there was no better way to take her mind off her heartache than to join Dexter's family. So she sat with them and ate a blueberry pancake, a few orange slices, and drank some coffee. Listening to Maribel and Mariana tell Dexter about all of their school club meetings and assignments for the day was inspiring. They had real schedules that they were excited about. Now she understood why during production, he had been so firm about video conferencing twice a day with his daughters. Their conversation was smooth, like clockwork.

"What about you? What are you going to do today?" Mariana asked Sonja.

"A lot… a lot of work."

"Do you want to do a lot of work?"

Sonja avoided Dexter's eyes when she said, "For now."

"What about later?"

Mariana rarely took vague answers for the final

answer, so Sonja dug into her dusty box of principles. "I've always felt life should be lived one day at a time. I'm always open to what's around the corner."

Mariana turned to Dexter, who winked at her. Then she looked at Sonja, who was smiling at her and smiled back.

Soon they all filed into Dexter's hired car. Their first stop was dropping the girls off at school, which looked more like a place of business than a regular campus.

"Mariana and Maribel like you," Dexter said when they were alone.

"I like them too."

"What you said about living in the moment? Is that what you've done all your life?"

Sonja shrugged. "I guess so. Why? Don't approve of Mariana subscribing to the philosophy?"

Dexter chuckled. "I'm not the mayor of my girls' minds. They like you, and you're more information for them to take in and process on the road of life."

"Ha. You sound like my gran."

A sheepish grin flashed across his lips.

"What?" Sonja asked.

"So how's Robin doing these days?"

Sonja pictured her cousin, feeling as though they were a million miles apart. "I don't know. We haven't spoken much. I talked to her a few days ago, but as usual, she was busy. I'm sure she's still traveling steadily at a hundred miles an hour."

He frowned inquisitively.

"I guess… it's just what she does. Go, go, go with no end in sight. My sister does it, and so does Robin's sister."

"You've been going pretty hard yourself," he said.

Sonja grunted thoughtfully. "Yeah, I guess we all have it in us."

Dexter nodded as though he understood exactly what she meant. "Well, the last we spoke, she decided we should talk again when things lighten up."

"That sounds like Robin."

He grunted. "Things are never going to lighten up, are they?"

Sonja studied Dexter. She thought about Robin and how if it weren't for Jay showing up at her place and bringing that contract to her, Sonja probably would've let the opportunity to be a real TV writer pass her by. But for a guy who had everything going for him—such as looks, smarts, and a genuinely kind and caring personality—Dexter was weak when it came to going that extra mile to seal the deal.

"Did your career just fall into your lap?" she asked.

He looked perplexed. "My career?"

"Yeah?"

"No."

"Think of Robin as that extra special somebody who's not just going to fall into your lap because of"—her pointed finger circled him—"all of this you have going on."

Dexter looked down at himself then back up. "All of what?"

Sonja cocked her head and narrowed an eye. "Come on, really?"

"Really what?"

"You look in the mirror, don't you?"

He threw up his hands. "I'm just a guy."

She chuckled. "Well, you're a gorgeous guy and that's not enough to land a woman like Robin. If you want her, then you have to convince her you're the best partner for her. But perhaps in the end, there lies the problem."

He jerked his head back. "Meaning?"

"If you're working all the time and she's working all the time, then that leaves the both of you unavailable. Robin needs someone who can show her what the pastures look like on the other side of the mountain. But I'm thinking you need the same thing."

Dexter pursed his lips and scratched the side of his mouth. After a while, he grunted then stared straight ahead.

"Did that make sense?" Sonja asked.

"It did," he said, although he still seemed troubled by what she'd said.

"And hey, everything I said could be totally wrong."

He chuckled. "You can't backtrack now. But don't worry, I can handle the truth. Plus, I'm positive you hit the nail on the head."

"I'm pretty sure I did as well."

They laughed.

AEE's offices were in the top six floors of an extremely tall building. Frankly, Sonja didn't like having the ability to look flying birds in the eyes. But thank goodness, she hadn't time to worry about how uncomfortable she was. As soon as they walked through reception, it was all systems go.

The first thing Sonja did was shake hands with

Vincent Adams. It was the first time she'd seen him in person since running out of their meeting at AMTA months ago. Like Dexter, he was an unusually good-looking guy. Vincent Adams also had a lightness about him that convinced Sonja he loved waking up and facing big days at the office.

After Sonja was shown her office and IT had set her up on the internet and given her a big monitor to attach her laptop to, she checked her emails, confirmed more meetings, then went straight to the editing bay.

The one thing she loved the most about working in production was that everyone got right down to business. There was no lollygagging. Within minutes of getting started putting together episode five, they were rolling along like a well-greased machine. Three hours later, the calendar on her phone dinged to let her know it was time for her lunch meeting with Delta.

"Shoot," she said, looking at the time on her phone. "I have to go."

"That's fine," Tony, one of the editors, said. "I'll work with the notes you gave me, and by the time you get back, I'll have something for you to review."

She accepted that and rushed to her office to get her purse before heading out into a city that was still and would forever be way too busy for her liking.

Her car was waiting for her in front of the building. At first she thought being driven around like the high roller she wasn't might be a little pretentious. But even making it to work on time had taken some very sharp skills by Dexter's driver, Victor. He had to know how to avoid congestion. Her driver was just as knowledgeable about getting her to her destination on time.

The restaurant, Tempter, was located at the top floor of a glass-walled building on Wall Street. Sonja rushed through the double glass doors. Even though the driver had managed to avoid several pockets of stalled traffic, she was thirteen minutes late, and she hated being late. Once she made it to the hostess station, she stood behind a group of men in expensive suits, waiting to be seated. She could feel them checking her out as though she were a museum exhibit, but she looked past them, searching the dining room for that one familiar face.

Finally, the hostess walked from behind the booth to show the men to their table. As they walked away, she heard one of them ask the hostess to put Sonja near them. Sonja didn't hear the hostess's answer, but another young woman stepped behind the desk.

"Welcome to Tempter," the new and unsmiling hostess said.

"I'm here to meet Delta Foster."

The woman perked up, smiling the way she should've before Delta's name was mentioned. "He's waiting. This way please."

She led Sonja past occupied tables. Most of the people were in suits, no matter if they were men or women.

Sonja finally saw Delta sitting at a table next to a window with a view of the Hudson River. She took and released a quick breath through her nostrils. Jay was back on her mind. Delta watched her with a smile that made his face glow, looking like an angel, not some lying, conniving jerk who sought to sabotage her relationship with Jay. And because of that, she didn't know what to think or how to feel. Should she heed Dexter's warning, or give him the benefit of the doubt?

He stood before she reached the table.

"You look beautiful," he said as they hugged.

"Thanks," she barely replied. Sonja didn't want to be nice to him until she knew the truth. So as soon as she settled in her chair, she leaned forward.

“Did you actually go to Ireland or are you bullshitting me?”

“Whoa,” he said, tilting back. “Where is this coming from?”

"You lied to me. That's where it's coming from." Even though being hostile wasn't her thing, she felt okay with letting him have it.

“How?”

“When we met, you pretended as though you never knew about *Pact of Lies*.”

“No, I didn’t.”

“I told you I was working on a show in Canada.”

He threw up his hands. “Okay?”

“When we met, Plume had already referred you to Dexter and Vince as a replacement for Jay’s character.” She shook her hands emphatically. “Plume! I can’t think of any scenario where she wouldn’t have mentioned me to you.”

Delta shifted forward. “I’m telling you, she didn’t mention you at all. The first I heard of your existence was from Robin.” He raised a hand. “Scout’s honor.”

Sonja narrowed her eyes. She didn’t believe him but had no way to prove it.

“And I did fly to Ireland. As a matter of fact…”

He took his wallet out of his pants pocket, opened it, snatched a slip of paper out of the billfold, and unfolded it. "This is my production pass."

He handed it to Sonja, and she read it. *Delta Foster – Visitor – The Reign of Masters*. She recalled they'd used the same sorts of passes on *Pact of Lies*. What she was holding could definitely be construed as proof enough. Pain soared through her as she handed it back just as the waitress stepped up to their table.

"Hello," she sang, keeping her attention on Delta. "Have you had a chance to look at the menu?"

"No, we haven't," Sonja snapped. She felt like lashing out even though it wasn't fair to the waitress. "Do you have any suggestions?"

Her smile faltered, but she recovered. "Um, the seared scallops on a bed of brown butter and fresh garlic risotto is good."

Sonja handed her the menu. "I'll have that."

The waitress seemed taken aback by her brusqueness. "Okay, thank you." She took the menu and wrote down Sonja's order.

"I'll have the smoked trout with artichokes," Delta said, grinning flirtatiously.

If he was trying to reclaim the girl's full attention, it worked. It was clear to Sonja he was a needy guy, which made her even more upset, since he was nothing like Jay.

"Is that all?" the waitress asked him, grinning from ear to ear.

"A bottle of your best champagne," he said.

"I'll have iced tea," Sonja said.

"Great." The waitress tucked the menus in her armpit. "A bottle of our best champagne."

Sonja snapped her fingers. "And?"

"I'm sorry?" the waitress said, definitely annoyed by the finger snapping.

"Champagne and what else?"

She read the food order off the order pad.

"I said iced tea."

The girl frowned. "Sorry, I didn't hear you."

Sonja pressed her lips together and smiled tightly. Goodness gracious did she want to light the girl up for focusing more on Delta Foster than her. Heck, out of the both of them, she was the one who had a job. From what she'd heard so far, Delta couldn't find one. But she had to get a grip and stop misplacing her anger. Delta was the heartthrob. Women came on to Jay all the time, but he was more respectful about it. Delta chose not to be.

"Iced tea, thank you," she reiterated.

"I'm sorry about your iced tea, ma'am," the waitress said. She sounded remorseful.

"Thank you, babe," Delta said.

The waitress's smile wavered as she looked at him then turned to Sonja. "You're welcome."

Sonja smiled back. "So," she said, returning her focus to her lunch companion now that the battle to be seen and validated was over. "You're saying Jay blew me off."

He rolled his eyes. "I told you what he told me."

"That doesn't sound like him at all."

"Maybe you didn't know him like you thought."

Sonja snickered. "It didn't take me long to figure out Plume. And the fact that you're hooked up with her—"

"Sonja, you gotta believe me, I'm not hooked up with Plume Ashbury. This is all coincidence. I only know her because we worked on a few movies together."

"I've never seen or heard of a movie with the two of you in it."

"Come on," he said sharply.

"You come on," she snapped back.

"Not every movie that's made gets released."

"I know that you and Plume command a huge

box office take and only an idiot wouldn't release a movie starring the two of you."

"Not seven years ago," he said, shaking his head adamantly. "And come on, Sonja, we're brand new friends, aren't we?" He seemed to be trying too hard to look sincere.

"I don't know. Are we?"

He pressed his lips together then sighed sharply. "Yes. We are. Listen, I don't know why Jay said what he said. He didn't look good. He wasn't happy. But he hasn't dropped off the face of the Earth. You'll see him again one day. When you do, ask him why he said what he told me."

Sonja closed her eyes to ponder what Delta said. She opened her eyes. "He wasn't happy?"

"No, he wasn't."

Jay had probably told him all of those hurtful things for the same reason he felt he had to create distance between them in the first place. But he'd said one thing about Jay that she would never believe.

"But you said Jay was high."

"I've known Jay West for a long time and he looked high to me." He shrugged. "He could've been tired though. It was late."

A server was back with their drinks, and Sonja

allowed herself to settle in her seat. Delta was pretty convincing. It wasn't farfetched to think that something had knocked Jay off the wagon. He had been determined to leave acting behind, but something had happened and he was now bound to another project. That could definitely send him careening off the wagon.

Sonja sighed deeply, allowing the air to clear the anger out of her head. "All right. Let's drop this for now."

He grinned slightly. "I'm all for that. Now let's talk about me being a lot more interesting to you."

She rolled her eyes. "I'm not in the market for a new boyfriend." She scrunched one side of her face squeamishly. "Sorry."

He watched her with smoldering eyes. "I like a challenge."

She shook her finger at him. "See, now I'm doubting you again."

Delta sat up straight as though he'd decided to be a good boy. "Then let's talk about something else. What are my chances of getting the part?" He inclined his body toward her, checked over his right shoulder, and whispered, "I still need a gig."

Sonja recalled Dexter saying Delta didn't have an honorable bone in his body. "Well, you get my vote. But this isn't a dictatorship. The decision of who replaces Jay is also up to Dexter Frampton and Vincent Adams."

He grunted. "Dexter Frampton is a nobody. But I know Vince's wife. She'll put in a word for me." He sounded like a whiny little kid.

Sonja widened her expression. "Wow, you know his wife?"

"Yeah. Her name is Maggie." He seemed pretty proud of it. "She used to be my publicist until she quit to raise a kid."

Finally their food came, and they dug in right away. After all, Sonja only had an hour and a half for lunch.

"So," he said, before taking a bite of trout, "you're the creator of the series."

She titled her head suspiciously. "And who did you hear that from?"

He rolled his head. "Oh come on. Are we back there again?"

"Not if you answer my question."

"You told me in the car the other day. Plus, it's in the trades now."

"The *Hollywood Reporter*?"

"And *Variety*."

"Okay, I'll let it go," she said, relaxing the

tension in her body. She couldn't stop grinning though. Having her name in *Variety* was actually a dream come true.

Now that she'd put her distrust of Delta on the backburner, Sonja told him about Ms. Jenkins, her crazy former tenant, and the relationship she had with Sonja's grandmother. Delta seemed entertained by the whole story. The fact that she referred to Ms. Jenkins as the general of the cat brigade made him laugh his head off.

Then he spent the rest of lunch telling her about his ex-girlfriend Rachel. Even though he was rarely in town, she wouldn't let him see the dog they had adopted together two years earlier. Apparently Rachel was a "spiteful bitch" who never had anything nice to say about him or anyone else. She was crazy too, and he claimed she used to lock him out of the house for no reason at all. Sonja didn't believe that.

Then he stopped dragging Rachel's name through the mud and started on how useless his agent was. Basically, Sonja couldn't get a word in edgewise. Finally, and thankfully, Delta motioned for the waitress. All it took was a slight wiggle of his finger and she came straight to the table. He asked for the bill and paid for their lunch.

"So what are you doing tonight?" he asked.

"Probably working."

"You can't work all night."

She slipped her purse off the back of her chair. "I'm not hanging out with you, Delta."

"But you have to. There's this great exhibit at the Met and it's invitation only. I have two tickets, and I want you to come with me."

The thought of getting dressed up for a chilly night out in New York City made her yawn. "Nah, I didn't sleep well last night."

She stood, and so did he.

"Come on," he said in a coaxing tone.

"I really am tired. I didn't get any sleep last night." She squeezed her eyes, trying to ease the headache she remembered she had. "But I think I'll sleep better tonight, and I want to get a head start on it."

"All right, then we'll go tomorrow."

She scrunched one side of her face. "I thought you said you only had tickets for tonight."

"I didn't say I *only* have tickets for tonight. I said I have tickets for tonight. But I can have my assistant call and make the tickets for tomorrow night."

Sonja groaned and looked away. The hostess

was across the room, staring at Delta with glossy eyes.

"Ask her." Sonja nodded at the girl. "She's really into you."

Delta kept his eyes fastened on Sonja. "Tomorrow night? Yes?" He didn't drop his intense expression, not even a millimeter of it.

Finally she relaxed. "How about I see how I feel tomorrow?"

He smiled again. "I'll take that."

"Good, because that's all you're getting."

Finally Sonja had her first real sit-down meeting with Vincent Adams. During lunch, he had viewed the changes she'd made to episode five.

He flashed his winning smile. "It has my approval. You have some sharp instincts."

She contained her excitement. "Thank you very much, Mr. Adams."

"Call me Vince, please."

"I will, thanks, Vince." Goodness, was she breathing? She wanted to take a deep breath just to make sure, but that would've shown how nervous she was.

"So…" He sat back in his large leather armchair and folded his hands on his chest. "How's your first day in the city going otherwise?"

Sonja tensed, trying to stay in the moment. For some reason, she wanted to lament about missing Jay and wanting to be with him or go back home. Instead, she put on a tight smile. "It's been pretty good, I guess. I didn't get much sleep last night. Oh, and I had lunch with Delta Foster."

His head tilted ever so slightly. "Is that so?"

She felt her eyes expand a little more. "Um, yes. He said he knows your wife."

His expression remained flat. "Yeah, he was a client of hers when she ran Mo&Ma. Ever heard of them?"

"No, I haven't."

Finally, he smiled. "My wife is a smart woman. She's principled too." Suddenly he clapped once, snapped his fingers, and shot two fingers in her direction. "Your grandmother is Lorraine Hester?"

"Yes." Not even hearing her grandmother's name, the person she missed as much as Jay, eased her nerves.

"My wife's cousin just bought your grandmother's company."

Sonja pressed a hand against her cheek. "Oh."

"Sorry. You didn't know?"

The day before Sonja left for Vancouver, her grandmother had mentioned that she was looking to sell LH Real Estate Group, but in all honesty, Sonja never truly believed her. That company had been Gran's reason for breathing for as long as Sonja had been alive.

Sonja dropped her hand and cleared her throat. "No, no, that's not it. She mentioned she was considering selling the company and moving to the desert. I just never thought she'd do it."

His smile was sympathetic. "If it's any consolation, her company has landed in good hands."

"Knowing my gran, I'm sure it has."

They smiled at each other, then Vince got right down to business. He gave her the rating numbers all over again, expounding on what he envisioned for the future of *Pact of Lies*, which included five solid seasons. He asked Sonja if she had any ideas how those seasons would play out. Of course she had an answer.

"Hey, what are you doing Friday night?" Vince asked.

Sonja looked at him with wide eyes, and Delta's face came to mind. She had been living in the moment so much that she'd forgotten the day of the week. *Monday, Tuesday, Wednesday*… it was Wednesday. "Um, I'm not doing anything."

"My wife and I are having a dinner party. I'd like for you to come."

Sonja struggled to contain her excitement. "I would like that, yes. Thanks for the invitation." She was proud of herself for staying subdued.

"Well… actually I'm inviting you because I do like you and I'm happy you're on my team and not anyone else's. But there's another reason."

Apparently his wife's family would be in town and three of them had watched the first four episodes of *Pact of Lies.* They were now addicted to the series and wanted a chance to meet the creator and head writer. Sonja couldn't retain their names because her nerves were through the roof and she was constantly trying to steady them.

"That means you're our first and only celebrity dinner guest. That's how much they're in awe of you."

Sonja couldn't stop beaming. "Wow, thanks! Yeah, I'm still in."

"Good." He released a small sigh of relief. "Very good."

Now that that was out of the way, he told her that he and Dexter had decided that for the next few seasons, she'd be working closely with them on casting, storytelling, and hiring key personnel. After that, they were hoping she could take the reins so that Dexter could move on to other projects.

"He's one of the best writers and producers out there when it comes to drama, but he prefers news and documentary. He spent the front part of his career as a journalist."

"Oh..."

Sonja's thoughts and feelings were bouncing all over the place. If her and Jay's plans had come to fruition, then she would have way less responsibility with the show, not more. But she hadn't known that Dexter preferred to be doing something else as well. *Pact of Lies* was her baby, not his. Perhaps running away with Jay was merely a dream. At some point, reality would've kicked in and she would have been forced to make room for not only *Pact of Lies,* but perhaps many other shows in the future.

"Well..." She readjusted in her seat. "This is my baby, and I'll be ready to cuddle it whenever it's my time."

He winked at her. "That's a creative analogy."

She grinned. "Thanks."

"And if you decide to create another show, then

just put the treatment on my desk and make sure you're able to juggle the work that goes with it."

Goodness, she was still grinning. She'd gotten it! The famous invitation to be a forever part of the AEE family. Her career was now set in stone.

After her meeting with Vince, Sonja was riding on cloud nine. For the next two hours, she sat in her office and banged out the first episode outline for season two. Every beat led up to Mia Faraday's, Plume's character's, death. It was time to write Plume out of her life for good. And the best part was she had the power to do it, no questions asked.

Next was a meeting with Taylor, who was still in LA even though she was scheduled to catch a flight to New York that night. Sonja yawned while planning her schedule for the rest of the week.

She needed to meet with her staff writers, but most of them were in LA. She didn't see a need to fly them in since they could easily work by videoconferencing. Taylor also had to schedule a whole host of budget and logistic meetings with different departments, all of which had to be coordinated with Dexter's assistant and Monica, Vince's right-hand woman.

Next Sonja reviewed the cuts to episode five Tony had made while she was at lunch. One thing was for sure, she was spread thin and was going to need some help. She'd thought active production were the busiest days of her life, but apparently she hadn't seen nothing yet.

Her final task of the day was a wrap meeting with Dexter. She let him lead, masterfully summing up all that they had done separately and bringing their undertakings together to show how much progress had been made.

Sonja slapped the arm of her chair. "And that's how it's done."

Dexter chuckled. "Yep, that's how it's done. We stay ahead of schedule."

"So," she said and uncrossed her legs, "I can do all of this from LA the week after next?"

"The offices in LA are even better, so yes."

She released a sigh of relief.

"Already homesick?" he asked.

"I was homesick the second I stepped off the airplane."

"The girls will miss you, but you can leave this weekend if you like."

She felt her face expand with excitement. "Then I'll do it. I hadn't even seen my gran since we left Vancouver." Nor had she called Gran. Once upon a time, she spoke to her gran every day. Had she been so busy that she was neglecting the ones she loved?

Dexter snapped his fingers. "Sonja."

She shook her head, pulling herself out of a stupor. "Sorry. I'm so damn tired, I could fall asleep right here in this chair."

"Then let's get this over with."

Sonja raised a finger pointedly. "Oh, and what about Delta? Is he going to be cast as a Michael Lockwood-like character? I need to know in order to finish episode one of season two." Thinking about replacing Jay broke her heart again.

"I don't know. The jury's still out on that."

"Well, I had lunch with him today."

The sides of Dexter's mouth turned down as he readjusted in his seat. "You did?"

"Yeah."

"And?"

"He really wants the part."

His frown intensified as he nodded.

Sonja placed a hand on over her heart. "I'm okay either way. If you don't want him, we'll find somebody else."

"How about we hold off on making that decision until next week?"

"I'm okay with that too."

He scrunched one side of his face as though he smelled something foul. “Are you guys involved or something?”

Sonja shook her head emphatically. “No. No, no, no, no. He wants to be friends, and I don’t see why we shouldn’t be.”

Dexter’s eyes narrowed in a way Sonja was sure he wasn’t aware of. He shifted abruptly. “As I said, we’ll table recasting a Michael Lockwood-like character for now. Our preliminaries suggest viewers are into Jay West as Michael Lockwood to the point where ratings may suffer if we lose him.”

Sonja sat up straight. “Really? This is the first time I’m hearing of this.”

“Yeah well, Michael Lockwood is going to be tough to replace. And it doesn’t look good if he’s gone after the first season.”

“But Jay abandoned us.” The pain of her broken heart smothered her, so she sighed deeply.

Dexter leaned forward, resting his elbows on his thighs. “I know you’re hurt, and I would be too if I were in your shoes. But you have to keep a level head.”

Sonja narrowed an eye. “What does that mean?” She couldn’t make the connection between

Jay abandoning them, her being hurt, and keeping a level head.

"Isn't it kind of early to be hanging out with Delta Foster?"

"I told you, he's just a friend."

"Does he know that?"

Sonja was going to say yes, but she smashed her lips together. A thought stopped her from speaking. Delta had been coming on to her since they met. She was used to men coming on to her, but she was also accustomed to not caring about it.

"I told him that we can only be friends," she said. "But he has asked me to attend some event at the Met with him tomorrow night."

Dexter's unamused expression didn't change a wink. "Then he asked you on a date?"

"No. He's into art, so he's going to show me…" No, he was going to prove to her that he could be a deep enough man to land a woman like her or Robin. She didn't dare tell Dexter that, so she sat back and crossed her legs.

"Show you what?"

She shrugged. "He likes art. That's all."

Finally, and to Sonja's relief, Dexter sat up as the tension left his body. "Okay. Just be careful. That's all I'm asking."

Sonja nodded, heeding Dexter's warning.

Dexter bowed his head graciously. "All right. How about we get out of here? We'll pick up the girls and go grab some dinner."

Sonja took a deep breath as she stood. "Sure. Let me shut down my computer and get my purse."

Dexter rose to his feet. "Cool. I have a call to make, but I'll stop by your office in five?"

"Five works for me."

When Sonja was at her desk, she had six more emails from Taylor regarding scheduling session times with the writing team. She also had a text message from Delta, asking if she had made a decision about joining him at the Met tomorrow night.

She sat back in her chair, thinking of all the reasons she should say no. But the one reason why she should say yes prevailed. So she texted: *I'm in. What time?*

Almost immediately, he texted: *Seven p.m. Where should I pick you up?*

Sonja looked at the time on her computer. It was 7:53 p.m. She felt as though tomorrow she would need even more time at the office than today, so she replied: *Eight p.m. Meet me in the lobby of the AEE building.*

7:30 p.m., he responded.

Sonja sighed and tersely tapped out, *Eight.*

I'll be in the lobby at 7:45 p.m. Join me then or at EIGHT, he replied.

She shook her head, wondering why confirming the time for a date she could've just as easily passed on felt like a power struggle. So she decided to stop engaging. She'd said eight and meant eight.

Okay, she wrote in her last text to him. He responded, but she slipped the phone into her purse before she could look at it. Dexter was standing in her doorway. It was time to go.

CHAPTER 28

ELAINE HESTER

Yesterday Morning

Elaine sat at her desk, staring out the doorway. She had just ended a phone call with a woman who'd told her they needed to meet immediately. When Elaine asked why and who she was, the woman said she was calling on behalf of AEE.

"Tell me who you are or fuck you," Elaine said.

"Stop trying to nullify your purchase of AMTA. As Archie told you at 10:33 a.m., 'It's a done deal, cupcake.' But if you want to reverse your fortune, then meet me at the address I'll text to your cell phone. I'll be waiting."

Elaine ended the call without agreeing to meet the woman or not.

"It's a done deal…." she whispered.

Jimmy from media management walked past her office then stepped back to look inside. "Hey, are you okay?"

She tried to straighten her frown but couldn't. "Yeah."

She cleared her throat as she waved him away. He left, and Elaine checked her cell phone. The text message had come through with an address she recognized as the Getty Museum. Then she checked the time of her last call with Archie Rubenstein, the President of AMTA, who was handling the sale of all five shareholders' interest. It had started at 10:33 a.m. and he had said to her those exact words—it's a done deal, cupcake.

"What the fuck…" Elaine whispered.

She jumped out of her seat and snatched her purse off the coat tree near the door. She told Eden she'd be back and high-tailed it out of there.

Elaine drove as fast as traffic would allow. Thank goodness the Getty wasn't far from her offices in Westwood. She parked and took the trolley up to the facility. It was the middle of the afternoon, so lots of groups were peppered across the grounds.

Elaine had been given instructions to go to a specific room. The door to the room was unlocked, so she opened it and was stopped by the sight of an extremely beautiful blonde sitting a few feet away, her long legs crossed. She wore a black sweater and pants with ankle boots. Elaine looked over her shoulder then back at the woman just to prove she wasn't a figment of Elaine's imagination. There was something illusory about her.

"Are you the one who called me?" Elaine asked.

The woman pointed at the empty chair across the table from her. "Please have a seat."

Elaine crossed her arms. Her first inclination was to resist and ask questions, but the look in the woman's eyes made a chill run up and down her spine. One didn't get as far as she had in her business without knowing who not to fuck with, and that woman was definitely one of those people.

Elaine unfolded her arms and carefully placed herself in the seat. "Why am I here?"

"My name is Maggie Adams. My husband is Vincent Adams."

Elaine touched her throat. "You're Vince Adams's wife?"

"Yes, ma'am."

Elaine wiggled her finger. "We're not that much different in age. I'm not a ma'am to you."

"I apologize if I've offended you, Ms. Hester. You asked me why I'm here. It appears you and my husband have a mutual problem."

"AMTA?"

Maggie nodded once. "I've seen the video with Jay West and used my resources to authenticate it. The footage has been grossly manipulated. Only seven percent of the video was captured on a single source recording device—an illegal recording device. The rest was manipulated with a specific type of technology that's also not on the market."

"And you know this because…? What are you, FBI?"

She'd never thought a guy like Vincent Adams would be married to such a woman. But apparently that was definitely the case because this Maggie had no reason to lie, so Elaine felt as though there may be hope for her to find a powerful, smart, and drop-dead gorgeous man of her own. She loved Gary, but he wasn't even close to falling into that category.

"No," Maggie said. "I'm who federal law

enforcement agencies call when they need to get shit done without bureaucracy and bullshit."

Elaine blinked at the face of an angel talking like a badass. "Then you have access to this technology?"

"I do."

Elaine closed her eyes and braced herself as the sweet feeling of relief flooded her.

"But that doesn't mean Jay West and the 174 other clients who have been framed in the same manner are off the hook."

Elaine nodded. "I know. Not unless you can locate and delete every single copy of the videos out there."

Maggie scooted up to the table and folded her hands on the desk. "That's correct, Ms. Hester."

"Call me Elaine."

She nodded briskly. "So I already have my team on—"

Elaine tilted her head. "Your team?"

"My investigative team."

"And who do you work for?"

Maggie smirked. "Myself."

"And how much are your services going to set me back?"

“Since my husband’s and your interests intersect, you’ll pay nothing. Vince is footing the bill.”

Maggie had put Elaine in a tight spot. She'd never felt so vulnerable in her life. Paying for help kept Elaine in the control of a situation.

Elaine twisted her mouth from left to right. There was no way she could give up the power. “This is my company. I’ll pay.”

“No.” Maggie sat back. “My husband will pay my fee. You will wait until the next time I contact you. Until then, you’ll go on with business as usual. Don’t let Archie think for a second you’re okay with them selling you a lemon.”

Elaine frowned. “You’ve heard me call AMTA a lemon?”

“I have.”

“Is there a timeframe in the day when you start and end invading my privacy?”

“We only listen into correspondence between you and those involved with the case.”

Elaine cocked her head. “Wait, is Archie behind this?”

Maggie kept her expression mute. “Perhaps.”

“Yes or no?”

“I said perhaps.” She set her jaw.

A flash of agitation soared through Elaine,

which made her look away and massage the back of her neck. Something was happening between the two of them. Maggie Adams had done her homework. She'd asked the right questions, used the right language, and spoken in the right tone. Something in her posture, and even her outfit, screamed, *don't fuck with me, Elaine Hester*. Maggie was discombobulating her, Svengali-ing her, and it equally disturbed and impressed her.

Elaine threw her hands up in surrender. "Apparently you're the one in control here."

"No," she said with a gentle headshake. "We control this situation equally. If either of us slip up, then AMTA will continue to hemorrhage seven hundred million—"

"Six-hundred fifty thousand dollars a year," Elaine said. She'd recited that number often. It kept her up at night and aggravated her ulcer.

Maggie nodded briskly. "That's a lot of money paid to criminals, and believe me, they would rather keep the payments coming than tarnish your talent."

Elaine cocked her head. "Damn it. Yes."

She shook her head. Why hadn't she thought of that? It made all the sense in the world. She had been worried about the wrong aspects of the situation. She shouldn't have backed off and let Jim Neely, the first person she was going to fire, make Jay end his affiliation with *Pact of Lies* and take a last-minute role in Ireland. The only reason why Jim had made him do it in the first place was because of his tiny wounded ego.

"Shit…" She rubbed her temples. "How close are we to catching these guys?"

"Close."

"Give me more. I need more."

"I'll give you this. There are two things I've learned since I've started doing what I do. A—always follow the money. And B—when the dollar amount is that exorbitant, people will do whatever they deem necessary to keep the cash flowing. Which means I get to continue following the money."

Elaine studied Maggie's perfect face. Back in high school, she would've been jealous of a woman as lovely as Maggie Adams. She used to believe girls who looked like her had no ambition in life other than becoming a man's dream. But there Maggie sat, proving that naive belief totally wrong.

"And you really know what you're doing?"

Maggie kept a straight face. "Yes, Elaine, I do." She reached down to the floor beside her, brought up a stack of papers, and slid them across the table toward Elaine. "I'm going to need you to give me permission to have all the documents that we've obtained from your company without consent."

Elaine snorted. "Does that mean I've already lost my plea to reverse the purchase?"

Maggie sneered. "You have, but only because I made sure of it."

She read something in Maggie's expression. "Could you have gotten me out of that contract?"

"Yep."

Elaine signed each paper then looked at Maggie with a crooked smile. She liked Mrs. Adams. She liked her a lot.

Maggie collected the signed documents. "But you don't have to worry about all the shit you were worrying about before this meeting." She reached down and pulled up another set of papers. "I'll find whoever's extorting your company and bring them to justice. And I'll do it sooner rather than later." She slid the new stack across the table. "Which is why I need you to sign these as well."

Elaine grimaced at the name and address at the top of the petition. "Wait, that's me." She read fast then looked up. "You were investigating me?"

"No one was exempt," Maggie said with a straight face.

Elaine tapped the documents. "Then I'm signing this because you found something?"

"We did."

"What?"

"Turn to page seventeen."

Elaine quickly flipped through the papers and read page seventeen. It was the start of a number of text messages and phone calls. Her mouth fell open, and she had to struggle to take deep breaths.

Maggie leaned toward her. "Do you need water?"

Elaine squeezed her eyes shut as she shook her head. "I'm fine." She cleared the frog out of her throat. "Explain this, please."

Maggie hesitated then sat up straight. "We identified a woman in thirty-six of the videos, including the one with Jay West. Her name is Sarah Rose. She worked in your fiancé's bar until two months ago."

Elaine chuckled bitterly as she thought about all the times she'd ignored her intuition when it came to Gary. He'd pushed her so hard to buy AMTA. Gary was one of three people who knew how wealthy Elaine actually was, especially for a single, thirty-five-year-old woman who wasn't an heiress.

Gran had taught her how to not only invest her money and draw interest off her assets but how to take educated risks.

Gary, Gran, and Sonja were the only people who knew Elaine was a major investor in ConnectUp, the biggest social media platform on the planet. She remembered the day she had been told that the company went public and she had made over three billion dollars. Instead of doing a happy dance, she'd poured herself a glass of wine, sat on the sofa, and thought, *No man will ever love me now.* She had always been, to her chagrin, too smart, too goal-oriented, and no matter how hard she tried not to be, way too ambitious. The day ConnectUp paid off in 2014, she was forced to add way too rich to the list. She never would have bought AMTA as a single woman because that would've made her too powerful as well. But she'd thought she and Gary were a done deal.

She took another breath. "Well, thank God for the family cellular plan." She signed both sets of documents.

Maggie gathered the pages and stuffed them back into whatever was on the floor beside her. "You know you're going to have to keep this between us for now."

Elaine was surprised her heart didn't ache. Actually, she was numb. She grunted bitterly. "Gary would've been my fourth attempt at marriage. Did you know that?"

Maggie kept a straight face. "No, I didn't."

It had been a long time since Elaine had felt so lonely. "Do you want to go grab a drink or something?"

"It's not in our best interest to be seen together. But definitely another time." Maggie stood.

"Damn it," Elaine said, pounding her fist against the table. "I thought I actually loved the motherfucker."

Maggie looked at her with the same poker face. "I'll be in touch."

Without another word, she walked out of the room, leaving Elaine sitting alone in her despair.

CHAPTER 29

SONJA HESTER

Dinner with Dexter and the girls was just as entertaining as it had been the night before. They went to an upscale Jamaican restaurant in Queens. The food was so delicious and the girls were so excited about Sonja trying all of their favorite entrées that they ordered just about everything on the menu. Then later, surprisingly, Sonja got the best sleep she'd had in a while.

Now she was back at the office and barreling through her day with no time to leave for lunch. So Taylor, who had arrived at the office later that morning, walked seven blocks to bring Sonja a sub sandwich for lunch. Having her own executive assistant toting and fetching for her felt strange.

Sonja wasn't quite sure if she liked it; however, she was darn certain she needed Taylor's help.

The hours raced by, and she let Taylor go at five o'clock. She didn't want her assistant to be overworked without overtime pay like she suffered while she was an assistant.

Of course, Sonja couldn't leave at five. She had to finish going through the final edits of the fifth episode and send her approval to Vince before eight a.m.

Sonja was rubbing her eyes after finishing the last scene when she heard, "I guess you were going to blow me off."

She blinked until she saw Delta standing in the doorway, dressed to impress in a white V-necked sweater that looked to be made of cashmere and black slacks that showed off his sculpted lower body. Her eyes fell to the time at the corner of her computer screen.

"Shit, it's eight thirty. Is it too late?" She hoped so.

"It's never too late." He was flirting again.

Sonja sighed. "Is the event over?"

"Did you think it was only going to last for thirty minutes?"

"Huh?" She was so confused.

Not one cell in her body wanted to go wherever Delta was taking her. She wanted to go back to Dexter's house, do some more work, and wait for him and the girls to come home. They had three hard-to-get tickets for the Broadway play *Hamilton*. If they'd had a fourth, she would've gladly blown Delta off again.

"You were supposed to meet me in the lobby a half hour ago. So we haven't missed much."

She grunted. "Oh, right. Then give me a minute."

"Gladly." He flopped down in one of the armchairs.

Sonja concentrated on drafting her email to Vince, letting him know that the final version of the episode was a go and she enthusiastically approved.

"What are you smiling about?" Delta asked.

Sonja hadn't realized she was grinning from ear to ear. "I guess I like what I do."

"Speaking of what you do, how close am I to landing the role of Michael Lockwood?"

She pressed Send, completing her final task of the day, then focused on Delta. "First of all, there can only be one Michael Lockwood, and that's Jay."

"But he's not coming back," he said as though he was sure of it.

She narrowed her eyes at him. His tone irritated her. "Well, it's out of my hands at this point. It's up to Vince and Dexter. I gave my vote."

"And what was your vote?"

"It was what I told you yesterday at lunch."

His naughty smirk was back. "Then that's all I need for now."

Sonja pressed her lips together. Something about his response felt odd, but she didn't understand why. Perhaps it was because she was trying to pretend as though Delta wasn't coming on to her. Her instincts were begging her to call off their date for the night.

"Are you ready?" she asked, her tone lackluster.

He sprang to his feet. "I was born ready."

He was doing it again, looking at her as though he had been lost on a deserted island for a decade and she was a Big Mac.

THEY TOOK SONJA'S HIRED CAR TO THE Metropolitan Museum of Art. She was beginning to like being driven everywhere and thought perhaps LA would be more tolerable if she had someone driving her around that city too. When she asked

Delta what he had done with his day, he went on a long diatribe about meeting with friends—one who owed him money, another who'd stolen his girlfriend once, and another who'd lied about him to the tabloids. By the time they reached the Met, Sonja realized that Delta was a "crisis" man—someone who was never happy unless he was involved in a crisis, usually those of his own making.

"Okay, well, are you ready?" she asked and turned to watch all the nicely dressed people trekking up and down the steps.

"Yep." He hopped out the car and opened her door for her.

Due to the fact that it appeared image mattered at the event, she let Delta hold her hand as they walked up the broad set of steps. There was even a press section, where photographers called Delta's name before snapping their picture. Sonja hated the hoopla. She would've loved it if she had been with Jay instead.

"So what's going on here tonight?" she said close to Delta's ear so he could hear over all the noise.

"It's a secret. And by the way, you look so damn beautiful tonight," he whispered in her ear before they entered the doors.

Sonja looked down at herself. She hadn't tried hard to please when she dressed that morning. She had on black skinny pants and a fitted sweater with extra-long sleeves to keep her hands warm in the cold building. The only fancy detail about her outfit was that the sweater had a peplum.

"All right then," she said dismissively.

There were so many people inside. She really wanted to force Delta to tell her why she was putting up with a crowd that size on a work night. She barely avoided yawning when Delta introduced her to a group of snobbish-looking people.

"I know you, no?" a woman with long black hair and wearing an extremely short cocktail dress asked. Her face resembled a bird, but not in a bad way.

"I don't think so," Sonja said.

"Oh." She rolled her eyes away from Sonja's face and started catching up with Delta and three other guys about what they'd done in the last few months.

Sonja was about to excuse herself and walk around. The longer she stood there, the more she was willing to look on the bright side of things. She had free access to the Met, one of the world's most famous art museums.

"You're Robin Hester," the woman said out of the blue.

Sonja flinched, surprised. "No, but she's my cousin."

"Ah. You look alike. Very beautiful."

"Thanks," was all Sonja could find to say.

"How about I give you my card, and you give it to her? Let her know I want to show her art in my gallery."

For the first time since the woman started talking, Sonja heard her accent. She looked at the woman's business card.

"Why don't you give it to Delta?" Sonja said. "He knows my cousin. He has her paintings in his beach house."

"I tried," Delta said.

Sonja looked at Delta. She hadn't known he was listening.

"Robin Hester is finicky," the woman said then shoved the card at Sonja's chest. "Take it please. She will not be disappointed. You tell her."

One thing was clear—Sonja was not meeting Claudia Francois by accident. She noted the giddy grin on Delta's face. For sure, a lot about him was off. Why the whole production? Why not just ask her to put in a word with Robin for a friend?

Sonja reluctantly took the card. She might or might not follow through.

"Thank you very much," Claudia said. Her eyes shifted to Delta then down.

"By the way"—one of the guys shot a hand in Sonja's direction—"I'm Cornelius."

They shook hands as he gave her the eyes. Yet another guy was subtly coming on to her, and it was strange. Or was it? Sonja looked down shyly, thinking about the days before *Pact of Lies.* She would go months without meeting someone of the opposite sex. Now that she and Jay were passé, she wondered if she should pay attention to other men.

Delta wrapped an arm around her waist, which threw her for a loop. Her skin ran hot. She didn't want to be rude and shove him away in front of his friends even though that was what she felt like doing.

"Um, excuse me." She stepped out of his clutches. "I need to go to the ladies' room."

"I will go with you," Claudia said.

Sonja hesitated. She would have rather gone alone, since the restroom was merely an excuse to escape. She figured ten minutes away and Delta might forget about her.

"Sure," she muttered and walked off.

“How long have you known Delta Foster?” Claudia asked.

Sonja kept a brisk pace. She planned to shake Claudia once they entered the stalls. "Not long."

“How long is not long?”

"I actually met him a few days ago. Robin directed me to him, so I don't understand why you need me and not him as a middle man to get to my cousin."

“Yes, she is very difficult.”

“She can be, but she’s not that hard to reach. She works at our family coffee shop in Culver City.”

“Culver City? Where is that?” She seemed irritated by having to ask for clarification.

“In Southern California, where Robin lives. I mean, she’s not like Picasso or anyone.”

“Picasso? Who compares an artist of today to Picasso?” she said snobbishly. “Robin Hester is the most popular artist in the country at the moment. That’s why I can help her.”

Sonja flinched as her feet came to a grinding halt. “She’s the most popular artist in America?”

“Perhaps in the world. She sold out at Emerald Hall last month. Three of her paintings were purchased by Hans Goleth.” She turned her head slightly. “You’ve heard of Hans Goleth?”

Suddenly someone tapped Sonja on the shoulder, and she turned to see a burly man in a security uniform standing behind her. "Yes?"

She was short with him because she was haunted by what Claudia had said about Robin. After all, Robin's fame was news to her, and Robin told her everything. Perhaps Robin was famous and didn't know it. That wasn't a farfetched conclusion.

"You're Sonja Hester?" the security officer asked.

"Yes."

"Could you please come with me?"

Sonja took a moment to regard him cautiously. "Why?"

"There's a message for you from Dexter Frampton of AEE. He says it's important."

Sonja slapped her chest, remembering she'd told Dexter where she'd be tonight. "Oh my God, is he okay? Are the girls okay?"

He threw his hands up. "I don't know what the message is. You're going to have to come hear it."

Sonja felt as though the room was spinning. She touched Claudia's shoulder. "I'm sorry, I have to go, but I'll give Robin your card when I see her."

Claudia held Sonja's arm. "Will you see her soon?"

"No." She shook her head frantically.

"Could you tell her before you see her then?"

"Ma'am, we should go," the guy said.

"Yes," Sonja said then nodded at him.

Everyone she passed looked as if they were existing in a different dimension, one that was fun, lighthearted, and stress-free. They reached a large staircase, and the security officer stopped.

"Up that way to the right, all the way down the hall, make a left, and enter the third door on the right. Was that clear?" he asked, chin down and eyebrows raised as though he was quizzing her.

"Up, right, end of hallway, left, three doors to the right."

He nodded. "You got it."

He hadn't mentioned what she would find in that room—a phone, a friend of Dexter's, the police? Was Dexter waiting for her and didn't show himself because he wanted to avoid Delta? She bet that was it as she scampered up the stairs, then made the right. She had to pass a velvet rope barrier before making the next turn. However, the person on guard let her through without question. Then she walked quickly up the hallway, counting, one, two, and three—she opened the third door.

Her eyes expanded at the sight of the tall, virile

figure of a man standing in front of the window. Before he fully turned, her nose had picked up his familiar scent and her soul was jumping for joy because it recognized his energy.

"Hey, babe," he said.

Sonja pressed both hands over her heart. "Jay?" she barely said.

"It's me."

CHAPTER 30

SONJA HESTER

Sonja's head floated as they kissed. Were his strong, eager lips really crashing against hers? Was she feeling his hard chest and solid manhood pressing against her? Or perhaps she had landed in the best dream ever as they moaned and fondled each other.

"What—?" Sonja tried to ask what had happened to him but her desire wouldn't let her.

"You smell good, baby," he whispered, his lips and tongue against her neck.

The erotic feeling of his strong and eager lips and wet warm tongue tasting her skin sent shivers down the insides of her thighs. Sonja opened her mouth to try to speak again, but all she could do was sigh.

"I missed you. God, I missed you," he whispered.

She couldn't stop kissing him. His hard body, soft hair, and his sounds of desire made her shiver. Never in her life had she wanted to have sex as much as she did then, but she struggled to let her practical self rise past her lust. After all, Jay had way too many questions to answer. The first was why in the hell had he left Canada without telling her? The second was why hadn't he gotten in touch with her since then? And the third was what in the world was he doing in New York on a random Thursday night? So she forced her lips to abandon his.

"Jay." Her voice was shaky.

"I know," he said as though he could read her mind.

"You know what?"

"If I could've handled it better, I would've." He drew her against him and wrapped his arms around her. "Can I just hold you for a minute?"

She embraced him tighter. "Yes."

Sonja pressed her ear against her chest and listened to his heartbeat—it was still her favorite sound in the world. The seconds ticked by. She knew that at some point, they would need to let go and move on with their night. She also knew that wherever Jay was going, she was following, no questions asked.

"I have a lot to tell you and something I have to show you."

She nodded. "Okay, well, let's go."

He didn't budge. "But I can't be seen here, because I'm not supposed to be in New York."

She ripped her face away from his chest. "Why not?"

Their gazes locked, then he kissed her lips. "Don't worry, I'm not leaving you again."

Her tense body released a spontaneous sigh of relief. "You better not."

He took her hands. "Here's what I need for you to do."

Sonja went out the way she'd come in. Jay had asked her not to disappear on Delta. Instead, she should tell him she had to leave because something had come up. If he asked what, say that the matter was private. That was nearly fifteen minutes ago. After saying goodbye to Delta, she was to meet Jay out front, where Dexter's driver, Victor, would be parked.

The number of people attending the event had doubled.

Sonja grabbed the first person who looked open to speaking to her. "What's this event about again?"

The woman's smile was bigger than the moon. "It's a pop-up exhibit!"

"Like a pop-up restaurant?" Sonja asked.

"Exactly!"

"Who's the artist?"

"We won't know until we go inside. The exhibit just opened."

Sonja turned to look at the double doors that had just opened. "Thank you."

"You're welcome," the woman sang. She was definitely happy.

Of course, Sonja had to stand in line, but it wasn't that long. When she entered the room, she could hardly believe what she was seeing. They were previewing Yayoi Kusami's new exhibit!

Sonja walked through the lights and mirrors with her hand over her mouth. She couldn't stop smiling. Perhaps Delta wasn't the self-centered, shallow person she had taken him for.

Everyone seemed to be in a state of euphoria,

experiencing the ambiance as if they were all high. After all, they had been drinking for the last hour and a half. Only a small part of Sonja wished she could stay and experience the rare event. Mostly, she wanted to get back to Jay. The longer she was away from him, the more she felt she might lose him again.

So she stopped focusing on the exhibits and searched the faces she passed. It didn't take long to see one she recognized.

"Claudia," she said then rushed over to touch the woman's shoulder.

"Ciao," Claudia sang as though they were old friends. "You are back." She hugged Sonja, and for some reason, it didn't feel weird.

"Hey, have you seen Delta?" Sonja asked.

She circled a hand in the air. "He's around somewhere. He's with Cornelius."

"Thanks, I'll go look for him."

Before she could walk away, Claudia gripped Sonja's arm. "This could be Robin Hester. I can make this happen for her."

Sonja stepped out of her grip and held up a hand, motioning her to remain a few steps away. "Don't worry. I'll let her know you want to talk."

"That's excellent!" She was ecstatic again.

Sonja pursed her lips then turned to exit as fast as she could. For some reason, she was stressed out again. Perhaps it was because not only was she eager to see Jay again, as well as find Delta, but she also had to think about convincing Robin to consider giving Claudia a call.

She walked from one end of the museum to the other. There was no Delta in sight. She was about to call it a night when she saw one of the guys Delta had introduced her to earlier, although she'd never gotten his name.

She walked up to him. "Excuse me?"

He looked at her as though he had never met her and therefore she was bothering him. He wiggled his head as if it was his way of sharply saying, what?

"Have you seen Delta Foster?" she asked anyway.

At first he rolled his eyes, then a devious smirk flashed across his lips. "Yes, he's that way and outside." He pointed at a long walkway. "Just follow the first exit signs you see."

"Thanks," she said.

She was confused by his instructions until she saw at least five exit signs up the hallway, but she did as she was instructed and made the first right she saw. Up ahead were two large glass doors. It was pitch black beyond them, and another guard was posted in front of them. As she walked slowly toward her next barrier, she wondered what in the world Delta and Cornelius were doing out there. He was probably getting high. Dexter had referred to Delta as a coke-head on a few occasions. Regardless, she wouldn't be facing him long. All she needed to say was goodbye and good night.

"Can I help you?" the unsmiling guard said.

"I'm looking for Delta Foster. I'm his date."

"Yeah, I saw you with him," the guy said in a lackluster tone and let her pass.

Sonja was eager to say goodbye and get going, but the silence and stillness in the air made her push the door open slowly. She walked onto the unlit patio, where cool air pressed against her skin. Then she heard almost animalistic grunting. She inclined her ear toward the sound. She also heard groaning and the distinct sound of man sucking air through his teeth. Clearly someone was having sex. And as her eyes adjusted to the night, she saw the participants.

Sonja stood paralyzed. Behind a large planter, Delta leaned against the wall while Cornelius gave him a blowjob. She gasped then pressed her hand over her mouth. They were both so focused on their actions that they didn't even sense she was there.

Slowly, silently, she walked backward toward the door. She almost made it, but she tripped over something and hit the ground hard. She got up lightning fast and ran into the building. After seeing that, she surely didn't need to tell him goodbye.

"Are you okay, ma'am?" the guard asked as she flew past him.

"Yep," she said.

Sonja kept moving until she reached the car where Jay was waiting for her.

CHAPTER 31

SONJA HESTER

Sonja would've loved to unsee what she'd just seen. Her adrenaline was still pumping and the car moving down the busy street when she told Jay about it.

"That doesn't surprise me," he said.

Sonja blinked at him as he looked at her hands.

"You're bleeding." He scooted to the edge of the seat. "Victor, do you have Kleenex?"

"Yes, I do." The driver reached over to open the glove compartment.

"What the hell happened?" Jay asked, taking the tissues from Victor.

Sonja raised her good hand to her face. "I fell getting the hell out of there." She wasn't bleeding that much, but when she hit the ground, she must've ripped a gash in her palm.

Jay packed the cut with tissue. The more her excitement subsided, the more she felt the stinging pain.

"That asshole Delta."

"It's not his fault," she said.

"The hell it isn't. You wouldn't have been out there if it weren't for him."

"Did you know he was gay? I thought he was coming on to me this whole time."

"He's not gay." Jay sounded sure of it. "Delta would fuck a lizard if he could. He has problems, Son. He came all the way to Ireland, never told me you're the one who sent him, and came back to New York to seduce you." He thumbed aggressively over his shoulder. "I should go back to that museum and kick his ass."

"He never told you I sent him?"

Jay explained exactly what had happened in his trailer in Ireland. Not only had Delta never mentioned her, but he'd also pretended as though he hadn't already been in touch with Dexter and Vince. The only reason Jay had found out was Delta's cell phone vibrated when he went to the bathroom. The fact he told Jay the lie that production had collected his device while he was on set hadn't surprised Jay either. So Jay decided to dig Delta's device out of his coat pocket and Jay was shocked to learn the caller was Dexter. Generally Dexter would've had an assistant make the call, but he'd decided to call Delta personally to tell him no, *Pact of Lies* didn't have a part for him, and also to go to hell.

"I knew he didn't like Delta, but I thought he was still considering him for the part," Sonja said.

"Let me see." Jay lifted the huge wad of tissue from her gash. "Delta's toxic, babe. It's not a matter of if he's going to fuck up production, it's about when."

"I guess that's why his agent wouldn't find him roles."

"It stopped bleeding," he said.

"Well, you packed enough Kleenex on it."

Jay chuckled then pressed his lips to get serious again. "Delta's toxic."

"Apparently."

They gazed into each other's eyes. It was almost surreal that they were sitting next to each other after all the heartache and stress she had endured while being apart.

He took her uninjured hand. "There's something I have to tell you and show you."

His grave tone alarmed her so much that her lips parted but she couldn't ask anything. She felt as though he was going to break up with her and give some justifiable reason for it.

"Have you spoken to Elaine?"

She jerked her head back. Her sister was the last person she thought he'd bring up right now. "No, why?"

"Then she still has you in the dark."

"Apparently so, unless you're referring to her buying AMTA. But she's trying to get out of the deal because according to her, the company is hemorrhaging money."

"She didn't tell you why?"

Sonja shook her head. "Do you know why?"

He nodded gently. "I do."

As the car bolted through the Holland Tunnel, she listened to a story about Jay being set up and filmed. The tale made her uncomfortable, and almost difficult to follow the details beyond that but she forced herself to listen and be open to the truth. According to him, he hadn't done anything wrong but had met some people he couldn't trust. The guys who'd invited him out on the night they presumed the video was made were two ex-actors who were now strung out on drugs. Vince Adams had hired his wife, who was an investigator, and she'd learned that the two guys had been paid a lot of money to lure Jay to the club.

"Who paid them?" Sonja asked.

"They don't know. It was someone they'd never seen before, but he paid them three thousand dollars up front and promised thirty more if they were able to follow through."

Sonja sniffed cynically. "Wow, that's a profitable carrot to dangle."

"Yeah."

"So you mentioned a video," she said.

Terror flashed in Jay's eyes, and she also saw shame. "Maggie confirmed that the video is a fake."

Sonja continued to study his expression. "It must be pretty awful."

"It's pretty bad, Son. But I didn't do any of it. It's all manipulation."

She held up a hand to stop him from talking. "Then I don't need to see it."

"Really?" He looked shocked.

"If it's not real, then why? Even if it were real, I wouldn't want to watch you do anything you're ashamed of."

He closed his mouth, and his Adam's apple bobbed as he swallowed. "If you don't want to see it, I'm not going to insist." He kissed the back of her hand. "I missed you."

Sonja felt her heart racing. "I missed you so much that I still miss you."

They kissed gently, and she got high off the familiar feeling of her head spinning.

"But why didn't you call me?" she whispered thickly.

He pecked her lips indulgently. "For some reason, Jim Neely wants me to stay away from you. The night we wrapped, he sent someone to the location to show me the video. They had already gotten into our room and packed my shit and told me I couldn't say goodbye to you. When I got into the limo, the driver asked for my phone." Jay shook his head as he gazed off. "It didn't make sense to me until I found out about Delta and Plume."

"Wait, what do you mean?"

"Plume is the one who referred Delta to Dexter on the same day Delta contacted Maggie to ask about an opening on the show for a guy like him."

"Who's Maggie?" Sonja asked.

"She's Vince's wife, and Delta knows her. But they did all of this on the day I arrived in Ireland."

Sonja frowned thoughtfully. "Right, I get where you're going with this."

"They knew way too soon."

Sonja shifted in her seat then told Jay about finding Plume having sex with Nick while she was looking for him.

Jay shook his head. "Fuck."

"What?"

"Nick is the one who came for me after the final scene."

"I know, I saw that." Sonja squeezed her eyes shut as too many questions and not enough answers invaded her mind. "So what do you think it all means?"

"I don't know, babe. Plume wants me because you have me. Jim never wanted me to work on *Pact of Lies* and I did it anyway. And that bruised his fucking ego, so now he wants me to feel his wrath and know that he's the alpha dog in charge."

"You mean to tell me he would ruin your life just because you chose to move forward on a project he didn't agree with?" Sonja asked.

"That's what I'm telling you. Also, I was leaving him for Elaine."

"Oh… that's right."

"But the night he sent me to Ireland, he was so

fucking smug about it. I was telling him I didn't do it, but he was too happy to have something that would give him control of me. Elaine was there."

Suddenly it all made sense to Sonja.

"She saw the video?" she asked.

"Yeah… and now she owns AMTA. I didn't know she had that kind of cash."

Sonja raised her eyebrows. "She does. She doesn't like that she's so wealthy, but she can't stop herself from making herself richer."

"That's the Laney I know and love. But buying AMTA must've cost her billions."

"She has billions."

"Wow."

"Yep."

They smiled at each other.

"So now what?" Sonja asked.

He curled an arm around her and nudged her to move closer, so she scooted over until they were so close they might have melted into each other. Jay kissed her forehead, her cheeks, her chin, and then her lips.

"We wait," he said.

After the dizziness subsided, she opened her eyes. "Really?" she said breathlessly. "Are you okay with waiting?"

"That's all we can do at this point. I'm not even supposed to be here. I was okay with waiting it out until Dexter told me how Delta was sniffing around you."

"But I thought you didn't have a phone on set."

"I didn't at first. When Vince found out where I was and what happened, he convinced Matthew Barbary to give me a phone."

"Who's Matthew Barbary?"

"The director."

"Oh… how did Vince convince him?"

"I don't know. I didn't ask. I thought about calling you every minute of every day, but what could I do? Four episodes of *Pact of Lies* have already aired. The ratings are high and they're eager for the next seven episodes. If that video was leaked, all the work we did would've gone down the drain. And my reputation? No one would look at me with respect after seeing that."

Sonja grimaced squeamishly. "The video's that bad, huh?"

A haze of sadness glossed over his eyes. "It is."

She rested her head on his shoulder. "I'll always look at you with respect."

He kissed her forehead. "Thanks, babe."

They decided to give all the circumstances

responsible for keeping them apart a rest for now and checked into a hotel in Hoboken, New Jersey. It was quieter than Dexter's place. Plus, since it was important that Jay stayed out of sight, hiding in Jersey was easier than in Manhattan. One photograph taken by some excited tourist of Jay West out in the city could go viral in seconds.

When they made it to the hotel, the first thing Jay did was ask the concierge for antibiotic ointment and bandages for Sonja's cut.

When they reached their room, Sonja felt as if she were having a spiritual experience. Her desire was through the roof. Whenever he looked at her, his eyes smoldered and when hers met his, she could feel the fire. Soon, they would let being famished for each other's touch direct their love making.

At the moment, he was focused on dressing Sonja's cut. But their skin touching and their closeness was making that difficult too.

"There," he said after pressing a Band-Aid over her wound. Jay looked at her with his mouth agape, then his Adam's apple bobbed as he swallowed.

It happened so fast. The next thing Sonja knew, his mouth was on hers. Her sweater was coming off over her head. She watched as Jay threw the garment aside and then he tugged at the front of her bra.

"Take that off," he said breathlessly.

Sonja felt herself getting wetter by the second. The way he looked at her—as though nothing was more satiating than seeing her exposed breasts—made her dizzy with desire. So she reached between her tits, unclipped her black lace bra, and slowly separated the material.

Jay took steps back to drink her in. Then he sucked air sharply between his front teeth. Gosh, he looked so sexy doing that. Slowly he moved toward her again, one step, two steps. She couldn't help but count. He curled an arm behind her back, and his breaths sped up as he lowered his head. When warmth, softness, and the delicate nibble of his teeth stimulated her nipple, Sonja's head fell back and she released a moan with a sigh.

Knock, knock, knock.

Sonja and Jay froze, looked toward the door, then at each other.

"I'm coming in," a woman said from the hallway.

Before they could respond, the door opened and in walked a tall, beautiful blonde in all black. Sonja immediately crossed her arms over her exposed breasts.

"What the fuck are you doing, Jay?" she asked.

He jerked his head back. "Maggie?"

Sonja grimaced. Was that Vince's wife, Maggie?

MAGGIE HAD KEPT HER COOL AS SHE WALKED IN, looked at Sonja and said, "I'm Vincent Adams's wife. Could you please put on a robe so we can talk? We'll be in there." She thumbed toward the sitting area.

That was almost a minute ago. Sonja found Maggie and Jay standing in the living room portion of their suite. Now they were all standing in the middle of the furniture but Sonja's legs were so shaky that she wanted to sit. However, she was too confused about what would happen next if she did so. Would Maggie snatch Jay away and make her have to wait forever to see him again?

"I was telling Jay he shouldn't have left Ireland." Maggie left a little space between two pinched fingers and said, "I'm *this* close to ending this, but if they get even an inkling that I'm about to shut them down, they could scramble and we could lose them." She narrowed her eyes at Jay.

"I know," Jay said, scratching the back of his head. "But I don't want to be in Cork while she's here."

She studied him for a moment then sighed, shaking her head. "Plume knows you're not there, and she just placed a call to Neely. He's looking for you. Does Barbary know you're gone?"

Jay shook his head.

She threw up her hands. "What the hell? You were supposed to work with us."

"I am working with you, Mags. Can't I do it from here though?"

She narrowed her eyes even more as she studied him, then she paced. Was she really Vince Adams's wife? She was intense and beautiful, very beautiful. And she was also in the best physical condition of any woman Sonja had ever seen. Her legs were strong but not overly muscular, and so were her arms. The way she moved said that you didn't want to fuck with her.

"I have a plane waiting to fly you back to the set," Maggie said.

Jay sighed dejectedly. "Is that my only option?"

She narrowed her eyes again while scratching

the side of her neck. "Actually, it's probably not the best idea to send you back. But you can't stay here either. Let's sit."

Finally, they all took seats. Maggie explained that the ten people behind the videos were running a sophisticated operation in a small office in Santa Monica. It had taken her people two days to figure out their operation. They recorded footage on a M-Max32030. Maggie said that that camera wasn't for sale in the public marketplace, but it gave a certain type of computer the ability to manipulate pixels and recreate images in any way they wanted. Basically, once they had a full body shot of a subject, they could show him on the toilet, jumping out of an airplane, or fucking someone he'd never met.

What the blackmailers didn't know was that each computer made that edited the video had three secret locater chips. They apparently thought there was only one chip.

The criminals never kept the videos on their in-office servers. They forwarded the material to another site, using encryption and anti-tracking software to hide the data. Once it arrived at its final location, they used more illegal software to rebuild the data.

"Which is great because that meant when we broke the bank, we'd find all the gold."

Sonja was literally on the edge of her seat. "Have you found the gold?"

For the first time, Maggie smiled, although it was slight. "Yes, we have." She sounded proud of it.

"Then who's behind this?" Jay asked.

"I can't tell you yet, but tonight, there'll be arrests. Tomorrow morning at eleven thirty, a memo will be emailed to all the employees of AMTA, letting them know they have a new owner and company president. If that email goes out, then you'll know all is resolved and life will go on as usual."

"Will Jim Neely be arrested or fired?" Jay asked.

"Your agent?"

"Yes."

"I don't know. Neely has nothing to do with the blackmail case, but I heard Elaine Hester isn't too fond of him."

Sonja couldn't read Jay's expression, but he didn't look happy or disappointed to hear his agent wasn't part of the blackmailing scheme. She believed that deep down, Jay liked Jim Neely. While they were in Canada, Jay had spoken of him often, saying he really wasn't that bad of a guy. He just had issues, like everyone else. Whenever someone opposed Jim, the guy took it way too personally, often going to battle over shit he should simply let go. The fact that Jay wanted to move to Elaine's shop was one of those skirmishes. Before Jim had declared war, they could've at least remained friends. Now that was no longer an option.

"But tomorrow is the blackmailers' payday. At nine a.m., the payment that was made today will make it to their overseas account. Then we'll cease that account, all other accounts associated with it, and eventually return the funds to AMTA."

Sonja couldn't help smiling. "By then Elaine will own the company."

"Right." She turned to Jay. "But listen. I just learned they've been sticking close to you and have access to calls made to and from your private cell phone."

"I haven't been using my phone," Jay said.

"I know, but you better believe someone on set was watching you. So you running to New York will make them think you have nothing to lose. And they need to believe that you think you're still being blackmailed to stay in Ireland. However, you running back to Neely will make them think you're still in crisis."

From her inside coat pocket, Maggie withdrew a device that looked like a handheld computer. After turning it on and grimacing while tapping on the screen, she looked at both of them. "Now you've left the set in Cork and are on the way back to LA."

After tapping something else on the device, she gave it to Jay and told him what to say when the call went to voicemail.

"And perform it, please," she added.

The device beeped. Jay cleared his throat and loosened his shoulders as a voice said, "It's Jim Neely. I'm unable to take your call. Leave a message."

Maggie nodded, keeping her eyes intense.

"Jim, I can't do this shit anymore. I'm on my way home. I'll talk to you in the morning." Jay ended the call.

"Good job. Now I'm putting you on that flight." Maggie turned to Sonja. "And you are going to be in a meeting at eight thirty a.m. with Delta Foster, Dexter, and Vince. But first…" She tapped on her device again. "He's been calling you all night. Tell him you don't care what you saw. Thank him for getting you into the exhibit. You left because you had a headache. Tell him you'll see him in tomorrow morning's meeting and that you're excited about it."

She handed Sonja her device. Delta picked up after the second ring. He sounded worried. Their conversation didn't go exactly as Maggie had mapped it out, but Sonja hit all the points.

Then Maggie gave them a few moments alone to kiss goodbye. However, she reminded them that they would see each other at her apartment in the city for dinner tomorrow night, so there was no need to make it a long goodbye.

"You think I'm going to be able to make it back to New York for dinner?" Jay asked.

Sonja didn't even know he knew about the dinner. She was going to tell him after they had made love and he was holding her close again.

"It'll all be wrapped up in the morning, as long as you stick to the plan," Maggie said and told Jay to meet her in the hallway in less than five minutes. She also told Sonja that Victor was parked in front of the lobby, waiting for her.

When they were alone again, Sonja and Jay stood before each other silently, gazing deeply into each other's eyes.

"I don't want you to go," she finally said.

"I don't want to go. But…"

"I know."

Their lips joined and his tongue slid deeply and indulgently into her mouth. Sonja closed her eyes to feel herself floating. Goodness, the dopamine was pumping and she was getting high.

"Okay," he said, breathing heavily as he ripped his lips away from hers.

"You should go."

"I should."

He turned without looking at her. She refused to watch as he walked to the door and left, closing it behind him.

CHAPTER 32

JAY WEST

FRIDAY

Jay stared out over the dark airfield through the small window of the airplane. He had been sitting there for a few hours because he had to time his arrival into LA with his phantom flight from Ireland. He was gripped by anxiety though, and of course he knew why.

His mind raced back to the afternoon he laid eyes on Sonja for the first time ever. That happened often. There was something fateful about that day. He'd only had two other days like it in his life. Once was during his final stay in rehab, when he'd first shaken hands with Dr. Reynolds.

The therapist had said to him, "If you're serious about wanting help, then I'm going to get you some life-changing results. But you have to be open to liberating your entire belief system. If not, then you might as well continue down the path to your destruction." And then he said something Jay had never heard before. "And don't think there's a rock bottom that's going to eventually stop you from falling. Rock bottom doesn't exist. You have to make a choice to change at any stage in your addiction."

Then he'd listed some Jay's peers who had actually allowed their addictions to take them to the grave, left them saddled with incurable diseases, or both.

Jay had been okay with either. He didn't give a fuck about his life or body. But Dr. Reynolds said something simple that, for some reason, resonated with him.

"Jay, why not give happiness a try for at least once in your life? I can help you do that. Try it on and see if you like how it fits."

"Okay," Jay had said. "Why not?"

So Dr. Reynolds had made him face the shadows of his past in ways he never had before.

Riley, his oldest sister, had always been allowed to pitch a tantrum, cry, and whine to get what she wanted. However, even during the first ten years of his life, Jay had been required to man up.

One day Dr. Reynolds had given him the shirt of a ten-year-old boy to stretch and hold up in front of him. "How in the hell is this kid able to man up?"

Jay had felt tears well up in his eyes.

That was when Dr. Reynolds said, "God gave men tears for the same reason women have them. Use them whenever and wherever the hell you want. They'll heal you."

That was the first time Jay had ever cried outside of his job of being an actor. He hadn't even cried when his parents died. And from that day forward, he'd ditched the practice of halting his tears.

He'd also started to understand that the women, drugs, and ruining his reputation as someone who could be relied on was him giving himself permission to pitch a tantrum, just like Riley. When he left rehab, he was happy to see a change in his brain. The shit that used to get him excited before didn't work anymore, especially the sort of women he used to go for. They were all frantic, demanding, and could pitch a good tantrum when they didn't get their way, just like his sister and mother.

Then he ran into Elaine at AMTA, and seeing her reminded him of how he used to hang out with Sonja. Sonja had been his best friend as a kid because she was the embodiment of the untapped peace and joy hidden somewhere in the depths of his soul.

The third and final time he'd felt that fateful feeling in the pit of his stomach was when Sonja walked into the first meeting at AMTA. When she ran out, due to being blindsided by his presence, he'd had to chase after her. He couldn't lose her again.

Finally the pilot had announced that they were ready for takeoff. Jay closed his eyes and relaxed into his seat as the airplane taxied to the runway then darted down it. He was making a lot of plans while they took off.

Jay had spoken to Vince twice since the night he'd answered Delta's cell phone in his trailer. A day ago, Vince had actually told him that Maggie estimated the blackmailing issue would be entirely resolved by Friday morning. Not only that, but it was set in stone that he would continue to play Michael Lockwood and finish up the five seasons of

Pact of Lies as part of the production team, alongside Sonja.

So when Dexter called Jay three hours later and told him Delta was making moves on Sonja, it was a no-brainer for Jay. He stuffed as much as he could into one duffel bag and walked off the compound.

The production camp was situated fifteen miles from Cork, but Jay didn't want to call a cab to meet him at the gate because he didn't want a soul to know he had left. He usually ran ten miles a day when his schedule allowed it, so with the aid of his adrenaline pumping, he had no problem speed-walking about six miles before using the cell phone Matt Barbary had loaned him to call a cab.

He froze his ass off for about a half an hour while waiting, and when saw the headlights of the cab approaching, he tossed the phone into a nearby field of wild grass and asked the driver to take him to a small hotel in town. He checked in as Jake Johnson, his alias, in order to remain low-key. Next, he contacted his personal pilot, who called a friend of a friend able to fly him out of Cork International Airport at six in the morning. That was how he made his escape from Ireland. When Jay arrived in New York City, Dexter had been perturbed that he hadn't stuck to the plan, but he knew what kind of rot Delta was, so he understood.

As his flight soared through the sky, taking him back to the West Coast, Jay stopped second-guessing his decision to return to the States. Something else was clear to him.

He opened his eyes and smiled.

Crystal clear.

After Jay's flight landed at the Santa Monica Airport, driving his car back home felt good. It had been way too long since he'd been behind the wheel. It was five in the morning, and the streets were nearly deserted. Activity in LA ran like clockwork, everybody doing everything at the same time.

A time existed when he would've taken advantage of the empty streets and broken all kinds of speeding laws on the way home. But now that he'd already kissed Sonja's soft lips after nearly a week of believing he wouldn't see her or touch her for months, the anger inside of him had diminished. His car rolled all the way home at the speed limit.

After entering the gates of his property, he understood for the first time exactly what Sonja had meant by his house being sterile. Buying the overpriced home in the Bird Streets used to make him feel like a man who had accomplished manly things. But as he drove up the driveway, studying all the glass and modern mid-century architecture, he felt only like putting the house on the market and moving wherever Sonja wanted to take them. She'd been dreaming about life outside of LA longer than he had.

When Jay walked inside, he felt as if a tremendous burden had been lifted off his shoulders. At least he was among his things. The door from the carport closed and locked behind him, then he stood totally still. He thought he felt something in the air.

Then he looked up the hallway. A slip of paper was lying on the floor. Jay walked over and picked it up. He unfolded it, read it, and grinned. It was Sonja's boarding pass for her flight from Vancouver to LA. He practically skipped down the hallway, happy to have a piece of Sonja from the time he had been forced to stay away from her.

Suddenly something hard hit him in the head, sending volts of pain through his skull. When a stinging sensation sliced through his neck, he knew he was under attack. His knees hit the floor, but he kept his wits about him. On one hand, his fingers were wedged between someone's forearm and his neck. His other hand fought to keep the blade away from his neck.

Whoever had attacked him definitely had the advantage. However, Jay had learned while training with Ty Leonard, a world famous martial artist and MMA fighter, that if he was ever in a fight he hadn't seen coming, his job was to keep his cool no matter what and outthink his opponent.

So Jay closed his eyes and felt exactly where he was in relation to his attacker's body. He felt the attacker's abdomen against the top of his back, so he couldn't head butt him. If it weren't for Jay flexing his neck muscles, the guy could've easily snapped his neck.

But Jay didn't know how much strength he had in reserves. He was losing steam fast, and not gaining an advantage. His arms were shaking. Was this how he was going to die? A loud *pop* filled the hallway, followed by another *pop*. All the pressure against his neck eased. He was no longer struggling to keep a blade from slicing through his neck.

He looked toward the figure down the hallway. "Maggie."

She shook her head and sighed with relief. “Damn, that was close.”

JAY SHOVED HIS HAND OVER THE GASH IN HIS NECK as he scrambled to his feet.

“You okay?” Maggie asked, standing over the guy bleeding and squirming on the floor. He was obviously in a lot of pain, moaning and groaning and asking God to help him.

Suddenly three other guys dressed in black ran down the hallway. Jay tensed up, getting ready for another fight.

“They’re with me,” Maggie said and walked toward the men. “How in the hell did he get this deep?”

The guy shook his head. “We lost him for a while.”

"I know that." She stuffed her weapon back in the holster strapped to her body. "Just take him already. Don't forget to read him his rights." She turned toward Jay's attacker. "You're under arrest."

Maggie's team swiped the guy off the floor and dragged down the hallway and around the corner.

They were exiting through the carport. As far as Jay could tell, he had been shot in the chest and leg.

"He'll live," Maggie said when they were alone.

Apparently she knew where to aim.

"Why was he trying to kill me?" Jay asked.

Maggie turned to look at him. Then she smashed her hands on her hips. "I have to show you something."

Jay nodded and followed her. Just they walked into the carport, a cleanup crew entered.

She told him to get into the passenger seat of a gray sedan. When he was inside, she pulled up a photo of a man on the monitor against the dashboard.

"Recognize him?" she asked.

Jay didn't have to study the face long. "Yeah. He's the guy who came to see me in Vancouver. He said he was a messenger."

"He's Frank Kaplan, Joe Spears, Douglas Sharp, and about twenty other people. But his real name is Harry Duke."

Blood dripped down Jay's hand, so they decided to go back inside and dress his injury. Maggie complimented him for being a real survivor. She had been scared as hell she wouldn't reach him in time. They sat in his living room as she explained that Nick, the production assistant, was actually part of the criminal network.

"They liked to keep people close to their high-paying clients, and the agency was paying 150,000 dollars a month to keep your video secret."

"So what does Nick have to do with this guy trying to kill me?"

"Nick is Duke's nephew. And for some reason, Harry Duke decided to show his face to you. We have Nick in custody, and he's not turning on anyone. He's chosen to go down with the ship. You're the only person, besides his nephew of course, who's ever seen Duke's face, and we were able to follow the money between one of Duke's identities and AMTA's president. Keeping tabs on those two was how we got wind that they ordered a hit on you tonight. They've already been apprehended."

"Archie's been arrested?"

"Yes."

Jay scrubbed his face with both hands. It was hard to believe what he was hearing was true. But damn if someone hadn't tried to stab him in the neck tonight. He guessed his attacker had been trying to make it look as though he were a victim of a burglary. That would've been plausible, since he'd been away awhile.

"Well, I'm glad I'm still alive."

"Me too." Maggie sighed with relief. "And by the way, you're still going to have to go into AMTA. It's still critical we not show our hand. We're putting their lights out gradually."

Jay felt the heaviness of having to go anywhere but back to Sonja. "What do you mean by gradually putting their lights out?"

"As we darken one part of their network, other parts are still live, operational, and making sure nothing out of the ordinary happens. For that reason, we haven't already confiscated their equipment, but we have an eye on all of it."

"But what happens when they learn Archie and this Duke have been arrested?"

"They won't know until it's too late." She smirked a tiny bit. "This is what I learned while doing this job. We know they're about to get caught, but no one ever believes they're going to get caught. So they continue their illegal shit like it's a regular ol' Monday. The footmen only hear from the generals when shit goes awry. The shit has hit the ceiling, but we've already put their generals out of commission, so there's no one around to warn them about what's coming next. But we have to act fast, or they'll figure it out."

Jay nodded. He understood. "What about Plume? Did she have anything to do with any of this?"

"Not to her knowledge. She was involved sexually with Archie."

"Rubenstein?" Jay asked, surprised.

"Yeah, she did it to get work. That's it. She had no knowledge of the blackmail scheme."

"And what about Jim Neely?"

She shook her head. "He's nowhere in the vicinity of this."

On the one hand, Jay found that to be a relief. On the other, it proved what he'd known all along. Jim was a real jerk who made every problem into a war, and he didn't care who had to destroy to win.

CHAPTER 33

ELAINE HESTER

FRIDAY

Elaine ended the call. She pressed the phone against her lap and took deep, steadying breaths because her head felt as though it was going to float away.

"Hell," she whispered.

Deep down, she hadn't had enough faith in Maggie to think she would actually pull off exposing AMTA's blackmailers, confiscate all the video footage, and tie Archie to the crime of blackmailing AMTA in order to pocket as much money as he could. But Maggie had done it, and even told her that Archie had been planning to release all the videotapes after the deal was finalized. He'd already stolen over twenty billion dollars and decided he'd had enough. He hated Elaine, so as soon as she was relying on his former clients for compensation, he would unleash hell on her.

But as Elaine sat in her car in the parking garage of AMTA, she felt like a caged bird that had just been released to the skies.

“Well, you bought it,” she said to herself.

Last night, she’d had a long talk with Gran, who’d told her not to worry about whether or not she’d made a mistake and take things one day at a time. Gran knew Elaine was afraid that Gary was the last man who would ever be in a relationship with her. No real man wanted to be taken care of by a billionaire woman.

Gary wouldn’t be arrested for his involvement in the blackmailing scheme because the girl who worked in his club had been hired by Archie and his co-conspirators to seduce him and convince Elaine to buy the company. So worse than a criminal, Gary was a weakling and a cheater.

A pervading feeling of loneliness washed over Elaine again as her smart-watch dinged. She closed her eyes, braced herself, and looked at the time. It was eleven thirty on the dot. Even though she knew the contents, she read the email that came with the alarm. All of the stolen money had been seized, and the memo regarding new ownership had gone out to each employee and client. Press releases had been sent to the media as well.

Elaine opened her car door and stepped out of her vehicle. The fumes and dreariness of the parking garage always made her feel dismal, but she didn't let the unpleasantness push to the back of her mind this one truth—it felt damn good being the head bitch in charge of AMTA.

Everyone who had ever tried to undercut her clients or get them fired altogether was under her control. She hated shady business, and in her solid career as a manager, she had never engaged in it. Today was a new day for AMTA.

Elaine patted her briefcase and raised her head high as she walked into the president's private elevator, used her key to unlock it, and hit the up button.

If the memo had been distributed, then Elaine couldn't tell. Everyone was hard at work. Those she passed said, "Hello, Ms. Hester," and that was it.

They were all assistants though. It finally dawned on her that the agents were hiding.

When she made it to Archie's old office, she was happy to see that Eden had already arrived. However, Archie's assistant was sticking firmly to her old desk. That's when Elaine realized that today was going to be a lot longer than she had planned, and she'd be working through the weekend. But first…

"Hi, Elaine," Eden said, jumping to her feet.

Elaine stopped in front of Archie's old assistant's desk. "Clara, right?"

"Yes," Clara said with a shaky voice while looking at her with wide, unsure eyes.

"Clara, could you call operations and have them set up two desks in the office next door?" Elaine said, pointing to the right.

"But that's Nancy Emerson's office."

Nancy was the vice president.

"Right. She's fired." She shifted her finger between Eden and Clara. "You two are my assistants. I want you to work together, always be on the same page, and figure out a system that helps you make my job easier. Got it?"

The girls said yes as they looked at each other.

"Good. Now Clara, show Eden how to get Jim

Neely on the phone and tell him he has five minutes to get his ass in my office or security will be escorting him out the building. And then call operations and have them set up those two desks pronto. You both need phones. On top of that, I need IT up here to set up our computers and our private network."

Elaine turned to Eden. "Have Davey from the old office get over here and train people on how I like it. Also get the director of HR in here in fifteen minutes. That's how long it'll take to handle Neely's tiny little ass."

She sashayed into Archie's office. His shit was everywhere. He definitely hadn't seen his arrest coming early enough to clear out. She had been to AMTA often enough to know how to work the phones, so she placed a call to Clara's desk and told her to get the cleaning staff up there to toss Archie's shit into the lost and found.

Then she remembered his spiteful plan to sink her after he'd got away with billions of dollars and told Clara to come in and take whatever she wanted from his office before then. Elaine knew Archie was a lecherous pig and had been sexually harassing the pretty young lady. The days of fucking assistants for sport, which AMTA was notorious for, were over.

Elaine was sending a text to Carrie Newsome, her vice president, at the law office when Neely walked in. Newsome was the only one who could confirm Elaine's purchase of AMTA, and it was time to put their huge transition plan into action. After she hit Send, she looked up. Of course Neely hadn't come alone, the coward. Jay was next to him.

"What are you doing here, Jay?" Elaine asked. She was disappointed to see him because knowing that he looked okay made her less of the ballbuster she wanted to be at the moment.

"Just escorting my ex-agent, right?" he asked.

"Is that what you want?"

"Yes," he said without pause.

"Ah, fuck you, Jay," Jim groused. "I made you, man."

"Yeah, I don't see it that way. I made my fucking self."

"Who do you want?" Elaine asked Jay. He had the pick of the litter.

"Who's your best?"

"Fiona's going to be my VP, so after her, Carl Dawson."

"What?" Jim exclaimed. "Really?"

"Then that's who I want," Jay said.

Jim snorted bitterly. "Fuck you, Jay."

Elaine smiled. Jeez, it was a genuine smile. "Then that's who you'll get."

"All right, Laney, see you soon." He turned to leave.

"Jay," she called before he was all the way out.

"Yeah?"

"I'm sorry. And um…" She looked at Jim. She didn't want him to think he was about to get the soft treatment. "Tell Sonja I love her and I'm sorry for letting this bonehead make me separate the two of you."

Jim shook his head. "See, that's not how I see it."

"And," Elaine said loudly, "I love you too."

Jay winked. "Always, Laney."

On that note, he darted off as if he had been called to put out a fire. It was only after he was gone that Elaine finally wanted to ask him what the hell had happened to his neck. She would have to wait and ask Sonja later.

Jim clapped his hands and rubbed them together. "All right, Elaine, so you want to destroy me?"

"Absolutely, you little elf."

He threw his hands up in surrender. "All right,

I'll absorb the short jokes only if you realize Tom Cruise and I are the same height."

She kept a steady face. She knew all of Neely's tactics. "Self-deprecation will get you nowhere."

"I wasn't self-deprecating, I was explaining." He pointed at the chair across from Elaine. "Can I sit?"

"No."

"Come on, Elaine. I might be a dick, but you know I'm a good agent."

"Your ego is too fragile. Jay is like a brother to me. I had to fight you and your fucking weak tactics for his contract for months, then you used an illegal and salacious blackmail tape to send him away from my sister because you hate me so much. So you, little man, are—"

He held up a hand. "Wait?"

She pressed her lips together. Truthfully, she was having too much fun firing him. Regardless of all the drama she had gone through since learning of the blackmail videos featuring all of her inherited clients, she'd fantasized of the moment when she would fire Asshole Neely.

"What?" she finally asked.

"I'm one of the best in the business, Elaine. So are you. We've been each other's nemeses for a reason. Listen, I've been a low, conniving asshole because that's the kind of ship Archie ran. If you're running a different kind of boat, then I'm going to be a different kind of sailor."

She scrunched one side of her face. "Do you think that helps you? That means you're just a squirrel."

"Come on, Elaine."

Gosh, he was begging. She considered him carefully. He was an enemy, but she'd always believed it was smart to not only keep enemies close but also under her control.

"Whatever, get out of here," she finally said.

He tilted his head. "What, I'm fired?"

"No, get out of my office."

"Then I'm not fired."

"Not yet, but pull your rat-infested-ship bullshit and you're out of here."

"10-4." He watched her with a big ol' grin.

"Leave."

As she waited for the head of HR, Elaine sat in Archie's oversized leather chair and swiveled herself around to look out the window. What a view of Santa Monica and the ocean in the distance. No wonder Archie had felt invincible. That seat was enough to make anyone believe they were king of the world.

Her phone buzzed. She swiveled around to answer it. "Clara?"

"It's Eden. HR's here."

Elaine looked around Archie's office, then patted the arm of his chair. "Put us in the conference room. Then get his furniture out of here and bring in my furniture from the Westwood office in here. Could that be done today?"

"Absolutely," Eden said.

A small smile formed on Elaine's mouth. "Thanks. And by the way, you're getting a raise. Schedule yourself a meeting with me about your next step, okay?"

Eden paused and then said, "Yes, thank you, Elaine."

Elaine hung up, slowly rose to her feet, and headed out to tame her new beast of a company.

CHAPTER 34

SONJA HESTER

Friday

Sonja's cell phone played Alice Walker's "Fool For You." She swiped the device off the nightstand and turned the volume down, but not off. Last night when she'd set the alarm to wake her, she'd wanted to hear something that made her cells gallop. It was six in the morning, but the song didn't quite work.

Last night, for the first time, Sonja had used her guest keys to enter Dexter's brownstone. The lights were dim and the house was quiet. On the drive back to Brooklyn, she'd called Dexter and he'd told her the girls had gone to bed but he was in his office working. After she locked all six bolts on the door, she went to the office to thank Dexter for saying whatever he'd said to make Jay leave Ireland and come to New York.

He sat back in his chair and laced his fingers behind his head, grinning. "It wasn't supposed to happen that way, but I guess he couldn't take the idea of Delta buddying up to you."

She grinned as she snorted. "I guess not." She looked up again. "By the way, Maggie Adams. Is she a real person, or was that a figment of my imagination?"

Dexter chuckled. "She's real, and interesting. She always makes me ponder what experiences in a person's background make them grow up into Maggie Adams."

Sonja yawned. "Yeah, I'd watch that movie."

"You should go to bed. It's been a long day."

She sighed tiredly. "You're right."

They said good night, but Sonja hadn't gone right to sleep. First she called Gran, and they talked about the sale of LH Real Estate. Gran promised that she was sure of her decision. She had given it a lot of thought.

"Darling, I only have twenty or so good years left on this Earth. I'm not going to spend them worrying about business."

"Then good for you, Gran."

They decided to have dinner on the day after Sonja was scheduled to return to LA.

Next, Sonja called Robin, who of course only had a few minutes to spare. Apparently she was finishing a collection for a new exhibit.

"Someone gave me a business card to give you," Sonja said.

"You know I make my own connections."

"I know. I told her that in a roundabout way. But I mean, could you at least take the business card so that I can fulfill my promise?"

She sighed. "Okay. By the way, I miss you and I love you."

Sonja beamed. "Same here. Oh, and I wanted to ask you—how in the world are you even friends with someone like Delta Foster? I would think the two of you would have nothing to say to each other, especially after he started spouting his crisis of the moment."

"Delta and I aren't friends. But someone told me he might be able to help you find Jay."

"Who?"

She went silent.

"Who, Robin?"

She grunted exasperatedly. "Plume."

Sonja's mouth fell open. "Ashbury? Plume Ashbury?"

"Yes."

"But I told you how much trouble she'd given me during production."

"You wanted somebody fast. I was with Janet Mosley."

"*The* Janet Mosley?" She was an at-the-top-of-the-food-chain actress.

"Jan made a good point about Plume always trying to find her way up Jay West's ass. Talk about a crisis? You were having one, so I called Plume and she gave me Delta's info."

"Then you've never met him?"

"Not that I recall. But that doesn't mean we never met. Plume said he was a fan of my work."

"Right, he has your paintings in his beach house. Recent paintings."

"Which pieces?"

Sonja described two of them.

"Oh, right. I sold those to Plume."

"Plume doesn't strike me as someone who's into art."

"She is, and I sold those to *her*."

"No way," Sonja said, shaking her head.

"Don't judge her. She can be superficial and

reactant, but people are always more than the sum of what we see or what they show us. But you know that already."

Leave it to Robin to bring some depth and humanity to Plume Ashbury's ball of mess. Only Sonja didn't want to hear her rationale at the moment.

"Whatever. It's late. I'm going to bed now."

"See ya," Robin said briskly. "Love you."

"Ditto and ditto."

Regardless of Robin humanizing Plume, Sonja slept well. But when her alarm went off and one of her favorite songs played, she was still so tired she could have slept for at least six more hours.

Then she remembered that tonight at dinner, she would see Jay, and that put some pep into her. They would have the weekend together. She planned to suggest that they mosey back over to their hotel suite in Hoboken and watch movies and make love for most of the weekend. With that in mind, Sonja sprung out of bed and rushed to the bathroom to brush her teeth, shower, and go through the rest of her morning ritual.

By the time she made it to the table for breakfast with Dexter and the girls, all of her worry was back. She hoped nothing went wrong with Maggie's plan, that the people who had been blackmailing Jay would be stopped cold turkey and there would be no negative fallout because of it.

"Are you okay?" Mariana asked.

Sonja gazed at the cutest, most purely empathetic face she'd ever seen and smiled. "I'm fine. Tired."

"Lots of work?" Maribel said.

She chuckled. "A lot."

"Mom and Dad always say when it's time to take a break, then you should take it." Maribel looked at Dexter.

"That's right."

"Then this weekend, I'm going to rest and relax." She omitted making love.

"We're going to Grandma's house in Hanford," Mariana said, her eyes lighting up. "You want to come with us?"

"Come on, you guys, you can't take Sonja everywhere with you," Dexter said.

"I do want to go, but I've already made plans with my boyfriend." Shoot, Sonja may have said too much. She checked Dexter's expression for concern, but he was still smiling.

"You mean with Daddy?" Mariana asked.

"No," Sonja and Dexter said at the same time.

"We told you we're just friends," Dexter said.

"But you make the perfect couple and we like her," Maribel said.

"Who's your boyfriend then?" Mariana asked.

Sonja's insides beamed as she leaned across the table. "If I tell you, then you have to keep it between us until Monday at least."

"Or Saturday," Dexter said.

Sonja narrowed her eyes curiously at him. It seemed as though he had all the faith in the world in Maggie's abilities to turn things around.

"Okay, what's his name?" Mariana asked, unable to contain her curiosity.

"Jay West," she whispered.

The girls looked at each other with wide eyes.

"You mean *the* Jay West?" Mariana asked.

Sonja nodded. "Um-hmm."

Mariana slapped her hand over mouth, and Maribel screamed.

"He's Daddy's friend too. Is he going to come over and stay too?" Maribel asked.

Dexter raised his hands in a motion reserved for stopping traffic. "No, he's not."

"But he has to come over to visit Sonja, doesn't he?" Maribel whined.

"He will," Sonja said and winked at Dexter. "Next week, we'll all have dinner. How about that?"

The girls waved their hands in celebration. Sometimes Sonja had to remember how big of a movie star Jay was. Unlike Delta, he never reveled in it.

AFTER DROPPING THE GIRLS OFF AT SCHOOL, SONJA and Dexter were driven to work. He told her that he'd received a text from Vince and he wanted them to meet with Delta first thing in the morning.

"He's tired of the guy trying to reach Maggie," Dexter said.

Hearing Delta's name made her cringe, though it wasn't because she hated him so much. "He's such an elaborate liar."

"That he is. The dude's uniquely damaged."

Sonja looked out the front window for a few beats. She was getting used to all the skyscrapers and general bustling about. "Are we meeting with him because there's a role for him?"

"That's where it gets tricky."

She looked at him with an expression that asked what he meant, and Dexter went on to explain the terms Vince and Maggie had decided to offer Delta. As she listened, Sonja realized Vince may have been the owner, operator, and CEO of AEE, but Maggie had more say-so in her husband's business than most wives.

The meeting with Delta was set for eleven a.m. Sonja had no time or space in her mind to worry about seeing him again, especially after getting a look at him receiving a blow job from Cornelius last night. She didn't know what to think about that. She'd grown up in LA, so she understood that in a lot of cases, sex didn't define sexuality. The act was used for a lot of reasons—to ease the pain, to fabricate love, and of course for power. She'd learned all of that by having many conversations with Gran, who always kept the lines of communications open for every subject under the sun, especially sex. Sonja only wondered what was Delta's poison.

Regardless, she had a budget meeting first thing in the morning. They had bagels, fruit, and a lot of good coffee. That meeting lasted an hour, then one of the ancillary actors wanted a call back to confirm that she would actually be cast in the next season.

Only then did Sonja realize that she had to have Taylor draft an email to the cast to put their minds at ease. So she did that; however, she instructed Taylor to not send the memo to Plume. Instead, she wanted Taylor to get Plume on the phone as soon as possible. She didn't want to leave it up to Jay, Dexter, or any of the other producers to tell her she was going to be written off the show.

Of course Plume didn't answer her phone. But that was fine, because before Sonja went into her meeting with Delta, Jay called to say that he loved her, missed her, and would be in New York for dinner that evening. Even though she was in a rush, she stayed on the phone with Jay until the very last minute before the meeting started, and her head felt floaty when she walked into the conference room. The only people present were Dexter and Vince.

"Where's Delta?" Sonja asked.

Dexter shrugged, and Vince crossed his leg as though he needed to do it in order to contain his frustration. She had been around Vince long enough to know that he liked for all of his meetings to start on time, which was why she'd rushed Jay off their way-too-short call. A lot had happened in LA that morning, but he'd had no time to tell her.

Sonja took a seat the table. "But he's been eager to hear whether or not there's a role for him."

Vince grimaced while checking his wristwatch. "He has two more minutes."

Dexter shrugged his forehead at Sonja.

"I'm only doing this for Maggie anyway," Vince muttered, then looked at his watch again.

Sonja realized she had nothing to do but wait. Before anyone could fill the awkward moment, everyone looked up to see Nicole, the receptionist, escorting Delta.

Vince uncrossed his legs and moved his chair closer to the table, although he hadn't dropped his frown. It appeared Dexter had no reaction to Delta whatsoever.

"Thank you, beautiful," Delta said, dazzling Nicole with his flirty eyes.

She turned bright red and giggled as she looked down and walked away.

Vince's frown intensified. "You're late."

"You're busting my balls over three minutes, Vince? It's the elevator in your building. It stops about twenty times before it gets to your floor."

Vince shook his head. "You always have an excuse."

"What should I have done?"

"Leave earlier."

Delta sniffed bitterly. "Do I have a fucking chance here, or am I just wasting my time?"

Dexter cleared his throat to get everyone's attention. "So—"

"Vince," Delta said, interrupting Dexter, "I'm talking to you, not him."

"Well, he's talking to you, so listen the hell up." Vince crossed his arms.

Delta shook his head, and his combative glare reluctantly fell on Dexter. However, there was a change in Dexter's eyes too. Sonja had never seen him look as though he was ready for battle. The two men obviously hated each other, and she believed there was a story behind it, even if Dexter said there wasn't.

"As I was saying," Dexter began. "We can talk about a future role in the series after you've completed a three-month cycle in rehab and have been sober for three months, complete with regular check-ins with Dr. Bradley Reynolds."

Sonja smiled to herself. He was Jay's therapist, the one who'd helped save his life.

Delta snickered harshly. His glare could set the polar ice caps on fire as it landed on each one of their faces and stopped on Sonja's. "You're part of this too."

"Um…"

"Leave her alone," Dexter snapped.

"You heard the terms," Vince said. "If it were up to me, I wouldn't have a damn thing to do with you. You're toxic, and I've already written you off. Maggie's the reason why you're sitting here and I have to look at you."

"Fuck you, Vince," Delta growled as he shot to his feet.

Vince shrugged as he snarled, a response that was aggressive and dismissive.

Sonja couldn't close her mouth as Delta looked at Vince as though he were a hurt child who wanted to pitch a fit, cry, and rip off Vince's face.

"Just wait," Sonja blurted, surprisingly having a real visceral reaction to the situation.

All the men looked at her, and she detected irritation and a gleam of hope that brought some calm in their eyes.

"Delta, come on. Is it hard to go away for a while and let someone help you?" She motioned with her hands in front of her chest because she didn't know how to say what she wanted to say without possibly offending him, especially since all she could see was his face while he was being pleasured last night.

"With all due respect, cunt, fuck you." Delta whipped around and stormed out before any of them could respond.

Sonja's mouth was caught open.

"Sorry about that, Son," Dexter said.

"Yeah…" Vince said with a sigh. The kind, gentle, yet serious and pragmatic Vince was back. "The guy is hopeless. I know you want to fix him, just like my wife does, but he's too damaged."

All Sonja could do close her mouth and nod. "I'm okay." Her words were barely audible.

"Good. Don't let him rattle you. Let's get back to work. We have a day here." Vince gathered his pad and what looked like a contract for Delta to sign and walked calmly out of the room.

Sonja and Dexter sat in silence for a moment.

"What just happened?" she said.

"Did you really think he was going to bite?"

"Maybe. There's so much animosity between the two of you. Has he done something to you personally?"

Dexter scratched the back of his head. "He's a bum who doesn't take responsibility for his shit. You haven't known him long enough to get where Vince and I are with him. But he's already started off on the wrong foot with you, lying and shit." He narrowed his eyes at her. "Do you get it?"

Sonja pushed her back against her seat. She wanted to be empathetic and hopeful, but she understood Dexter's point. "I get it."

And on that note, they rose from the table and went on with their day. One meeting ran into the next until Sonja sat with Taylor to watch the full fifth episode of *Pact of Lies*. They both agreed it was everything it should be and more, so she passed it on to Dexter, who would watch it and give it to Jay before it reached Vince's desk.

Sonja spent the rest of the afternoon in the editing bay, putting together episode six. That was going a lot faster since she and Tony had figured a system to work together more efficiently. It wasn't until Alice Walker sang "Fool For You" on her phone again that Sonja was able to detach from her work and look forward to the rest of the evening.

In two more hours, she would be at Vince Adams's house for dinner. Finally she would see Jay again. They had been texting each other all afternoon. She knew when he'd arrived at Santa Monica Airport, when he'd bought a sandwich and coffee, how the food had tasted, and when he'd boarded. That was six hours ago, so when she and Dexter arrived at Vince's house together, she expected Jay to be there. He wasn't.

However, Sonja hadn't expected to see what she saw. She thought Vince would have a butler of some sort answering the door. Instead it was Maggie, and she was wearing loose-fitting vintage-style jeans with holes on both knees, a white V-neck T-shirt, and white slip-on tennis shoes. She looked nothing like the James Bond-like character Sonja had met last night. The transformation was jarring.

"Welcome," Maggie said with a fantastic smile.

First she hugged Dexter, then Sonja. It was an embrace long enough to be friendly and inviting but stopping short of saying "we're best friends." She imagined that with a woman like Maggie Adams, that status had to be earned over time.

Sonja heard music playing in the direction Maggie was leading them.

"What a stunning apartment," Sonja said, taking in every detail of the open living room beyond two large, white brick pillars.

The floor was light wood, but the carpets were fluffy with colorful patterns that matched the unique pendant lights, furniture, throws and pillows, shelving, and wall art. The wall of windows showcased a wide open view of the city beyond and mostly darkened Central Park. The environment felt warmer than she'd imagined, like a contemporary yet traditional New York City country-house.

Maggie pointed out where the bathroom was, then mentioned the night's menu: prime rib, chicken Marsala, pasta with creamy garlic and mushroom sauce, glazed carrots, and a lemon-and-pepper roasted vegetable medley. Then she announced that she'd helped cook by boiling some water, but Daisy had cooked the rest.

Sonja didn't have to ask if it was *the* Daisy Dexter had been in love with. Nearly all the life drained out of his gorgeous face as he smashed his lips together. He only did that when he was nervous.

"It smells delicious," Sonja said, because the scent was making her hungrier than she already was.

"I'm glad, and I've been wanting to congratulate you on the success of your show." Maggie said that louder because the beautiful guitar music was filling the air.

"Thank you!" Sonja said.

They'd made it to another large, west-facing family room. It spanned the entire length of that side of the apartment and even had outside space with a swimming pool enclosed in glass. A few kids were in it, splashing around and diving in. Way on the opposite end of the deck, a guy was playing guitar while a sexy woman dressed in black stretch pants and a sleeveless black turtleneck sweater was doing modern dancing. But she wasn't alone. Two kids, a boy and girl, were beside her, holding hands and turning each other around. They laughed their heads off whenever the dancer gracefully kicked her heel over their heads. The guitar player seemed to be torn between watching her and laughing with the kids, who had to be about two or three years old. Sonja couldn't help but watch with a smile.

"That's Charlie on guitar, Angel dancing like an angel." The most heartfelt smile Sonja'd ever seen made itself across Maggie's lips. "And Angel's two sidekicks are her daughter, Abigail, and Jack and Daisy's son, Ed."

Sonja stole a peek at Dexter. Thank goodness he was grinning at the kids too.

Then suddenly out of nowhere, one of the most stunning creatures Sonja had ever seen came walking in their direction. She wore her curly brown locks short, almost the length of Robin's, and she had on a navy blue maxi dress with long sleeves and a boat-neck top. The dress clung to her curves, and the hem touched the floor. With her posture and the elegant manner in which she carried herself, the woman looked regal.

"Dexter, you made it," she said.

"Daisy!" he sang and opened his arms to receive her.

They hugged. Dexter turned red again, and Sonja could see why he had the natural inclination to fall in love with her. Hell, she was falling for her and hadn't even met her yet.

Dexter pointed at Sonja. "Daisy, this is Sonja." Then he directed his hand toward the goddess. "Sonja, Daisy."

Daisy put her hands together as if in prayer and bowed slightly. "It's my honor to meet you."

She was definitely one of the fans Vince had mentioned.

"Well thank you," Sonja said. "And thank you for cooking and for including me."

Then the doorbell rang again. Maggie excused herself and walked down the hallway as fast as she could. Sonja heard Dexter and Daisy getting caught up on what had been going on in their lives, but Sonja kept her eyes on Maggie. And finally she saw who had arrived. Her heart filled with joy as her jaw dropped.

CHAPTER 35

SONJA HESTER

THE BIG DINNER

Sonja turned toward Dexter to make sure she was seeing what she was seeing. For the first time since Daisy showed herself, she lost his complete attention.

Walking in step with Maggie, and smiling as much as she was able to, was Robin. Jay was behind her, grinning proudly. He deserved that expression too. He'd done well for sure.

After hugging Robin, Sonja embraced Jay then leaned back to get a look at the bandage on his neck. "What happened?"

He pecked her lips. "I'll tell you after dinner."

Sonja frowned as he took her hand and led her into the family room.

THINGS WENT FAST FROM THERE. MAGGIE AND Daisy announced everyone had arrived, and they went off to prepare the table. Finally Sonja saw Vince and Daisy's husband, Jack Lord, sitting near the pool, engaged in a conversation while watching the three boys, who were probably six or seven years old, enjoying themselves in the pool.

But now they were ushering the boys out of the water for dinner, something she'd thought they would have nannies do. It was strange, because all of them had a job, either watching the kids or preparing dinner, and she wondered if that was planned or occurred naturally.

When Angel and Charlie ended their song and dance, the two little kids scurried to the middle of the room to play with some large plastic building blocks. As Sonja and Robin shook Charlie and Angel's hands, Angel explained that the kids had already eaten dinner but were so excited to be around each other that they were fighting sleep. Sonja couldn't stop smiling while watching them play. They reminded her of how close she and Robin had been.

Jay never let go of her hand as they sat on the humongous sectional with Dexter, Robin, Charlie, and Angel, who kept most of her attention on the kids. Sonja learned that Charlie worked with Jacques Blanchard, the famous musician and composer. Angel was Blanchard's daughter. Sonja tried to contain her excitement—after all, she was huge of fan of the man. His song "Swing By Night" was one of her alarm ring tone favorites.

While Dexter, Jay, and Charlie reminisced about a project they had worked on together, Sonja took the opportunity to ask Robin what in the world had prompted her to come all the way to New York for dinner. That wasn't like her at all.

"And why hadn't you mentioned it last night?"

"If I told you, then it wouldn't have been a surprise," Robin said. "And I just made the decision to come today."

"But how did you even get the invitation?"

"And scene," Angel said and shot to her feet.

Charlie chuckled, and when everyone saw what was so funny, they laughed too. The two kids had fallen asleep on their building blocks and each other. Angel explained that they'd had a full day of swimming, attending a street fair, and generally being excited.

Jack Lord—strapping, handsome, and triple sexy—came to carry Ed off to bed. Angel collected Abigail as well.

"Dinner time!" Maggie called.

And as everyone made their way to the table, Jay made sure he and Sonja lagged behind. "I haven't kissed you properly," he said.

Sonja cracked a naughty smile before his mouth indulged in hers, sending flames of desire through her body.

"I love you," he whispered when their lips separated.

"I love you too."

Her legs wobbled as she walked to the dining room. Even though Sonja was seated next to Jay, she couldn't help but notice that all the other couples were sitting nowhere near each other, which confirmed what she had been feeling all along. This wasn't an average couples' dinner party; it was a family gathering.

They passed the dishes around, and everyone served themselves. Three conversations were happening at once, but Sonja couldn't help but listen to Daisy and Angel discuss planning a party in France next year for their father's birthday. It took her a while, but she could definitely see the resemblance between Angel, Daisy, and Jacques Blanchard.

Daisy noticed her watching them and smiled. "So I don't think you know, but Angel, Maggie, and I are huge fans of *Pact of Lies*. When it's on, we like call each other and talk about what happened and try to figure what's going to happen next."

"How did you even come up with that story?" Angel asked.

Sonja couldn't help but turn to Robin for permission to reveal any parts of their grandmother's past. But Robin wasn't even paying attention to them, although she was definitely studying everyone at the table in her own unique way of socializing.

So Sonja told them about her grandmother and how she'd come to California and started her own business, which turned into an empire. "And she has this weird friend, who she never really socialized with—Ms. Jenkins. She has, like, a million cats in her apartment and, knowing that I was allergic, she would call me in to fix stuff that she broke on purpose."

Maggie snapped her fingers. "Ida Lawry!"

"Yeah. How did you guess that quickly?"

"Because Ida doesn't care for people, including herself. But you're not on the nose with it. You have to watch her and listen to what she says and the subtleties in her actions. What you do is damn near expert, Sonja." Then Maggie explained that when Vince had asked her to read the screenplay, she'd put her life on hold to finish it in three hours. "I didn't even have to make any edits in my head. It was that good."

Sonja felt herself squeezing Jay's hand tighter under the table. All the adulation and attention was making her extra nervous.

"But what about you all? You're such a big, beautiful family. How did the couples meet?" she asked. That was what she really wanted to learn. She wanted to file their lives and who they were into the index in her brain and pull them out as characters in future stories.

First, Daisy and Jack spoke about how they'd met in Martha's Vineyard. They told their story in conjunction, with her saying something and him telling the next part. Then they passed the tale onto Maggie and Vince, who told their story in the same way. Sonja could tell they'd been asked the question before because their narratives were smooth and contained all the plot points of a well-told story. By dessert, it was time for Angel and Charlie's story.

"So what about the two you?" Angel asked, meaning Sonja and Jay.

Sonja and Jay looked at each other. Just thinking about how they began made her soul flutter.

"We actually met for the first time when I was eleven and she was ten," Jay said.

Sonja felt his pulse racing and hand moisten. He was nervous.

"We became best friends and started writing and producing all of these neighborhood plays together. And we would charge the neighborhood kids to see them."

"Robin, did you buy a ticket?" Dexter asked.

Since they sat down for dinner, Robin hadn't made a peep, although she had followed a lot of the conversation and smiled every now and then—as much she would allow herself anyway. What Sonja so appreciated about the people at the dinner table with them was that they allowed Robin to be herself, never asking her a question to get her to say something.

Then Sonja remembered what Claudia had said about Robin. She was famous. Perhaps they already knew about Robin's natural temperament, or maybe they were all intuitive enough to sense it. However, Sonja had noticed Dexter being unable to keep his attention off Robin, who simply ignored him. It was clear he was biding his time, waiting for the perfect opportunity to gain her attention. Now he had found it.

"A ticket to Sonja and Jay's puppet shows?" she said in a cynical tone.

Dexter must've liked how she said that because his face lit up. "Yeah."

"No."

"Oh, come on, Robbie. You were a fan," Jay said jokingly. He let go of Sonja's hand and leaned forward, ready to address the table.

"You've been pretty quiet," Dexter said, his focus still on Robin. "How are you enjoying dinner so far?"

Her eyes narrowed a bit as she studied him. "I'm enjoying dinner very much."

They seemed to have captured the attention of everyone at the table.

"Why? What do you enjoy about it?"

Robin adjusted in her seat and glanced at Sonja, who knew her cousin was expecting her to bail her out of the awkward situation.

"Well, she—" Sonja said.

Dexter raised a hand. "No. Let her answer."

Sonja jerked her head back. For the first time since she'd met Dexter, he had done something that made her want to smack him across the face. After all, it was her job to swoop in and protect Robin.

Sonja watched her cousin with her mouth agape.

After a moment of glaring at Dexter, Robin grunted thoughtfully. "You ever notice family portraits from earlier decades? How unsmiling and miserable the participants appear? Take Grant Wood's *American Gothic*. They used to forbid smiling in photos as being socially unacceptable."

Sonja's gaze fell on all the faces at the table. Robin had their complete and undivided attention.

"Then they went from frowning to faking it in the 50s," Robin continued. "Which I think is worse. I always wondered why—until recently, and certainly at this very moment." She smiled thoughtfully as she always did when she was living in her analytical mind.

Silence lingered for a few seconds. Jay had taken Sonja's hand again and that relaxed her some.

"Are you going to tell us what about now gives you answers to what you've been pondering?" Daisy asked. She seemed to be on the edge of her seat, eating up everything Robin had said.

"I'd like to know the answer to that too," Dexter said.

"Well, the idea of killing joy, making it irrational, evil, or even ungodly, allows this"—she raised her hands demonstratively—"power that we as humans create, we give it the ability to maintain control. But if we embrace joy, happiness, and love, well, that creates freedom and that scares people. We're used to living in bondage. And so..." Robin raised her glass of wine to her lips. "We continue therein. Except you all, of course. It appears you've unlocked the box and stepped out of it."

"You're pretty severe, aren't you?" Dexter asked.

"Am I?"

Sonja squeezed Jay's hand under the table again. "When we were younger, we used to call her Wednesday."

"It's okay, babe," Jay whispered in her ear. "Robin's handling herself well."

She quickly turned to look at him. Was it that obvious she couldn't help herself from riding to her cousin's rescue?

"Why do I feel like saying something funny to ease the heaviness?" Charlie asked.

"I have something to say," Jay said.

Sonja turned toward him. He had a finger in the air. Then he cleared his throat and looked at her, beaming. Right then, she knew whatever he had to announce was about her.

"Sonja." His gaze landed on her face, and the intensity in his eyes made her feel as though she was having an out-of-body experience.

Robin, who was sitting on the other side of her, took Sonja's bandaged hand. When Sonja turned to look at her, she was grinning in a way that wasn't Robin-like.

Jay got down on his knees.

Sonja's gaze jerked from one smiling face to the next. "Oh my God."

"We were always meant to be," he said. "I loved you from the moment you told me your puppet's name was Skinny Pig."

Robin let go of Sonja's hand so she could cover her mouth. Were those tears rolling down her cousin's face? Yes. She was crying.

"We've spent fifteen years away from each other. I'm sure that was God's plan, because during that time, I had to learn to understand that I want to spend the rest of my life with you. I hope you want the same." Her heart nearly stopped when Jay brought out a tiny ring box and opened it. "Sonja Lorraine Hester, will you become Sonja Lorraine Hester-West?"

She snorted, chuckling. They were having an inside joke moment. When they were kids, they used to talk about one day having to marry somebody. She'd never liked the idea of having a husband, mostly because she thought changing her name would define her whole life.

"Why can't the man change his identity and not the woman?" she would say.

"Jeez, Sonja, it's just tradition and not a law. You don't want to change your name, don't change it."

It was a weird argument for thirteen-year-old kids to have, but now that she looked back, it was clear Jay had taken her stance against marriage personally.

Everyone was quiet and smiling.

"You know I will. Yes, every day, yes!" Sonja replied.

The next thing she knew, she was swept off her feet.

"Congratulations, darling!" came her grandmother's voice.

Sonja ripped her attention toward the sound. A monitor had risen out of a console behind her. Gran and Elaine were waving at them from the screen and sending them kisses and their blessings.

Soon, dessert resumed. Dexter and Robin squared off some more, and everyone had a front-row seat to their back and forth over politics, religion, and every other subject one wasn't supposed to bring up in polite company.

It was nearly midnight and everyone at the table was involved in Dexter and Robin's mating ritual—by chiming in and egging them on—when Sonja and Jay decided it was time to go.

"So what happened to your neck?" Sonja asked as soon as they were riding down the private elevator to the lobby.

"Someone attacked me in my house."

She gasped. "What?"

"It was connected to the blackmail scheme." He told her all about it on their way to Dexter's place to pick up her things.

"I could've lost you," she said while the car parked in front of the brownstone.

"I could've lost the opportunity to love you forever. But, baby, I don't feel like our time together is going to end any time soon. Let's just live a nice safe life from this point out."

She cracked a smile. "No skydiving?"

He smiled too. "None."

"Not even if we're together?"

"That's no guarantee we'd die together."

Sonja grimaced squeamishly. "Yikes, that's kind of morbid, isn't it?"

He gently kissed her, making her mind do back flips. "It is," he said breathlessly. "That's why I changed the subject."

They went inside Dexter's home to collect her suitcases. She told him the funny story of her first day she arrived in the city, which included being trapped in a stinky train car with a guy for an hour and struggling to walk to Dexter's house from the subway. She also told him about Maribel and Mariana.

"Ah, great girls," he said before they headed back to the car.

"We're going to have dinner with them a few times this week, okay?"

"I'm in," he said and locked the door behind them.

They kissed and groped each other all the way to their five-star hotel in Manhattan, where Jay had reserved a luxury suite for the whole upcoming week.

They couldn't avoid cameras snapping pictures and girls exclaiming when they saw Jay. Sonja had learned that New York truly was the city that never slept. The good thing was that inside the hotel, they entered a special elevator that took them straight to their suite.

Once their luggage was brought up and they were alone, they wasted no time stripping each other out of their clothes and falling into bed. Sonja was ready for Jay to make love to her, and that was what he did, over and over and over again.

It was hard to sleep, even though they were both exhausted. They'd had as much sex as they could, but only a few minutes ago, Jay had run out of steam.

Sonja chuckled as she rubbed Jay's penis. "He's retreated."

He laughed. “But he’s gotten a lot of mileage tonight, so he deserves it.”

“True.”

He held her tighter, and Sonja sighed in heavenly happiness as she pressed her ear against his chest and engaged in her favorite activity, which was listening to his beautiful heart.

“We were once friends, and now we’re forever lovers.”

Jay kissed the top of her head. “You’re still my best friend, baby.”

“And you’re still mine. Who would’ve thought those two kids we were from our old neighborhood would be getting married?”

“I always knew. Then I forgot. But when I saw you again, I remembered.”

“Ah…” Sonja lifted her head to gaze into his eyes. Gosh, she loved him.

As they kissed… kissed again… kissed some more, they did some laughing about Dexter and Robin snapping at each other throughout the night. They talked about how much they liked the Lords and Adamses.

After laughing at how Ed and Abigail had passed out while playing with building blocks, they decided they wouldn’t be opposed to starting their own family. They talked about how different they would be from their own parents. They admired how hands-on Jack Lord was, and admired that the family didn't talk business at the dinner table.

Then Jay renewed his decision to take private culinary classes while working on *Pact of Lies*. The sun was coming up when Sonja yawned. Jay snored lightly, his head resting on her breasts. Finally he had fallen asleep, so she closed her eyes and did the same.

TAMING THE SHREWD EXCERPT

Elaine Hester paced in front of the glass wall of her penthouse office, which displayed a view of the west side of LA. She checked her watch again. Zachary Lord was eleven minutes late. She presumed that, like most men of his stature, he grasped the importance of being punctual. Her mind conjured up an image of a balding, ball-bellied man who wore a permanent frown from constantly pursing his tension-filled lips. That was the look of most billionaires she knew. She pictured him sitting in the back of his limousine, telling his driver to take his time, no rush, because he was sending her a message, which was that he was the one with the upper hand.

Unfortunately, she hadn't had time to conduct the appropriate research on him. Two days ago, Butch Benjamin, the man who owned thirty-nine shares of her company, had died suddenly. She still didn't know what had killed him. Perhaps his evil and self-serving heart had finally given up.

Anger and frustration raced through her, emotions she'd felt ever since learning more about what a sucker she was for purchasing AMTA a month ago. She studied her watch again. Butch's nephew, Zach, the trustee of his estate, was now twelve minutes late. She wanted to wring his neck. But then she heard her grandmother's voice telling her to use the extra time to do something constructive.

Elaine returned to her desk and looked over all her notes regarding her purchase of AMTA. The firm was the second-largest talent agency in the world, but with her at the helm, it could soar to number one. At least that was what she believed. It had been difficult to charge forward since taking over the company, but her next step would be the one that would get the wheels turning. However, she'd always believed an offer could be too good to be true, and that was definitely the case when it came to the purchase of her brand-new company.

Banker Dale Henley had given her a valuation, which presented sixty-one percent of the company stock as though it were a hundred percent. She didn't know that then, but he had found loopholes that legally allowed him to word the deal in such a way that he could hide the truth within the language. Normally, Elaine would've caught the manipulation and saved herself some grief, but she was given twenty-four hours in which to purchase before other buyers were approached. Granted, her emotions had taken over. Archie Rubenstein, the then-president, was running AMTA into the ground, and she knew she could manage it a lot better. Archie was the classic Hollywood scoundrel, with no business or creative instincts, but loved to use his power to get shit for free and sexually harass young women.

The day after Elaine signed the deal and wired the money to the bank, she learned not only that had she had bought a lemon but also that Butch Benjamin owned thirty-one shares of her company. Not too long after that, she learned AMTA was the victim of extortion by blackmailers who were running a sophisticated operation. Videos showed top-tier talent engaging in salacious, career-ending acts.

One casualty of the extortion was her soon-to-be brother-in-law, Jay West. Elaine would've been licking her wounds that very moment if Jay hadn't been valuable to mega media mogul Vincent Adams and his enterprise, AEE. The pre-release episodes of a new TV series starring Jay had been the highest-rated show a cable network had ever seen. No way was Vince going to allow scandal to ruin the acclaim and validation the series would bring his company. So he hired his wife, Maggie Adams, to fix the problem. Not only did she stop the extortionists, but she also made it appear as if the whole ordeal had never happened. Apparently Maggie was a secret agent of some sort.

Elaine was curious to learn more about the woman who'd saved her ass. But she had been too busy to connect with Mrs. Adams and invite her out for that drink Maggie had promised that the two of them would share one day.

Even though the criminals had been stopped, and in a deal to keep his mouth shut about the truth, Archie was now in jail on a lesser charge—rather than conspiracy to commit murder, extortion, and insider trading—it hadn't taken long for

Elaine to figure out she had been set up and expected to fail. The extortionists were supposed to milk her dry, which would've forced her to sell her devalued stock to the first willing buyer, and that more than likely would've been BLB, Butch's investment firm. She never would've recouped the money she spent to purchase her portion of the company, nor her dignity.

It took another week before Butch would answer any of her calls. Then he'd agreed to come to her office on Wednesday morning. She was waiting for him and stewing because he was over an hour late.

At 10:10 a.m., she called his office and was informed that he had passed on Tuesday morning. Elaine could hardly believe what she was hearing. But she was in survival mode when she consulted the obituaries. She had already missed the funeral, so she hightailed it to the burial service with the purpose of figuring out who was Butch's beneficiary and arranging a meeting with him or her before the day was over.

Elaine arrived at the burial service just in time to see Betsy Benjamin sashay up to the casket during one of the prayers and spit three times on Butch's pine coffin. There was a collective gasp.

Elaine's eyes widened. Not because of what Betsy had done—Elaine had heard Butch Benjamin was a womanizing cheater who had an appetite for barely legal girls—but because she felt Betsy's timing was off. She could've at least waited for the prayer to end, but then her actions wouldn't have been so rabble-rousing. Elaine had attended enough memorial services for men like Butch Benjamin to know that the widow didn't show out in that way unless her deceased husband had given her a reason to hate him. It rarely had to do with a mistress but always had to do with money. The gold leaf design, which covered all the walls, the white marble floors with gold swirling through them, and the solid-gold lampposts surrounding the pine box—a comical paradox at best—were evidence that a lot of that cash had gone to making sure Butch's ego was still alive and well, tainting the room even on the day he was laid to rest. Elaine's instincts told her that it wasn't Betsy's ass she needed to kiss in order to secure the thirty-nine shares she was owed.

After the service, Elaine had first tried talking to Mike Falk, who actually attempted to shame her for asking questions about business at the cemetery, in the presence of Butch's grieving friends and family. She could see his reverence for the dead was merely bullshit by the way his eyes smiled naughtily. He was hiding something, and more importantly, she suspected he was looking to blindside her somehow. So when she saw Betsy walk past Mike and look at him as though she wanted to push him in the grave with his client, Elaine knew there was an opportunity for her to figure out what the hell Mike was cooking up.

She was on her way to track down the latest Mrs. Benjamin when a guard approached her and asked to see her invitation.

"I'm here on behalf of the Hester family," she said.

The guard took a wide stance and crossed his arms over his chest. "This is a service for the Benjamin family."

She scoffed. "Are you trying to insinuate that the last name of everyone here is Benjamin?" She thumbed behind her. "Because I just spoke to a Falk, who I suspect told you to come tell me to leave."

"This is a private service for family and close friends only, ma'am."

Elaine narrowed her eyes and studied his intense frown. She could tell he was the kind of guy who didn't like being pushed around by women.

But he also hadn't said another word, which let her know perhaps there was a way to make him see things her way.

"One moment." She opened her purse then her billfold and took out a hundred-dollar bill. "How about we make a deal?"

He scrunched one side of his face.

She took out another hundred-dollar bill. "How about this kind of deal?"

He grasped one end of the bills, but she wouldn't let go of hers.

"I'll give you this, and you get someone to stop the grieving widow from leaving." She pointed across the grass and at the black limousine where Betsy was at the back passenger-side door, speaking to a couple.

"I'll take that deal," the security guard said.

She paid him the money, and he ran off to stop Betsy's car. It all worked out. When Elaine told Betsy who she was and what she was seeking, the widow ordered the driver out of the car and told Elaine to get in the back seat with her.

Betsy's ice-blue eyes regarded her shrewdly. Elaine recognized that look. Heck, she'd trademarked it. The expression was designed to convey not only that was she willing to wheel and deal but also that she meant to come out on top.

"You're very beautiful," Betsy said.

Elaine pursed her lips and nodded. Her response spoke for her, saying, *So fucking what? I'm here to play, win, and stay*.

Betsy grinned as though she was amused by Elaine's nonverbal but very loud communication. "So, you want your shares?"

"Yes, that's why I'm here."

Betsy tilted her head to the left and studied Elaine some more. "You're very young, Elaine. How old are you?"

"Does it matter?"

"You look like one of those poor girls who came to Hollywood to become a star but failed miserably, so you became a lawyer."

"I don't come from anywhere but here."

"Yes…" She grinned some more. "I know you're Lorraine Hester's granddaughter." She shifted in her seat. "I didn't say you were one of those girls. I said you look like one. But anyhow, may I ask you something?"

Elaine was getting annoyed but knew she couldn't show it. Maintaining her cool composure, she nodded.

"Have you ever fucked my husband?"

Elaine kept her poker face. "No."

Betsy eyed her scrupulously. "That's right. You're a Hester. Your grandmother would probably disown you if she knew you were using your pussy to get ahead."

"My grandmother would never disown me," Elaine said brusquely, realizing Betsy had finally said something that momentarily broke her resolve.

Betsy paused and then chortled. "Of course, I see. Zachary Lord, Butch's nephew. He owns your shares."

If it weren't for the fact that she couldn't allow Betsy to see her relax, Elaine would've sighed with relief. At least she had a name. "Do you have his number?"

"My husband left it all to him. You see, Elaine, a woman doesn't marry a man like Butch for love or stay with him because she's devoted. Do you understand?"

The worst thing Elaine could do was answer that question. She had to convey they were not friends, and she wasn't empathetic to Betsy's gold-digging ways. "Zach Lord. What's his phone number?" Elaine asked firmly.

Betsy cracked a tiny smile, then she said the number so fast that if Elaine weren't so sharp, she would've forgotten it and had to ask again. She was sure that was what Betsy was hoping.

"Thank you," Elaine said and opened the door.

"Wait," Betsy said.

Elaine looked back.

"You want your company, then you get that fucker to put it all in my hands, and I'll give you your thirty-nine shares. You'll pay nothing for them."

Elaine took a moment to study her and then smirked. "Oh, I'll be paying something for it."

"Zach is not Butch. Fucking him will be fun."

It didn't surprise Elaine that someone who appeared to be the typical kept wife had such motives. She'd met many wives like Betsy ever since she'd hit the big leagues in her career. What hardened them the most was learning they had kissed a frog and he was never going to turn into a prince or a king. No, the man she'd married was just a rich frog. And what the wife hated the most was that she couldn't delude herself into thinking she wanted anything more than his money, because every morning when she looked at him—at least on the days when he chose to sleep in their bed—she was reminded that she was in the relationship because of the standard of living he provided.

"Goodbye," Elaine said and opened the door.

Betsy grabbed her by the shoulder. "Or don't fuck him. You're a smart thirty-five-year-old woman. Convince him to give me what I fucking earned, and I'll give you your shares."

Elaine didn't say yes or no. This time when she moved to get out of the car, Betsy didn't stop her. Perhaps she knew Elaine was going to think about her proposition and use it to her benefit if need be.

It was never Elaine's intention to interject herself into their family issues. She wanted to convince this Zach Lord to sell her the shares at a reasonable price, or else she would be forced to take him to court. But if that happened, she wouldn't be looking to keep the company—she'd be reversing the purchase. Her odds of winning such a suit were favorable. To emerge the victor, she would have to expose the blackmailing scheme. She wasn't ready to go that far, not yet at least.

Elaine stayed up all night devising a plan to get what she wanted from Zach. She wondered what Betsy meant by saying that having sex with Zach wasn't like banging Butch. Elaine guessed it sure wasn't like fucking George Clooney or someone of that stature. It was probably more like boning Jim Neely, the short little cocky, annoying agent who worked for her at AMTA. They used to be bitter enemies before she became his boss, and she had every reason to believe he was the reason everyone hated her so much. She'd finally fired his ass last week.

So she deeply pondered the question of whether she could fuck someone like that to get what she wanted. Absolutely not. Seducing Zach Lord wasn't an option. She'd never used sex to get anywhere in life, and she wasn't going to start now.

No, she had to outthink him. She had to offer him a deal he couldn't refuse, even if she had to dupe Betsy, whom she didn't trust, anyway. There was no way the not-so-grieving widow was going to essentially give away an asset worth $1.2 billion.

At five o'clock that morning, two things happened: Elaine finally came up with a plan, and she fell asleep. Her alarm blared at seven. Elaine yawned. It was another day where two hours of sleep was all she was going to get, and that bummed her.

Finally, her desk phone chimed rapidly, twice, which let her know that it was one of her temporary assistants. Eden, her assistant of six years, was now in the agent trainee program, which put her in the mailroom all day long. Eden had reported to her regarding the effectiveness of the curriculum. As far as Elaine was concerned, the trainee program needed some serious revamping, and she would start the process of doing that very soon.

And Clara, Archie's former assistant—whom she'd kept on as her second assistant—was out yet again. This time she claimed to have the flu. In one month, Clara had racked up ten workday absences, which was alarmingly excessive. It was definitely time to replace her, but not with either of the two daft temporary assistants working Elaine's desk at the moment.

"Yes," she said.

"Mister… Um…"

Elaine could faintly hear Zachary Lord telling the assistant his name.

"A Mr. Zach Lord is here to see you." Even though he'd told her his name, the girl still sounded unsure about it.

Elaine closed her eyes as she shook her head. Why in the hell did she have the worst assistants in the building? She was the head honcho and should have had the best! "Send him in," she said tetchily and ended the communication.

Elaine stood then quickly sat right back down, preferring to sit. How she presented herself was important. She didn't want to seem too eager or weak. The objective was to strike a deal that favored her wants and needs, so sitting in the big chair made her look more dominant.

But when the door opened and in walked Zachary Lord.

The Hester Girls love stories continue in **Taming The Shrewd**. Don't miss it!

ABOUT THE AUTHOR

Z.L. has been writing romance full-time since 2011, which has allowed her to amass quite a catalog of romance novels. She loves what she does, and as she's evolved, so have her stories. Now, she's focused on writing brooding, boss billionaire heroes, and the smart, plucky heroines they can't live without. She has always loved writing great, intense heroes that readers can't help but fall in love with.

www.ingramcontent.com/pod-product-compliance
Lightning Source LLC
La Vergne TN
LVHW010049110826
845155LV00028B/262

* 9 7 8 1 9 5 2 1 0 1 0 8 3 *